YVES CORVER

From New Orleans to D-Day

The double war of a Black GI

Historical fiction novel

Yves Corver

This book was independently published by the author, and printed by IMB, Bayeux, France
Revised edition, January 2023.

ISBN: 978-2-9580279-3-3
For information, address the author at yves.corver@laposte.net

YVES CORVER

From New Orleans to D-Day

The double war of a Black GI

The Double Victory Campaign
Democracy at home and abroad[1]

Historical fiction novel

Foreword by Alice Mills,
former maitre de conférence at Université de Caen,
former W.E.B. Du Bois Fellow, Harvard University

---

[1] Campaign launched on February 7, 1942, by the Afro-American newspaper *The Pittsburgh Courier*

Yves Corver

Langston Hughes (1902—1967), poet, social activist, novelist, playwright and columnist of the Chicago Defender wrote in his column on June 17, 1944:

"Invasion!!! The invasion has begun! American troops are in France. [...] The France of the great mulatto writer, Dumas. The France that made Félix Eboué a Governor General in Africa. The France that ever welcomed Negro students and artists and musicians and tourists. [...] American Negroes are part of that invasion, moving in blood and death and determination into Europe. Men from Harlem and Chicago's South side and Pittsburgh's Hill and Savannah's Yamacraw and Rampart Street and Tuskegee and Dallas and Los Angeles and Seventh Street in Oakland and Beale Street in Memphis and U Street in Washington DC. [...] This is our War because we are dying in it. This is our country because we are dying for it. This is our invasion because we never did believe in slavery and race hatred and the strong-arm methods of subjugation that Hitler and others like him believe in [...]"

Yves Corver

Warning to the Readers

The first reason why I decided to write this novel was that I wanted to pay tribute to all the young African American soldiers who came over to France and fought for our liberty, whereas their own freedom was not guaranteed in their own country. My initial research lead me to discover the 320th Antiaircraft Barrage Balloons Battalion, an all-black fighting unit, besides a few white senior officers.

Over the course of my investigations in books and on the internet, I got to know bloggers and other people very interested in the involvement of colored troops in the U.S. Army, and their relation with the people of the countries crossed by our American allies.

It is through a British web site—*Reminiscences of Old Pontypool*—that I discovered that another person was working at the same time on a book dedicated to the 320th VLA.

In her book *Forgotten, the Untold Story of D-Day's Black Heroes*, Linda Hervieux tells the story of this black battalion through the testimonies of several veterans whom she had the chance to meet in their homes in the United States. The names of a few of them appear on some occasions in my novel. This is the case of Wilson Monk and Waverly Woodson. Other real people are mentioned, like Lieutenant Colonel Leon John Reed, commanding officer of the battalion, his second in command, Captain William Taylor, or chaplain Albert White. All the other characters, soldiers and civilians, came out of my imagination.

Several years of research on the employment of Negro troops in the U.S. Army led me to the following observation: there is no detailed official record which could help me to thoroughly trace the life of this battalion, which I used as the backdrop of this story.

However, I tried, as much as possible, to piece back the journey of the main characters inside battery A, in the respect of the historical truth. This made it necessary to collect and cross-check elements coming from many different sources. Yet, the currently available information is both fragmented and partial, which forced me to take some narrative license. On the other hand, I cared about recreating, as faithfully as possible, the atmosphere and the general spirit at the time, in the Army and in the civil society, in the United States, as well as in Great Britain and in France.

The induction of African American soldiers occurred in a context of racial segregation and racist prejudices, which seriously complicated the recruitment, the training and the distribution of Negro troops in the different U.S. military forces.

Simultaneous pressures came from all sides and turned into a real headache for the Administration of Franklin D. Roosevelt who, in November 1940, was running for a third presidential term. On the one hand, the Southern segregationist states, the Air Force and the Navy. On the other hand, black organizations like the NAACP and the Brotherhood of Sleeping Car Porters, and the African American press.

Yet, one person had a strong influence, and would

sometimes slightly tip the balance in favor of the Negroes: the first lady, Eleanor Roosevelt. Her involvement in the fight for the civil rights of colored people earned her to be accused by the Southern White press to be accountable for the Detroit race riot, in June 1943.

The different Army Corps had the obligation to hire a nine percent quota of Negroes, consistent with the share of colored people in the whole population. Nevertheless, the staff continued to deny to black recruits access to combat units, based on deeply anchored prejudices.

However, in order to meet the requirements of African American lobbies, all-black combat units were created. A few among them shone on the theater of operations. The 761st and the 784th Tank battalion, the 92nd Infantry division, the Tuskegee Airmen of the 332nd Fighter group, and the 320th Antiaircraft barrage balloon battalion, on which this novel is based.

For the rest, most of the colored soldiers were assigned service and logistics tasks. Later, on the front, black volunteers would be authorized to join white combat units, provided that they accepted to be demoted to the rank of privates. Indeed, a regulation in the Army denied a Black the right to command a White. These black volunteers, coming from service units, proved very brave and earned the recognition and admiration of their white counterparts.

This book is a historical fiction novel, loosely based on the story of the soldiers of the 320th VLA, which was the only all-Black combat unit to take part in the D-Day landings on June 6, 1944[2]. Nevertheless, this book is a tribute to all the African Americans who fought for our

---

[2] Source: https://aaregistry.org/story/d-day-and-the-vla-barrage-balloon-battalion/

11

freedom in France and in Europe. Whether fighters or service men, they all deserve to be honored.

<u>Regarding the use of the words *Negro* and *nigger*</u>:

At the time when the story takes place, the Americans were using words like *Negro* and *colored* people to refer to African Americans. The word Negro comes from the Spanish which means black. Although today nobody in the USA would use the word Negro, at that time, it had no pejorative meaning nor negative connotation. Therefore, I deliberately let my characters use the words *Negro*, and *colored*.

On the contrary, the derogatory epithet *nigger* was used by many white Southern officers when talking to or about African Americans, intending to humiliate and outrage them.

For my wife Nathalie

and my sons Antoine and Yann.

Yves Corver

Foreword

The amount of data available on D-Day is enormous and yet some historians may find it insufficient to portray the reality of the landing. The existing information is heterogenous, its elements may be fragmented, contradictory and overabundant in certain respects and, at the same time, lacking in others.

In order to construct narratives which are both coherent and scientifically acceptable, historians often resort to making chronological presentations of facts they consider major and supported by quantitative data, technical descriptions and verifiable quotations. Much of what is considered to be minor or cannot be checked is eliminated in the process. Details such as silences and deafening sounds, smells of spring or death are often omitted. Needless to say, unrecorded thoughts and feelings are considered irrelevant. This is probably why those who were actually part of the Landing, whether active soldiers or bewildered villagers, often have trouble relating to the historical accounts of D-Day. The personal human element is missing.

Novelists have more freedom.

In his thoroughly documented novel Yves Corver restores elements of the Landing's history that was often ignored by official narratives until the mid 2000s, such as the participation of black American troops in the storming of the Normandy beaches. The story focuses on the role played by the black 320th Barrage Balloon Battalion whose courage and determination in the assault was praised by General Eisenhower.

The novel shows the struggles of the battalion through the fictitious 19 year old corporal Firmin Bellegarde whom the reader follows from a Tennessee training camp to his return to the U.S.

Corver's tale is built on impeccable facts and portrays the dramatic circumstances the battalion faced as well as illustrating the smaller details such as the presence of static electricity stored up in the balloons, the collapse of the ground under the weight of the equipment, the crunch of the sand imbedded in ration packs or the cold mud penetrating under the soldiers' blankets.

For example, the allegedly unsinkable LCVP is, in reality, made of plywood. Firmin knows that the barge cannot protect him from the shooting and the explosions and yet he stubbornly clings to it because it was made in the very factory where his mother works

In many ways Firmin's story is that of every other GI fighting for the Normandy beaches. Whatever their origins the soldiers were torn between the desire of being part of the great adventure and the fear of not surviving it. Like the others, Firmin suddenly realizes that his life has shifted, that he cannot step back and that he may die at any minute.

All the young American recruits caught under German fire experienced confusion and terror. Yet within their shared story there is one which belongs to black GIs only. They not only had to fight the Germans but their own bigoted comrades as well.

Corver's characters face blatant racial discrimination starting in bootcamp where no recreational area is provided for the black soldiers who must sit in the back of buses behind curtains. They know that any White man may mistreat them and accuse them of misdeeds, such as rape, for which they will likely be convicted. Even in the course of the landing when solidarity is a matter of survival for all Americans, black soldiers are often left out. The novel shows a story of a few Whites sabotaging the cables of the balloons manned by their black comrades and even turning them away from shelters on the beach.

Corver's hero is a gentle, quiet young man who respects the authority of both his parents and the government. He dreams not so much of glory as of getting an education and a decent life. The sudden confrontation with brutal, complex wartime situations tears his soul apart. Having joined the army out of a sense of duty he struggles to keep faith in an America which inflicts pain and humiliation on its own troops. Yet, unlike his comrade Ed who defiantly criticizes the ambient racism, Firmin hopes that keeping quiet and doing their jobs well will earn black soldiers the respect they deserve.

Firmin's attitude probably reflects that of a large segment of the black community which, at the time, instinctively believed that a country whose land they cleared, whose roads, railways and bridges they built owed them a fair share of its prosperity. Conversely Ed represents the other part of the community which felt they did not belong to a country which mistreated them from the very beginning.

Yet in spite of their opposite points of view, Ed and Firmin face German fire in unison.

More important than ending up victorious or discovering the extent of their own bravery, it is probably the attitude of the French and English populations towards them which marks a turning point in the lives of the young soldiers. The Europeans do not see them as Blacks but as Americans.

Being treated as equals stupefies the GIs and changes their view on the world, opening up new possibilities. It is not in Firmin's nature to ever become a Martin Luther King and much less a Malcom X but his deference for the established order definitely vacillates after the war, reflecting a general shift in the attitude of the black American community.

Yves Corver presents us with a beautiful fictional narrative. May *From New Orleans to D-Day* encourage the potential holders of manuscripts written by black GIs themselves to publish them. Their testimony is invaluable.

Alice Mills,
former maitre de conférence at the University of Caen (Normandy, France), former W.E.B. Du Bois Fellow, Harvard University, author of *Black GIs, Normandy, 1944* (Éditions Cahier du temps, 2014)

*This book is dedicated
to Corporal Stith Brooks,
to Corporal Henry J. Harris,
killed in action on Omaha Beach on June 6, 1944,
and to private first class James M. McLean
killed in action in Normandy, France, on July 16, 1944,
and all their comrades of the 320th VLA, among whom
the combat medic, Corporal Waverly B. Woodson who,
despite his heroic actions on June 6, 1944, never received
the Medal of honor, and to all the soldiers of the service
and logistics units, without whom the Allied armies
wouldn't have been able to defeat the German Nazi
armies.*

Yves Corver

CHAPTER 1

New York Harbor, November 16, 1943

The nineteen year old corporal, Firmin Bellegarde, scanned his misty eyes all around him. The six foot and almost one inch tall and burly soldier looked like a young fan meeting his favorite actor for the first time. His lower jaw hung in amazement. A beatific smile enlightened his milk chocolate skinned face.

Firmin wouldn't miss a thing of this awesome scenery, in which he was both an observer and an actor. Actually, a mere extra among thousands of others. Wherever he looked around him, he felt like in the middle of a stage set. One of those Technicolor Hollywood super-productions which overwhelm your senses and nail you to your seat in a movie theater. Except that in this case the screen was all over the walls and on the ceiling as well. Besides sight and sound, it called upon his perception of smell and touch.

No film director could have imagined a more striking staging. The night was pitch-black and the visibility restricted by a slight mist. Oil fumes mingled with the faint scent of the sea breeze.

Under the yellow glow of the street lights, thousands of soldiers were stamping their feet on the cobblestones of Pier 86. Whiffs of vapor exhaled from their mouths.

A brass band was playing *Roll out the barrel*[3] with gusto, trying its best to give this dramatic setting a festive

---

[3] *Beer Barrel Polka* song on a tune composed in 1927 by the Czech Jaromir Vejvoda.

atmosphere. Firmin Bellegarde had already played this tune in his father's instrumental ensemble. But he was too awed by the sight of the Cunard White Star Line flagship to get carried along by the music. The mighty, stately shape of the *Aquitania* stood towering in front of him. A nine hundred feet long ship, ninety-eight feet wide, with a capacity of forty-five thousand tons. It was a British cruise ship recently restructured for the second time in her career to accommodate the transportation of American troops from New York to Scotland. Firmin immediately recognized her. He could remember seeing her picture on company ads. At the time, he couldn't even have imagined setting foot on it. It was a dream reserved for city Whites.

Almost eight thousand soldiers stood on the Manhattan West Side Dock, ready to board the ship. Among them, two thousand black men, many of whom had prayed for this moment to happen. It meant they could now start serving their country as soldiers. They were willing to fight America's enemies wherever they were.

For Firmin Bellegarde and the six hundred and eighty-six men of the 320th VLA[4] gathered at the foot of the steel behemoth, this moment was even more special. Not so much because they were all Negroes, besides their top-ranking officers, but because as such, they were aware of their exceptional privilege of belonging to one of the rare colored combat units of the U.S. armed forces. Since the country had been at war, the African American press had relentlessly protested the reluctance of the various headquarters to send colored troops abroad.

In an attempt to calm their nervousness while waiting

---

[4] Very Low Altitude. Another name for the Antiaircraft Barrage Balloons Battalions (AABBB).

their turn to board the ship, some soldiers were trying to flirt with the girls clad in Red Cross uniforms who had come to comfort them with drinks, donuts and cigarettes. Others were lost in their thoughts about their families or their girlfriends, whom they sometimes had not seen for months.

All his senses on alert, Firmin was focusing on every detail in his surroundings that he would etch in his memory. Despite his youthful exuberance, he was aware that this was a once-in-a-lifetime moment. He could still picture the Statue of Liberty, which was standing out in the mist a few hours earlier, as their ferry was going down the Hudson River after it had left Camp Shanks.

He looked for a few minutes at the distant halo of midtown Manhattan lights, several blocks away. He regretted he hadn't been granted a leave. He would have enjoyed the pleasure of a night out. He vowed he would come back after the war and have a few drinks at the Copacabana in Spanish Harlem, or even better at the Cotton Club in Negro Harlem. He hoped the legendary area would have regained its joyful liveliness by then. With some luck the race riots which had disrupted it throughout 1943 would then have become a thing of the past.

Corporal Bellegarde suddenly felt the ground give way under his feet. The column of men of the 320th Coast Artillery Barrage Balloon Battalion had ultimately started to move forward on instruction of its commanding officer, Lieutenant Colonel Leon John Reed.

Firmin got carried away, half-lifted, half-drifted, by the flow of young soldiers. He didn't resist nor accompany the movement. His heart was torn apart between his fear of never coming back, and his desire to live to the fullest an adventure, which would leave him lifetime memories.

His late maternal grandfather had told him about the horror of WWI in Europe, its millions of dead, its veterans psychologically harmed or severely maimed. The old man also used to denounce the ungratefulness of the Whites after his return to America, when not their outright hostility. In southern states, Negroes who came back from the war were spat upon when they wore their uniforms on the streets.

In December 1918, one of them, Private Charles Lewis, was lynched in Kentucky just because he was wearing his soldier's outfit when he arrived in Taylor Station, his hometown. Deputy Sheriff Al Thomas allegedly arrested him for theft. Then, while Lewis was waiting in prison to be handed over to the District Judge, a mob of about a hundred hooded people dragged him out of his cell, slipped a noose about his neck, and hung him to the limb of a tree.

And yet, like millions of Negroes, Firmin now nurtured the hope that this time victory against Nazi Germany would bring them more than low-ranking medals and nasty wounds.

While climbing the gangway, a few soldiers began to feel slightly nauseous. Almost none of them had ever set foot on a boat before. Very few could even swim. Firmin peered for the last time at the dock, then at the city in the distance. With great care, as if he wanted to incise the image in his memory, before being gobbled down in the entrails of the monster.

Firmin didn't have a chance to gaze at the splendor of the upper decks, which access was reserved for white officers. He followed the flow of his battalion, slowly descending to the lower decks.

Since their departure from Camp Shanks already, rumors had been spreading among the men about the places they should avoid by all means on board of a ship. Particularly in times of war. The worst being the engine room, in the ship's hold. Given that it was beneath the waterline, it would be instantly flooded if the ship were hit by a German torpedo, thus inevitably drowning all the machinery mechanics inside. Next on the list was level F, also under the waterline.

Firmin looked at his boarding pass. He read the indication: "Deck E." Would the *Aquitania*, by misfortune, cross the route of one of those damned German *U-Boote*[5], Firmin would be closer to the upper deck, and would still have some chance to get out of it alive! At least, he needed to believe it, to feel reassured.

The smallest free space of this ship had been used to board all these soldiers, besides the crew. Firmin and his comrades occupied four rows of narrow berths, in tiny compartments. A few soldiers were undressing while sharing jokes to overcome their sense of claustrophobia. Some were singing in shaky voices. Others were praying. Firmin's thoughts were for his parents.

The young corporal felt exhausted after the incredibly long day. He fell sound asleep after a while, comforted by the certainty that the *Aquitania* wouldn't leave the wharf before noon tomorrow. He would have time to write his feelings in his diary in the morning.

---

[5] From the German *Unterseeboot* (sous-marin)

CHAPTER 2

F irmin George Bellegarde was born to George and Celestine Bellegarde, on March 21, 1924, in Baton Rouge County, Louisiana. He spent his first years with both his parents and his mother's parents, on the same small family farm. Cultivating the land was harsh and ungrateful. Yet, the two couples could make a living with it. Their two houses were separated by less than three hundred yards, at equal distance from the farm's windmill water pump.

Firmin's parents' home was a shack, made of recovery boards for the walls, and rusty metal sheets for the roof. It had no partition. A stove stood in the middle of the only room. It would serve for heating and cooking. Provided they had firewood and some food to fill the stewpot.

Above what served as his parents' bed, Firmin used to sleep on a canvas bag filled with hay, lying on a mezzanine. In winter, the heat of the stove raised warm air towards him, but in the middle of the night, when the wood was entirely consumed, the icy cold of the iron sheets of the roof would make him shiver, and finally awaken him.

In summer, the temperature up there was sweltering. Sometimes even suffocating. Then, his father eventually allowed Firmin to sleep downstairs on a bed of straw covered with a rush mat.

In a corner of the house, a curtain was hanging that his mother Celestine would draw when she wanted to wash herself in a metal washtub, which she also used to do laundry. His father never closed it … until Marie's arrival.

To reach the latrine, they had to get out of the house and walk to a wooden hut across the garden where Firmin's mother used to grow vegetables to feed her family.

When his wife complained about the lack of comfort of their home, Firmin's father, George Bellegarde, used to reply, "Maybe it's a slum, but it's ours!"

George and Jean-Baptiste Duvivier, Firmin's grandpa, shared all the farm work, while Celestine and her mother took care of their vegetable gardens and households.

Firmin enjoyed visiting his grandma, Rosalyn, in the afternoon. Every day of the week, she would bake oat cookies, stuffed with season nuts or fruit. After she had taken the cakes out of the oven, she would spread them on a plate and let them cool down on the table. Through the open window, Firmin would smell the delicious scent of warm crispy rind. Rosalyn would then let Firmin come in, and sit for a while around the table, gazing greedily at the cookies until they had cooled. Firmin liked their taste and smell. But, not as much as his mother's Sunday cookies.

The young boy felt a mingle of admiration and fear for his grandpa. He never got tired of wandering with him in the fields. Jean-Baptiste taught him much more about the local wildlife and flora than his own father could have done. Moreover, Firmin loved to hear him recall his feats of arms during the Great War. However, the old man didn't always realize that he was talking to a very young boy. Sometimes, he wouldn't spare him sordid details about the dreadful life of the soldiers in the trenches of France. Firmin would strive to hide that he was scared. He would refrain from crying. Nonetheless, it would cause him nightmares in the following night, making Celestine angry at her father.

Firmin's most distant memories went back to the year when Marie was born. It was in 1928. What he knew about the years before was what he had heard from his mother.

Marie was his little sister. Her arrival had been welcomed by everyone like a blessing from the Lord. After Firmin's birth, Celestine Bellegarde had had two miscarriages. Celestine and Joe wondered what kind of sin they had committed to deserve such a divine punishment.

Immediately, Marie was at the heart of all their attention.

Yet, Firmin didn't lose his central position in his grandfather's mind. Warfare is a men's issue. He couldn't discuss the matter with a little girl.

Firmin was a very protective big brother for Marie. He would do everything he could to make her happy and let her forget the extreme poverty of their living conditions. And indeed, the six of them were happy. Firmin loved to see her burst out laughing, when he was dressed up in funny costumes, or when he was pulling the wheeled crate that their father had built, inside which she would sit on a pile of hay.

Sadly, this happiness hadn't lasted. Because of this damned drought that had hit all the Southern States in 1930.

And in the following year.

And in the year after, again.

Besides, the winter and spring rains didn't suffice to refill the groundwater. Water became so scarce that there was just enough left to water the garden and cook the vegetables.

In the summer 1932, Firmin's grandfather eventually decided to leave the farm, and let his daughter and her husband run it. The farm couldn't feed all of them any longer. So, he and Rosalyn would move to Baton Rouge.

Jean-Baptiste had other skills, besides being a farmer, that he could make a living with. He used to be a blacksmith and an iron craftsman before he went to war in Europe, and for a while after he came back in 1919. Unfortunately, the mechanization of agriculture had taken a lot of work away from blacksmiths. However, the constructions of new hotels and large buildings in Baton Rouge required skilled iron craftsmen. Besides, the explosion of the number of cars in circulation gave a lot of work to car body repair mechanics.

The land had become so arid that it had disintegrated into a fine dust. Then violent storms had come that had lifted this dust and blown it away, accelerating the soil erosion.

As a result, they could not harvest anything, three years in a row. His father had to get in debt to feed them and buy seeds. Until no more banks would accept to lend him money anymore. Eventually, like thousands of families, his parents had had to resolve to sell their land to pay back their creditors.

From farm owners, they became sharecroppers. They were allowed to work the soil that used to be theirs, in exchange for half of the crop. Their only source of income.

Weakened by the lack of food, Marie died in the early summer 1933. Firmin would never forget this cursed day.

It was on the Fourth of July. On Independence Day. Like every year, the celebration was an opportunity for all the negro families of the parish to gather for a giant picnic on the east bank of the Mississippi River. The kids were playing together on their side. Some fathers were enjoying fishing, while others, drunk, were taking a good nap under the refreshing shade of a big tree.

The mothers were chatting and laughing together, while keeping an eye on their babies and their younger children.

As Firmin was playing baseball with his boyfriends, a powerful and shrill cry tore the air. He immediately recognized his mother's voice. He threw his glove away, took off his peaked cap, and ran towards the group of women as if he was possessed.

When he saw from afar his mother's silhouette kneeled in the grass, surrounded by other women trying to support her, he understood. He rushed to them. When he arrived, breathless, he saw Marie, leaning against the trunk of a cypress. Her eyes wide open. She still had on her face the same amazed smile that she had every time she would see anything or anyone she loved. Her Mom, her Dad, her brother, a flower, a funny cloud... She probably knew she would not live long. So, to compensate for the pain she would cause her family the day she passes away, she had decided to offer them her joy of living, each and every day God would grant her.

Joe arrived a few minutes later. The tumult of the Mississippi River had prevented him from hearing his wife crying out. Firmin attended this scene that would haunt his nights for months after. Joe's eyes were flooded with tears. Firmin had never seen his father cry before this day. He couldn't stop the trembling of his chin. His mighty hands were clasped to the fabric of his eternal canvas jumpsuit covered with multiple patches. His entire body looked seized with pain and despair. His fixed gaze seemed to get lost in Marie's eyes. While Celestine was weeping and wailing in the arms of a girlfriend, Joe slowly came closer to Marie, like a robot. He fell on his knees, gently took her in his arms, one behind her back, the other under her knees, and lifted her lifeless body with extreme delicacy. As if he was afraid to hurt her.

Firmin then found refuge in his mother's arms. And they started weeping together, and they kept on for a while.

The whole community returned home with the Bellegardes. Each family with its wagon pulled by a mule. Celestine was sitting on the bench of their carriage. She was pressing Marie's inanimate little body, wrapped in the picnic table cloth, against her breast.

Joe was walking ahead of the cart, firmly gripping the bridle in one hand, and holding his son's hand, who had insisted on walking next to him. Firmin was struggling to imitate his father's dignified and courageous demeanor. He wanted to look like a man. Perhaps was he also trying to stifle his pain. Half an hour later, Firmin eventually jumped on board of the wagon. He sat near his mother and cried his eyes out in her skirts.

The next day, Firmin's father went alone by bus to Baton-Rouge to inform Jean-Baptiste and Rosalyn of the tragedy. Celestine was too devastated to go with him. The whole parish attended the funeral under a blazing sun.

Celestine, who was expecting another baby, would have a new miscarriage two months later. After that, she would never be pregnant again. Firmin would become the cement of the family. His parents' only child and only reason to keep on living.

CHAPTER 3

F irmin was filled with admiration for his mother. He considered her the bravest woman he had ever met.

Unlike most of the other ladies of her parish, Celestine had always stayed slim, to the greatest despair of her husband, who was more attracted by generous curves. Her friends often mocked her.

"One of these mornin's, a tornado'll carry ya 'way till the far end of the State."

Intending to frighten her, they used to tell her that one day her man would leave her for a more curvaceous woman. Firmin was convinced that they were jealous of her young woman's silhouette.

Celestine had a passion for flowers which she used to prepare small quantities of various perfumes for herself. When she hugged him early in the morning, Firmin felt like he was breathing the scent of a bouquet of wildflowers.

Born Duvivier, she hailed from a Haitian family who had fought Napoleon's troops under the command of Toussaint Louverture. She was proud of her ancestors, and therefore gave her son the first name Firmin, in honor of Joseph Antenor Firmin[6].

The Duviviers had emigrated to Louisiana, right after the French colony had been sold to the British by Napoleon. Despite her humble origins, Celestine was

---

[6] Haitian politician and writer (1850–1911), author of "The equality of human races. Positivist anthropology"

highly educated. Firmin owed her that he had attended
school until he was eighteen. That he could read and write
English fluently, and, furthermore, had good notions of
French. Not the Creole of the Antilles nor the Louisiana
Cajun, but the French of the White masters. Even if he
sometimes happened to drop some popular sayings, here
and there. She had also taught him respect, perseverance
and dignity.

Her husband was all the opposite. His first name was
George and his second Antonin, but he wanted to be called
Joe. He was a force of nature. He was nearly six feet and
one inch tall. His weight varied with the season, and
depended on what kind of food was simmering in the
stewpot. No need to say that he had lost a lot of weight at
the time Marie passed away. Still, Joe had always stayed
muscular. He wore the same jumpsuit every day, his
peaked cap screwed on the top of his skull.

He was descended from a lineage of griots natives of
West Africa. He also was very proud of his roots. Griots,
he used to say, are the guardians of the memory of the
elders. One of his ancestors had been abducted by
traffickers outside his village in Upper Volta, and sold as a
slave in Virginia. Around 1700, according to the story that
had been orally handed down in his family. The following
generations had been successively resold in Alabama and
Mississippi, before settling permanently in Louisiana.
Griots had mostly become musicians, like fiddler, banjo or
harmonica players.

Joe had also inherited another family tradition, which
he carefully kept secret when he met Celestine: gambling.
He was an inveterate gambler.

One of his uncles had secretly introduced him to

cockfighting. A highly appreciated pastime among the men in rural areas of the deep South. When the drought of the 1930s combined with the effects of the Great Depression, Joe had jumped at the chance to give up fieldwork and start acting like a bookmaker. It must have been right after Marie's death. Or a little before. Firmin could not remember exactly.

The difference of nature and temperament that opposed them gave rise to heated domestic disputes. It also tore Firmin apart, all through his adolescence, making him hesitate between the austerity of studying and the sparkling glitter of partying. Now, Firmin thanked God for giving him a mother like his. With enough strength of character to resist both her husband and their farm owner. At that time, it was customary to withdraw a child from school every time fieldwork required it. Namely during the sowing and harvest seasons. Celestine had always fiercely refused it.

The first school Firmin had attended was just a large shack, as dilapidated as his parents' home. But he felt good about it, although he missed his mom in the early days. Long after, he would remember with nostalgia the wood stove standing on the right side of the teacher's table. In winter, he enjoyed being requested to come to the black board. Some of his school friends even would come too close to it and get their buttocks burned.

There was only one single class. It was the pastor's wife who taught them to read, write and count. All the schoolchildren were mixed. Boys and girls, aged six to ten, divided in the first four school grades. Most of them couldn't have hoped for more. Only the most gifted or the luckiest would study beyond primary school. Thanks to his great intelligence, and to his mother's insistence, Firmin had been part of the lucky few. Despite the extreme poverty of his family.

In 1934, many Black folks had fled the South towards the North, in an attempt to build a better life. But the Great Depression[7] had already considerably lessened the chances to get a job in the industrial North. Celestine had heard of the *Straight College*[8], in New Orleans. So, she had inwardly vowed that she would enroll Firmin there.

One day, she had decided to drive to the big city, intending to find a position as a domestic worker for a White family. She had traveled by a *Teche-Greyhound Lines* bus, that connected the parishes of the east side of the Mississippi River from Baton Rouge to New Orleans.

The pastor of her congregation had sent a recommendation letter to one of his colleagues in New Orleans. The latter would serve as a moral guarantor, and the same day, Celestine got a job.

She had had no trouble convincing her husband to follow her. It had sufficed to suggest him the possibility to work as an orchestra musician in the French quarter of the city. That is how the three of them had settled in the Lower Ninth Ward, in the summer 1934.

They shared a large wooden house with two other African American families. On the left side of the ground floor lived an elderly couple: the Robinsons. The opposite apartment, on the right side, was where the Bellegardes lived.

Zachary Robinson, the husband, rarely spoke. And when he had to, he would often stutter. He had

---

[7] 1929 crisis.
[8] University of New Orleans, reserved for colored students.

Parkinson's disease. His wife, Rosa, was very devoted and caring to him.

Rosa loved Firmin very much. She would always have a candy or a cookie for him when he helped her carry her shopping basket up to the kitchen.

All the first floor, above, was occupied by the Davises and their three boys. The youngest son must have been fifteen, and the oldest twenty-one. Celestine avoided them like the plague. Her maternal instinct made her fear that they could have a harmful influence on her son. Thus, Firmin hardly ever dealt with them.

The change from their dilapidated shelter, in the middle of a barren landscape, had been radical for Firmin, and for his parents. But it could never compare to the shock the ten-year-old boy had felt the day he had been enrolled in *Holy Cross Junior high school[9]*.

A majestic brown brick three-story building. Every level was pierced by high-vaulted plate-glass windows, which white muntin bars resembled crosses. Girls and boys were in different classrooms and each grade was clearly distinct from others. Firmin joined the school in the fifth grade and would stay until the end of the twelfth.

To reach the school from his home, Firmin had to cross the canal that separated the Lower Ninth from the Upper Ninth, on St. Claude Avenue, then take North Rampart Street up to Elysian Fields Avenue, heading north. Even when using two streetcar lines, he would spend nearly one hour for each trip.

During the first two years, his mother used to travel with him early in the morning from home to her

---

[9] Catholic high school of N.O.

employers' house, in the Seventh Ward.

Firmly determined to ensure her only son a better future, Celestine hadn't hesitated a second to relegate her Protestant education to the background, to allow her son to join this Catholic school. It had earned Firmin to review all his religious upbringing, from the very beginning. However, despite the strict discipline imposed by the fathers, he loved learning all the new teachings he could study. And it was a point of honor for him to never disappoint his mother, who worked hard at the Letelliers, a family with French origins that had made a fortune in the trading of cotton, sugar cane and rice.

Monsieur Letellier had felt the wind change before everybody else. Long before the harvest of 1930, he had bought several cargoes of two basic food commodities from regions less exposed to drought. As of the next fall, he had made a substantial profit. The requirements of the Letelliers had risen accordingly. Their domestic staff had been reinforced.

Very soon, Madame Letellier had appreciated Celestine's courage and natural authority. And, of course, her language proficiency in French as well as in English. Celestine had been entrusted the supervision of two other household servants, and her wages had been increased.

CHAPTER 4

Bellegardes's financial situation had improved significantly compared to what they had experienced in Baton Rouge county. A comfortable housing, with running water and a bathroom. Well aligned houses. Streetcar lines. Everything was looking beautiful and modern. The city was teeming with activity. It provided both parents good jobs and enough income for a very decent life.

However, in their parish near Baton Rouge, they were among Negroes. They knew the deep contempt of White people, but they only felt it on rare occasions. When their farm owner came, once a year, to claim his share of the crop. Or when they happened to cross a White man driving his car. Then they would have to take off their hats and lower their heads and gaze.

In New Orleans, segregation was everywhere, well and truly present, reminding them, constantly, their status as inferior beings. When they walked out of their neighborhood. In the street, in shopping areas, at school. Every day, every minute, something or someone would remind them of their condition of colored man or woman.

In 1935, the case of a man had grabbed the headlines. A light-skinned African American mailman, named W.W. Kerr[10], on his way to work, had had the unconsciousness or the guts to get in a streetcar and sit on one of the front seats, in the "Whites only" section.

---

[10] Source: Better day coming: Blacks and equality, 1890 – 2000, chapter 9 The NAACP's challenge to White supremacy, 1935 – 45.

His offense eventually reached his manager's ears, in the post office where he worked. His boss censured him officially. Still, Kerr persisted in sitting at the same seat of the streetcar, every morning. When his boss asked him: "*Are you a White man of the Caucasian race?*" Kerr answered: "*Yes! [...] My hair is smooth and dark brown, and my skin is as white as that of a great majority of people in this community.*"

Then, Kerr added that, because he looked Caucasian, his "*presence in the black section of the street car might cause confusion and disorder, the very thing that the segregation law was designed to prevent.*"

The argument made his hierarchy turn mad!

Despite all their reprimands, Kerr persisted in his attitude, and stubbornly refused to sit beyond the curtain that separated the Whites' section from the Colored one. Kerr would justify his decision by claiming the fourteenth amendment[11].

"*As a federal employee, he represented a function of government that cannot be circumscribed by the limitations of race, creed or color.*"

This conflict opposing Kerr[12] to the U.S. Postal Service had led the way to other protest movements against the segregation policy and *Jim Crow*[13] Laws. Kerr was also

---

[11] The 14th amendment of the U.S. Constitution aims at protecting the rights of former slaves, particularly in Southern States. It guarantees the citizenship of every person born in the U.S.A. and asserted the necessity to guarantee an equal protection to everyone on its territory.
Source: Fourteenth Amendment to the United States Constitution - Wikipedia
[12] Nearly everyone has forgotten his name, but everybody has heard of Rosa Parks who was arrested by the police of Montgomery, Alabama, in December 1955, for refusing to leave a seat to a White passenger in a bus.
[13] Jim Crow laws were a series of regulations and ordinances generally promulgated in municipalities and Southern States between 1876 and 1965.

the head of the postal workers' union: the NAPE[14].

In the 1930s many Black trade unions were founded or reinforced, among which the famous and first colored union: *The Brotherhood of Sleeping Car Porters*. Kerr's action earned him to play a major role in the NAACP.

Celestine, who used to hate agitation, and blamed her husband for trying to drag their son to his inclination for union actions, often used Kerr's example to remind Firmin of the major importance of a good education to defend himself in his life. More pragmatic than idealistic, Celestine had chosen to deal with the segregation policy imposed by White people.

One day, as Firmin had let his anger burst out against this injustice, his mother told him, "Things will eventually work out! Before the Civil War, we were slaves. Today, we're free! Now, we just need to show the Whites that we're worth as much as they are... Some of them already know it, and are giving us the means to achieve this goal. Like the Catholic fathers who welcome you in their beautiful school. And like others... It's only through knowledge that you have a chance to succeed! Do you hear me, Son? Through knowledge!"

His father saw things differently. He would never lose an opportunity to let his wife know.

"Ya oughtn't work for the whiteys! Behind their big smiles and their beautiful speeches, they'll always despise you. The only thing they like from you ... is your resignation..."

In Joe's mind, segregation was a good thing, somehow.

They set the terms of racial segregation.
Source: Jim Crow laws—Wikipedia.
[14]National Alliance of Postal Employees.

"We, Negroes, ain't got nothin' to do with 'em! We're gettin' along awright like we are now!"

Celestine would answer: "Oh yeah? And what kind of school are you able to offer our children, you and your negro friends? What chance would they have to work it out better than we do, without the education from the white fathers, and without the goodwill of some wealthy white patrons of the north?"

"Separate but equal," claimed the white segregationists. Joe used to reply : "segregated, for sure, but equal, God knows it's a lie!"

One day, Joe had proudly shown to his son his member's card of the NAACP. The annual fee was one dollar. In the middle of the printed text, his names and address had been added with a type writer. The card issued by the office in New Orleans certified that George A. Bellegarde had become a member of the *National Association for the Advancement of Colored People* for the year 1936.

After that, Joe had had to reconsider his opinion about segregation, because the NAACP was ferociously fighting it. They argued that the Constitution was indifferent to the color of your skin and didn't recognize nor tolerate the existence of classes among its citizens.

On her side, Celestine couldn't blame him for being a member of the NAACP, because their first demand was the right to equal opportunities through education. The association campaigned for a free and free public school, open to everyone, Whites and Blacks.

However, Celestine feared that Madame Letellier could discover it and may lay her off.

CHAPTER 5

T hanks to the WPA[15] and to Celestine's persuasion, Joe had accepted to be hired in 1935 as an unskilled worker on the City Park Stadium construction site. Four months long, he had to pour concrete with a shovel for the building of the new twenty-six thousand seats outdoor bowl. A back-breaking work.

Afterwards, Joe had found a series of day jobs as an earthwork laborer on various road repairs, or as an unskilled worker on new public building construction sites.

Celestine would ensure that her husband's pay wouldn't end up in drinking booze or gambling. But when it came to his job as a musician in the French quarter on Saturdays and Sundays, she didn't have her say. This was his secret garden. His personal world, from which Celestine wanted to keep her son away as long and far as possible.

The only moments she would allow Firmin to see his father play the saxophone or the harmonica were during family or community gatherings of their neighborhood. Including at funerals. The yearly highlight of these events was *Mardi Gras* in February.

Firmin would never forget his first *Mardi Gras*, in the Lower Ninth Ward. It was in 1936. Nobody would have missed this opportunity to party. Even in these difficult

---

[15] Works Progress Administration created in 1935 under the Administration of F. D. Roosevelt, intending to revive the economy during the Great Depression.

years, his mother had never had the heart to deprive him of it. Watching all these brass bands parading with dance steps in front of you would fill your heart and ears with joy, and make you forget all your daily concerns.

When, finally, Firmin had seen his father in the first row of his band, blowing like a devil in his sax, he had felt swelling with pride and admiration. In the following nights, the child he was dreamed of himself dancing at the head of his own band, bewitching the crowd with the warm sound and the syncopated rhythm of his sax.

Two years later, on his tenth birthday, Firmin had succeeded in getting his mother's approval to let him learn from his father to play an instrument. On this occasion, Joe had offered him one, adapted to his size and at a reasonable price. A ten holes harmonica. A Hohner *Marine band* key of C.

Joe had carefully cleaned and polished it to make it shine, before putting it back in its original packaging. However, Firmin had noticed a few light scratches that had made him think the instrument wasn't new, but he was too happy with his gift to say anything.

The deal with his mother was very clear. As long as he would bring home good report cards from school, she would let him have two hours of training with his father. These weekly sessions soon became the only true father-son tie. The rest of the time, Joe was absent or non-existent. The days he had worked on one or another site, he would come back home so late and tired that you couldn't speak to him.

On Saturdays, by the end of the afternoon, after Firmin's harmonica lesson, Joe would leave home and go to the French quarter to perform in a bar. Firmin and his mother wouldn't see him back home before Sunday late. Most often drunk and hilarious. By chance! Because in such case, Celestine would arrange to undress and put him to bed, before he started to sober up. But if, by misfortune, Joe refused to let her touch him, he would stay in his armchair, unable to fall asleep. Then, while the effects of alcohol were gradually fading, he would successively turn sad, angry, and eventually brutal with his wife. He would blame the world for his being both poor and a Negro. He would shout: "If only I was white! I would become rich and famous! And I would be respected!"

When he woke, the following day, Joe couldn't remember anything. But when he noticed the bruised forearms and the swollen face of his wife, he would apologize profusely. Firmin deeply resented his father for the pain he inflicted to his mother. But Firmin wasn't strong enough to protect her, when it all started, early after they had settled in the Lower Ninth.

When Firmin finally could play most of the local folk tunes, his father offered him a personal saxophone mouthpiece. A brand new one, this time. An alto sax one, handmade with hard rubber, together with a set of five bamboo reeds. The boy must have had a curious gaze when he saw the object, because his father hastened to specify that it was the same model used by "Bennie Bonacio himself." The first saxophonist of the famous Paul Whiteman's jazz orchestra.

Of course, his big band was exclusively composed of white musicians. Nevertheless, Paul Whiteman hadn't hesitated to ask Duke Ellington to write a series of pieces of music that would be recorded with the singers Paul Robeson and Billie Holiday, both colored.

At this moment, Firmin understood why his father sometimes said, under the influence of anger or alcohol: "If only I was White…"

Joe knew his son would have preferred the complete instrument. But he couldn't afford it. So, he explained to him that, one day, he would be able to plug his personal mouthpiece into any alto sax he could borrow. Starting with his father's.

Still long after, Firmin would spend a lot to live this moment, once again, when he felt his father's saxophone for the first time in his hands. When he had managed to get first three notes out of this magical instrument!

Initially upset by this present that might possibly turn their son away from studying, Celestine would soon appreciate its virtues. The average marks on his report card rose by two points within a month. The boy was so scared to be deprived of his weekly saxophone lesson that he would show an increased zeal in doing his homework every afternoon when coming back from school.

During the years following their settlement, the Bellegardes became real city dwellers. Thanks to the cumulated incomes of both parents, everyone home could eat his fill and stay warm in winter.

George kept on working dressed in his dungaree, but from Saturday evening to Sunday night, he would swap it for one of his nice musician suits. Loose lapel pants. Two-tone patent-leather shoes. White starched shirt. Wide suspenders. Silk bow tie, and loose breasted jacket with large shoulder pads.

Celestine had also enriched her wardrobe. Her position at the Letelliers required her being always well dressed. To the greatest pride of her son, when she accompanied him in the morning on his way to school. At least, during the first two years. Afterwards, Firmin had let her understand that he would rather travel with his boyfriends.

CHAPTER 6

E urope was at war since September 1, 1939, but a law[16], signed by Franklin D. Roosevelt on August 31, 1935, compelled the United States to remain neutral. After France's and Great Britain's defeats, the Congress and the American people started to fear for the safety of their borders and for their economic interests. Several amendments had been voted, which allowed supplying military equipment to countries at war against the Nazis.

Then came Pearl Harbor, on December 7, 1941. A day no American would ever forget.

Without previous warning, the Japanese Airforce struck the American base of Oahu Island, near Hawaii, devastating most of the U.S. naval forces in the Pacific.

The following day, December 8, 1941, President F.D. Roosevelt declared war on Japan, Germany and Italy.

This event was the third-biggest upheaval in the life of Firmin and his parents, after the death of Marie, and their settlement in New Orleans.

The country's entry into the war would have huge repercussions on their existence, and on millions of American lives. Particularly on Black people.

It had started with the announcement by President Roosevelt of the *Victory program*, on January 6, 1942.

His ambition was to restart the American economy, still weakened by the aftermath of the Great Depression, by launching a large armament program, which would turn

---

[16] Neutrality Act.

the United States into the arsenal of the Allies.

The aim being to quickly defeat the Axis Powers, the program intended to equip, progressively, eleven million American soldiers with all the necessary equipment. Which would make thousands of factories run at full capacity, and give a job to millions of workers.

As the army was recruiting more soldiers, it became essential to call upon other people available to replace them in factories. Therefore, a large number of jobs, traditionally reserved for Whites, were then given to colored workers.

A talented entrepreneur of New Orleans would take a great advantage of the war and of the Victory program. Mr. Andrew Higgins, founder and president of Higgins Industries.

In the beginning, his factory was manufacturing small shallow-draft boats, designed to be used on the shallow marsh areas of Louisiana. He usually hired seventy to eighty employees. The generals of the U.S. armies must have predicted they would beat their enemies through great amphibian attacks. Because the know-how of this man earned him a contract with the government for the production of about twenty thousand LCVP[17], and around two hundred PT boats.[18]

One year after, Higgins industries would have seven plants and hire twenty thousand people. His needs for manpower became such that Andrew Higgins decided to call, indistinctly, upon women and men, Whites and Blacks. He was the first to do so.

For women and colored workers, the wages were far

---

[17] Landing Craft Vehicle & Personnel.
[18] Patrol Torpedo boats.

more attractive than anywhere else. Celestine had immediately seized the opportunity to get hired there as a riveter. A job usually held by white males.

For white females, these jobs offered a chance to escape from their condition of housewives devoted to their husbands and children, and win the status of independent and self-sufficient women. Moreover, while their husbands were serving their country under the Stars and Stripes banner, they had the feeling of taking a full part in the war effort and in the victory against the Axis Powers.

For Firmin's mother, as for all her colored friends, it was a chance to significantly increase the standard of living of their households.

On this point, the positive effects of the program didn't take long to be felt at home. Celestine had bought her son nice clothes and two pairs of shoes to go to school. The girls of Firmin's high school soon would look at the elegant teenager with an admiring gaze. In the same year, Firmin had kissed a girl for the first time. On her mouth, like in the movies. An experience that Firmin would remember for a long time. Her name was Shirley.

But the most exciting change came with the arrival at home of their first table radio. An Emerson AX-212 that Celestine had paid nearly twenty dollars! A great deal of money at the time.

More than watching his father play the sax in amateurs and semi-professional orchestras had done before, the musical programs on WWL 870 AM led Firmin to discover the greatest jazz musicians of the country.

There were also live radio broadcasts of Joe Louis boxing matches. The professional boxer from Alabama was a hero for all the African American community. After he had been defeated by a knockout in the twelfth round, by the German Max Schmelling, in their first encounter on June 6, 1936, Louis became a heavy-weight world champion, one year later. Then, on June 22, 1938, Joe Louis managed to take a brilliant revenge at the Yankee Stadium, by defeating Max Schmelling by a knockout after only two minutes and four seconds of fight[19].

His victory against the icon of the Nazi regime earned him the admiration and the respect of a large part of the white audience.

Unfortunately, the day the radio set had entered Bellegardes' home, Joe Louis had already joined the U.S. Army as a volunteer. He would then only fight in military charity boxing matches until the end of the war.

Such was the impact of the war and the Victory program.

But they also had another influence on their lives. Far more important than the material aspect.

Some members of the Black community saw them as an unprecedented opportunity to express and share their demands. The trigger had been an article in the African American press.

Referring to a letter sent by a reader to the editor in chief, the *Pittsburgh Courier*[20] had launched in February 1942 the *Double Victory* campaign. Victory inside the United States against segregation and racial inequality, and victory abroad against the Axis Powers. The same newspaper had already stood out, four years earlier, by publishing a letter to Franklin D. Roosevelt, asking him

---

[19] Source: https://fr.wikipedia.org/wiki/Joe_Louis. Joseph Louis Barrow remained world champion until 1949.
[20] Biggest newspaper published by African Americans.

for the establishment of a new Negro division in the army.

The headline of the Pittsburgh Courier showed the logo of the campaign. Two Vs overlaid and topped with a bald eagle, and the slogan: *Double Victory, Democracy at home and abroad*. The idea had immediately been passed on by two other big African American newspapers: the *Chicago defender* and the *Afro American* in Baltimore. Soon followed by all the Negro press.

The requirements of this campaign were very clear. As the African Americans would be requested to go and fight for democracy abroad, they should have the right to expect in return an equal treatment in their country.

Unfortunately, the campaign didn't last more than six months. Many Blacks benefited from the Victory program. They feared they might lose these economic advantages if they had continued to campaign too frontally for their civil rights.

The Negro press eventually adopted a more positive attitude and tone in regard to the war effort. As a compensation, they started publishing many articles about the role played by colored soldiers in the defense of their country, and on the theaters of operation against the Nazis and the Japanese.

Firmin's father had quickly subscribed to the Baltimore newspaper, by the advice of his friends of the local section of the NAACP. Every week, Joe would ask his son to read him the articles of a reporter named Ollie Stewart[21]. The man who would make Firmin want to become a journalist.

---

[21] African American journalist (1906–1977). He became the first Black reporter accredited by the U.S. Department of War, as a war correspondent in North Africa and in Europe.
Source: https://en.wikipedia.org/wiki/Ollie_Stewart

CHAPTER 7

F irmin deeply admired Ollie Stewart. He particularly liked the tone of his articles, in which he told the life of American colored soldiers. All the more that this guy didn't mince words to denounce the segregation applied in the U.S. Army, and all the racial prejudices against the Negroes.

In one article published in November 1941, one week before Pearl Harbor and America's entry into the war, Ollie Stewart had already severely criticized the behavior of white officers towards colored soldiers. He challenged the idea that only a White man could make a good commanding officer of Black troops.

At the time, his father was not yet a subscriber of the Baltimore Afro-American Newspaper. It was one of his school friends who had let him read it. The boy used to collect all articles of this kind that he would clip from the newspapers thrown in the trash by their readers.

Known for its provocative headlines, the weekly newspaper had titled the article: "*White Faces Making Lee Soldiers Sick.*" Which had angered Edgar Hoover, then FBI's head, over the editor in chief. Yet, Stewart had remained very moderate in his analysis. From then on, Hoover had sought to stop the publication by all means. Without Roosevelt's intervention, he would surely have succeeded.

Actually, Ollie Stewart was just advocating on behalf of the intelligent and educated negro soldiers he had met, and who felt deeply offended by repeated humiliations and discriminatory measures. Not to mention the absence of recreation organized for them inside the camps. No theater, no library, no relaxing room! Nothing of what the Whites were offered.

In this article, Ollie Stewart wrote:[22]

"The truth of the matter is, these white officers at Camp Lee do not understand their men at all. They mean well— but they just don't know. They live in a different world, and it is my honest opinion that they will never get as fine response and results from their units as colored officers would. [...]

Let's reverse the order. White officers here could learn why their men work so hard to 'have a world of fun' by taking the same treatment their men take — just for one week. It is extremely doubtful that they could be so convincing afterward in telling a visitor how well the colored 'boys' are being treated!

White officers should be chased back to the rear of the couch every time they paid their fare and entered a bus. They should have to abide by the orders that forbid colored soldiers to even walk through certain streets in Petersburg, and to walk but so far on other streets. [...]

They should know by experience how it feels to be forbidden entrance to hotels, bars, theaters and clubs in Petersburg—and even segregated on the U.S. Army post."

Which Firmin and his friends would soon discover by themselves.

Stewart concluded his article in these words:

"In short, the colored men in this camp are strictly on

---

[22] Excerpts from Ollie Stewart's article of Nov 29, 1941, in the Baltimore Afro-American newspaper.

their own when it comes to spending their leisure hours. Jim crowed in their neighboring town, Jim crowed on the post, they retreat to their areas and make a splendid effort to find happiness among themselves. Anything to keep from going nuts."

Despite Edgar Hoover's threats of a trial for sedition against the Afro-American, its editor in chief kept on publishing Stewart's articles. From then on, Firmin followed his school friend's example and started clipping and collecting all the papers signed by Stewart.

These kinds of publications could only galvanize Negro youth like Firmin, and push them to demand the repeal of Jim Crow laws. This probably also encouraged Firmin to graduate high school, and consider going to college.

As of spring 1942, these papers had convinced the teenager, like many others, that the best way to fight segregation was to prove his patriotism and follow the example of hundreds of thousands of Negroes who had already enlisted in the U.S. Army[23].

Like Joe Louis on January 10, 1942.

Like his mother who was building landing craft boats at Higgins, he would fight against the Axis Powers.

But he had decided to wait until the end of his last school year before he would ask his parents' permission, especially his mother's, whose reaction he feared.

---

[23] 93,000 in 1941. 331,000 in 1942.
   Source: special studies by Ulysses Lee *The employment of Negro troops.*

CHAPTER 8

November 21, 1943

F our days long, the *Aquitania* had been sailing across the North Atlantic Ocean. Four days and as many nights that seemed endless to all the guys confined in every nook and cranny of the huge metal structure.

The ship had cast off on November 17, at 13:30 hours. She had left the harbor, pulled by two powerful tugboats. Many soldiers had stayed on the upper deck and watched the shape of the Statue of Liberty fading until it had disappeared behind the horizon. Surrounded by his comrades, Firmin had prayed, in communion with his mother he thought. But he didn't know, then, that he would spend all the crossing time begging for the Lord's mercy.

Off the American shores, the Ocean was already restless. Nothing too bad, according to the crew members. Still enough, however, to make the captain order the last stragglers to return to their berths right off the bat.

The *Aquitania* had to reach a minimum speed of twenty knots to have a chance to escape German *U-Boote* strikes, especially without a Marine escort. But at such a speed, the ship was dangerously swaying, and walking along the passageways would require a strong sense of balance and quite a good physical coordination. A difficult exercise for those who have sea legs. Hardly feasible in practice for others.

From then on, the *Aquitania* turned into the antechamber of hell.

It didn't take long until the more seasickness-sensitive ones started to vomit. No time to reach the washrooms. Too far. Already occupied. Some would throw up into their helmets, as suggested by the crew. Then the smell of vomit would cause all others to spew their guts out.

The first evening, Firmin and several non-commissioned officers of the 320th VLA had tried to take their meal in a lunchroom, intending to escape from the stale air of their cabin. They never managed to reach it, as it was already full. When they had returned to their berths, the food distribution was over. They had to be satisfied with a few crackers to fill and ease their stomachs, which had been seriously battered by the nausea of the day.

The second night had been a further descent into the depth of hell. The slop served on board by the British cooks turned out as appalling as its smell had let it foreshadow, causing an epidemic of diarrhea. The putrid stench of the washrooms would soon add to the stink of vomit.

By chance, Firmin had come through this first food poisoning. But he wouldn't avoid the following ones. Spewing when your stomach is empty is a real torture for your guts.

To kill time, when they were not seized by nausea or diarrhea, most of the guys were gambling, despite the outright ban from their senior officers. Or they would read some popular comics or their personal mail. Fewer were those who, like Firmin, would record their feelings or state of mind in their diary. Firmin didn't have the heart of telling his parents about the daily ordeal he was enduring.

Later, when returning home after the war, if God grants him to survive until then, Firmin would probably laugh about it. But, for now, he was cursing the day he had announced to his mother his intention to join the army.

During the previous night, the alarm had sounded. All the men had been ordered to climb up to the upper deck. The presence of a nearby *U-Boot* had been detected. Terrorized and numbed with the cold, their life jackets around their necks, they had attended the dropping of dozens of depth charges, which by exploding would make the metal structure of the *Aquitania* resonate. They had been waiting for hours under this unbearable tension before they had been allowed to return to their compartments. The alert had ended, but the fear of being sent to the bottom had remained, and would remain until the end of their journey.

Exhausted by this forced vigil, as much as by their continuous seasickness, the men of the 320th AABBB were sleeping like the dead during the night of November 21, when suddenly the ship was violently shaken. The four rows of hanging berths detached from the wall at once, crashing Firmin and his comrades down to the floor in a deafening racket.

Still dazed with sleep, most of the men were convinced they had been hit by a German torpedo. They immediately feared they would be locked in their watertight compartment; sacrificed to save the ship and the lives of the occupants of the decks above them. Petrified with fear of dying, some were whimpering and beseeching the Lord to save them. Others, driven by their survival instinct, rushed to their life jackets and tempted to reach the upper decks, uttering howls of terror. Firmin felt panic overwhelm his entire body. Dying like this, without having even fought! The idea was unbearable. So, he recovered and decided he would struggle to stay alive. At all costs. He grabbed one of the straps of his berth and straightened himself up on his legs.

But the ship was swaying so much that Firmin could hardly stand on his feet. Amidst the confusion, he recognized a familiar shape. It was Albert White, the chaplain of the 320th VLA who was trying to calm his flock down, while overcoming his own fear. When they all realized the *Aquitania* was keeping on swinging back and forth, and heeling over, but no leak was to be found, the passengers soon recovered their composure.

Later, they would learn from the crew members they had only faced a violent storm, with a wind speed between forty and seventy-five knots, and up to thirty-three-foot waves.

Firmin was then unable to go back to sleep. To banish his blues, he recalled the day when he had received his high school diploma.

CHAPTER 9

Seventeen months earlier.

T he date of June 26, 1942 would stay engraved in Firmin's memory forever. The day of the graduation ceremony. The reward for eight years of hard work at high school.

More than a mere card sheet that would give him access to a college, it had been the pride on his parents' faces that had given the teenager the most intense emotion.

Before he even went on the stage to receive from the hands of the principle the precious document that would soon be framed and hanged on one of the walls of their living room, Firmin had already made the decision of postponing the college projects his mother had dreamed of and hoped for him. But he refused to deprive her of enjoying her happiness until the next day.

She was so proud of him and so happy with this first outcome of all the sacrifices she had made until then.

Firmin had already let his father in on the secret. The latter had approved his decision, as it was in compliance with the political line of the NAACP. Firmin had made him promise he would not let Celestine know, for the moment.

Always worthy, like on the day Marie died, Joe was striving not to weep. But actually, he was as moved as his wife. In their neighborhood, the kids who managed to reach this level of education were rare. Many at the same age could hardly read and write. Joe would brag to his fellow musicians and other workers on the construction sites where he used to work.

Firmin understood his father had bet a few greenbacks that his son would get his diploma with highest honors, as written on the document. This is what he guessed when he saw his father fold and cram into his pocket a wad of cash, that his fellow musician had given him.

Besides this, Joe was convinced that the war would soon be over, and that his degree would earn his son an officer's rank in the army. Therefore, Joe had no reason to worry about Firmin.

Celestine organized a dinner at home. She invited their neighbors, but only the Robinsons came. The Davises had claimed a family impediment not to join. The truth was that they couldn't stand to see the Bellegardes' son succeed, when their rascal sons would be condemned to live from thankless odd jobs until the end of their lives.

On the other hand, other nearby families came with their children, hoping they would want to follow Firmin's example. Beyond his air of modesty, the boy was proud like a peacock. He spent the evening strutting around among a dozen of appreciative kids.

He even seized the opportunity to seduce a girl, whose parents Celestine had invited. She must have found him pretentious, because she rapidly lost interest in him.

Firmin waited until the following morning to announce to his mother his decision, on their way to St-Paul's Lutheran church, on Annette street. She suddenly stopped walking, stood in front of him, stared at him, straight in the eyes, for a few seconds, and slapped his face. Without saying a single word. Then, she resumed walking towards the church, with a quick and purposeful stride. Firmin followed her. Quietly. His head downcast. His eyes pointing to the ground.

It had been eight years since he last had set foot in a Protestant church. Because of his new Catholic education. He recognized some of the neighbors who were looking at him with a watchful and admiring gaze.

He understood why, when he listened to the pastor's sermon. Celestine had already told everybody about the news. His speech was devoted to the virtues of knowledge, and aimed at encouraging the parents in the church to follow the example of Celestine and another mother, whose children had just graduated high school. The teenagers could feel the gazes of all the faithful turning in their direction after the pastor had pointed his hand at them.

On their way back home, Celestine just asked Firmin if he had informed his father of his decision. When she learned that Joe had not opposed it, she gave up making him change his mind.

That was how Firmin had joined uncle Sam in August, 1942. While they were waiting for the bus which would drive them to their military base, a crowd of several hundred people had gathered around Firmin. Young recruits like him, of course. Probably less than fifty. But mostly their parents and some next of kin.

Fathers were playing tough guys. His father would tap him on the shoulder, from time to time, repeating to him "Ah'm proud a'ya, son! Yuh naw it?"

When the bus finally arrived, he hugged him for long. Without saying a word, this time.

Celestine, on her side, had never stopped containing her emotion by flooding him with the recommendations of a protective mother. "Did you take your toothbrush? And the cookies? Didn't you forget them in the kitchen?..."

Before letting him step into the bus of the *Southern Interstate Lines*, she encircled him with her arms, and implored him to take care of himself, to write to her, as often as possible, and not to forget saying his prayers every evening. She didn't cry. Not in front of him, at least.

Intending to reassure herself, she thought well adding: "your general'd better bring you back alive and in perfect shape. Otherwise, I swear I'll personally kick his ass! Hear?"

Firmin was not the only one who heard this. It would earn him constant mockery during several days. Until he decided to put it an end, by knocking one of his comrades down with a right jab.

Luckily, no one noticed what his mother secretly slipped into his pocket, while whispering in his ear, in French:

"Ne t'en sépare jamais ! Tu m'entends ?"[24]

Firmin fingered the object inside his pocket. He instantly recognized a Haitian lucky charm. Knowing his mother, so respectful of her pastor's teaching, Firm felt stunned. Almost shocked.

When she noticed his embarrassment, she added, still in French:

"Ça ne m'empêchera pas de prier pour toi, tous les jours. Et de toute façon, ça ne pourra pas te faire de mal."[25]

Firmin smiled at her and promised he would always

---

[24] "Don't you ever part with it! You hear me?"

[25] "Of course, it won't stop me from praying for your sake, every day. Anyhow, it won't do you no harm!"

keep it with him. Since then, when dark thoughts crossed his mind, he would grasp the fabric bag in his hand, and his blues would soon vanish, like by magic.

The four-hour drive to Camp Claiborne, south of Alexandria, Louisiana, went smoothly and very quiet.

The time of contemplation followed the excitement of their departure. Most of the guys had never lived away from their families. They had no idea of what a soldier's life looked like. On his part, Firmin still had in mind the articles of Ollie Stewart about the living conditions of the colored soldiers in the army. So, he was striving to comfort himself by thinking that they had surely been improved in the meantime by the military staff.

By chance, Firmin was sitting near a boy of his age, who had also graduated from another high school of New Orleans. Like him, he had chosen to postpone his plans of university studies, until the end of the war. The two boys didn't need to expand on their respective political motivations, as they were induced by their decision. Moreover, both of them were aware that any displayed political stand would earn them serious trouble with the military hierarchy.

Firmin would really have liked to sympathize further with this boy. Having a friend in a foreign and even hostile environment would have been a priceless help to overcome moments of solitude and despair. Unfortunately, the army would decide otherwise. They both would be assigned to two separate units.

Camp Claiborne, where all the volunteer soldiers of Louisiana were sent, was housing the Engineering Unit Training Command. Firmin joined a small transportation unit called Engineer Dump Truck Company, which counted one hundred and twenty men, of which four white senior officers and nine black non-commissioned officers.

Camp Claiborne was a gigantic military camp, located a few miles away from Forest Hill, Louisiana, which construction had started in 1940. The first regiments, mainly attached to the 34th infantry division, had arrived early 1941. The camp also saw the birth, in the same month of August 1942, of the 82nd and 101st Airborne. Before them, two other famous units had emerged in the camp, in February 1942. The 784th and the 761st Tank Battalions. Two among the rare colored combat units in the U.S. Army. The 761st would later be distinguished in Europe under the name of *The Black Panthers*.

Firmin and the passengers of the bus were impressed by the size of the camp and the number of new facilities, which included a post office, a bank, several post exchanges, seventeen chapels, six movie theaters, three guest houses, five service clubs, a large sports arena and a bus station[26].

But they would soon come down to earth. All this was designed for the white soldiers and officers.

The colored sector was located far away from the command center.

Segregation laws in this Southern State applied inside as well as outside the camp. And of course, as far as possible from the area reserved for the white battalions. Firmin and his colored comrades would be housed in tents. Nothing had finally changed since the first articles by Ollie Stewart. The white officers justified their decision by

[26]Source:https://www.alexandria-louisiana.com/camp-claiborne-louisiana.htm

alleging that they wanted to avoid unrest caused by racial tensions.

CHAPTER 10

The recruits were confined inside the base for ten weeks. Their bodies were put under severe strain by daily twenty-five miles forced marches. Sometimes by night. Besides the physical exhaustion, they had to withstand the nervous tension caused by the repeated jeers and taunts from white officers, most often from the South and overtly racist, who strove to insult and humiliate them.

Most of the African Americans at Camp Claiborne were from Louisiana and other Southern States. As such, they were used to both verbal and physical assaults, and they knew they would rather not answer them.

The words of a "nigger" didn't weigh much when opposing those of a white officer. Challenging an order, or even responding to insulting comments, would have been considered as an act of rebellion. In times of war, this would have earned them to be court-martialed. The soldiers had to champ at the bit, not to bust out with anger.

Firmin and his tent mates welcomed their first furlough with a great relief. They were deeply disappointed when they realized the fierce resentment of the white local population towards colored soldiers.

It started from the bus stop, not far from the entrance of the camp. Two buses passed along, without stopping, although half empty. Firmin and three fellow soldiers managed to get on a third one. They mechanically walked to the rear of the bus, and sat beyond the curtain which indicated the end of the section reserved "for Whites only."

Another Negro, unknown to them, stepped in and sat on one of the free seats in the front zone. The bus driver, who was keeping an eye on him through his rearview mirror, turned around and started to shout at him.

"Hey, you nigger! You're gonna move your ass from there, and you're gonna join your fellow niggers in the back of my bus!"

The soldier didn't move. He calmly replied to the driver: "what allows you to call me nigger? I'm a soldier of the U.S. Army!"

Then, the driver stood up, put his hand on the gun hung on his belt, and answered to the guy in a threatening tone:

"For sure, you're a nigger! A fuckin' nigger! You're under the Mason-Dixon line here! And on this side of the line, you're all little niggers. So, either you're gently gonna sit in the back with your friends, or you get the fuck out of my bus!"

While saying this, the bus driver never stopped fingering the butt of his handgun.

The soldier struggled to contain his anger. He was aware of the consequences his resistance would have. The least being a fine, the worse being an all-out beating, or, who knows, a hangman's noose. He turned his head and looked questioningly at the soldiers sitting in the back, with a gaze in which you could read his thought: "So, you won't move your asses to help me?!"

There was no need for Firmin and his comrades to reply. Their absence of reaction betrayed their embarrassed powerlessness. The man eventually stood up, hesitated a few seconds, walked back to the front and got off the coach. He waited until the bus had restarted, and addressed Firmin and his neighbors a gaze of contempt, and spat on the ground, conspicuously.

This excursion outside the military compound deterred Firmin and his friends for ever from asking any further overnight leave near Alexandria. Although recreation possibilities and facilities for colored soldiers inside Clamp Claiborne were limited, while the Whites could benefit from several movie theaters, recreation clubs, and even a swimming pool.

The access to the Exchange store was strictly regulated. When it was not purely denied to Negroes, it was available to them for only a few hours. And even then, colored soldiers couldn't claim drinking a soda on the spot like their White counterparts did it.

Afterwards, Firmin attended training related to his job in the unit. The transportation of military stuff in multi-purpose dump trucks, with a loading capacity of two and a half tons. Ninety-one horse power GMC[27] trucks, which could reach a speed of forty-five miles per hour.

His command and mechanical skills earned Firmin to rapidly be appointed an engine repair team leader, with the rank of corporal.

He had hoped to stay in this unit, because of its relative vicinity to New Orleans. Yet, he had had only two opportunities to pay a visit to his parents, since his enlistment in the Army. The first time was by the end of October 1942, on the occasion of a seventy-two hours' furlough. The second time, one month later, after he had been informed of his coming transfer to another unit.

Educated and graduated African Americans were rare. Especially in the Southern States. Most of the enlisted

---

[27] General Motor Company.

colored soldiers could hardly read, and even less could write. Besides a few rudiments. The most educated were therefore wisely divided in various regiments, as they would serve as a link between the white hierarchy and the black troops.

Firmin was granted a one-week leave before his transfer to Camp Tyson in Paris, Tennessee. This new separation was a real heartbreak for his mother. But for Joe, it was, above all, a great pride to learn his son would actively participate in the defense of his country.

CHAPTER 11

Camp Tyson, December 1942

P aris, Tennessee, and the whole Henry County, had been chosen as of August 15, 1941, to house the new training center for the anti-aircraft barrage balloon units of the U.S. Army. Its construction, started on September 4 of the same year, had been completed on March 14, 1942.

When Firmin arrived at Camp Tyson early December, the facilities were still new. The site was stretching out one mile and nine hundred yards from north to south, and two miles and eight hundred yards from east to west. An area of about nine hundred acres occupied by nearly four hundred fifty white buildings, including a four-hundred-bed hospital, a twenty-five-hundred-seat theater, a hotel to receive visitors, a recreation center, two chapels and a library.

Before the United States' entry into the war, barrage balloons weren't considered as an efficient defensive weapon against air strikes. The disaster of Pearl Harbor radically changed the opinion of the U.S. Army. The absence of balloons in the sky above the naval base of Oahu Island in Hawaii had encouraged the Japanese to launch their surprise attack on the morning of December 7, 1941.

It was agreed later, at a high level, that, had the harbor been protected by a few dozen balloons, the Japanese dive-bomber strikes would have been impossible, or at least less efficient, and the bulk of the U.S. naval fleet would have been spared.

Since this cursed day, barrage balloons had become a strategic priority.

Camp Tyson would train thirty battalions of this new weapon. Twenty-six of them would be composed of white staff. Four others would be colored units under white command. The 318th, 319th, 320th and 321st CABBB.

Firmin Bellegarde joined the 320th CABBB.

He would never forget the show he had seen at his arrival on the camp. Oblong shaped balloons, as big as buses, floating in the air. Sunbeams reflecting on their metal casing.

As he was getting closer, he could notice the long steel ropes that linked them to the solid ground. He had already seen some pictures of British balloons flying in the sky of London, over Tower Bridge or the House of Parliament. But seeing them in real life, projecting their protective shadows on the ground of Camp Tyson, was far more spectacular.

Firmin arrived at the same time as another group of soldiers, coming from various Northern States. Unlike him, they weren't volunteers, but draftees.

They didn't like the idea of serving their country in a segregated and often racist army. Moreover, they feared they may end up in a Southern State subject to Jim Crow laws. The commandant himself, Lieutenant Colonel Leon John Reed, welcomed the newcomers. The thirty-four-year-old officer, born in South Carolina, graduated at fifteen, had won a scholarship to the Citadel, the prestigious military college of Charleston. He belonged to the rare white officers capable of leading colored soldiers efficiently. Unlike many of his counterparts, he knew how to impose his authority without showing disrespect to his Negro subordinates.

He never used racist epithets like "nigger" when talking to them. In return, they showed him a deep deference.

Unfortunately, Reed's second in command was a Texan using a less refined language. Captain William Taylor, nicknamed *Wild Bill*. When talking to one of his men, he used to call him "boy," as if he was speaking to an immature child.

Dressed to the nines in his service uniform, Lieutenant Colonel Reed read to the recruits a welcome speech written by Brigadier General John Blackwell Maynard[28], commandant of the base. The latter wanted to remind the rookies the great honor and immense responsibility that laid on his shoulders, in this unique training center dedicated to the handling of anti-aircraft barrage balloons. The first men trained at Camp Tyson, he said, would enlighten the path for all those who would succeed them. The solemn tone of Lieutenant Colonel Reed and the silence that was reigning at this moment gave the speech a strength that swelled Firmin and his comrades with pride.

As he had already undergone a basic military training at Camp Claiborne, Firmin was exempted from the nine weeks of forced marches and physical pain the others would have to endure.

He was directly attached to the battery A of the 320th CABBB, as a balloon crew leader. He would follow a series of technical training. Starting with six weeks to

---

[28] August 12, 1887 — February 2, 1945. Source :
https://www.findagrave.com/memorial/49259947/john-blackwell-maynard

learn how to operate a balloon. The men quickly realized the complexity of this defensive weapon. They took their mission even more seriously.

The risk of accidents was high. The balloons were tethered to the ground by steel ropes which could be broken off when the wind was too strong. In such a case, a valve device would open up to let the gas escape and make the balloon go down. But meanwhile, the casing would accumulate static electricity. And to bring the balloon back to the ground, the operators had to grasp the mooring lines with their hands protected by special gloves, made from leather outside and from rubber inside. Without them, the operators would be injured by deep cuts and violent electric shocks. However, this protection sometimes turned out to be insufficient. Therefore, they had to wait until the last wire had touched the ground to be sure that all the electricity was gone. Lightning as well could strike a balloon down through its lines, as would happen later, causing the death of a crew member.

The men constantly needed to watch out that no wire would wind around a leg or an arm during the ascending phase. Otherwise, the balloon could lift an operator to considerable heights.

Twelve more weeks were required to learn to read the sky and make weather forecasts. Balloons were indeed very sensitive to wind and storm, and could quickly become uncontrollable. The crews had to keep their balloons facing the wind.

Then, they had weapon handling training, especially with the Garand M1 rifle, which would accompany them on the field. They also learned hand-to-hand fighting with a dagger, disarming an enemy, surviving in a hostile territory.

This intensive training program reinforced the *esprit de corps* that welded the men together. Although he couldn't know, nor appreciate, each of the twelve hundred guys of the 320th CABBB, Firmin managed to build a circle of friends with whom he enjoyed talking, laughing, having a drink or taking a trip outside the camp. Although the local white population didn't welcome the colored soldiers.

CHAPTER 12

Camp Tyson, May 1943

L ike many other military compounds, Camp Tyson was far from lively cities where colored soldiers could enjoy recreational activities when they were on leave.

The nearest town was *Little Paris*, which had the only club available for thousands of Black soldiers based at Camp Tyson. To get there, you had to take a twenty-five-seat bus that passed before the base only once an hour. Needless to say that for Firmin and his friends it wasn't easy to get to the town and relax for a few hours. To top it all off, alcohol was prohibited.

Paris, Tennessee, housed a Black community, which would welcome the soldiers who behaved correctly. Some families even happened to invite a few of them for dinner, after the Sunday mass.

Further, halfway from Memphis, were Jackson and the Lane College, where the soldiers could buy a hamburger and a glass of punch, and dance the jitterbug or the swing with a girl. As there was no hotel accommodation in the town, the smartest guys managed to get hosted for the night by some inhabitants. However, Firmin quickly got tired of this place and started to save a part of his monthly thirty dollars' pay. He intended to make an unforgettable stay in the city of Memphis, Tennessee. He had to provide enough to buy the round-trip ticket and pay all the extra costs. Drinks, two or three movie sessions in one of the ten theaters allowed to colored people, where he would admire the gorgeous Lena Horne in the musical *Cabin in the sky*. And of course, hotel accommodations for two nights, at least.

Located about one hundred and twenty-five miles west from Camp Tyson, Memphis was a mythical place for all the blues lovers. Where giants like Cab Calloway, Louis Armstrong and Muddy Waters used to perform in the south side clubs.

A few weeks earlier, Firmin had been told, by one of the guys the HQ battery, that the *Palace Theater*, on Beale Street, organized evening events. Amateur musicians were given the chance to perform in front of an enthusiastic audience. Like Firmin, William played in a brass band of Harlem, New York. Both friends had mutually challenged themselves to get registered on the list of the participants of one of these events, and play together with two other guys of the 320th some blues standards.

The challenge was ambitious for Firmin, as he hadn't touched an alto sax since his departure from New Orleans. Plus, the only instruments that he had brought in his duffle bag were his *Marine band* key of C harmonica and his hard rubber mouthpiece with two spare bamboo reeds. During the rehearsals, Firmin had to sing the notes while handling an imaginary saxophone with his two hands.

After three hours of travel by train in the colored compartment, Firmin, William and the two other soldiers of the 320th VLA went in search of a restaurant, nearby the station.

They soon noticed a snack bar, almost empty. One of the four tables behind the window was occupied by a couple. At the bar, a man sitting on a stool was staring at his glass of beer. The bar owner was talking to him, while cleaning the counter.

The four soldiers hesitated shortly to enter in the place that was free of any colored customer. But they were too hungry to look for another one.

Bill was the first to overcome his apprehension. He opened the door and got inside, inviting his friends to follow him. "Good evening" he said, with a neutral tone. The bar owner stared at the newcomers with a pout of disgust and contempt. The customer at the bar ventured a glance over his shoulder, wagged his head, and turned back to his silent monologue with his glass. The four soldiers refrained from reacting to the particularly chilling reception of the owner and directly sat down at one of the free tables. From behind his counter, the boss made them understand they would have to come and pick up their orders by their own. "Without those uniforms, wouldn't even let you in. So, pay me, hurry up eating up your meal, and get the hell outta here!" he said.

Bill started to stand up, but Firmin held him down by the jacket. It was out of the question to ruin the furlough they had prepared during several weeks.

The four GIs ordered the same meal. A hamburger with fries, a glass of chilled beer, and a cup of coffee. They tasted their meal silently, and very slowly, to piss off this asshole.

One hour later, on their way to Beale Street, fifteen minutes walk from the train station, the four friends witnessed a scene that might have disgusted them, once for all, to serve their country. A small group of civilians was joking loudly with white officers in uniform, outside a restaurant. Passing along one of the guys, one of Firmin's friends recognized a few German words. Firmin had heard of German POWs that were kept in custody in military bases, on the American soil. But when they saw the whole group entering the restaurant, which displayed a sign mentioning "For Whites Only," the four African American soldiers felt deeply humiliated. They started wondering if they weren't completely wrong when they imagined that their involvement in this war against the Nazis would earn them one day the recognition of their rights as full American citizens. The enemies of America and democracy were better considered and treated than Black Americans.

Luckily, their goal for this evening was very close. The four of the 320th VLA didn't wait long until they could hear the muffled sound of music coming out of each bar, each club or performance theater that dotted Beale Street. They stopped in front of a large poster announcing an exceptional concert by the Cab Calloway Orchestra, on the following day.

They continued their way until they reached the number 324 of the street, and stopped at the entrance of the *Palace Theater*. The evening headliner was Earl "Fatha" Hines and his Orchestra, featuring prestigious soloists like Charlie "Bird" Parker, playing the alto sax, Dizzy Gillespie, playing the trumpet, Sarah Vaughan, the piano and vocals, and the singer Billy Eckstine. The promise was tantalizing. A waiting line of over one hundred yards was already stretching on the sidewalk. Firmin and Bill looked at each other for a few seconds, with wide and shining eyes, then rushed to the end of the line. They couldn't miss such an incredible gathering of talented musicians.

They came out of the *Palace Theater* three hours later, stunned and firmly decided to wait a bit longer before they would perform on a stage. They weren't ready to compete with those jazz heavyweights. They wouldn't come back the next day to register the *Amateur Night*. However, they vowed they would attend Cab Calloway Orchestra's concert, whatever it may cost.

CHAPTER 13

Camp Tyson, November 6, 1943

This first unforgettable excursion to Memphis was also the last one. Firmin transcribed his memories of that day in his diary. One day, he might use them to write a few articles for the African American press. Wouldn't any newspaper accept to publish them, Firmin would write his memoirs or, who knows, a novel like those of Richard Wright[29], or poems, like Langston Hughes[30].

Like in many cities in the country, racial tensions lead to violent outbursts.

One night of July 1943, a Black soldier of the 320th CABBB, Herman *"Hank"* Hankins, was shot dead in the back by a .22 long rifle bullet[31]. According to the official version, Hankins had been mistaken with a prowler and had refused to obey the injunction of the police that came to arrest him. Despite the virulent protest of his fellow soldiers, the high command of Camp Tyson refused to launch an internal investigation. The news was reported in the African American press on August 14, mentioning two other suspicious deaths of black soldiers. One of them in South Carolina had also been shot in the back.

---

[29] Writer and journalist (1908–1960), author of *Native son* published in 1941.

[30] Poet, short story writer and columnist (1902–1967), involved in the Harlem Renaissance movement.

[31] Source: Forgotten, p. 128, by Linda Hervieux.

Fearing that riots may break out inside the camp, the staff decided to ban the colored soldiers outright from going to Little Paris and Jackson, Tennessee. Regarding Firmin, it made no difference. He had anticipated the troubles and already given up venturing outside the compound, because of the tensions between black soldiers and white police officers.

Previously, in June 1943, following a strike in a *Packard* factory in Detroit[32], Michigan, riots had erupted, leading to the death of thirty-four people, of whom twenty-five Blacks, and nearly six hundred wounded. Seventeen of the victims had been killed by the police.

Although a Northern liberal State, New York applied *Jim Crow* laws in some areas. The Blacks of Negro Harlem were banned from some nightclubs and theaters, sometimes even in their neighborhood. White-owned shops along the 125th street refused to hire colored employees. Despite the ban on racial discrimination, factories of Long Island under contract with the War Department claimed not having jobs vacant for colored workers, whereas they were looking for white workers.

After the Great Depression, Negro Harlem had seen its population increase by six hundred percent in thirty years. Outside the bourgeois neighborhood of Sugar Hill, with its elegant houses, the rest of the inhabitants were crammed in sordid, dilapidated and unhealthy buildings. Harlem had turned into the largest slum of the country.

All the conditions were met for an imminent explosion. Rumors predicted a large-scale riot for the 4th of July celebrations. It was another rumor that set the fire in the

---

[32] Source: http://www.detroits-great-rebellion.com/Detroit---1943.html

night of August 1st to 2nd, 1943.

James Collins, a white police officer, had shot a black soldier, named Robert Bandy, and wounded him. Right after, rumors had spread in all Negro Harlem, saying that the young man had been killed. It was enough to make groups gather and organize a vast retaliation offensive against White-owned businesses. At dawn, the authorities counted six dead, five hundred fifty arrests, and fourteen hundred shops and businesses destroyed or damaged[33].

During the following months, racial tensions inside the camp kept on worsening.

In October, sixty-four colored soldiers of Camp Tyson seized two trucks to go chasing a white police officer who had killed one of their fellow soldiers. The mutineers were arrested and court-martialed. They got from one to five years' forced labor.

Like many of his comrades, Firmin feared that the situation might go out of control and that he would get involved in a riot. This could end up with him being killed or, at least, tied to one of the chain gangs he had seen along the roads of Louisiana and Tennessee. And without the integrity of Lieutenant Colonel Reed, things would probably have ended this way for Firmin and his friends.

Fortunately, there were plenty of opportunities to busy the soldiers' bodies and minds to prevent them from brooding over their bitterness or doing silly things. Close combat. Rifle shooting training. And above all, night marches, loaded like donkeys, under the orders of a pitiless lieutenant who pushed their limits until his men would faint.

---

[33] Source : https://www.revolvy.com/page/Harlem-riot-of-1943

Intending to motivate his soldiers, Leon Reed reminded them of the great utility of their mission. He told them, in a detailed manner, the performance of another barrage balloon battalion, which had illustrated in the invasion of Sicily, Italy, in July 1943.

The relief eventually came, one morning of October, when Lieutenant Colonel Reed informed them that the best of his soldiers would soon be given the chance to shine on the theater of operations. On this occasion, they discovered their new model of balloons, named VLA[34], which would accompany them on the field. They would fly at an altitude ranging from six hundred to forty-three hundred feet, to be compared to sixteen thousand feet with the current model.

The size of the first balloons made their production very expensive. But also hard to use. Their volume required huge quantities of gas to be inflated, and large crews of operators to be maneuvered.

Thirty-five feet long and fourteen feet wide, the new balloons had a volume of twenty thousand gallons. As a consequence, they required only ten percent of the gas needed by the previous models. They could be tethered to a ship or a truck driving at the speed of forty miles per hour. As it weighed only one hundred and thirty-three pounds, it could be handled by a crew of four men and transported on a Jeep.

The announcement of the upcoming departure of the 320th VLA came as a surprise for everybody in the unit. Due to the recent unrest, Firmin and other colored soldiers at Camp Tyson had feared they would never be sent

---

[34] Very Low Altitude.

abroad for a real mission. Besides, it sometimes happened that colored units received a new assignment. Most of them were eventually disbanded before they had served.

This uncertainty had a very negative impact on the morale of Negro troops, hence on their motivation.

More than six hundred of them would be selected to go and fight somewhere on the other side of the Atlantic Ocean! In Europe or in Africa? They would learn it later.

When Firmin had the confirmation that he would take part in the journey, he couldn't tell if he should rejoice or lament. He knew the grief it would cause to his mother, and he was aware of the dangers of war. However, staying here, in Tennessee, among a hostile White population and Negroes at the end of their ropes, wasn't safe either.

If he had to risk his neck, he would rather do it fighting for his country. A more glorious way, for sure.

This trip to the unknown commenced on November 6, 1943. The men of the 320th VLA got in a train and had to keep the curtains down during a long part of the trip. It wasn't meant to keep their transfer secret, but to protect them from the demonstrations of resentment of Southern White mobs along the railroad.

Two days later, on November 8, the convoy reached Camp Shanks, in Orangeburg, Rockland County, twenty-four miles northeast from New York. One of the three staging areas of New York City. The place which had already seen dozens of thousands of U.S. soldiers transit, and as many thousand tons of war material, was named *Last-Stop, USA*.

The men of the 320th VLA spent eight days there, during which they had to undergo a series of medical tests. They received dental care and got vaccinated. They were given a complete set of new equipment: two pairs of shoes, a precision wristwatch and a Garand M1 rifle. Not to mention a gas mask and a set of clothes impregnated with some chemical solution which stank like hell.

The gas mask reminded Firmin of his grandfather who told him about the horror he had seen in the trenches in France, during World War I. Which made Celestine very angry. "Stop tellin'm all these horrors. That kid's gonna have nightmares for weeks!"

This thought pushed Firmin to write to his mother a letter to reassure her. A letter longer than the previous ones, which more or less looked like telegrams, in which he reported some anecdotes of his soldier's life. Without telling her his deep feelings. He knew that all the mails were closely examined by the military censorship. He could write: "last night, we had a twenty-five-mile march in the woods. We came back exhausted early on the following morning, but we had to wait until the evening, before we could sleep." In no way, he could have specified that their lieutenant hadn't stopped undermining them by calling them "incapable fucking niggers"

This time, Firmin lingered for a long time staring at the sheet of paper, before he could start writing. He wanted to say how much he missed her. How deeply grateful he felt to her for all what she had done for him since she had given birth to him!

The guys spent their free time playing basketball, softball or football. Others watching movies, reading or writing letters to their families. Some, challenging the commandant's ban, would gamble their pay on poker games or shooting craps.

Others, much wiser, preferred to invest in life insurance

or in War Bonds. Firmin, for his part, always spared a moment of privacy to write something in his diary.

Training sessions were less intensive than in Camp Tyson, however, still physically exhausting. The soldiers discovered on this occasion a new kind of exercise: descending a rope ladder to a dinghy floating in a swimming pool.

For the rest, physical drills consisted mainly in marching in step while singing.

On November 16, they wrote their registration number with a piece of chalk on their helmet, and everyone received an inflatable cotton coated life jacket. Then, they took a train that would bring them to a harbor in New Jersey. From there, they boarded a first ferry which traveled down the Hudson River to New York Harbor, in the boarding area of Manhattan West Side.

The night had already fallen when they saw the majestic shape of the *Aquitania*, docked at the Pier 86.

CHAPTER 14

November 24, 1943

Every morning on board, an alarm would sound inside the passageway to announce alert exercises. All the men had to put their life jacket on, and climb the stairs to the upper deck as fast as possible. But the practice, which was supposed to reassure them, eventually increased their anguish. The vastness of the Ocean, spreading out all around them as far as the eye can see, reminded them how vulnerable they were.

What would be their chance to survive if the ship were sunk? The lifeboats of the *Aquitania* could contain four thousand two hundred passengers, whereas the ship had boarded eight thousand of them. And what about those inflatable jackets that they had to wear almost constantly? Would they prevent the survivors from dying by drowning or of hypothermia?

But that morning, the scenery that appeared to the eyes of the soldiers almost instantly erased all the fear and pain they had suffered in the past eight days.

During the night, the *Aquitania* had bypassed Ireland to northwest. She was now traveling up the firth of Clyde.

The sea mist was slowly clearing, allowing them to glimpse the rugged hills of Scotland, covered with snow. As the ship was approaching her destination, the sun progressively lifted the mist veil, revealing new details of the enchanting landscape, that would be engraved forever in Firmin's mind. The men of the 320th VLA recognized the familiar shape of the British barrage balloons floating in the sky above the bay.

The captain's voice resonated through the loudspeakers. He announced the end of the journey and the imminent docking at Gourock Harbor. All the soldiers had to return to their berths and pick up their duffle bags, and make sure they wouldn't leave anything on board.

Descending the boarding bridge, Firmin was struck by the contrast between what he was seeing and what he had imagined about Europe. He had expected to discover a scene of desolation, and ruins among piles of rubble in a town destroyed by the war. He discovered instead a peaceful life in a little green corner surrounded by mountains.

A few German airplanes had indeed bombarded the neighboring harbors of Gourock and Greenock in May 1941. Two hundred fifty civilians had been killed, and thousands of houses had been razed. But they had since been rebuilt.

Now, the estuary was well protected. From an air strike by barrage balloons; and from an incursion of German submarines by giant nets hooked across the bay at big metal floating buoys.

At the very moment he set foot on the soil of Scotland, Firmin knew his life had been turned upside down. Into another time. Another world. That it was impossible to step back. By crossing the immensity of the Atlantic Ocean, he had passed the point of no return. He felt kind of weird. A feeling that the more pessimistic would easily consider to be a bad omen. He remembered his mother holding him tight in her arms at the door of the bus which would drive him to Camp Claiborne. He even felt as if he could smell the fragrance of wild flowers of her perfume. Was she thinking of him at this moment? Did she receive his last letter, posted on the American soil?

The different units were separated and redirected to their respective destinations. The men of the 320th VLA marched to the town's train station, where they received their food rations for two days, before getting on a first train.

On the way, they saw, for the first time in their life, approving eyes on the faces of white civilians. Girls were smiling at them. Boys much less. But what they could read in the gazes of these British youth wasn't the hateful contempt of the racist Whites of their country. It looked more like jealousy of those Black GIs to whom their girl friends were paying so much attention.

When they arrived in front of the station, Firmin and other guys of the 320th VLA searched in vain a sign indicating the waiting room and the washroom for colored people. They had heard that the UK didn't apply segregation, but they wanted to check it by themselves.

After they stepped on board of the train, the American way resumed. The white officers reserved the exclusive use of the first-class compartment for themselves. They would do the same at each train change.

Inside the other cars, Firmin and his comrades were too busy dreaming of their next furlough to challenge the behavior of their superiors. The soldiers had learned their destination: Checkendon. A small village of the Oxfordshire, in England. Small but with a significant advantage: it was less than forty miles west away from the heart of London.

Of course, they all had in mind the images of whole

precincts of London littered with debris of buildings destroyed by German bombings, during the *London Blitzkrieg* between September 1940 and May 1941. But they also knew that since the end of the Battle of Britain, the British anti-aircraft defense, which counted hundreds of barrage balloons, provided the city and its inhabitants an excellent protection from German raids. Especially thanks to its radar system named *Chain Home* AMES[35]. Knowing that Jim Crow laws didn't apply in the kingdom of George VI, the soldiers got excited by the idea of a night trip in the red light district of London. A prospect which, some said, was worth all what they had endured in Camp Tyson and during the crossing of the Atlantic.

---

[35] Air Ministry Experimental Station.
  Source: https://fr.wikipedia.org/wiki/Chain_Home

CHAPTER 15

Checkendon, England. November 24, 1943

The excitement immediately subsided in the morning, when the soldiers discovered their settlement. A large field in the middle of the woods, less than one mile away from the village of Checkendon. At its center stood several dozens of *Nissen* huts[36]. Prefabricated small constructions of corrugated steel, half-pipe shaped, planted on a brick foundation.

Those intended to house the soldiers were all identical. Twenty-three feet wide, forty-three feet long and ten feet high at the center. Others, wider and longer, housed the officers' mess and the soldiers', a hospital and the management services. The contrast with the masonry constructions of Camp Tyson was striking. Firmin had the feeling he was sent back to the time of his childhood, when he used to live with his parents in a shabby wooden cabin. Some joked about it, pretending they regretted their good old Dixie.

The huts housing the soldiers contained twelve beds. Six on each side. A coal stove in the middle was supposed to heat the whole of it. At the head of his bed, each soldier had a shelf to put his helmet and other stuff, and three hangers to hang his uniforms. At the foot of the bed, a wooden box contained all the rest of his equipment and personal things.

---

[36] British equivalent of U.S. Quonset huts. Nissen huts were conceived during WWI in 1916 by Major Peter Norman Nissen, engineer in the British Army.

The facade of the hut was pierced with a door and two windows that supplied a unique source of natural light. Suspended at the top of its vault, three electric lamps provided the artificial lighting of the room. Firmin's was housing three crews of balloon operators.

Firmin managed to take one of the two beds in the second row. At equal distance from the daylight and from the warmth of the stove. His second, of a chillier nature, Private First-class Edward Washington chose the following bed in the third row. Right next to the stove. The other teammates took the beds on rows one and four. Private James Stevenson, from Goose Creek, North Carolina, on the left side of Firmin. Private Douglas Murphy, from Richmond, Virginia, on the right side of Edward.

Edward, who preferred to be called Ed, was a muscular and handsome guy. A bit less than six feet tall and one hundred fifty pounds. He was a native of Atlantic City, New Jersey. He was the second of six children. His father was a train porter of the *Philadelphia and Atlantic City Railroad* company. His mother worked as a maid for two hotels of the city. They all crammed together in a two-room apartment on the first floor of a house in the north side.

As a child at school, he was unable to stay quiet on his chair. Despite real skills, and unlike his elder brother, he had decided to leave school right before his fifteenth birthday. "The most important," he said, "is that I can read, write and count fluently. The rest of it, I'll discover myself."

He wanted to earn his life quickly to take full advantage of all the pleasures offered by his city, renowned as the capital of vice. Sex, drugs and booze. Indeed, he was attracted by the lights of the night and by music clubs, like the *Harlem* or the *Paradise*, where Count Basie, Duke Ellington, Sarah Vaughn or the stand-up comedian and actress Jackie "Moms" Mabley used to perform.

Their common taste for blues and jazz brought Firmin and Edward together, of course. But it was only one stone of the foundation of their friendship.

Thanks to his great energy, his charming smile and his incredible glibness of tongue, Ed had managed to get a job as a salesman in a retail shop of Apex News and Hair company[37].

He had finally been summoned to military service in November 1942, at the age of twenty-one.

On Firmin's left side, was private E2, James Stevenson, a native of Goose Creek, Berkeley County, South Carolina. Five feet and nine inches tall, he was only a few pounds lighter than Ed. Jimmy was the youngest of three brothers, and had two sisters as well. His parents owned a forty-acre farm, on which they grew corn, potatoes and cotton, which hardly sufficed to feed the family. Like many other black children, he had left school at the end of the fourth grade. Jimmy was rather rough, with a trend to be rebellious to authority. Nonetheless, he was good-natured and proved it by his unwavering team spirit, and his friendship. Firmin could ask him anything. But when the orders came from a white officer who, moreover, yelled at him, punctuating his instructions with racist invective, Jimmy had great difficulties in containing his rage. Without the presence near him of Corporal

---

[37] A chain of beauty shops founded in 1919 by Sarah Spencer Washington, an African American cosmetics entrepreneur.

Bellegarde, he surely would have flipped out and been court-martialed.

For the rest, Jimmy was taking this military experience as an adventure. Without it, he would never have gone out of the United States, or even of Berkeley County. He seemed unaware of the dangers of the war.

The last member of Firmin's crew was private El Douglas Murphy, from Richmond, Virginia. He was as tall as Jimmy, but much bigger than the three others of the crew. His mother was a worker in a cigarette factory. His father was hired as a handler in an armaments factory. Like New Orleans, Richmond had prospered a lot, thanks to arms deals from the army, from which many black families had benefited.

Doug had also left school very early. Anyhow, he didn't have the intellectual capability which would have allowed him to study further. On the other hand, he demonstrated his goodwill in applying Firmin's instructions. He was typically a follower. The kind of person who easily gets influenced to do something silly. He was also quite greedy. At each meal, he would ask around who would give him up his dessert. His protruding belly had earned him the nickname of Dough-belly, which made him sometimes fly off the handle. Once, as he was harping on about his mom's donuts, one guy started to call him Donut. Doug found it affectionate, and even flattering. Since then, everyone called him Donut.

All the privates and the non-commissioned officers spent the day installing the battalion. Six hundred and thirty-eight men selected from the originally nearly twelve hundred in the beginning at Camp Tyson. In order not to bend the rules which prohibited a Negro from commanding a white soldier, the top of the hierarchy was exclusively composed of Whites. Lieutenant Colonel Reed was assisted by forty-eight officers, of whom only seventeen were African Americans.

The prejudices of the American army, challenging the commanding ability of black officers, were so rooted that even in an All-Black unit like the 320th VLA, it remained unthinkable that its command could be entrusted to a Negro. To the point that Brigadier General Benjamin O. Davis Sr, the first black general in the U.S. Army, appointed in January 1941, at Fort Riley, Kansas, at the head of the 4th brigade, 2nd cavalry division, was soon reassigned in Washington as an inspector of the Advisory Committee on Negro troops policy. His mission was to verify that colored soldiers were fairly treated.

The African American press, and the leaders of the NAACP, were convinced that the white counterparts of Benjamin O. Davis had put pressure on the headquarters staff in that way, because they feared a black general might accomplish a military feat which could question their racist prejudgment. It was probably the same reason, Firmin thought, why colored soldiers were almost exclusively confined to support and logistics tasks.

Firmin thanked heaven for having led him to an anti-aircraft defense battalion, and especially the 320th VLA. Not only because he would have an opportunity to prove his valor and that of all colored soldiers, in the service of democracy. He had read many articles denouncing the inappropriate behavior of white senior officers towards black soldiers. Lieutenant Colonel Reed knew how to be obeyed and still be respectful with his subordinates. Most of the men on the 320th VLA were aware of their luck.

They never lost sight of the fact that a lack of discipline under his command would cause Reed to be transferred. He would then be replaced by one of these Southern commandants who terrorized colored soldiers, like in Camp Stewart, in Hinesville, Georgia.

Besides dormitory huts, Checkendon's temporary base provided all the conveniences of an American camp. A mess housed in several Nissen huts put together. A mess for white officers. Another one for their black equivalents. Several sanitary blocks. A small field hospital. Not to mention recreation units.

However, something essential was still missing in this camp. The VLA balloons and all the equipment to operate them. The deployment of one hundred and thirty-five balloons required huge logistics means. Several dozens of 2½-ton dump trucks, a truck-mounted hydrogen generating plant, two ambulances, sixteen Jeeps, sixteen ½-ton command trucks, twelve motorcycles with sidecars, sixteen 1½-ton cargo trucks and thirty-four 2½-ton cargo trucks. Some of them had .50 caliber anti-aircraft machine guns.

The bulk of the equipment hadn't yet arrived. And neither Reed nor his men would accept to be compelled to give up their mission.

For their first lunch, they had to satisfy with a food ration M. Pork stew and butter beans were at the menu. But the cooks performed a culinary prowess. They managed to get enough fresh food from neighboring farms to prepare the soldiers' first decent meal in two weeks. The guys were still traumatized by the food served aboard the *Aquitania*.

CHAPTER 16

Checkendon, November 25, 1943

As of the first night in the camp, the soldiers discovered the joys of the English climate. A little taste of what they could expect from the upcoming winter.

The corrugated iron of the Nissen huts was an illusory protection against the night chill. Like the rooftop of the shack in which Firmin and Marie had spent their early years. Except that here, in the middle of England, one element amplified the effects of the cold: moist air.

During the day, it would seep into the huts and permeate the bed sheets and blankets. In the evening, after supper, when the soldiers had returned to their hut, the man in charge of the stove had to fill it with coal and keep it heating until the curfew. Each man received a daily ration of coal, hardly enough to fill half of his helmet, which was pooled together by the roommates. Then, everyone snuggled under his blanket. Some fell sound asleep, almost instantly. Others read under their sheet by the glow of their flashlights. A letter, a comic book or a newspaper. Firmin used to write a few lines in his diary.

The night before, the twelve balloon operators had rapidly fallen asleep, in a concert of loud snoring. Early in the morning Firmin was awakened by the coughing of other roommates, as much as by the damp cold of his sheets. Mist was exhaling from his mouth. Despite a furious urge to pee, he stayed in bed until he heard the hoarse sound of the bugle wake-up call.

They needed a strong motivation to get out of their beds, quickly wash with ice-cold water, and put on their damp cold clothes. Edward was shivering so much that Firmin had to drag him out of his bed and help him get dressed.

Then they went to the mess, where they had a ration B breakfast, composed of high-calorie crackers, three lumps of sugar, three dextrose based energy bars, one dose of instant coffee and one of dehydrated orange juice.

They didn't even have time to warm up their hands with their coffee-filled canteen cups, before they were ordered to get up and run outside the camp for a test of endurance in the nearby woods. However, nobody complained. Even the laziest ones. Everything was good to prevent you from freezing to death.

At noon, the thermometer indicated 45 Fahrenheit. The guys of the weather forecast advised them to enjoy it, as in the coming days they expected a light and continuous rain, and a temperature drop.

After lunch, the training went more intensive. Walking in the mud. Running an obstacle course with a backpack filled with stones and a rifle in their hands. And finally, disassembling, cleaning, lubricating and reassembling of their rifles. Then only, they were allowed to take a cold shower and take care of their bodies.

They all had made it through, without grumbling so far, because they could dream of the warm meal which would be served in the mess for supper.

"Ah can't stop dreamin' of a thick and juicy half-poundah," said Donut. "Ah believe ah'd gulp down a couple of'em!"

"Dang it, Dough-belly! You never stop thinking of gorging, do you?" shouted Ed. "Look at you, fat-ass!"

"Eh? What? Ah'm just starvin'!" grunted Donut. "Can't help it. Ah'm always hungry."

"Duh, if you say so!" mocked Ed. "Anyhow, don't ask me to leave you my share."

While the others were bent double, laughing, Firmin announced the bad news that the two other crew leaders already knew.

"Nobody will have to leave his share to Donut. 'coz there ain't any special menu tonight!"

The guys felt all the more disappointed that they thought they had really earned the reward of a true warm meal.

"Suck it!" yelled Donut, punching his mattress.

"Won't do ya no harm to be on the diet, for once," said a guy from another team.

His leader ordered him to shut up, which cooled the others as well. Firmin started to unpack his M ration of the day.

"Let's see what uncle Sam has cooked for supper," he said in a serious tone.

He took a can in his hands and read the description printed on it. "Beef goulash, potatoes and carrots."

Said like this, it didn't sound appetizing. So, Firmin stood up and began improvising a recipe that would make their mouths water.

"Tonight, the chef suggests his tender beef meat, gently stewed three hours long in its onion, tomato and red pepper-based sauce, enhanced with sweet paprika. This delicacy comes served with delicious boiled potatoes and carrots."

Both other crew leaders applauded. So did the other roommates. Except one, who shattered the illusion, by saying:

"But it's much less tasty, when it's cold."

"Not with a double ration of fuel," replied Corporal Bellegarde, pointing at a bucket filled to the top with slack coal.

Everyone stood up at once and hustled to the stove. They managed to warm their bodies, while heating their canned meat inside their mess kits turned into a *bain-marie*.

Was it due to the attractive presentation made by Firmin or because of the beneficial effect of the extra fuel? Anyhow, this supper appeared to all much better than usually.

Before the curfew, one guy was ordered to add a few handfuls of coal into the stove between two and three o'clock, the next morning.

Corporal Bellegarde was the last man to fall asleep that evening. It was around 21:00.

CHAPTER 17

Checkendon, November 27, 1943

That Saturday, balloons still hadn't arrived, and it hadn't stopped raining since the night before, making the woods almost impracticable, even for a routine march. All drills were canceled. Lieutenant Colonel Reed decided to grant free time to everyone, save a small team which would stay on duty for services and night guard.

On Saturdays, most of the soldiers used to write a letter to their girlfriends or their families. Firmin hadn't written to his parents for the last three weeks.

All the incoming mail of the week was delivered at once. In the parcel from Celestine, Firmin found, besides her letters, two pairs of socks, wool gloves and a scarf, on which she had poured a few drops of her perfume. He wrapped the muffler around his neck, unfolded the sheets, and started reading:

Dear Firmin,

When you read this letter, you'll be in GB. Yr father and I pray to the Lord every day that your crossing goes safe. We're so scared by all the news about our ships sunk by German submarines in the middle of this immense Ocean.

After the mail you sent before departing for Europe, I bought a blue star flag which yr father hung behind our window, so that everybody in our street knows our beloved son is serving the country. The Davises are green with envy. Their youngest is still too young, but both elders scored V at AGCT[38] tests, and 4-F on the SSS[39] list. And a rumor says they got the kind of disease you get by going with scarlet women. I hope you'll never let one of such evil creatures make you lose yr mind. It'd kill me, for sure. How are the Brits? Do you eat enough, at least? I was told it's quite cold there, so I send you these woolen gloves and scarf. Hope to read you soon. We miss you so much. Love. Mom and dad.

As predicted by the battalion's meteorologists, the temperature dropped lower. At 13:00 the thermometer indicated 39 Fahrenheit. But, during the day, it was strictly prohibited to light the stoves inside the huts, as smoke might reveal the presence of the camp to an enemy aircraft. The guys would soon miss the training sessions of the previous two days, which had helped them stay warm.

Concerned by the morale of his men, the commandant had ordered that his troops be served a hot meal prepared with fresh food. Besides, one hundred and twenty soldiers, including Firmin, Edward, Jimmy and Douglas, were granted an overnight leave in the village of Checkendon. Fearing overflows due to alcohol abuse, the lieutenant colonel had chosen to limit their number. He also explicitly warned the lucky beneficiaries that he wouldn't tolerate any inappropriate behavior of his men towards the villagers, especially with females.

To make sure everything would go smoothly, the soldiers were asked to watch a little movie titled

---

[38] Army General Classification Test. Intelligence test for recruits.
[39] Selective Service System. 4-F means the person is unfit for service, due to physical, mental or moral reasons.

A Welcome to Britain, released by the Ministry of Information on behalf of the U.S. War Office. The film intended to remind the GIs of some essential differences between American and British cultures.

The film began with the description of a typical British place: a village pub. "*An English pub,*" said the presenter, "*isn't like a saloon. It's more like a club for men and women who haven't a great deal of money, and who don't drink for the sake of drinking, but for the company. Pubs are real institutions that sometimes have seen several generations of customers and owners. People come in the early evening to have a drink, chat together, or play dart game, smoke a pipe, read a newspaper, always in a very sedate way.*"

The footage reminded the GIs of the rules to be respected with the British. "*Never be arrogant nor ostentatious. Don't pull a wad of cash out of your pocket to buy a pint, even when offering a drink to everyone around. These people work hard and earn little. Moreover, they're severely rationed. They're short of many things. So, when you have the privilege to be invited by some of them to share their supper, don't rush on the food like if you were starving!*"

One point of the movie interested the soldiers of the 320th VLA more particularly: segregation. As they had noticed before, since their arrival in Gourock, Blacks were welcome in the U.K. like the Whites were. The presenter reminded them all that they weren't at home in this country, and therefore had to comply with the local customs and abstain from importing their racial prejudices.

This sequence was welcomed by approving comments, and a few scathing sarcasms towards white officers, especially Wild Bill. On this subject, the presenter interviewed General Lee, head of the Services of Supplies in the U.K. The man had lots of colored troops under him, who were doing a big job there.

Firmin and the others listened religiously to the speech of the general. "*America,* he said, *has promised the Negro real citizenship, and a fair chance to make the best of himself. When the army needs Americans to fight for the country, it takes Negroes along with Whites. Every one is treated the same when it comes to dying, and so, the army wouldn't be true to America, if it didn't try to live up to the promises about an equal chance.*"

"*Still,*" the general added, "*You don't get over a prejudice that easily. There's no use pretending we're different from what we are. But we can try to live up to our American promises. I go further and say, we can't do less. We still feel ourselves patriots. We have promised to respect each other. All of us. That's one of the reasons that makes our world worth fighting for. But we're all together in this small country, with the same surroundings, the same amount of pay to spend, in the same sort of places to spend it. And we're all here as soldiers. Everything we do, we do as American soldiers. Not Negroes and White men, rich or poor, but as American soldiers. It's not a bad time, is it, to learn to respect each other, both ways.*"

At the end, the presenter reminded the soldiers they weren't there for a good time, but for a job or work. About security rules as well. "*Don't tell anyone where you are or what you're doing. And always wear your dog tags. At all times.*"

Braving the cold, Firmin and the other lucky ones

washed themselves with lukewarm water, around the stove. They finally put on their service uniforms, under the bawdy remarks of their comrades.

CHAPTER 18

All the guys on leave that night were dressed to the nines. In Firmin's hut, the last one to be ready was Doug. "Tonight," he said, "Ah'm gonna pick up my first English gal." He sprayed his body profusely with *Old Spice* aftershave, making his roommates' heads spin.

Firmin, Edward, Jimmy and Doug agreed they would go and come back together as well. They walked to Checkendon village, side by side, in the double file procession. Ten white officers, split in two groups, were meant to supervise the ninety African American soldiers. One of them, in the front, had a flashlight, which glow could hardly light up the ground ahead of his feet. Another one, in the rear carried a red light to reveal their presence to a vehicle possibly coming from behind.

The group eventually reached a long stone building. On its facade hung a sign. But the night was so dark that you needed to get very close to it to read the black letters on the red and green background. *Black Horse pub*[40].

Behind the wooden door, two thick black curtains ensured that no light could be seen from outside, in compliance with the very strict blackout rules applied in this country at war. Still, muffled laughs and voices betrayed the presence of people inside. The officer in the front raised his hand to order the procession to stop.

"Why don't we get in?" muttered a soldier, burned with impatience.

---

[40] Le *Black Horse* pub is 350 years old. It still existed in 2019. Source: https://whatpub.com/pubs/SOX/0140/black-horse-checkendon

"This place is reserved for Whites!" replied an officer. "You keep on going this way," he added, pointing his hand in the continuation of the street. "There's an excellent pub over there which serves colored people. Six hundred yards from here. It's called the *Four Horseshoes[41]*."

This coarse and sneaky attempt to apply *Jim Crow* laws on the English soil didn't fool anyone. It instantly raised the disapproval of all the colored soldiers. The officer's initiative was all the more clumsy, not to say provocative, that the soldiers still had in mind the movie they had watched in the afternoon.

Hearing their strong and loud protest, a man came out and stood on the doorstep, barring the entrance with his legs spread out and his clenched fists pressed on his hips. He roved his eyes over the street until they got used to the darkness of the night.

When he saw all these guys gathered in front of the entrance, a large smile lit his face.

"Gentlemen!" He said with a loud voice. "Be welcome in my pub!"

These few words made Firmin and his comrades' hearts swell with joy and pride. For most of these black men coming from a country where you see signs everywhere reading *No Colored Allowed* or *Whites only*, being called gentlemen by a white business owner was an unprecedented experience.

Two white officers tried to deter the pub owner from letting the soldiers in. But the man held on and said:

---

[41] The *Four Horseshoes* pub was closed, since then. It was in use since the 1840s.
Source: https://historicengland.org.uk/listing/the-list/list-entry/1368910

"You're here in England, not in America. We don't apply segregation in the United Kingdom."

Maybe he was simply a pragmatic person. Like any self-respecting businessman, he didn't want to reject so many clients because of the color of their skin. Anyhow, whatever his motivation was, his reaction would earn him a nice revenue for this evening and others to come.

In a sudden and irresistible move, all the guys started to elbow their way while pushing the ten white officers inside the pub. Firmin was literally lifted and dragged by the human wave. In the rush, they almost tore off one of the two black light proof curtains.

Inside the pub, the officers had to raise their voices to be respected. From the sheer force of habit, they gathered around two tables, close to the exit. Black soldiers, on their side, stayed away from them. Some used the overcrowding of the room to taunt them by raising their pints conspicuously in their direction.

Firmin beckoned his teammates over to the bar.

"First round is on me," he said to the barmaid, while pointing his hand at the three men.

"Thank you, Corp.," Jimmy said. "Double scotch for me, please!" he added to the woman behind the counter.

"Aw! Calm down with alcohol!" Firmin said. "I don't wanna see you being arrested by the MPs[42]."

Jimmy gave him a reproachful stare.

"Alright," Firmin agreed. "But only one. Who'd like to try a brown beer with me?"

"I," replied Edward.

As usual, Doug joined the majority and raised his hand.

---

[42] *Military Police.*

"So," said Firmin to the waitress, "it'll be one scotch for him and three draft beers for us."

He paid immediately with his first pay in local currency and raised his glass. When he saw the size of his scotch and compared it to the size of the pints, Jimmy couldn't hide his disappointment.

"Cheers!" said Firmin. "May God bless us and lead us all back home, safe and sound."

"God bless us, and bless America!" added Edward, raising his glass in turn.

"Which America?" quipped Jimmy, before swallowing his whiskey in one gulp, while Doug was staring at the content of his pint with great caution.

Firmin spotted an empty chair, which no one dared to use, as it was very close to the one occupied by the battalion's doctor, a white captain.

"See you all in one hour outside," said Firmin, "and don't get drunk as a skunk until then."

Firmin walked to the chair and sat, turning his back to the captain, without even asking his permission. The officer didn't react. Firmin eventually could taste his first English beer.

Although he had been warned, the experience earned him his second shock of the evening. Before this, he thought that all the beers should be like those he was used to drinking in New Orleans. Like the *Falstaff* amber or the *Jax*, served fresh, of course.

Firmin couldn't withhold a grimace of distaste when he felt in his mouth the bitter taste of that brown lukewarm beer. He almost spat it out. So, it was true. The British didn't do anything the way the Americans did. But there was something else they didn't do like the Americans.

They respected the Negroes. Firmin thought they were probably right about beer too. So, he carefully observed his pint of brown beer. Darker than his skin. And he started to enjoy it. Slowly sipping it, first. Then, he swallowed mouthfuls of it. He eventually liked it.

When he saw the barmaid passing between the tables, replacing empty glasses by full ones, Firmin felt like ordering his second pint. At the same moment, Edward appeared in front of him.

"It's my turn this time, Corp. What would you like?"

Firmin raised his head. He looked at Ed wonderingly, but didn't answer. He seemed to be lost in his thoughts.

"What's up? Anything wrong?" Ed worried. "Shouldn't you better take a scotch? Would do you good, for sure."

"No, thanks. I'm all right. And I'd love to drink one more pint of this!"

Edward stared at Firmin with wide open eyes, his mouth opened in astonishment. He shrugged his shoulders, turned round and went to the bar to order their drinks. He came back a few minutes later with a glass of scotch and a pint of beer. A second chair had been freed in the meantime. He pulled it towards Firmin's, and sat.

"Where are the two others?" asked the corporal.

"Jimmy's playing dart game with two old villagers. Seemed he was being clobbered."

"What about Doug? Tell me you didn't leave him alone!"

"I saw him at the bar, about five minutes ago. He told me he needed to relieve his bladder."

"You know him! He's unable to keep control when he's drunk. He's so easily influenced. He may follow anyone to have sex in a brothel."

"All right," Ed sighed. "If he's not back in five minutes, I'll fetch him."

The two men toasted together again.

"May I ask you something, Corp.?"

Firmin raised his head and gazed at Ed.

"Is it a question for Corporal Bellegarde or for your buddy Firmin?"

"For both, Corp."

"Go ahead!"

"Do you believe, one day, Whites... I mean, White Americans, will treat us the way the Brits do today?"

Firmin smiled. He was precisely wondering the same thing when Ed showed up. He gently rubbed his forehead with the palm of his hand, as if his head was aching, and sighed deeply.

"I hope it. Like you. Like every Negro. But I seriously doubt it. Especially after seeing what happened earlier. You saw it like me. Despite official recommendations explained in GI movies, our white senior officers can't resist imposing their racial prejudices here in Great Britain."

"You're right. But there are still Whites of goodwill, like Reed."

"Indeed. But they won't weigh much when opposed to all the Wild Bills[43] of the deep South, I'm afraid."

"So why should we risk our necks for people who ain't worth more than Hitler and those damned Nazis?"

Firmin frowned and sighed.

"Probably because if we won't, we'd agree with all these racists who assert that we, Negroes, are deadbeats.

---

[43] See above. Nickname of Captain William Taylor, second in command of Lieutenant Colonel Reed.

That we are cowards, unfit for fighting. Wild animals ruled by their instinct and their urges."

The corporal stood up and roved his eyes around him.

"I can't see Doug. I don't like it. Go and see what the hell he's still doing outside."

Donut had vanished. From what other guys said, Ed understood that Donut had followed a group of fellows, as drunk as him, looking for another "good place."

Firmin decided to leave and go to look for him. He asked Ed and Jimmy to come with him. Ten minutes later, the trio ended at the *Four Horseshoes*. The pub was as crowded as the *Black Horse*. Its owner, Debbie, granted them the same warm and respectful welcome as the owner of the first pub. However its atmosphere was much more relaxed.

Firmin quickly understood why. There was no white officer of the 320th VLA in the room. The only Whites, besides Debbie and her husband, were inhabitants of the village.

Firmin made to Debbie a description of Doug. She hadn't seen him before, but could easily guess where he might be at this moment. "You, soldiers, are all the same. Especially when you're far from home. When the urge itches you, you always find the place to go, don't you?"

The corporal agreed with a forced smile, but the image of Donut busy screwing a prostitute in the middle of a dark street or in the nearby woods made him shiver with disgust. He quickly wiped off this dirty vision by carefully observing the people around him.

Villagers were toasting with black soldiers, thanking them for helping to give a good beating to this bastard named Hitler. They even tried to teach them some of their local folk songs. One of the villagers took a violin and started to play. Firmin who had given up running after Donut, instantly saw himself back in the French quarter of New Orleans. The day when his dad took him to attend a jazz parade on South Rampart Street. Amateur bands were marching together with professional orchestras. Among them were the trumpet player Willie "Bunk" Johnson and his New Orleans Jazz Band.

It was in 1942. At *Mardi Gras*. Despite the country's entry into the war, the Carnival had been maintained. It would be Firmin's first public performance as a saxophonist in his father's band. The latter had asked his son to accompany him to the gathering place at the departure point of the parade, claiming that he needed him to carry his spare suit protected by a white sheet.

When they arrived there, his dad asked him:

"What're ya waitin' for? C'mon! Giddy up! Put on your suit now!"

Under the sheet, Firmin discovered a new outfit, completed with two-tone shoes and a straw hat. Joe had bought the set without telling Celestine. Firmin almost hugged his father to thank him. But Joe hated outpouring of feelings. Particularly in public. When Firmin was finally dressed up, from head to toe, Joe eventually handed him his saxophone and asked: "Still git yaw mouthpiece with ya?"

Of course, he had it. He always kept it with him, unless he was going to school.

"So, it's your turn to play," his father said. "Now, make me feel prouda'ya, son!"

Remembering this, Firmin wished he had brought his harmonica. He would have loved joining the old fiddler.

The evening went on, with more or less philosophical discussions between GIs and villagers, punctuated by rounds of brown ale beer or whiskey. The young soldiers listened to veterans of the Great War telling them their feats of arms. With careful ears in the beginning, but less and less attentive as alcohol was accumulating in their bodies.

As Firmin was getting ready to return to the camp, Donut appeared in the entrance doorway. His disheveled hair and sloppy appearance sufficed to betray him. But, in case Firmin was ready to give him the benefit of the doubt, Doug's fly was still wide open.

"Did you use a condom, at least?" the corporal asked, with a disgusted expression.

Doug didn't react.

"What about your pro-kit? Did you use it after?"

Doug stared at him with a cow-eyed look. The last illusion Firmin had about Doug's common sense instantly vanished. Donut was desperately immature. However, it was out of the question to let a man of his team contaminate the others with his horrible bacteria. He would personally bring him to the health care unit for a complete disinfection.

When he woke in the following morning, Firmin couldn't tell how many pints he had drunk nor at what time they had returned to the camp. But what he could tell for sure was that he had had a wonderful night, which he would remember for a long time.

While the others were still sleeping, Firmin was thinking of his parents. Of his mother, particularly. It was Sunday. If she had been there, she would have asked him to go to church with her. He realized he had tended to move away from God, in the last weeks. He felt he could hear Celestine lecture him.

Daylight was finally dawning. It was time to wake up everybody for breakfast. After that, Firmin would attend the eleven o'clock religious service. Not only to please his mother.

Since they had arrived in Europe, the soldiers were progressively getting aware they had come here to fight. That many of them may be killed before the end of this damned war, although they weren't expected to combat on the front line.

CHAPTER 19

D oug wasn't the only patient of the medical unit, during the following days, due to many suspicions of venereal disease. At the point that the battalion's doctor had been ordered by Reed to review the whole education of the soldiers regarding sexual hygiene.

From the early 1940s, recruiting campaigns of the army had revealed a high rate of infected people among African American volunteers[44]. Yet, a prevention program of sexually transmitted disease had been launched in the 1930s by the public health service. It intended to inform people about the danger of such kinds of infections, and the ways to prevent and cure them. The program pointed out that most of the infected people ignored the names of the diseases, and that they could be cured.

This health problem was taken all the more seriously that, besides the sanitary impact, it also made it more difficult to reach the quotas in soldiers recruitment. The American Negro press, unions and political organizations, were putting a constant pressure on the army to ensure that they would hire the same percentage of Blacks as in the whole population. Indeed, the great number of cases detected by the recruiting tests compelled the army to reject many of them.

The army couldn't afford to lose a precious time in curing the recruits after their conscription. Until early 1943, the treatment of gonorrhea required thirty days of

---

[44] Source: *The employment of negro troops*. Author: Ulysses Lee. Center of military history. United States Army.

hospitalization, whereas syphilis led to a six-month disability.

The widespread use of penicillin and sulfonamide in May 1943 considerably reduced the medical care length, and allowed the army to recruit infected people who would eventually make very good soldiers.

However, the healthcare services still had to cope with great difficulties to inform less educated people, especially in the Southern States. More than the lack of education, superstitions were making their task quite complicated. Among others, a popular belief said you couldn't get such illness by full moon nights. Others claimed that drinking lemon juice sufficed to cure the clap. Unless they used raw and slang terms, the lectures made by medical staff about the dangers of syphilis and gonorrhea didn't impress these soldiers. The epidemic of STI started to decrease by the middle of 1943, when the army had enough prophylaxis kits. Every man of the 320th VLA had received one at his arrival in Camp Tyson, together with an illustrated pamphlet[45] reminding of sex hygiene rules. The STI issue was a major concern of the U.S. armed forces stationed on the British islands. They cooperated with the local authorities, mainly by setting up prophylactic stations inside the military bases, and by tracking the likely contaminated sex partners.

Local American units were instructed to use indirect expressions when referring to such clinics, like *U.S. Army Aid station*.

Despite all these precautions, STI continued to spread. And although the use of penicillin and sulfonamide

---

[45] Sex Hygiene and Venereal Diseases in 16 pages (US GPO:1940 Ref 254247°).

accelerated their treatment, the impact remained very significant in terms of failure of infected staff and of health service occupation. The matter was a source of political and social tensions between the American forces and their British hosts.

The battalion's doctor organized a series of compulsory lectures. Each one intended for a group of about one hundred soldiers.

Firmin and Ed warned Doug that he'd better listen very carefully to the doc's advice. Besides, he had been punished with the suppression of all further overnight passes for the rest of their stay in Checkendon.

Two medics distributed one pro-kit to each soldier. Then, the doctor reminded them of its detailed content and how to use it.

"This," he said, showing a little tube held high in his hand, "contains five grams of ointment for internal use. Which doesn't mean that you should swallow it!"

The comment triggered raucous laughter. The captain let the guys laugh out a few seconds, then shouted.

"Enough now!"

A deafening silence fell on the assembly.

"Venereal diseases," he continued, "are extremely expensive for the army. Not only in terms of medical care and drugs. If you keep on behaving like walking cocks, we'll soon be short of beds in our health unit. And we'll need to turn our post into a hospital."

The doctor paused and gazed around him at his audience with a slowly roving glance.

"Do you really think we can win this fucking war with an army of syphilis infected soldiers?"

He paused again and frowned heavily.

"Let me tell you this! If one day I need to choose between taking care of a guy with the clap and a man wounded in action, even slightly, I swear I won't give a damn with the first one."

No one wanted to laugh anymore.

"So, for those who can't read, let me start from the beginning. The pro-kit is meant to be used after you had sex. Inside, you'll find a soap impregnated cloth for carefully cleaning your penis. Then you dry it up with this cleaning tissue, also included. Last but not least, comes this little tube. It has a thin ending that you have to gently introduce inside the urethra."

The doctor pointed his finger at the board behind him, showing the drawing of a penis.

"Then, you press the tube to fill the urethra with the full content of ointment. And finally, you massage your dick a few seconds and let the drug do its work. And therefore, you have to wait half an hour at least before peeing."

The doctor gazed intently at his audience again.

"Is it clear for everyone?"

He continued his lecture by inviting the soldiers in need to go to a nearby prophylactic station to get checked or ask individual pro-kits. Like a teacher, he read out loud the instructions written on a poster. The same kind of poster was displayed in various places inside each post and in army aid stations. He punctuated each sentence by hitting the edge of his desk with a metal rule.

"*STI can be avoided.*

A girl who'll let you use her is probably infected.

The surest way to avoid venereal disease is to stay away from sex relations until you marry.

If you can't stay away from women, use prophylaxis.

Nine out of ten men who get VD failed to use prophylaxis.

So, after you've had sex, don't forget it!

Wash you peen carefully with soap and water.

Use your pro-kit systematically.

Don't take any risk!"

After the doctor had finished, Firmin turned towards his neighbor and nudged his flank with his elbow.

"Hope you've listened thoroughly, Doug. Because next time you come back with one of these damn diseases, I'll write a report and get you out of my team. Hear?"

"Yes, Corp."

"Can't hear you. Louder!"

"Yes, Corp.!" Doug shouted.

CHAPTER 20

Checkendon. December 24, 1943

A ll through December, the soil was soaked by relentless rain. Thick mud bogged their trucks and stuck to their shoes. It made their daily ten mile marches pretty exhausting.

The guys welcomed the end of the year holidays with deep relief. Lieutenant Colonel Reed asked his senior officers to lower the frequency and intensity of the drills during the week before Christmas. He was aware that this period would awaken a mingle of longing and homesickness among his men. Maintaining the same work pressure as usual could undermine the battalion's morale and it's cohesion.

For the second time in his life, Firmin would celebrate Christmas far from home. The year before, he had been transferred to Camp Tyson in early December and therefore deprived of this family celebration. Never, since his induction into the army, Firmin had felt his parents' absence so painfully.

Mrs. Griffiths, her husband and their four children must have felt it, because they had bent over backwards to offer their guests some peace and comfort on this Christmas Eve 1943.

The cohabitation between several million American soldiers and the British people wasn't easy every day. Even though the GIs were generally welcome. Intending to keep the climate as friendly as possible until the Big

Day, both British and American authorities strongly encouraged exchanges, all around the year. Civilians provided the American soldiers with the family environment that they missed. In return, GIs would offer them all kinds of things which they needed so much. Especially on Christmas Eve.

The guys of the 320th VLA had done their very best to prepare this event. For a few months, a choir of two hundred colored soldiers had been very successful in Britain. The *Negro Chorus* of Roland Hayes, the lyrical tenor from Georgia. His chorale had even performed at the Royal Albert Hall in September. The villagers of Checkendon had imagined that all the Negroes were very good singers. So, they had asked Reed insistently if they could enjoy hearing on Christmas Eve a Negro choir composed of soldiers of his battalion.

Knowing Bellegarde's musician skills, Lieutenant Colonel Reed asked him to form and conduct a group of twenty members. The singers would be exempted from all chores during the whole week of the concert rehearsal. Needless to say that Firmin didn't lack volunteers. Far from all of them, however, could sing in tune. Firmin eventually managed to find his twenty voices.

The next step was to get Reed's approval with the choice of the titles. The Negro spiritual repertoire was full of songs about Black slaves. In order not to offend the sensitivity of the white officers, Firmin was forced to exclude songs like *Nobody Knows the Trouble I've Seen*. Nonetheless, he managed to keep *Go Down Moses* by Harriet Tubman, although its author sympathized with the plight of the slaves fleeing north. For the rest, the pieces on the concert program included traditional Christmas songs like *Silent Night, Holy Night* and *All the way my savior leads me.*

The chorale performed in St. Peter and St. Paul, a little church of Checkendon, at the end of the afternoon. The chapel was crowded with villagers of all ages. At the beginning of the performance, Firmin noticed the strange gaze on the singers' faces who were facing the audience. The choirmaster quickly turned his head and looked over his shoulder. He saw the people, seated as still as stone, smiling and quietly listening. Firmin realized that the British weren't used to sway in rhythm to the song inside the house of God. They couldn't even sing with them, as they didn't know the lyrics. So, Corporal Bellegarde made an insisting smile to the singers, who smiled broadly at the audience.

When the choir began to sing *Amazing Grace*, the whole assembly started to sing in chorus with them. Sometimes, Firmin would turn round to watch all these people sing this ode to the glory of Jesus, along with his Negro chorale. A long shiver ran up and down his spine. Still, Firmin knew, like all his singers did, that this anthem had been composed in 1779 by a poet and Anglican cleric named John Newton, who had been a captain of slave ships until 1755.

After the mass which followed the concert, many soldiers of the 320th VLA were invited for supper by families of the village. That's the way how Firmin and Edward ended at the Griffiths.

Located at a hundred yards from the church, on the opposite side of the road, the house was a patchwork of various building materials, attesting its long history. The half-timbering was filled here by raw stones, there by red bricks, elsewhere by millstones, here again by cob or mud. The small plot of land which separated the house from the pavement was a gathering of squares forming a kind of checkerboard of vegetable crops. Only one square of lawn had escaped the patriarch's spade and rake blows.

On this occasion, Mrs. Griffiths had decided to burn a few extra logs. The house was still filled with a moist heat when Firmin and Ed came in, confirming the absolute destitution in which these people lived, like most of the British, since the beginning of the war.

Both friends had brought the best ingredients they had saved from their Thanksgiving's rations of the previous month. Canned turkey. Chocolate bars. Candies and various chewing gum for the children. *Wrigley's Juicy Fruit* flavored with fruit tastes and *Beech-Nut Brand* flavored with green or peppermint. And even a bottle of *Coca-Cola* for each of the four kids. Besides, they discretely handed over to Mr. Griffiths a Lucky Strikes cigarette pack each, plus a pair of nylon stockings which he would eventually offer to his wife the next day without feeling embarrassed.

The children were standing near the wood stove, aligned in descending order. They were waiting, as quietly as they could, to be introduced to their guests by their father.

The three elders wore a floral printed velvet dress specially made by their mother, with a fabric likely cut out from curtains.

Patricia, thirteen years old, had the same coarse face features as her father. Jaimie, ten, and her sibling Janet, nine years old, looked alike almost as if they were twins. They had inherited the best from their mother. Long red hair, green eyes, and a constellation of freckles.

When he introduced them to the last one, Billie, four years old, the father couldn't hold back a deep sigh, and said: "a girl again!"

Despite her white dress, enhanced with a collar and a marine-blue belt, the little girl still looked like a tomboy. Her little dark look reminded him of her father, as if she wanted to soften his disappointment of not having a son. At last! How could she ignore it, since her father had given her a first name, which could fit a boy as well as a girl?

Firmin could read a small touch of sadness in Billie's eyes. The image of his little sister Marie suddenly appeared before him. The vision was so real that he felt like he was reliving the day Marie passed away. His lips started to quiver, and his eyes grew misty. He covered his face with his hands, but it didn't stop his tears from gushing out of his closed eyelids. He was terribly confused, as he didn't want to spoil their evening. But he couldn't stop weeping.

"Supper's ready!" said Mrs. Griffiths with a loud and joyful tone, intending to free Firmin from his sad thoughts.

Firmin wiped his eyes with the back of his hands, took a long and deep breath, and flashed an appreciative smile at Mrs. Griffiths.

They all huddled around the table. The two parents were facing one another at each end. Firmin and Ed took a seat on each side in the length of the table. The kids sat between them. Billie insisted on sitting on Firmin's right side. Mrs. Griffiths asked around who wished to say grace. As none of the two GIs reacted, Patricia, sitting on his left side, volunteered.

Firmin felt Billie's hand grasping his. While Patricia was praying to the Lord to bless their meal, Firmin was observing alternately Edward, Jaimie, Janet, Mrs. Griffiths and her husband. Two colored soldiers sharing the same table with this white family. All linked together by the hands, without feeling embarrassed. Without racial prejudice. He could feel Billie's watchful gaze on him. He turned to her. She smiled at him with compassion, as if she knew what he was feeling at this very moment. Then, she gave him an accomplice wink.

"Enjoy your meal!" she said, immediately after the grace, before holding out her plate to her mother.

Watching these four kids feasting on all this good food was for Firmin the most beautiful present he had received for a long time. Anyway, it succeeded in dissipating his melancholy.

Of course, he missed his parents. As well as his friends and the Lower Ninth ward in New Orleans. However, he didn't feel this nostalgia, sweet and painful at once, which overwhelms you when you're far from home in such circumstances.

Everyone was striving to make this special moment of conviviality stretch as long as possible. Billie, however, eventually fell asleep on the edge of the table. Mrs. Griffiths carried her to bed.

When she returned, her husband stood up and started to sing *Auld Lang Syne,* a Scottish world famous traditional song. His two guests stood up at once and accompanied him in an improvised chorale.

It was late, and Patricia, the oldest of the girls, seemed to be the only one able to stay awake any longer. The two GIs warmly thanked their hosts and wished them a Merry

Christmas, one more time, and took leave of the Griffiths.

The warm welcome of this English family moved Firmin deeper than his first experience in the town's pubs had. Even his first kiss with Shirley didn't have such an effect on him.

Something was seeping into his mind. A strange feeling which looked like misgivings. Of course, his wish to fight the Nazis remained undiminished. But if he had been asked, at this very moment, why, and, moreover, for what he was ready to risk his life, he wouldn't reply as categorically as on the day he had joined the army.

At that time, he wanted to fight for his country, hoping he and his colored brothers would be rewarded with the same civil rights as the Whites had. But the Negroes continued to suffer from the same segregation in the army as they did in their home towns and neighborhoods. So, considering the gap that separated America from Europe in this matter, the reason why he was ready to fight the Nazis now was different. At this moment, he wanted, first of all, to help the British, the French, the Belgian, the Dutch and all the European victims of the Nazis, who were ready to consider the Negroes with respect and fairness.

"How can I still be proud to be an American," Firmin thought, "if America persists in applying segregation? When we have beaten the Nazis, will I still wish to return to New Orleans, knowing that I would only recover my condition of a second-class citizen?"

CHAPTER 21

Checkendon. January 3, 1944

That morning, the whole battalion was gathered in the middle of the camp to attend the raising of the American flag and listen to the new year's speech of Lieutenant Colonel Reed.

"The last six weeks have been disrupted by logistics problems. You couldn't touch a single balloon, and I know how frustrating it was for you. And, above all, that you are worried. I was even told that some of you were wondering if they hadn't been sent here to Great Britain just to deceive the Negro press and public opinion. If, actually, the army's headquarters simply didn't trust this colored battalion."

These words raised murmurs of approval, which Reed silenced by continuing his speech.

"Did you believe, even one second, that I would have accepted to command a junk battalion? No way, of course! I fully trust each and every one of you. And you will soon get the opportunity to prove me, and our whole army, and the American people, your valor and your bravery…"

A thick and heavy silence wrapped the parade ground. Firmin was seized by a strange feeling. A great pride mingled with fear. Were they going to be led into battle although they weren't fully prepared?

"Essential elements of our balloons went astray during our trip from Camp Tyson. Fortunately, they are now on their way to our next post. In two weeks from now, our battalion will be transferred to a place which is better fitted to balloon training."

Firmin sighed of relief. Death would have to wait for a while. Others around him reacted more loudly. They longed to recover their jobs as balloon operators, meteorologists or maintenance mechanics. It would reduce the frequency of the forced marches they had to make almost every day in the nearby moist and frosty woods.

"This year, we're gonna defeat our enemies. And you will get your share in the fight, and in the victory as well."

A great clamor rose. Lieutenant Colonel Reed raised his hand. Everyone went silent again.

"But your role will not be limited to a static presence far behind the front line. You will have to face the enemy sometimes. Then, you will need to be able to defend yourself. To sell your life quite dearly. And, preferably kill your enemies before they kill you."

It was an abrupt but necessary way to remind these men they had come to Europe to fight, which implied that some of them may not return home alive.

"Therefore, to make real soldiers out of you, we will use the remainder of our stay in Checkendon, until our transfer, to teach you man-to-man fighting techniques. With a knife or barehanded. You will learn how to kill, not to be killed! How to kill an enemy before he kills your fellow soldier or yourself!

I'm aware that for some of you the idea of killing a man doesn't cause a moral dilemma. I know that many of you have been confronted to violence, injustice and humiliations since their younger age. Some may have witnessed the murder in cold blood of a member of your community. Men like you need to be extremely wise, on the contrary, not to yield to the temptation of revenge.

I still do hope that your faith in God and your religious education will help you so!"

The first training session commenced right after lunchtime. Four hours non-stop of self-defense drills, to learn how to disarm and put out of action an enemy who threatens you with a rifle, a hand gun or a dagger. Two instructors were assigned for each battery. The result of this session didn't prove convincing. Firmin and many others were virtually killed a dozen times each by their drill sergeants during the afternoon.

The guys ended so exhausted that they fell asleep before the curfew hour.

January 4, 1944

The awakening turned out to be quite painful for many. The brutal and repeated falls in the day before, the twisting of the arms and the improvised parries against the attacks from their instructors had left traces on their bodies. Bruises, tendinitis, aching joints and muscles.

However, it was unthinkable to expect any compassion from Wild Bill, Reed's second in command. You could count on his usual outspokenness to put even more pressure on the soldiers.

"Whenever you are facing the enemy, be sure that he will not give you any respite. And so, neither will I. I carefully watched you yesterday, and what I saw was just a bunch of pussies. You wouldn't even hold on one hour on the battle field. All the money, the time and the energy spent by the U.S. Army for training you would be reduced to nothing in just one hour's time... If it depended on me,

I would transfer you all to a service unit. You, niggers, are good for nothing but that! Right? But I've got orders and I'm a soldier. And as such, I obey. I was asked to make fighters out of you. Men. Real ones. So, believe me. I'm gonna give you a hard time. You're gonna curse me. But I don't care, as long as I can turn you into fearsome warriors before the big day!"

What Firmin feared the most came right after Wild Bill's earful. The self-defense lessons of the previous day left room to offensive techniques.

It started with a lecture of the most efficient ways to kill a man noiselessly. Methods borrowed from the British SOE[46], and developed by a major named William E. Fairbairn, who was also the inventor of a double-edged knife specially designed to slit the throat of an enemy as quickly as possible.

"Forget about fair play, gentlemen," warned the sergeant major. "It may look cruel to you, but it would be even more to take more time to kill your enemy. Even if you already crippled him by breaking his arm, don't stop! Rub him out! Take advantage of his disability to kill him even faster with your dagger!"

He didn't leave them any time to mull over his introduction. He immediately continued with a description of the weapon they would have to use for that.

"The U.S. M3 knife is a dreadful and silent weapon, which can easily be hidden and from which there is no efficient parry when it's used by an expert. Except if you've got a firearm or if you can run away bloody fast!"

For the practical exercises, they used harmless wooden

---

[46] Special Operations Executive. British secret services responsible for the support for the members of the resistance in Nazi-occupied countries.

replicas. However, Firmin could easily imagine the blood spurting out of the jugular vein severed by the blade. The yawning trachea preventing the victim from screaming. He had once seen his mother slaughter a chicken. The poor bird had kept on flapping its wings for a few more seconds after.

The most painful part of the morning was the anatomy lesson of the abdominal region of the human body. Liver, stomach, spleen, kidneys. All the vital organs.

In the evening again, the men were knocked out. They snored like bears. The last one awake as usual, Firmin wondered how he would manage to sleep in the middle of this concert. He would have liked to stuff his ears with cotton, but, as a crew leader, he wasn't allowed to. He had to remain capable of jumping out of his bed when the alert sounds.

CHAPTER 22

January 5, 1944

Despite their protests and supplications, the men of the 320th VLA couldn't escape from a new challenging day of close combat drills.

One at a time, they had to attack their instructors from behind, using the techniques learned on the previous day. The slightest hesitation, the tiniest synchronization defect earned the poor apprentice killer to be projected onto the ground by one of the many moves developed by the major William E. Fairbairn.

As far as he was concerned, Firmin took the lesson into account, at his second attempt. When the evening came, however, he still could feel the dull pain caused by the violent contact with the frozen ground of the camp.

Others had been less successful. Like Edward. Ten times—maybe more—the poor guy had been floored down by his drill sergeant. Every time, the latter ended his demonstration yelling, "You're dead!" Then, he would add "Because of you, the sentry will give the alert, and all your comrades will be killed!"

This man seemed to have an inexhaustible energy. Watching him, Firmin wondered if the guy didn't find pleasure in making his friend suffer.

During the supper in the mess, Firmin talked a long time with Edward. He worried a lot about his friend. He was afraid that he might not survive very long after having landed on the continent during the big day, which everyone knew would come soon. Yet, no one could tell when or where.

Edward confessed to him that he couldn't resign himself to killing a man with his hands. "At some distance, when you shoot at a man with your rifle, you don't see his life turning off in his eyes. But here…"

Firmin decided to strive to free him from his scruples.

"You must think of yourself first, and of your buddies as well. You're not alone in such a situation. It's not your life only which is at stake. In a unit, every man must be able to count on each of his comrades. Swear to God that you wouldn't hesitate to drive your knife into the heart of one of these damned Germans if he were on the brink of killing me!"

January 6, 1944

This morning, Lieutenant Colonel Reed had given free time to all the battalion. Those who wished it could attend the religious service of Epiphany by chaplain Albert White. The others were allowed to go about their business.

At first, Firmin was stunned but the unusual attendance for a mass celebration. Walking his way towards the altar, he noticed some faces that he hadn't seen in a church before. Among them were firm atheists, or even impious men who never lost an opportunity to swear like a trooper, or blaspheme the Lord, except in the presence of Reed who couldn't condone any disrespect for God.

Edward's scruples were shared by other soldiers of the battalion. Did they really have the right to kill in cold blood? Wasn't killing a man a deadly sin? These questions, which had been tormenting the souls of some soldiers since they were taught how to kill in silence, eventually reached the ears of Lieutenant Colonel Reed.

Reed feared the consequences it might have on the morale of his troops and on their efficiency in combat. Therefore, he decided to ask the chaplain to prepare a homily intended to restore the men's confidence in their mission and in the blessing of the Lord.

This was what Firmin could understand when he heard the sermon sprinkled with biblical references, which had no link with the encounter of the Three Kings with the Christ Child.

(Ecclesiastes 3 :8) "… There is a time for everything, and a season for every activity under the heavens:

… a time to love and a time to hate, a time for war and a time for peace."

(Romans 13 :4) "… For the one in authority is God's servant for your good. But if you do wrong, be afraid, for rulers do not bear the sword for no reason. They are God's servants, agents of wrath to bring punishment on the wrongdoer."

(Numbers 31 :2) "Take vengeance on the Midianites for the Israelites. After that, you will be gathered to your people."

The true believers who attended this mass, like Firmin and Edward, felt reassured by the chaplain's words.

Atheists were expecting something else. Reed's New Year's speech and these fighting training had revealed to them what they had been striving to ignore or reject since they joined the army. The possibility of a near death. *Their* death!

It was one thing to claim you're atheist or agnostic. It was a far cry from accepting the idea there is nothing after death. That, whatever you've done in your life, you won't be held accountable for it! Was life supposed to have neither sense nor reason? But if God exists, what would occur to my sinner's and unbeliever's soul after my death?

Such were the questionings that pushed the newcomers to join the faithfuls on that day.

January 7, 1944

The pastor's sermon had the effect Lieutenant Colonel Reed had expected. Even Edward showed an unusual aggressiveness during the exercises given by his drill sergeant. This dramatic change surprised his team leader as much as it reassured his friend Firmin.

In the same evening, the latter learned that he would leave on the following Monday with a group of soldiers of the 320th VLA for a maneuver training in the harbor of Cardiff, Wales.

Of his crew, only Ed and Jimmy would join. Doug would have to stay inside the camp of Checkendon, for sanitary and disciplinary reasons.

As a compensation for their coming mission, all the participants were granted an overnight pass for the next evening in Checkendon. Firmin longed to have a pleasant time at the *Black Horse* and at the *Four Horseshoes* among the villagers.

CHAPTER 23

Cardiff, Wales, January 10, 1944

The delegation of the 320th VLA arrived at Cardiff station in the middle of the afternoon. From there, it was driven by military trucks to the RAF[47] Pengam Moors, a few miles away. The air base housed the 43rd Maintenance unit RAF and the 587th RAF anti-aircraft cooperation squadron.

The balloon operator crews were eager to have their first effective training since they arrived in Europe. All the more as they hadn't had much time in Camp Tyson to get familiar with their new equipment.

The drills would have to be carried out in coordination with the British balloon units, in real conditions. The purpose was to defend Cardiff Port facilities. But for Lieutenant Colonel Reed, the issue of this mission was not only military or strategic. The honor of his battalion, hence of all the Negro troops, depended on the behavior of his men.

Firmin and his comrades of the 320th VLA were all the more motivated as they sincerely held their commandant in high esteem.

***

Unfortunately, on January 12, their equipment was still

---

[47] Royal Air Force.

missing! Lieutenant Colonel Reed was furious. The British started openly making fun at them.

Needless to say that the Tommies and the Yankees didn't love each other. For the British soldiers, their American counterparts were "oversexed, overpaid and over here." Their pay was three times the British one. Fifty dollars a month for the first, fifteen for the second ones. The yankees received half more meat daily. Besides the pay, GIs were getting large quantities of chocolate and cigarettes. Not to mention the nylon stockings.

They took advantage of this fashion accessory, which was impossible to find elsewhere in Great Britain, to curry favor with some young British girls. Which didn't fail to irritate the Tommies.

Moreover, their uniforms didn't flatter the British. Actually, they had only one, whereas the Americans had three different ones. One for each specific use.

The Americans sometimes wondered how the Tommies could bear to constantly wear their combat suit, made of this coarse woolen fabric. When the GIs were on leave in town, they wore their service uniforms, which consisted of olive drab wool trousers, jacket and cap. And, height of refinement, light leather shoes, with rubber soles, as opposed to the British, who wore those ugly hobnail boots, which made a loud crunching sound. It was no wonder that the Tommies were jealous of the Yankees.

Firmin and his friends of the 320th VLA hoped they would get an overnight leave to make a trip to Cardiff on the following Saturday. But a rumor asserted that the white American officers would deny the colored soldiers going out in town. The whole area around Cardiff was occupied by a large number of support and logistics troops. GIs were all over the place. The 117th Port battalion in Cardiff, the 756th Railway shop battalion in Newport, the 111th Ordnance company in Barry, the 5th Engineer special brigade in Swansea, and many other units.

While waiting for the arrival of their equipment, the operators of the 320th VLA were given from their British counterparts a few demonstrations of their anti-aircraft batteries and defense systems.

They also had the privilege to visit the maintenance workshops of the 43rd MU[48]. They saw dozens of aircraft being overhauled. Hawker Hurricanes which had distinguished themselves in 1940 during the Battle of Britain. Some Hawker Henleys and Miles M.25 Martinets used to tow targets designed for anti-aircraft shooting drills.

January 13, 1944

Lieutenant Colonel Reed was finally forced to inform his men that their balloons would no longer arrive on time.

They wouldn't train either on their British colleagues' material. Their balloons were more voluminous. They used different inflation and mooring systems. As a consequence, it was deemed counterproductive to teach them how to use the British equipment.

It appeared, once more, that the Tommies didn't do anything like the Americans did. It didn't bode well for the coordination between American and British troops.

---

[48] Maintenance Unit.

January 14,1944

Firmin hadn't slept well. There had been a continuous procession of emergency landings of Spitfires, Hurricanes and Mosquitos returning from night bombings over Germany.

Lacking a successful military cooperation, the commanding officers decided to organize a friendly sports meeting matching up the 320th AABBB[49] with their counterparts of the 587th SRAF[50].

Intending to ensure fairness, two different sports had been chosen.

The meeting started with a baseball game, which undoubtedly benefited the Yankees. Accustomed to playing cricket, another bat-and-ball game, the British never managed to get used to the thinner barrel shaped bats used in the American game. Not only were they thoroughly defeated, but their opponents took great pleasure in mocking them. The guys of the 320th VLA hadn't laughed that much for a long time. That was until the second event started: a rugby game.

The British players were dressed in rugby outfits. Their American opponents had their baseball suits on, over their fleece cotton underwear.

The revenge of the Tommies vs. the Yankees quickly turned into a stinging humiliation. The GIs were literally and figuratively crushed.

In American football games, players wear thick protections. The crazy British didn't use any, besides a mouthguard. Nevertheless, and despite a very hard ground,

---

[49] Anti-Aircraft Barrage Balloon Battalion.
[50] Squadron RAF.

they didn't show any restraint whatsoever when tackling the opposing ball carrier. As a result, the team of the 320th VLA had to replace half of its players before the end of the first half. And at the same time, the British team had scored six tries and a dozen penalties. The Yankees resisted a little better in the second half. However, they didn't score any point. Because of this "stupid rule" that bans forward passes. In American football, long distance forward passes are precisely what makes the strength of a quarterback and its team.

The GIs ended the game completely burned out. Every time one of them made a forward pass, their front and second rows were getting more exhausted in the scrums, although their forwards were tough guys. Stronger and better fed than their opponents. But the Tommies had no intention to concede a single point in this revenge, especially after the humiliation they had suffered in the baseball game.

At the end of the match, the British explained to them that rugby was "a thug's game played by gentlemen." And they proved it by respectfully greeting their guests with handshakes and applause, whereas the Americans had expected to be laughed at. Even better, the Tommies invited them all to play the title decider in the evening in the red-light district of the area. This lesson of fair play made a great impression on Firmin and his comrades.

They were advised to bring some precious gifts like nylon stockings and American cigarettes. And condoms, of course.

Against the battalion's white officers will, the British command succeeded in convincing Reed that it would be a bad idea to miss this opportunity to weld together both

American and British troops. Thus, Firmin and his comrades were granted an overnight leave.

CHAPTER 24

Saturday, January 15, 1944

The government of H.M. King George VI had asked, as of September 1942, that any kind of segregation towards colored troops be officially banned on the British soil. However, as they didn't want to offend their American allies, the memo of the Ministry of the Interior was more nuanced. It said actually that the British authorities *ought not, by any process, visible or invisible, to try to lead our own people to adopt as their own the social attitude to the American Negro...*

The colored soldiers of the 320ᵗʰ VLA had indeed experienced it in the village of Checkendon. However, they had been informed that things were not always going so smoothly in large agglomerations which hosted numerous units of the U.S. Army. Measures were taken by the U.S. commanding officers to prevent black and white GIs from mixing in the same neighboring towns by alternating passes.

Brawls weren't unusual, and most often started by white soldiers. But when the MP[51] came and took action, they were particularly violent with colored soldiers. Which came as no surprise as one third of the MP staff were natives of Southern states.

Firmin didn't want to take any risk. So, he, Edward and Jimmy decided to join a little group of other guys of the

---

[51] Military police.

320th VLA and ten soldiers of the 587th SRAF, who didn't look hotheaded. The base had made two of their personnel carriers available for their transport. QLT Bedford trucks.

On two occasions, the whole group was denied the entrance of a dancehall by white American soldiers, despite the indignant protests of their British counterparts. As the latter had no intention to abandon their African American guests, one of them, native of the region, eventually suggested a fallback plan. Somewhere in the little port city of Barry, twelve miles away from Cardiff.

They grudgingly hopped back aboard their terribly noisy and uncomfortable trucks. When they reached their destination, half an hour's drive later, Firmin and the others were numbed with cold. Although their Welsh hosts had done their best to warm them up with their traditional songs and their jokes. But it was sometimes difficult for the Yankees to understand their sense of humor, not to mention their dreadful accent.

No matter, at the very moment the group reached the entrance of the dance hall, the guys of the 320th VLA knew they were going to have an unforgettable night.

From the street, you could hear the wild rhythm of swing. The place was definitely made for them. When they saw their cheerful expressions on their faces, the Tommies uttered shouts of joy. Firmin and his African American fellows paid all the entrance fees and entered. Easily. Without a problem.

The two highest-ranking British officers set the time limit at three a.m., before letting everybody disperse into the crowd.

Firmin, Ed and Jimmy looked at each other with wide-open eyes. They hadn't seen anything like this before.

145

They hugged and roared with laughter. They needed to shout to have a chance to understand each other.

The hall was jam-packed with people. A human tide was rippling to the rhythm of *In the Bag* by Lionel Hampton. In the opposite end of the hall, the musicians of the band were standing on a platform. In front of them, dozens of dancers' couples were twirling, forming a moving shadow.

Firmin turned round to make sure his two partners still followed him. Then they struggled to make their way to the bar. Knowing where alcohol could lead them, they ordered three cold sodas and walked closer to the stage.

They couldn't believe their eyes. White girls were dancing indiscriminately with white or colored soldiers. Something that was inconceivable in America.

In the Southern States, a mere glance at a white woman could be enough to earn a black man to be lynched by a mob of Whites. Firmin hadn't ever witnessed it, but his father once told him that one of his uncles, living in Alabama, had been found hanging from a tree, near his town. The poor man was alleged to have looked up at a young white girl who was driving to church in a drawn carriage with her parents and her brother.

Right before he was told this sad and revolting story, Firmin had heard on the radio a song by Billie Holiday. A poem titled *Strange Fruit*[52], that talked about:

Southern trees [which] *bear a strange fruit*
Blood on the leaves and blood at the root
Black bodies swingin' in the Southern breeze
Strange fruit hangin' from the poplar trees

[52] A song recorded in 1939 by Billie Holiday, from a poem by Abel Meeropol, alias Lewis Allan, composed in 1937.

Pastoral scene of the gallant South.
The bulgin' eyes and the twisted mouth
Scent of magnolias sweet and fresh
Then the sudden smell of burnin' flesh.

Firmin had felt outraged, shocked and marked forever by this revelation. But his father had warned him against the idea of rebelling. "These folks are too powerful to be defeated by strength."

Edward was fascinated by a pretty and curvaceous brunette. Her skirt's hemline was lifted in circular waves and unveiled her knees every time she twisted her waist. Firmin, on his side, couldn't take his eyes off the musicians playing Duke Ellington's *It don't mean anything if you ain't got that swing*.

The orchestra's name was *Barry's Jazz-Band*, but judging by their varied ways of dressing, Firmin deduced that its composition changed according to the availability of each musician. They didn't have the same level, but they all played in tune. They had managed to gather all the elements of a good jazz band. A drummer, a trumpet player, a clarinetist, a trombonist, a double bassist, three saxophonists, and even a pianist. While looking at the alto saxophonist, Firmin was squeezing in his hand his mouthpiece which he hadn't forgotten to bring.

As the orchestra started to play Benny Goodman's *Minnie's in the Money*, Firmin felt someone was pulling him by the sleeve. It was Ed who had just hooked the pretty brunette. Firmin found her really lovely. Her great green eyes were lighting up her face. Her lips were enhanced with a red lipstick, matching with the color of her nail polish.

While poking into her pocket a pair of nylon stockings

147

that Ed had offered her, the girl dragged him onto the dance floor. They soon vanished in the crowd of the other couples.

Firmin turned again towards his favorite show. The musicians of the band. Especially the alto sax. A medium-sized white man, who seemed of his father's age. He wore a panama hat and a very loose light colored zoot suit with padded shoulders. "Plus, that guy moves pretty well on the stage!" Firmin thought.

The saxophonist noticed the young brown-skinned soldier staring at him with wondering eyes. So, he started gazing at him in return. He could appreciate the way Firmin was moving to the rhythm and sometimes closing his eyes to let the music creep into his body and soul. When the alto sax started to perform his solo, Firmin couldn't refrain from wiggling his fingers as if he were holding an invisible instrument. When the solo ended, he stared at the artist with a moved and admiring gaze.

At break time, the saxophonist intercepted Firmin's gaze and smiled at him with a friendly wink. The young GI made him understand he had appreciated as a connoisseur. He took his mouthpiece out of his pocket and showed it with his outstretched hand. The musician beckoned him over to the stage. Then, he asked him what piece he could play well. Intimidated, Firmin whispered:

"In the mood by Glenn Miller."

"This, son, is our finale," the saxophonist replied. "No way to let you play it in my place."

Firmin, then, suggested *Summertime* by George Gershwin.

"Can be," said the musician, offering his hand to lift him onto the stage.

Then, he took off his mouthpiece and handed over his saxophone.

"Let me hear how you play!"

Firmin wasn't prepared to find himself on a stage, so suddenly. He felt stage fright rising. But he couldn't back out anymore. He wouldn't let himself be intimidated.

While adjusting his mouthpiece to the instrument, Firmin strove to calm his fear down with long breaths. Then, he moistened the reed with his tongue, inhaled deeply, and took a plunge.

Firmin had played this piece dozens of times, before his father told him, "Now, son, you got it!" It was also the opinion of the saxophonist. Alfonso was his name. He asked the young and promising musician his name and walked to the conductor. He whispered a few words in his ear; then turned round towards Firmin, smiled at him, raised his thumb and nodded.

When the break was over, the conductor took a mike and announced the following title: *Summertime*, and his alto sax guest: Corporal Firmin Bellegarde.

The young man could feel all his fellow soldiers of the 320th VLA and those of the 587th SRAF turn their heads towards the stage and gaze at him. Edward and his young brunette were only a few yards away. Firmin refrained from looking at them, to keep concentrated on the music. Most importantly, he focused his eyes on the tenor sax and the conductor. He didn't want to play out of tune or even with a slight rhythm lag. But he quickly felt in perfect harmony with them. The notes came out in a natural and smooth flow. While playing, he thought he could see his father among the musicians. He could have stayed playing for hours. But Alfonso didn't mean it that way. Four minutes of performance and thirty seconds of applause! That was all what Firmin could expect. But it was already huge! Absolutely terrific!

When he jumped down onto the dance floor, Edward and Martha came to congratulate him. There was also a girl friend of Martha. Sheila. A pretty girl with long curled brown hair, a very white skin, almost milky, spotted with freckles. When she smiled, her hazel eyes would squint and her nose wrinkle.

As Firmin remained silent, Sheila started a conversation.

"You're brothers, aren't you?"

It wasn't the first time people thought so. They had indeed some resemblance, besides similar height and weight.

"No," he answered laconically.

She immediately thought that the young man who looked so self-confident on stage was probably reserved, if not bashful.

"Can you dance as well as you play?"

She didn't wait for his answer and dragged him among the dancers, on the first measures of a Lindy hop tune which Firmin recognized instantly. *Savoy*. The latest hit by Lucky Millinder.

It didn't take long for Sheila to spellbind her partner. She danced the jitterbug like no one. She performed the craziest pirouettes with an amazing ease. "And she's so light, too!" Firmin thought. He had never had such a dance partner before. Soon, the other couples would expand the circle to leave only the three better in the middle of the floor.

Seeing the excitement rising among the public, the

band followed up with the biggest hit by Johnny Mercer: *One for my baby and one more for the road*. Sheila was out of breath. Firmin could feel the frantic beating of her heart when she clung to his neck to perform a new acrobatic move. But she kept on with the same energy, without weakening.

There were only two couples left at the end of the song. A white soldier with an English girl. White too. And them. The conductor asked the public to determine the winning pair with an applause meter. Sheila and Firmin won hands down.

Good sport, the other couple came closer and congratulated them. On the spur of the moment, Sheila took Firmin's brown face between her alabaster hands and kissed him long and hard on the mouth.

Surprised by Sheila's carelessness, Firmin didn't have the reflex to push her away. Instead, he kissed her back. Without worrying in any way about the people around. Those few minutes of frantic dance with a beautiful white girl had made him forget about his condition of a black man in a white world.

A white soldier eventually reminded him where his place was.

"Hey, you, darkie!" he shouted. "Get away from the white girl!"

The remark immediately aroused anger among his friends of the 320th VLA and the other African Americans in the hall. Their British hosts of the 587th SRAF rushed to stop them from answering the taunt. Many of them had drunk a lot of alcohol, unlike Firmin, who remembered what his father used to tell him. "These folks are too powerful to be defeated by strength."

He instantly released Sheila's hand.

Firmin had to face the fact. Unwillingly, he had reached the limit of the tolerance of white people for Blacks, here, in Great Britain.

After this incident, Sheila went back to a group of British soldiers and wouldn't leave it anymore. She was probably afraid they might make her pay for her liberality.

On several occasions, Firmin's eyes met hers, in the opposite side of the dance floor. He had the feeling, for just a moment, that she smiled at him. But he couldn't smile back. He didn't want to give her friends a reason to start a brawl.

Firmin spent the rest of the night dancing alone while watching the musicians play. Sometimes, he would stop to catch his breath. He watched Martha and Ed with envy, and wished he was in Sheila's arms. The sweet dream continued until the early morning, after he returned to Pengam Moors airbase.

CHAPTER 25

Bulwark Camp, Chepstow. January 18, 1944

The delegation of the 320th VLA had left Cardiff two days earlier to join up with the bulk of the battalion which had been transferred meanwhile from Checkendon to Bulwark camp in Chepstow, on the northeast riverfront of the Severn Estuary.

A few balloons arrived short after that. Enough to ensure the operators to get four hours of daily training. The first ones since they had left Camp Tyson.

The drills were limited, however, as the battalion still missed one essential element. A hydrogen production unit. The balloons were inflated with air; hence, they couldn't fly. In such conditions, the training had a poor educational value. Like learning to drive in a pedal car.

The men of the 320th VLA hence returned to their routine of exhausting marches, by day, by night sometimes as well, which length was increased to twenty-five miles a day. Besides came the obstacle courses, the rifle shooting and the hand-to-hand bayonet fighting. Every activity which helped to protect them from the severe cold of the Welsh winter.

Not far from there, in Sudbrook, was the entrance of a tunnel connecting both banks of the Severn. There were also docks and shipyards. These strategic facilities were under the protection of the South Wales Borderers and a Scottish regiment. Firmin and his comrades of the 320th VLA used to cross their path almost daily during their military step marches alongside Camp Road.

There was also a tunnel pumping station which was under the constant protection of four soldiers. It had to run continuously to evacuate more than thirteen million gallons[53] of infiltration water per day out of the tunnel.

The destruction of the station would have led to a rapid flooding of the tunnel, interrupting at once all train connections between the west of England and the south of Wales. German airstrikes over Cardiff, eighteen miles away, were less frequent than at the beginning of the war. However, the threat remained a serious concern.

The area was constantly swept by strong wind gusts, which increased the sensation of cold and made the guard duties particularly trying. At the pump station, the sentries had to be replaced every two hours to shelter inside a Nissen hut.

The soldiers of the 320th VLA were glad to learn, a few weeks after, their transfer to another nearby town. The old Bulwark camp was very uncomfortable. Besides, recreation was limited to the Sunday mass in Portskewett church, and a few pubs in the village. Firmin and his fellow soldiers were eager to find back the kind of entertainment they had enjoyed in Cardiff.

---

[53] About eleven million gal Imp.

CHAPTER 26

New Inn Camp, Wales. February 21, 1944

The 320th VLA was transferred by train on that day to Pontypool, ten miles north of Newport, and twenty-one miles drive from Cardiff.

During the trip, the GIs could read a short guide about the British way of life and customs[54]. This thirty-eight-page pamphlet was more detailed than the movie *A Welcome to Britain* they had seen on their arrival in Checkendon. Lieutenant Colonel Reed had insisted on them carefully reading it and assimilating the basic notions, as some soldiers of the battalion would have the chance to be billeted in people's houses.

The booklet reminded them of the living conditions which local people had to endure.

"You are coming to Britain from a country where your home is still safe, food is still plentiful, and lights are still burning. So it is doubly important for you to remember that the British soldiers and civilians have been living under a tremendous strain.

It is always impolite to criticize your hosts. It is militarily stupid to insult your allies. So stop and think before you sound off about lukewarm beer, or cold boiled potatoes, or the way English cigarettes taste.

If British civilians look dowdy and badly dressed, it is not because they do not like good clothes or know how to

---

[54] *A short guide to Great Britain*. (Page 22) Published in 1943 by the War and Navy Dpt in Washington, DC. A Short Guide to Great Britain (olpl.org)

155

wear them. All clothing is rationed and the British know that they help war production by wearing an old suit or dress until it cannot be patched any longer.

One thing to be careful about—if you are invited into a British home and the host exhorts you to 'eat up, there's plenty on the table,' go easy. It may be the family's rations for a whole week spread out to show their hospitality."

When they got off the train, the soldiers were seized by the pungent smell of sulfur emitted by thick black smokes pouring from armament factories. The latter were indeed running at full capacity since the beginning of the war. So did the mines of this coal basin, after they had suffered a considerable drop of their activity during the interwar period. The pay was meager, but people of the area still rejoiced in finding a job again.

Then, the guys were driven by truck to their new post: New Inn's military base, one and a half miles southeast from the town.

In the afternoon, Firmin and several non-commissioned officers learned they would be billeted in family houses, in the small town of Abersychan, two miles north from Pontypool. Others, like Edward, Jimmy and Doug, would be accommodated in various buildings of the town, including church basements, converted into dorms.

The driver stopped the bus in front of a house in Station Street, and honked. "Family Jones," he said loudly, pointing his hand at one of the terraced houses aligned and stuck to one another.

They were all built on the same model. Functional and solid. With their street facades made of unequal-sized raw stones, contrasting with their crenelated window embrasures of carved stones. The door, in the center, was flanked by two windows. Behind the lace veiling, one could guess the thick blackout curtains, which the occupants had to keep closed during the overnight curfew. The second floor had three windows.

Firmin mechanically checked the name written on his billeting document. Reassured, he grabbed his duffle bag, stood up, walked to the front of the bus, and got off.

"And don't forget," said the driver. "Be right here tomorrow at 7:30 sharp. The bus will pick you up and drive you back to the base."

Firmin adjusted his tie and the collar of his jacket. He had no idea of who would host him. For the first time in his life, he would be alone with white people in their house, which made him feel very nervous. He flashed a last glance over his shoulder, to make sure the bus was still there in case the Joneses would refuse to let him in.

As he was lifting the knocker, the door opened. A man came forward. Firmin reckoned he was in his early fifties and about two inches smaller than him. He was stocky, with sloping shoulders. He had dark brown close-set eyes, and a thick mustache with curved up ends that gave him a sort of permanent smile.

Firmin handed over his official letter of introduction.

"Good evening, Son. Come in. We were expecting you," the man said, without even reading the document of the U.S. Army.

Then, he made a friendly hand sign to the driver.

"I'm John Jones, and this is my wife Maggie," he said to Firmin, introducing a woman behind him, hardly visible in the shade of the vestibule.

"Good evening, Mr. Jones. My name is Firmin Bellegarde," replied the GI, intimidated, extending his right hand to the man.

John clasped Firmin's hand with a grip that surprised the young soldier. "Welcome to our home," he added in a hoarse voice.

John quickly shut the door behind Firmin and switched on the light. The ceiling electric bulb projected on Maggie its weak yellowish glow. She seemed older than her husband. Her emaciated face accentuated the traces left by time and, moreover, by the deprivation and concerns related to the war.

However, something bright was lighting her face. A soft mix of melancholy and compassion underlined by a slight smile, which reminded Firmin of his mother.

"You must be exhausted, I presume," she said. "Follow me, I will show you your bedroom."

Firmin climbed the narrow stairway behind her. On the upper floor, a small staircase landing gave access to five doors. The left one opened on Maggie's and John's bedroom. On the right side, two others opened on the rooms of their children, Liz and Brian.

"Both have joined the army of our King George VI," she explained. "So, we don't see them often, nowadays," she added with a deep sigh.

The function of the last two rooms was indicated by enameled metal signs hooked on the doors: *Toilet* and *Bathroom*.

"Here is your room, Mr. Bellegarde, Maggie said after opening Brian's door. It's not large, but I have emptied the closet so that you can use all of it to store your belongings during your stay."

"It'll be fine, Mrs. Jones, thank you," Firmin replied while roving his eyes in the room. "But please call me

Firmin," he added looking at her with a broad grin.

"I'll leave you now, Firmin. Take your time. We usually have supper at seven. John and I would enjoy your presence … if you don't mind, of course."

"It would be my pleasure, Mrs. Jones!"

After Maggie was gone, Firmin pushed aside the curtains and opened the window. The declining sun would soon disappear behind the skyline. The window was overlooking a small garden adjoining the backside of the house.

Leaning outside over the guard rail, Firmin saw the alignment of vegetable gardens, which occupied most of the surface of each individual plot.

Joneses' patch was covered with vegetable squares. Mrs. Jones would soon make him the inventory of her personal cultivation. Two rows of leeks, as much of spinach, one of cauliflowers, one of broccoli, and one of Brussels sprouts. Plus a few fennel bulbs, a rhubarb plant, a square of rutabaga and one of Jerusalem artichokes.

During his stay in Pontypool, Firmin would taste the range of recipes, which Maggie had imagined or adapted to the harshness of the war. They would accompany the ham and beef cans which Firmin would bring her every evening.

After he had freshened up a bit in the bathroom and put on a clean shirt, Firmin came down to the ground floor, with an armful of gifts and victuals for his hosts.

Judging by the smell of Jerusalem artichokes gratin wafting in the house, supper time was about to come.

CHAPTER 27

New Inn Camp, March 8, 1944

Wild Bill was furious. The battalion had landed three and a half months earlier in Great Britain. And it took all this time to organize the first large-scale drill with a minimum of equipment. All the new VLA balloons had arrived, at last. The public authorities of New Inn had made their polo grounds available to the battalion. Weather conditions were acceptable, at least in terms of wind strength. They had succeeded in inflating three dozen balloons. Twelve units for each of the three batteries.

However, Captain William Taylor wasn't satisfied. The change of altitude wasn't fast enough for him. This defensive mode couldn't be effective when all the balloons were flying at the same altitude. It required the balloons to be flying at different heights to disrupt enemy airstrikes.

Therefore, Wild Bill never stopped yelling at the balloon crew leaders. Firmin and his colleagues cursed him. Wind was blowing at eight knots, and the thirty-six balloons were very close to one another over the polo fields. With wire lengths ranging from six hundred to two thousand feet, the risk of entanglement of several balloons was very high. Not to mention the possible accidents due to the lack of space. With wires lying on the ground, an operator could easily get his ankle caught in a loop and be lifted up by the elevation of his balloon.

To ensure that the operator crews and their logistics

supports would do their very best, Wild Bill put the highest pressure on each battery leader. He would give them marks according to the general performance of all the men under their command. Several criteria were taken into account. Of which the deployment speed, how quick the balloons reached the requested altitude, the orientation control according to the wind strength and direction, and the speed in which the balloons were brought back to the ground.

With just twelve balloons instead of forty-five per battery, Firmin was convinced that only the best crews would be selected to participate in the great invasion. He had no intention to be left on the sidelines.

Like a baseball team leader, Firmin gave his instructions to his three teammates before the exercise started. He made certain that Ed, Jimmy and Doug still remembered the commands and the related technical moves they had learned in Camp Tyson. He particularly insisted with Doug who tended to be slow on the uptake. Eventually, Firmin reminded them of the safety instructions. Checking that the antistatic gloves were in good condition and correctly put on. Never grasping a mooring wire before the four of them were in contact with the ground. Always watching your step to prevent from being carried away by a balloon in its ascension phase. Watching the sky, the shape and the size of the clouds, the strength and direction of the wind.

"Always keep an eye on each other. And listen carefully to my commands! Is it clear?"

"Yes, Corp.!" shouted Ed and Jimmy.

"Is it clear, private Murphy?" the corporal repeated in a louder voice.

"Yes, Corp.!" screamed Doug, standing at attention.

Firmin's crew made it through better than the average, despite some deficiencies regarding coordination and automatism. As feared, Doug remained the weak link in the chain, but Firmin didn't despair of turning him into a reliable operator. Provided that Captain Taylor would leave them enough time to do so.

This morning, no one found favor in his eyes. He would have liked to keep the exercise running until the end of the day.

Luckily, Lieutenant Colonel Reed was there. And he felt that the result of this first attempt was satisfactory. So, he made a sign to his second in command to put an end to the training session.

Donut would at last recover some strength by pigging out everything he could get his teeth into, during the coming lunch.

The following day was devoted to an assault maneuver on foot. The aim was to get up to the top of the hills surrounding a vast plain, southwest of New Inn, between Cwmbran and Newbridge. An ideal training ground to prepare the near invasion of the European continent.

After one and a half hour march, with their full combat equipment on their shoulders, the balloon crews arrived on site. The thirty-six balloons had already been delivered at dawn. They were linked to their winches carried by special trucks. The purpose of the exercise was to bring the balloons up to the ridgeline of the two hills, which ran, north and south, along the plain.

Three flags of different colors had been positioned on the heights, indicating the target of each battery. Once again, Wild Bill would rely on the competition between them to motivate his troops.

The positive altitude change wasn't great, but the vegetation covering the hills was dense enough to make the ascent of the crews painful. However, it was hardly comparable with what they would endure in real conditions on the theater of operations.

"Today, you'll depart from a clear field on a solid ground," warned the first lieutenant commanding the exercise. "But when the big day comes, you'll have to land from the sea. And you'll have to walk in chest-deep water, then run on wet sand, before you reach a hill like this one. So, I don't want to hear any of you complain about being tired, that it's too hard, or anything like this. Understood?"

The target of battery A was a yellow flag standing on top of the western part of the north hill. Perched on the roof of the truck cockpit, Firmin took some time to observe the terrain and spot the best path towards the ridge. Then, he went down and stood on the running board to give the driver his instructions.

While the truck was driving on a rutted trail, Ed was ready to unwind the steel rope to let the balloon progressively reach an altitude of six hundred feet. As a powered winch operator, Jimmy stayed on board until the truck reached its goal. Firmin, Ed and Doug followed walking, guiding the balloon with the mooring wires. Doug would have liked to take off his backpack and throw it on the truck bed, but Firmin refused it. The orders of the lieutenant were clear. The ground staff had to keep their full equipment constantly on them. Goof-offs and their teammates would be punished with a night march in battle gear. Every time he stumbled on a stone or a root, Doug would hurl a volley of curses and cusses, and threaten to ditch it altogether.

"Shut up, Donut, and move on!" replied one of the three others.

"If only I could get rid'ev this fuckin' bag that weighs a hundred pounds at least…" Donut grunted when he fell for the third time.

"It ain't your bag that weighs so much. It's all the donuts that you stick in your stomach all day long!" Ed rumbled.

Despite their desperate efforts, two hours long, none of the crews managed to reach their target.

The day before, coordinating three dozen balloons over flat polo grounds had already been a tall order. Now, bringing balloons up to the top of these bushy and wooded hills turned out to be a true nightmare. Mainly because of the cumbersome equipment required to maneuver the balloons. Especially the thousand-pound gasoline-powered winches used to bring them up and down. Despite their powerful engines and six driving wheels, the trucks would slip on the bushes, sink into the ground, or get stuck between the trees. They considerably slowed their movement.

The officers then realized that in a combat situation, during their progression from their landing on the sea shore up to the hills, the balloon crews would become easy targets under heavy enemy fire. Like sitting ducks in an amusement park's shooting gallery. It would endanger not only the men, but also the position defended by the battalion.

Therefore, they would have to find a solution to significantly lighten this essential accessory. Indeed, considering the volume of the new balloons, they had become particularly oversized. The first balloons used by the U.S. Army were more than ten times bigger and flew at a much higher average altitude. Hence, they required these imposing gasoline-powered winches to wind the very long steel cables which tethered them to the ground. But with the lighter VLA balloons, it was possible to dramatically reduce the wire lengths and, as a consequence, the size and power of the winches.

This first test drill resulted in a complete failure. However, it had at least highlighted this crucial problem, which would be reported to Lieutenant Colonel Reed right off the bat.

CHAPTER 28

Abersychan. March 12, 1944

Since his arrival in New Inn, Firmin felt like he was living in a dream.

Every evening, after a strenuous working day, he would enjoy the warmth of the Joneses' home. Not that of the charcoal burner which ran sparingly, due to rationing, but the human warmth of John and Maggie. The Joneses were so caring with him that it almost made him forget the absence of his parents.

When coming in, Firmin would give Maggie the canned meat of his ration K[55] *Supper* box, which she would serve with her dish of boiled vegetables. Sometimes, he would add a few rare foodstuffs bought from the PX[56]. After supper, Firmin used to share his cigarettes with John.

John was too old to serve in the army, but he early volunteered in the *Home Guard*[57]. He would watch the sky for three hours, one night in a week. Then, he would

---

[55] *Ration type K*, contained three meals: breakfast, dinner and supper. Source: https://en.wikipedia.org/wiki/K-ration. The *supper* pack contained canned meat (pork or beef stew with carrots), a bouillon packet, a tropical or sweet chocolate bar, a packet of toilet paper tissue, chewing gum, and a four-pack of cigarettes. In total, the three meals of a ration K would provide each soldier between 2,800 and 3,000 kilocalories.

[56] Post eXchange.

[57] Armed citizen militia founded in 1940. It gathered volunteers, mainly involved in guarding coastal areas and strategic places such as airfields, factories and explosives stores. I was nicknamed Dad's Army. Source: https://fr.wikipedia.org/wiki/Home_Guard

always keep one of the two cigarettes for smoking during his guard duty.

Every evening of the week, Mr. Jones used to listen to the BBC news, to stay informed about the war. Then, he would read a page or two of the *Abergavenny Chronicle's* last edition.

John was delighted to discuss current affairs with Firmin. Since his daughter and especially his son had left home to join the British Army, he had no one to talk politics with. He was inexhaustible when talking about the working class and the union actions. In the past, he had started to work in the mine for the same company as his father. Unfortunately, after the Great War, the mining industry had had to close several mines, successively. Many coal miners had lost their jobs. The luckiest had managed to convert to metallurgy. John was among them and eventually became a foreman. Since the beginning of the war against the Nazis, there was plenty of work.

"It's indeed true that today we make a living of it," John lamented. "However, I know that I sweat blood five days a week to manufacture cannons and bombshells that'll kill tens of thousands of people and make our bosses wealthier. And that makes me angry! See what I mean, Son? In the end, the same ones are getting screwed, whereas the others win every time."

Listening to him, Firmin felt like he could hear his father.

As he felt confident with John, Firmin told him in return about African American unions, the NAACP and the Brotherhood of sleeping car porters.

"You see, Firmin," John said, "actually, we, the Welsh miners, the workers, we're like you, the Negroes.

Exploited and despised. We, by corrupt English bankers and industry owners, you by racist and segregationist American Southerners, aren't you?"

"And by American bankers and industry owners as well," dared Firmin. "And not only from Southern States."

The comment made John laugh heartily.

As far as she was concerned, Maggie didn't like talking politics. She was too pious to let herself be perverted by evil feelings of revenge or jealousy.

"Prayers," she said, "are my only weapons to fight injustice in this world!"

One night, she asked Firmin if his mother was also religious. He told her of the Protestant church Celestine was attending and how she had consented to send her son to a Catholic school in New Orleans. He also told her, with some nostalgia, of his life. Of their first house in the parish of West Baton Rouge. Maggie felt truly sad about the loss of his little sister.

Then, he told her of their move to New Orleans Lower Ninth ward. How it positively changed their lives. How courageous Celestine was.

"I'm convinced your mother is also a very nice person," said Maggie. "Later, when this terrible war is over, I'd be delighted to meet her!"

Firmin knew that it was hardly possible, because of the distance separating their two families and of the cost of the trip. None of the two mothers could afford it.

"You could start with writing to her," Firmin suggested. "I'm sure she would be glad to have a correspondent in Great Britain. I can give you her address, if you wish!"

Mrs. Jones immediately accepted.

On the same day, Maggie offered him to attend the Sunday mass with her at the Trinity Methodist church on High Street. Her husband felt much less concerned by "all this bigotry." He restricted his church attendance to the Christmas and Easter celebrations.

Firmin had first accepted in order not to hurt Maggie. But then, in the following weeks, he felt some kind of comfort in singing in chorus with this woman who reminded him so much of his mother.

At night, Firmin went to bed earlier to write to his parents a longer letter than previously. He had so many things to tell. To the point that he would need several V- mails to put them all down.

320ᵗʰ VLA

APO, New Orleans, LA

Somewhere in Wales[58]

Sunday, March 12, 1944

Dear Mom, dear Dad

No word can tell how much I miss you. I'd love to share with you what I've been living since we arrived in our new post. Drills are very tiring, but they make us tougher and more determined for the big day.

As you know, I was billeted by a couple in their house. In a small town, a few miles away from the base. The Joneses are lovely. They welcomed me like their own son.

You'd surely get along with them. When John and I discuss together, I feel like I hear you, Dad. His wife Maggie is like a surrogate mother for me. I told her a lot about you, Mom. She said she'd love to meet you when the

---

[58] It was strictly forbidden to the soldiers to specify in their mail neither their exact location nor what they were doing on military level.

war is over. This morning, I went to church with her, and we prayed and sang together. It's amazing how much you both look-alike. Besides the skin color, of course.

The funny thing is that, for the first time in my life, I feel privileged compared to white soldiers who are housed inside the base. All the facilities they get from the Army will never be worth the warmth of a household.

In the town too, we are welcomed by most people. I regularly spend an hour with them in their pubs. I can enjoy one or two pints of their bitter brown beer, or playing darts. People also play Three card brag, which is like our poker game.

People here have no reluctance to mingle with colored soldiers. It's strange and pleasant at once not to feel judged or loathed because of the color of our skin.

British cooking is mostly bad, and I terribly miss your good food. Still, there is one thing I will surely regret when I am back home: their fish and chips. Every time we're off duty, we feast on a fried breaded fish fillet at Mark Belli's. Fish is the only food which is not rationed here. So, we can enjoy them at will.

This afternoon, I met with a girl of the American Red Cross, at the USO[59] of the village. Her name is Ethel and she comes from New Orleans like me. She's gorgeous. She volunteered after she graduated high school. She's very educated and considers starting medical studies right after

---

[59] United States Organization (for National Defense). Founded in February 1941 by a presidential decree. Its mission was to provide recreation for on-leave members of the U.S. armed forces and their families. USO recreational clubs supplied a place for everything from dancing, movies, and live entertainment to a quiet place to talk, write letters, or find religious counsel. Source: The United Service Organizations Was Chartered (americaslibrary.gov)

the war. I invited her to spend the afternoon with me next Saturday and she accepted. I'm looking forward to seeing her again.

That's all for now. It's late and we're starting a week of drills tomorrow.

Love. Write you soon. Firmin.

What Firmin would never write was the kiss with Sheila, a white girl, in Barry's dance hall. Even though he would remember it forever. Neither his mother nor his father could understand it. "You're gonna get in deep water," Celestine would say. Joe would have seen it as a betrayal. Firmin probably would tell them later.

His greatest fear was censorship. All the soldiers' mail was scrutinized and censored before it was copied on a microfilm. It then would be printed on paper upon arrival at their destination. Every word considered unacceptable or a threat to some military secret was concealed with black ink. As far as he was concerned, Firmin feared that his "inappropriate" relation with a white girl would earn him retaliation from white soldiers.

It took Firmin a long time to fall asleep. He wondered how he would react if he had to face the same living conditions as before when returning to New Orleans.

CHAPTER 29

Pontypool. March 19, 1944

F irmin attended the Sunday morning mass in Trinity Methodist church with Mrs. Jones. Then, he met his crew mates, billeted in different places of Abersychan, at a bus station.

Firmin, Edward, Jimmy and Doug had decided to make a trip to Pontypool, to celebrate the upcoming spring.

One of the things that war teaches you is that you shouldn't postpone an opportunity to have fun. In that regard, it had transformed Firmin. To be true, it wasn't so much war, but the discovery of a world without racial prejudices or segregation which had made him another man.

In New Orleans like in Camp Tyson, his mind was almost entirely filled with two intense feelings. One was the fear of the behavior of Whites, when he had to go out of the Lower Ninth ward, or out of the camp. The second was a sense of anger and revolt caused by the injustice of segregation and by the contempt and sufferings inflicted to colored people in his country. They didn't leave much space for lighter, yet precious, thoughts.

Here, in Wales, he had found a country where he could move freely among Whites, without fearing for his life. Where he didn't suffer the humiliation of being expelled from a public place because of his brown complexion.

His fear and anger had progressively subsided. Firmin had recovered the capacity for wonder, which he had as a kid watching the show of nature, or gazing at his little sister bursting out with laughter when they played together.

Opening his senses to all these simple things which, put end to end, looked like happiness. Such was Firmin's philosophy, whereas others around him never stopped grumbling against the "damn white officers," while longing for the next leave to get drunk and have sex with a white call girl. Keep drinking until you slip into a coma, and wake up the next morning with a terrible hangover, with no remembrance of what you did in the night. Firmin hated the idea.

Still, he wouldn't content himself with grasping the opportunities of happiness passing along at arm's reach. He would also incite them, making use of every minute of the few leaves the Army granted him.

Therefore, he had planned with Ed and Jimmy a schedule of activities for the afternoon. Needless to ask Doug. He was always up for it. As long as he could get enough to eat.

First: eating fish and chips for lunch. Then one or two movie screenings at the *Empire Picture House*. Then, having fish and chips again for supper. And last: spending the night at the *Palais de Danse*[60], where orchestras were performing.

What he hadn't told them, yet, was that he had asked Ethel to meet him at the movie theater between 13:30 and 14:00. He was afraid that she may not come. His friends wouldn't stop making fun of him, in such case.

The four soldiers ordered their hot fried fish, wrapped

---

[60] French name given to dance halls in Great Britain.

173

in a newspaper, and a cone of French fries. They kept on walking in the streets of Pontypool, while eating. Donut stopped on the way to buy a second set of fish and chips.

"You eat like a pig," Firmin blamed him.

"C'mon! Eat it up, now!" Firmin insisted as they were getting closer to the *Empire picture house*.

"Tell me you don't intend to get inside the theater with this stuff that stinks of grease!"

To tell the truth, Doug's bad manners put Firmin to shame. He was afraid that they could drive Ethel away from him.

Firmin carefully washed his hands at a public drinking fountain and took out of his pocket peppermint chewing gum to refresh his breath. A few people were already lining up for tickets at the theater's entrance. The four buddies approached without hurrying and looked at the two posters above the doors.

Doug pouted with disgust at the poster of the first film. *Lady in the dark*. A Technicolor Paramount musical with Ginger Rogers and Ray Milland.

"No dice! Ain't gonna put up with that mushy movie for Whites!" Doug muttered.

Then, gazing at the second poster, he added:

"Awready seen this one, but I can see it once more."

It was *For Whom the Bell Tolls*, another Paramount production released in June the year before, featuring Ingrid Bergman and Gary Cooper. The film was perfect to boost the motivation of American and British troops.

Firmin didn't like the idea of Doug hanging out in the streets of Pontypool, during the first film's projection. Still, he couldn't force Doug to watch that musical against his will. He may have been less reluctant if the featured actress had been colored. Like Lena Horne in *Cabin in the sky*.

All things considered, Firmin felt relieved that Doug would be gone when Ethel arrives and he introduces her.

"Well," sighed Firmin. "You'll join us here at the end of the second screening."

Doug recovered his smile. The smile of a kid who is spared from a punishment.

"But don't booze up and mess around, or…" Firmin added. "You know what's in store for you! Don't you?"

"Yes, Corp.!" yelled Donut, before he walked away.

"Hurry up, corporal! or we're gonna miss the first session."

Firmin instantly recognized Ethel's voice behind him. Ed and Jimmy observed him with an amused smile. Firmin was obviously caught off guard. He took a deep breath and slowly turned round.

Ethel stood in front of him. Slightly behind on her left, another girl was waiting to be introduced. Both young women were dressed in their American Red-Cross uniforms. Jackets and skirts in thick cotton crepe. The jacket was closed by four buttons. It had four patch pockets. Two on the chest and two on the hips. The tips of their collars wore three letters. A.R.C.[61] A Red Cross enhanced with a golden edging was pinned on their caps. They looked great, each in their way.

Ethel was shorter and thinner than her colleague. Her hair was pulled back. Beneath her cap appeared the beginning of a hair parting. Her eyes were deep brown. She had a hazelnut complexion, and fine features softly

---

[61] American Red Cross.

175

enhanced by a light makeup. All the opposite of her taller and busty girlfriend.

With a lighter complexion, she had opted for a bright red lipstick and a deep pink blush. An enticing beauty which, nonetheless, left Firmin cold. He had a crush on Ethel. He stood motionless before her for a few seconds, as if he were paralyzed. Ethel kept smiling at him.

"Don't you want to introduce me to your friends?" she asked, stunned.

"Hmm … sure," Firmin mumbled. "This is private first class Edward Washington, and this is private James Stevenson."

"Delighted!" she said, keeping her hand crossed in her back and looking at each of them.

Then, talking to Firmin:

"I allowed myself to come with my colleague Clarisse. I hope you won't mind."

"Not at all!" Edward exclaimed. "I love your name," he added, getting closer and extending his hand.

Jimmy was dumbfounded. He observed his crew mate, but couldn't react.

Offering Clarisse his right arm, Ed continued:

"I'd be immensely honored if you accepted to spend the afternoon with me!"

"As long as I'm your guest," Clarisse replied, with a broad grin.

"Of course, Ms. I'm a gentleman, you know."

Clarisse took his arm and pulled him towards the theater's entrance, behind Firmin and Ethel. Passing by Jimmy, Ed gave him a wink. Jimmy didn't want to stay alone. So, he walked along the queue, in search of some pleasant company.

Firmin and Ethel didn't see much of the first movie.

During the *Moviestone* news projection, their fingers brushed past each other. Then their hands. Firmin first apologized. But she wouldn't take her hand away. So he wrapped his fingers around hers. They gazed at each other from the corner of the eye, and eventually smiled together. As soon as the film started, Firmin extended his arm behind Ethel's back and gently placed it about her shoulders. She didn't protest. She buried her head on Firmin's shoulder, instead. She smelled of amber cologne, with a little touch of rose petals. A mutual attraction then rose, which they briefly pretended to resist. By shyness, or because of their religious education. No matter. Their desire was too strong. So, under cover of darkness, they finally yielded to the temptation. Their mouths got closer, inch by inch, like in slow motion. Their lips reached. They kissed each other long. With an increasing passion. Long before the actors on the screen, who would have to wait until the very last scene of the film to do the same.

Before the second session started, Firmin suggested to Ethel to leave the theater and get fresh air. None of them wanted to stay for the second movie, were it a master piece directed by Sam Wood.

Outside, Firmin crossed Doug who was waiting in the line for the second film. Seeing him, Doug rushed to present his conquest. A young English red-haired unattractive girl named Lindsay. When she smiled, she would show her terrible teeth.

"See you here, as planned, after the movie! Alright?" Firmin reminded him, before walking away with Ethel.

Firmin felt like he was falling in love with this young woman. And he liked the feeling. He didn't want to spoil this early relation with her. He had nothing in common with Doug, and he was afraid that she could misunderstand his intentions because of his bad company.

He had probably been chilled by his experience with Sheila. Anyhow, he was pleased to flirt with a Black American girl, who had less chance to be different from him. In terms of color, social status or geographical origin.

Firmin looked at his wristwatch.

"We still have two hours free before the movie ends," Firmin said. "If you're cold, we could take shelter in a pub, until then!"

"I'm fine. Let's walk further and enjoy this moment," Ethel suggested.

The streets were teeming with life. Other couples were also strolling aimlessly, arm in arm. Some of them, indifferent to the passersby's gazes, were kissing languidly. What the British public tolerated inside a dark room or a dance hall was considered shameless in the streets, if not rude. Whereas for Americans, kissing appeared as natural as drinking or eating.

While walking, Ethel took Firmin's hand in hers. Their fingers crossed. Their hands wrapped. Corporal Bellegarde gently pressed the young girl's palm. Then he cleared his throat and coughed.

"Have you got a boyfriend?" he asked.

Ethel endeavored not to smile, but an instinctive move betrayed her emotion. She squeezed her hand unwittingly. However, Firmin's inexperience prevented him from grasping the meaning of it.

"I guess you've got many potential lovers, at home," Firmin continued.

"None who drew my attention, anyway."

"You mean there's no boyfriend waiting for you in New Orleans?"

"Right! That's what I mean."

Ethel was used to the rude and tactless manners of young boys of her neighborhood, who wanted to flirt with her. She quickly learned many ways to get rid of those dumbasses.

However, she never stopped hoping that one day she would meet the right person. Today, her instinct told her that this man was holding her hand. But she hadn't foreseen he could be so bashful. Should she let him beat around the bush and eventually get out of her life for ever? She knew, as much as him, that he could be sent any time to the continent. Who could tell then how many months or years would pass until he's back home? Would he still remember her? Would he still be free?

Ethel was firmly decided not to let her chance go by.

"What about you? Haven't you left behind you the future woman of your life?"

"Me?" Firmin asked, surprised. "I was just eighteen when I joined the Army. Since then, I never stopped changing locations with our battalion."

"How old are you, now?"

"I'm gonna be twenty in two days. Why?"

Ethel suddenly stopped walking. She turned and got closer to him. She gazed at him a few seconds with admiring eyes, and smiled.

"Twenty years in two days! Hope you'll invite me to celebrate your birthday!"

"You think I'm too young for you, don't you?"

Firmin saw Ethel's eyes roving over his face, gazing at every detail. As if she wanted to engrave them in her

179

memory. He was intimidated to the core. He could feel his blood throbbing in his temples. His face flushed hot and his throat went dry.

"You're younger, indeed, than I had imagined! But you're so much more mature than many men that I meet every day at the USO! So much more delicate, too! Much more…"

Firmin was caught in a swoop of emotions. Far more powerful than after he had kissed Shirley. He felt flattered, moved, embarrassed and excited at once by the words of the young Red Cross volunteer. No girl before had told him such nice things.

"In short, I like you very much, Corporal Bellegarde," Ethel concluded, in a tone filled with emotion.

The young soldier could read in her eyes the strength of her feelings. She had a crush on him. She loved him. No doubt. He blamed himself because he didn't have the courage to tell her his own feelings before. But it was too late for regrets. Moreover, he had no more reasons to be afraid to declare his love.

He laid his hands on Ethel's cheeks, and looked into her eyes, while he was struggling to control his breath and calm the wild pounding of his heart.

"I think I love you, Ethel," he said, in a strangled voice.

"You think so?"

"No. I don't think… I'm sure," he confirmed, on a confident tone, this time.

He didn't leave her time to react. He took her head between his two hands and pressed his mouth on Ethel's lips. She responded to his kiss, long and hard.

Their mutual desire was so powerful that they ignored the British rules of decency. Until two ladies passing by expressed their deep disapproval.

Both lovers mumbled apologies and walked away in the search for a pub, where they could share a drink and wait until they could join the others at the Empire picture house.

CHAPTER 30

Sunday, April 9, 1944

T he daily program of physical and technical drills had been very intense in the past two weeks. Firmin was so exhausted, sometimes, that he had to give up going to the pub before going back home at the Joneses'.

In the days following his first outing in Pontypool with Ethel, he went three evenings in a row at the USO club instead of the pub. He expected to spend an intimate moment with her. But the rules of the USO prohibited a staff member from devoting her working time to only one soldier. Firmin could understand this. But he couldn't stand seeing her carefully serving other soldiers with a broad grin. It would make him madly jealous. Which didn't escape some of his fellow soldiers, who didn't deprive of joshing him and making him go off the deep end.

He waited for her twice until the end of her work shift. He would tell her how much he missed her. How much he suffered from knowing she was surrounded by all these potential rivals. She would strive to reassure him by swearing she loved him with all her heart and soul. Nevertheless, she felt he could flip his wig if a soldier went too close to her. So, she begged him to stop looking after her at the club. In return, she promised she would find a way to free herself up to spend the day with him in

Pontypool or Abersychan, when he gets a day off. Which she did twice.

Being in love didn't undermine his effectiveness as a balloon crew leader. He remained fully aware of the importance of his mission, here in Europe.

But when the evening came, he didn't resist daydreaming. Especially around the table with the Joneses. He, who used to be so talkative, would answer their questions unenthusiastically in bits and pieces. When John asked him why he hadn't seen him at the pub for a while, Firmin replied that the drills and training were so intense that they didn't leave much time for recreation. Mr. Jones said he understood, and stopped asking further.

As a woman and a caring mother, Maggie's intuition made her understand what her husband hadn't seized. Firmin didn't blame anyone. He was neither sick nor angry.

He was just in love.

One evening, when Firmin got home before Mr. Jones, Maggie seized the opportunity to make him feel confident, and talk. She offered him to have a cup of tea with her. As she insisted, he didn't have the heart to refuse her invitation.

While filling their cups, she cut to the chase.

"You're in love, Firmin, aren't you? Don't say no. It's as plain as the nose on your face. What's her name?"

Firmin was so stunned that he didn't even try to deny it.

"You're definitely like a mother for me, Mrs. Jones."

"If your mother had been here, she would surely have noticed it much earlier."

Firmin then rushed telling her about his feelings for Ethel. Which he could never have done in John's presence. This half an hour free chatting with Mrs. Jones did him a world of good. Especially when she suggested him that he invites the lucky winner of his heart for lunch, on Easter Sunday.

***

Ethel had attended the mass in another church of the village. The Saint Alban's Catholic Church. Firmin had offered to join her, as he had received a Catholic education from his high school in New Orleans, but she deterred him from doing so. She didn't want to upset Mrs. Jones before being introduced to her.

As agreed, Ethel walked alone to the Trinity Methodist church, and waited there outside until the service ended.

Maggie recognized her at first glance, from the faithful portrait Firmin had made of her. The young woman was terribly impressed. Corporal Bellegarde had told her about the Joneses in such respectful and glowing terms, that she felt like having a practice test before the official examination. She was convinced that she absolutely needed to succeed in this test to hope being later presented to his true parents.

She felt relieved when she heard Maggie warmly greeting her.

"We're so delighted to make your acquaintance, Miss. Firmin spoke to us so well of you."

"So am I, Mrs. Jones. It's so generous of you to invite me. I'm deeply touched."

"Please call me Maggie, will you!"

Ethel waited until they were inside the Joneses' house to offer to Maggie all the good things she had managed to

184

put aside in the past two weeks. She also offered to help her prepare the lunch and set the table, which Maggie was happy to accept. She would have a chance to have a confidential discussion with Ethel, and make sure of her morality and her real intentions about Firmin. Ethel didn't get fooled. Nevertheless, she played the game willingly.

On his side, John offered Firmin to drink a glass of his best whiskey. He didn't miss congratulating the young corporal for his taste regarding women.

"Your girlfriend is good-looking, indeed! And well mannered too!"

"Maggie was also good-looking at the same age!" John added, to clear up any misunderstanding.

On Maggie's request, Ethel said grace, as she had learned from her devout Catholic parents. It was still a double first time for her. The first time she celebrated Easter with Protestants, and the first time she was invited for dinner in a white people's home.

The atmosphere of the lunch quickly relaxed. The conversation about the differences between Catholic and Protestant celebration of Easter rapidly slipped to less sacred, however important, issues.

Maggie showed a genuine interest for her guests. As she knew almost everything about Firmin, she couldn't refrain from asking Ethel a lot of questions about her civilian life in the United States. Ethel told her of her intention to continue her nursing studies after she's back home. She had started training on the sidelines of her activity as an American Red Cross volunteer, and she was decided to go further.

"I'm certain you'll become an excellent nurse," Maggie approved. "And even a good female doctor, who knows?"

185

Hearing that, Firmin felt an immense pride. He put his hand over Ethel's. Mrs. Jones, who was sitting in front of her, smiled tenderly.

"When I look at you both," she said, "so charming and well educated, so courteous and cheerful, God forgive me, but I can't help blaming all the white racist sinners who treat you so bad and contemptuously in your country. I don't even dare imagine the suffering you endure in America."

From their embarrassed gazes, Maggie understood that it was a touchy issue, and that Firmin and Ethel didn't want to linger over it. Actually, they feared they could get carried away by their emotion, and hence lose their self-control and let their resentment blow out. Which could spoil the meal and disappoint Mrs. Jones.

"Have you thought of getting engaged?" Maggie asked, out of the blue.

"Jeez! I'm afraid you're becoming indiscreet, my dear," said John with an embarrassed smile.

Ethel turned towards Firmin and looked at him with an interrogative gaze.

"Don't worry, it wasn't indiscreet," replied Firmin. "But we must let our parents know, first. So as to make them feel that they still have the choice to accept or not."

They lingered at the table half an hour more with a cup of tea. Ethel asked them about their children and what they were doing in the British army. Maggie replied with emotion. As she feared she may cry, she decided to put an end to the lunch.

"I guess our two lovers have plenty of things to talk about, haven't they?" she said with a knowing smile.

"Come on, do me a favor!" she added while getting up.

"The weather is beautiful and mild, today. So enjoy it with a nice walk together."

Before letting them leave, Maggie hugged Ethel and whispered in her ear:

"Take great care of Firmin. He's a very nice person. So are you, dear! So, be happy, together!"

CHAPTER 31

Friday, April 14, 1944

The issue of the weight and size of the powered winches had been taken very seriously. After various attempts, the engineers had the idea to adapt a telephone wire reel borrowed from the Signal Corps, by adding to it two handles. The whole, including its winded rope, only weighed fifty pounds. One tenth of the original equipment. This new hand-powered winch could be carried by a single man. Which would greatly simplify their amphibian landing from a boat onto the beaches, during the invasion of Europe. This change would also allow reducing the balloon crews from four to three men.

Firmin was asked to choose which of his teammates would leave his crew. He immediately thought of Doug, whose blundering temper made him rather uncontrollable. So as not to offend his sensitivity, Firmin explained to him that he would gain a more valuable place in another three-member crew. The new organization would indeed lead to the building of five more crews in each of the battalion's three batteries. From then on, each battery of the 320th VLA would count sixty balloons instead of forty-five.

To help him swallow the pill, Corporal Bellegarde offered Donut three cans of fruit cake he had spared from previous rations.

The men of the 320th VLA learned that they would be split into three operational groups, then be transferred to marshaling camps along the south coast of England.

There, they would practice training maneuvers in real condition.

One hundred and ninety-five soldiers and five officers of each of A, B and C batteries. Four officers and a small detachment of the headquarters battery would join. The others would stay in New Inn camp. Doug was transferred to the battery C.

Previously, some officers had been sent to different camps to undergo special training on waterproofing of vehicles, signal communication, aircraft recognition, logistics and map reading.

The tensions in the 320th VLA ranks increased as its mission became more concrete. But the intensity of the drills didn't leave much room for mulling over dark thoughts. And Albert White, the chaplain, was always available to listen to those who started to fear for their lives.

Knowing that his troops would soon be deprived of any recreation opportunity, Lieutenant Colonel Reed decided to grant them a last overnight pass on the following Saturday. However, they would have to be back to the post on Sunday morning before eight o'clock. Any latecomer would be severely punished.

On Friday morning, the soldiers had to get their individual gear packs ready for an upcoming departure to an unknown destination. After the midday meal, the men could spend the afternoon inside the base to write to their families and rest.

Before he returned to the Joneses', that evening, Firmin stopped at the USO to inform Ethel of his next day off. He gave her an appointment on the following day at noon, for their last outing together.

Saturday, April 15

It was a balmy day. Firmin decided he would wait the following day to announce the news to the Joneses. He feared that Maggie would shed tears when Ethel would appear in front of her.

Therefore, he went out of the house before Ethel knocked at the door. Maggie could only notice the young woman briefly through the window and wish the two lovers a wonderful day.

Edward, Jimmy and Doug, like most of the soldiers, had planned to spend their last overnight pass in Pontypool, which offered more recreation possibilities. So, Firmin thought they would be more quiet if they first stayed a few hours in Abersychan.

He invited Ethel for lunch. They went to Mark Belli's on High Street, and took away a delicious fish and chips they would eat in Glynsychan Park.

They sat on a bench, in the shade of a plane tree, and devoured their still hot fish and fries, with an appetite of lovers after a sexual intercourse. Something they both had dreamed of, but wouldn't do before their official engagement.

Between two bites, they would compare their worse culinary experiences since they had arrived in Britain. The game triggered some uncontrollable giggles. They happened to discover another common point: a shared disgust for Brussels sprouts. Maggie had cooked them once, shortly after his arrival in the house. He hadn't dared telling her that just the smell of this boiled vegetable made him feel sick. Not to offend her, he had even taken a second portion of it. He had suffered from intestinal disorder all night long. In the following morning, Firmin just told her: "I think I don't digest Brussels sprouts easily." The message was duly received. Never again, would this food appear on the Joneses' table.

The two lovers ended their meal with the sweet note of a canned cake. Ethel then brought their conversation back to an issue which had caused her a great concern for a few days: their common future.

"Did you write to your parents about us?" she asked.

Firmin turned and took her two hands in his. He looked at her in the eyes and said:

"Of course, I did, darling! Since the first time we met, actually!"

Ethel smiled with emotion.

"You mean … since we first met at the USO club?"

"Indeed! Why? Are you surprised?" Firmin worried.

"Yes! I mean… No!" Ethel mumbled.

"And you? Firmin asked. 'Did you tell yours?'

"Right after our Easter lunch at the Joneses'!" Ethel replied with enthusiasm.

"What did you tell them?"

Ethel gazed long at him with moist eyes, then answered.

"That I had met the man with whom I hoped to live for the rest of my life. Both serious and funny. Thoughtful and kind. Handsome. Very handsome, even!" she added, seizing the collar of his jacket. "Who could give them beautiful grandchildren…" she continued, while approaching her lips from Firmin's.

Corporal Bellegarde felt the sap of desire rising inside him.

"Four, at least!" Firmin added, before getting rid of his peppermint chewing gum.

Then, he pressed his mouth on Ethel's. Their tongues searched, found each other, and mingled in frantic moves. Quickly, their bodies merged into a long and passionate embrace. They felt as if they were walking in the air, ignoring everything around them, until the stupid and embarrassed cackle of children brought them back down to earth.

Confused, and yet happy, they adjusted their parade uniforms and left the park, on the search of a car, which would drive them to Pontypool. Firmin intended to offer Ethel an evening there, she would remember until their reunion after the war.

All through the afternoon, Firmin carefully avoided all the places which might be frequented by his crew mates or other members of his battery. However, he was aware that, when getting into the *Palais de Danse* after supper, he would surely bump into Ed and Jimmy.

During their first evening at the dance hall, one month earlier, Firmin hadn't told Ethel of his passion for music. He hadn't told her that he played the saxophone. He even had made his buddies promise not to say a word of his performance at the Barry's *Palais de Danse*. He didn't want her to see him as a bragger searching to monopolize people's attention on him, and eventually seduce the prettiest girls around.

To ensure he wouldn't yield to the temptation, he hadn't taken his mouthpiece. But, on that day, Firmin noticed that they loved the same works of music . Sometimes, they would stop dancing and just move to the beat, looking at the musicians play. Firmin had vowed that the next time he would bring her here, he would make her an amazing and wonderful surprise.

While dancing together, Ethel and Firmin were called by two other dance couples. Ed was with Ethel's girlfriend Clarisse. Jimmy had ditched Lindsay and was now with a white brunette. Rather good-looking. She screamed her name. However, Firmin couldn't hear it, because of all the noise around. He just smiled at her and gave her an admiring wink.

Soon after that, Firmin pretended he wanted to order drinks, and left Ethel dancing near the four others. He made certain she couldn't see him, and got closer to the stage where the orchestra was performing. Under the stunned gaze of the musicians, he jumped onto the stage and sneaked to the alto saxophonist.

As he was murmuring something in his ear, showing his mouthpiece, someone in the audience yelled:

"C'mon, Firmin! Play us some good stuff!"

One, two, then three voices started to chant Firmin's name. They were soon followed by a dozen others, and eventually all the guys of the 320th VLA present in the hall, who had recognized him.

Considering the enthusiasm of the public, the orchestra's conductor grasped a voice mike to make an announcement.

"Well. I believe we have a new alto sax tonight. So, if Wilson agrees…"

The alto sax confirmed it by raising high his instrument.

"And if our dear audience agrees, too…"

The public replied with deafening cries, accompanied by a round of applause and shrill whistles.

"Alright!" he said, bowing respectfully. "What kind of stuff would you like to play, Son? Sorry. Firmin? Is that your name?"

Corporal Bellegarde came closer to the choir members and leaned over one of the mikes.

"That's correct, sir! And I'd like to play *In the mood* by Mr. Glenn Miller."

"Jeez! Are you kidding?"

"No, sir!" Firmin replied, while putting around his neck the strap of Wilson's instrument. "But, before we start, I'd like to dedicate this piece to someone."

The conductor agreed with a curt nod, while his musicians were searching in their partition books the corresponding one.

"We owe a monster named Adolf Hitler to be here! Right? But every cloud has a silver lining. At least it came true for me. Because here, in Pontypool, I met someone. The kind of meeting that changes your life for ever. It's here, indeed, that I met the woman of my life…"

Long whistles covered Firmin's voice. He waited a few seconds and continued.

"And she is here among us, tonight…"

The corporal gazed around at the dance floor. He eventually saw her surrounded by Ed, Clarisse, Jimmy and her partner. Ethel buried her face in the palms of her hands, to hide her emotion.

"Ethel," Firmin added gazing at her, "it's for you!"

A row of applause greeted the announcement of her name.

"But it won't stop me from kicking the Krauts and their damn Führer in the ass!" concluded Firmin before giving his mike back to the chorister.

These last words triggered thunderous cheers and the stamping of a hundred pairs of shoes. Meanwhile, Firmin moistened his reed with his tongue.

The conductor, looking at his drummer, announced the tempo. Firmin hardly had time enough to fill in his lungs. His eyes focused on the leader, he was waiting for his signal. The legendary hit by Glenn Miller, composed in 1939, started precisely with the saxophone section. On his right side, the tenor sax was watching him from the corner of his eye.

As from the very first measures, the dance floor was crowded with dancing couples. Their rippling reminded Firmin of the waves shaking the surface of the Lake Pontchartrain by strong winds. Ethel must have drowned into it. He couldn't see her any longer, but he gave up searching her, as he feared he would lose the thread of his partition. He had only three minutes and a half to shine in the eyes of his beloved. Even the two tenor sax and trumpet solos were strictly marked and time limited. Twenty seconds for the first one; the same for the latter, after five seconds of transition, in which saxophones and brass played together. Behind the trumpet solo, one could hear the bass and drum, and a few riffs of Firmin's alto sax. He stayed focused until the very last measure, during which he would play the same musical phrase as in the introduction theme. He ended his three minutes and thirty-one seconds performance, as breathless as at the end of an obstacle course.

CHAPTER 32

Finally, Firmin saw Ethel back, at the foot of the stage, under the protection of Firmin's crew mates. Ed and Jimmy were struggling to stop other soldiers from making insistent advances to her. Her eyes were shining in the glow of the stage lighting.

Under the applause of the musicians and the public, Firmin took off his mouthpiece and handed the sax over to Wilson. He thanked him, and jumped down the platform, right before Ethel. She was still stunned by his surprise. She remained voiceless for a while, but her sparkling gaze betrayed her emotion.

"I've never had such a stage fright before. Hope I wasn't too bad," Firmin apologized, while struggling to catch his breath.

The young woman wrapped her arms about his neck and cried of emotion. She squeezed him as hard as she could.

"No one before made me such a beautiful declaration of love." Ethel whispered in his ear.

Firmin's heart raced. He circled her waist with his arms, and started covering every inch of her face with kisses. Their lips met, and eventually merged.

Meanwhile, the band continued with a piece of slow foxtrot. The two lovers, welded together, were shaken from all sides by dancers' couples. They were irresistibly pushed outside the floor, while sketching some clumsy dance steps.

Ethel took Firmin by the hand and dragged him to a

dark place of the building, away from the turmoil.

She stuck her back onto the wall and grasped Firmin's jacket collar. Then, she drew him against her with all her strength. Firmin could feel her heartbeats resonate in his chest. Her eyes were roving over his face, in search of the slightest thrill.

"Did you truly believe all what you said on stage?"

Firmin opened his mouth, but Ethel cupped it with her hand.

"Think it over, before you answer, corporal. Would you repeat what you've said, while looking at me straight in the eyes?"

She relieved the pressure of her hand on his mouth. Firmin sucked his breath in, and looked at her with the gaze of the distraught lover who is about to answer "yes" to the ritual question of the priest. He waited a few seconds, as a matter of form, and took a deep and trembling breath, which revealed his emotion. Doing so, he felt strange. A feeling he had never experienced before. As if he were drunk with elation. He couldn't say if his vertigo was due to his being in love or to Ethel's heady perfume. No matter. He was ecstatic, and he loved it.

"You're the woman of my life, Ethel. I don't have any doubt about that. I've been dreaming of you every night, since we met. And now that I know I have to leave, far from you, I realize how much you mean to me. I believe I could die if I couldn't see you again."

Ethel was unable to speak, but her eyes showed her intense emotion. She was deeply moved by Firmin's words. Firmin was reassured. Their feelings were mutual.

At this moment, Firmin remembered their conversation with the Joneses, about their engagement. They didn't have time, any longer, to wait for their parents' approval. He didn't want to risk losing her to a bolder rival.

So, he poked his hand into his pocket and fished out his mouthpiece. Then, he looked at her with misty loving eyes, kneeled down and asked:

"Ethel, would you marry me?"

A bright smile lightened her face.

"Yes," she whispered.

Her voice was muffled with emotion.

Firmin slowly stood up and looked at her in the eyes.

"Really?"

She brought her face near Firmin's and covered it with a bunch of kisses. After each one, she whispered "yes." Firmin felt Ethel's warm tear drops rolling on his cheeks. Fearing he could crack, he gently withdrew from her embrace and showed her his mouthpiece in his hand.

"You see this little object?"

Ethel nodded in approval.

"It looks minor, but actually, … it's one of the dearest things to my heart. Besides my parents and you, of course! It's a gift from my dad. He taught me to play the sax with it. I always keep it with me. Do you understand?"

"Yes," Ethel confirmed in a sob.

"I'd like you to keep it. As a pledge of my commitment. It should replace the traditional engagement ring, shouldn't it?"

Again, Ethel wrapped her arms around his neck and kissed him all over the face, whispering words of love. Their embrace was so tight that it rekindled in their bodies an irrepressible desire. Firmin squeezed her harder, making him hunger more keenly for her.

"Now, let me offer you my dearest treasure," Ethel

whispered in his ear.

Firmin felt her body growing less stiff. He instinctively understood.

"Are you sure? You don't have to, you know."

"I've got nothing more precious to seal our love with… And… I'm burning with desire … so … what are you waiting for?"

"Hmm, I've never…" Firmin stammered.

"You've never done it before? You mean I'm your first time?"

"Yes," he whispered, confused.

"That's great!" she reassured him. "Consider this also as a present for your twentieth birthday!"

Ethel carefully looked to the left and to the right, to make certain they were alone. Then, she rolled up her skirt. And with a few undulations of her hips she got rid of her underpants.

While Firmin was kissing her with passion, she unfastened his belt and the buttons of his fly. His pants eventually felt down. He pulled his boxers down.

Like he had seen other soldiers do it with girls in some dark streets of Checkendon and Barry, Firmin leaned over her, grasped her thighs from under, lifted her up and pressed her onto the wall. Ethel didn't know anything about the subject, but what she had heard from coarse discussions between older colleagues at the USO club. However, she endeavored to overcome her ignorance, not to spoil this first experience.

With one hand, she pulled up her skirt further, while she wrapped the other arm around her lover's neck. Then she pressed her cheek to his and whispered in his ear:

"Please be gentle, my love."

The pressure of their mutual attraction would soon overcome their prudery and fear. They eventually succumbed to their too long contained desire. She struggled to muffle the pain of her defloration, not to spoil her lover's pleasure. Then, she gave herself, body and soul, without resistance nor restraint. He stayed in her several minutes after he had reached orgasm. Meanwhile, she kept on snuggling into his arms, caressing his hair, and whispering words of love.

They only stopped when they heard bursts of voices reminding them they were in a public place.

They dressed in a hurry and left the *Palais de Danse* before their friends could surprise them. After a few minutes of walk, the driver of a military truck accepted to drive them to the USO club in Abersychan, where Ethel and other Red Cross nurses were housed.

Sitting face to face in the back of the dump truck, they didn't exchange a word, but they never stopped gazing at each other. They waited until the truck was out of sight to embrace again.

The embers of their unfulfilled desire soon reignited. In other circumstances, they would have made love all night long, anywhere. But it was so cold outside. And they got less than fifteen minutes left before the USO would be closed for the rest of the night. Moreover, the Red Cross volunteers were forbidden to host men.

On his side, Firmin had promised Mr. Jones he would be back home before midnight. Besides, he would never allow himself to bring Ethel and put her in his bed. If John could understand it, her religious education defended Maggie to conceive that her beloved Firmin may have a sexual intercourse with Ethel before getting married.

Moreover in her house. She would have been profoundly shocked and terribly disappointed.

Firmin fished out of his pocket a sheet of paper torn from his diary. He had written on it the contact information of his parents and his battalion, including his military records and identification.

"I'd like you to promise me two things," Firmin said.

"Anything you wish, my love."

"First, promise me you will go to my parents, as soon as you're back in New Orleans. You probably will return before me. Tomorrow, I'll write to my parents that we are engaged. I'm sure they'll welcome you like their daughter-in-law, even when I'm still away. In case they have a doubt, just show them my mouthpiece. They'll understand."

"I promise, my love. And better... I'll introduce them to my parents."

"Great!" Firmin approved.

He kissed her lips and continued.

"Then, I want you to write to me once a week to tell me about you. I have no idea where ever war will lead me from now on, but I'm sure the army's postal services will always know where to deliver my mail. So, promise me!"

"I'll write every day, my love. I swear! And doing so," she added loudly, "I'll think of your eyes, of your smile, of your smell and our entwined bodies!"

Then, coming closer to Firmin's cheek, she whispered:

"I'll think of your sex sunk inside me, to maintain my desire of your body until our reunion. And this time, I won't satisfy with a single intercourse. I'm warning you! You'd better keep enough strength and stamina for that day. See what I mean?"

Firmin took Ethel's face between his mighty hands.

"I'll never cheat on you! I swear, my love!"

The door of the USO opened.

"We're closing, miss!" a woman dressed in a Red Cross suit said curtly.

CHAPTER 33

Sunday, April 16

After he had left Ethel at the USO, Firmin went straight back to the Joneses'. John was dozing off in his armchair while waiting for him. Maggie had already gone to bed two hours earlier. Firmin invited John to join her immediately, while he would use the bathroom to wash a bit and brush his teeth before going to sleep.

Although he was tired, Firmin couldn't sleep. He was too excited by the emotions he had gone through. Every time he shut his eyes, he saw Ethel's beaming face appear on the inner surface of his eyelids. He could even smell her perfume, and the warm contact of their bodies sealed together.

He desperately needed to talk to someone and express his feelings to ease the strain. In the absence of his mother or Ethel, what better confidant could he find than his diary? He couldn't think of telling some details to Reverend Albert White. Nor to his best buddy Edward.

Since he had moved in at the Joneses', he had confessed many things to his diary. But he always had to hide from his roommates or wait until they were fully asleep, before he could write a few lines under the yellow glow of his flashlight. He was afraid someone could steal it and show it around to mock him. Its integrated lock wouldn't protect his secrets.

Therefore, Firmin sometimes used a coded language. The names of some people would be replaced by letters.

Not the initials of their real names, but those of the nicknames he secretly gave them. Others were easily identifiable. People who were of the highest importance to him. Those to whom he devoted the best pages of his diary. His parents, Mom and Dad. The Joneses, Maggie and John. And now Ethel.

Every time he opened it, he would think of the day when his mother offered it to him before his enlistment in the Army. A leather-backed diary which he would fill at will along his journey, with the pump fountain pen he had received as a reward for his high school graduation.

In the beginning, he recorded his experiences of the segregation in and outside the Army, in the way Ollie Stewart wrote his articles, however without revealing the true identities of the officers. But also anecdotes related to his life as a soldier inside the camps, or outside during a furlough. He would also express his nostalgia for his neighborhood, or how much he missed his parents. Sometimes he would give up writing for one or two weeks.

However, since he had left Camp Tyson, he had never stopped writing for more than two days in a row. He would at least scribble a few words or some sketches. Or stick a theater or dancehall ticket stub. He started with the concerts he saw in Memphis, in May 1943. Of Earl "Fatha" Hines and Cab Calloway.

Firmin was aware he would soon lack the minimum of intimacy he needed to write his thoughts. So, he took out of the closet of his room a waterproof khaki bag, in which he kept his diary away from moisture. He opened his fountain pen and checked the ink level. "I'd better buy some ink at the PX tomorrow," he thought. He put his diary and the flashlight on his bed.

He switched on his flash light, turned off the ceiling electric bulb, and sat up comfortably in his bed with his back leaning against the headboard. He used his pillow as a stand, and unfolded his diary on it.

On top of the last half-filled page, a light-blue blotting paper covered with darker blue spots and signs testified to the frequent confession sessions.

Firmin carefully positioned his flashlight in the middle crease of the note book, with the beam oriented from top to bottom. Squeezing the pen between his fingers, he shut his eyes to better recall the best moments of this day with Ethel.

Then, he started writing. Slowly, at first. Hesitating on each word. Then, faster, as he was moving forward in his memory, from the moment Ethel had fetched him outside the Joneses'. His script soon became more fluid, quicker, then eager, even frantic. Like the script of a novelist brimming with inspiration and seized by a sudden and irresistible urge to write. Write as long as his strength would allow him.

After he had transcribed everything his prudishness and his education allowed him, he firmly applied the blotting paper onto the last page. Then, he shut the diary and locked it before placing it back into the waterproof bag.

It was past three on his wristwatch when he eventually switched off his flashlight. He soon fell asleep and dreamed of Ethel and him making love together.

***

Firmin woke at the first light of day, but he remained very silent, not to disturb the Joneses. After he had washed, he put on his outfit and went downstairs to have his breakfast before going to the camp.

Mrs. Jones was already in the kitchen. She had put three cups on the table. She was watching over a kettle of simmering water heating on the coal stove.

"Good morning, Maggie!" Firmin said, a bit surprised. "You shouldn't have gotten up so early. It's Sunday!"

"I couldn't sleep any longer," she lied. "And I didn't want to let you leave with an empty stomach."

"You're definitely like a second mother to me."

He was profoundly moved by her great concern about him. So, he wondered how he would tell her of his upcoming departure.

"You look worried, Firmin, don't you? Is something going wrong?"

He strove to smile, but Maggie didn't get fooled.

"Something went wrong with Ethel, last night, didn't it?" she asked, anxious.

Firmin's face lit up at the sound of her name. Maggie felt relieved. She grasped the kettle by its handle and poured the hot water over the instant coffee in the GI's cup. Then, she filled a little tea pot with the remaining water, which would stay hot on the stove's plate, while the precious tea gently infused.

She sat in front of him.

"Do you mind if I stay with you whilst you're drinking your coffee?"

Firmin smiled and shook his head.

"What worries you so much, then?"

He raised his head and put down his cup on the table.

"I didn't want to hurt you. So, I didn't dare telling you before. But I will soon have to leave you."

Maggie gave him a faint smile. Then, she moved her hands forward on the table, and put them on Firmin's. She looked at him with a compassionate gaze.

"We both knew that our encounter was doomed to end soon. It's been a great pleasure for John and me to host you in our home. Be sure that we'll never forget you. And we'll link you to Liz and Brian in our prayers."

Firmin breathed a deep sigh of relief, and eased back into his chair

"Does Ethel know?"

"Yes," the GI replied.

"How did she react?"

"Badly. Like me. We're gonna fear for one another until the end of the war. And if the war drags on, she'll eventually forget me."

"This will never happen!" said Maggie, squeezing Firmin's hands tighter. "She's sincerely in love. I could see it in the way she would gaze at you, yesterday again. What about you? Did you tell her you loved her? I mean, straight in the eye?"

"Yesterday, I asked her to marry me!" Firmin replied.

"What did she reply? Maggie asked, impatiently.

"Yes. Yes. Yes… I wouldn't say how many times she said yes."

Mrs. Jones sighed deeply of relief.

"With such a passionate love, I'd bet she'll never forget you! Anyhow, you can write to each other until then, can't you?

"Sure," Firmin confirmed. "I gave her my parents

address, just in case she would return to New Orleans before me."

"When are you leaving, actually?" Maggie asked.

"From Pontypool? Next Friday. But I was told that every soldier housed by civilians would have to return to dorms, by Tuesday evening."

Maggie stood up and turned round, pretending she would like to have some more tea. Nonetheless, Firmin instinctively understood she was trying to hide her sorrow.

"Well! It leaves us this evening, then, to say goodbye," Maggie said in a pretended cheerful tone, while the steaming tea was flowing into her cup. "Will you share our supper?"

"I wouldn't miss it for anything in the world, Maggie! Unless our commandant confines us inside the camp, of course!"

***

Corporal Bellegarde went through the individual combat gear inspection like a robot. Edward and Jimmy didn't fail to make the connection between his acting like a zombie and his sudden vanishing the night before at the *Palais de Danse*. They started teasing him, but he wouldn't react. So, they quickly got enough and stopped.

By the end of the morning, Firmin attended a mass celebrated by Reverend Albert White.

After a quick lunch without appetite, Firmin went to the PX to buy a block of lined paper sheets, a bottle of ink to refill his pen, and a 2B grade lead pencil that he would use to illustrate his diary with a few drawings and sketches. He also bought some good things he would offer to the

Joneses for their last meal together.

As planned, all the battalion was confined inside the camp for the rest of the afternoon. Lieutenant Colonel Reed feared incidents with some of his troops may occur in town, which would seriously compromise their last week of drills and training. No presence of his men in the streets after 20:00 would be tolerated. The MPs received instructions to arrest anyone who would disobey his orders.

For now, everyone was free to go about his business. Several sports competitions were organized. Football, softball, basketball, and even a boxing tournament. But the latter was canceled at the last minute, as the commandant feared that the inevitable bets coming with such events may end up in brawling and fighting outside the ring.

Others could watch a movie in the officer's mess.

The last ones, like Firmin and Edward could use the tables of the soldiers' mess to play checkers, backgammon or Monopoly. To read newspapers or comic books of *Batman* or *Captain America*. Or write to their families.

Firmin used his free time to tell his parents about his feelings in a long letter. So long that he had to use two V-mail forms.

320ʰ VLA
APO, New Orleans, LA
Somewhere in Wales
April 16, 1944
Dear parents,
Hope you're both doing fine. I miss you more than ever.
I'd rather tell you all this orally. The coming week will

be the last one here, before the battalion's transfer to a marshaling area. It's a real heartbreak for me to leave this place where I had two unforgettable experiences.

The Joneses' welcome was a great help for my morale. Like all the British I had a chance to get along with in the warm atmosphere of their pubs. But I told you before.

I hope you'll forgive me, but I couldn't wait until you'd meet her in NO before getting engaged with Ethel. Yesterday, I declared my love to her from the stage of a dance hall in front of the crowd. I played sax with the band, on "In the mood." The conductor let me replace his alto sax just for this piece. I believe you'd have been proud of me, dad. I'm glad I rehearsed this tune so many times with you.

Ethel looked deeply moved by my declaration. So, when she asked me if I was sincere, I couldn't resist. I asked her if she'd marry me after the war. She instantly said Yes! As I didn't have a ring, a gave her my mouthpiece instead. Hope you won't mind, Dad. It was the dearest thing I could offer her.

I did this because I'm sure you'll love her as much as the Joneses did when they invited her for lunch on Easter Sunday.

Now, I'm alone, far from you, without her. All the battalion is now in operational readiness. We'll have a last week of drills before our departure to the unknown. What we feel for sure is that we'll soon leave GB for the continent. We don't know where or when, which scares us. So, we try everything to ease our anxiety. Some pray. It's funny how some discovered their faith in God when they realized they may die anytime! I've always had faith, but I must admit I became more fervent after I landed in

Europe. Moreover, since I met Mrs. Jones. We went to church together, several times. And I prayed a lot, asking the Lord his protection on you. Asking to spare me and bring me back home soon and safe.

But don't worry, mom! I'll always keep on me the lucky charm you poked in my pocket the day I left NO.

I'm looking forward to introducing Ethel to you.

That's all for now. It's late and I must wake up early tomorrow.

Love you. Write you soon.

Firmin.

CHAPTER 34

F irmin jumped in the first truck driving from the camp to Abersychan. He was impatient to see Ethel again at the USO. But he didn't have much time to spend with her, as he had promised the Joneses he would be home for supper at 18:30 sharp. Therefore, he would have to give up his half-an-hour pause at the pub which he usually enjoyed with John and his friends.

When Firmin entered the Red-Cross club, Ethel was still on duty and wouldn't stop before 20:00. He couldn't monopolize her. He sat at a table and watched her do her job. He renewed his order twice to have a chance to get her come closer. But she wasn't allowed to take a seat and talk. In order to stay longer with Ethel, he would take time to look for change in all his pockets to pay the bill. He would then put the money in her hand and whisper words of love.

"Do you think we can see each other again, before you leave?" she asked.

"I don't know, darling. Not tonight, anyway. The commandant has forbidden all his troops to stay out after 20:00. The MPs have been ordered to arrest any offender.

"Tomorrow, then?"

The thirty minutes they managed to spend together was for both of them a delicious torture. They died of envy of embracing and kissing. Their frustration was growing together with their desire. However, as the end of their meeting was approaching, the two lovers realized that the war which had made them meet, was now taking a sadistic pleasure to tear them apart.

Before leaving, Firmin slipped in Ethel's hand a sheet of paper carefully folded in eight. The first of the letters he had promised. He had written it in the afternoon after writing to his parents.

"This one, at least, will not go through censorship." Firmin whispered, while withholding his lover's hand.

***

When he arrived at the Joneses', Firmin immediately went to the kitchen to bring the good food he had bought at the PX. Canned meat, fruit cakes, condensed milk, instant coffee and dehydrated orange juice, two chocolate bars and a few cigarettes and chewing-gum packs. Maggie was busy looking after the cooking of the meal. Steamed fish served with a turnip and potato gratin.

"Golly! There's too much for the three of us," she said, embarrassed.

"You'll think of me, while enjoying it," Firmin replied. "I'll get upstairs to refresh and put on clean clothes. I'll be back in ten minutes!" he added in a rush.

Firmin reappeared with a clean shirt on, under a sweater. He carried in his hands a pack of smoking tobacco and three bottles of beer, which he handed over to Mr. Jones, who was busy reading the last edition of the *Abergavenny Chronicle*.

"Good grief! This is way too much! Maggie told me you already spoiled us."

"Bah! You've coddled me like a child, since the first day. Besides, it's my pleasure!"

Maggie came in the room. Firmin pointed a finger to

the three bottles on the low table.

"Do we still have time to enjoy a beer before we eat?" Firmin asked.

"If the hostess of the house doesn't mind…" said John.

"Great!" said Maggie cheerfully. "Make yourself comfortable, Firmin. I'll fetch the glasses from the kitchen."

The meal lasted longer than usually. Maggie could hardly conceal her emotion. She would never let the silence settle. Right after Firmin had finished to reply to a question, Maggie would ask another one, sometimes interrupting her husband.

When she felt the tears coming to her eyes, she pretended to fetch the next dish in the kitchen to dab at her eyes with her apron.

For the dessert, Maggie had cooked a bread and rhubarb pudding. "A delicacy which had become too scarce in this house," according to John. This remark moved Firmin. It reminded him of the cakes that his mother used to cook on Sundays and on celebration days. Pecan nuts brownies and dried fruit cookies. Not to mention her matchless cheesecake topped with a blueberry or strawberry coulis.

At the end of the meal, John invited Firmin to taste a little glass of his personal whiskey, while listening to the BBC's evening program. It was an unmissable ritual for the Joneses.

On Sundays, Maggie would first listen to a mass broadcast at 20:00 in the *Evening service* program.

That evening, as the meal had extended, Maggie had missed the beginning of the service recorded at Westminster Abbey. The mass was celebrated by the

Reverend Doctor Garfield Williams. It was followed at 20:40 by an appeal for *War service funding* on behalf of the National YMCA, in the *Week's good cause* program. At 20:45, *Into Battle* reconstructed a decisive action of the war, like a battle or a feat of arms. John and Maggie always hoped they would once hear of Brian's regiment.

After that, they never missed the nine o'clock evening news.

BBC radio was a very popular evening companion for many British, since the beginning of the war. It allowed them to enjoy themselves and remain informed at the same time. On Mondays, the BBC Home Service would broadcast a play after the nine o'clock news. On Thursdays, after the news, Maggie and John used to listen to the *War commentary* magazine. It was followed by *Appointment with fear*, a weekly half-hour mystery and suspense story, written by John Dickson Carr and played by actors.

The Saturday evening program was for the Joneses the opportunity to have a pleasant time together. At 20:00: *Vaudeville of 1944*, a variety show. At 21:00: the news. And at 21:20: a play in *Saturday-night theater*[62].

While the two men were making themselves comfortable near the table radio, Maggie insisted on offering a farewell present to her guest.

"It's not much, I know, but I'm convinced that this copy of the Bible will bring you protection and spiritual help during the terrible ordeals which await you."

Firmin's first reaction was to smile. Although a fervent believer, his own mother hadn't thought of offering him a

---

[62] Source: http://genome.ch.bbc.co.uk.

215

bible to accompany his prayers. Instead of this, she had given him a Haitian *gris-gris*[63] as a protection against misfortune. Then, the young GI opened the book. On the flyleaf, Maggie had written:

"*With all our affection. May God bless you and bring you safe and sound back to your parents and your beloved Ethel. Marie and John Jones. April 1944.*"

These few words moved Firmin deeply, as they expressed his dearest wishes. Seeing his parents back, and being with the girl he loved. Besides, they confirmed the genuine affection of the Joneses, who had offered him so much more than a bedroom, in the past two months.

Firmin pressed the book against his heart. Then stood up to thank Maggie.

"It moves me so much, really! It will stay by me every day until I'm back home again."

Driven by the momentum, Firmin hugged Maggie and kissed her on both cheeks.

"Be careful, soldier!" John intervened. "I know my Maggie. If you keep on embracing her like this, she'll soon start to cry and then, we'll never stop her. Come over here and take a seat, instead, and taste this nectar."

Maggie went out, discreetly. John turned up the volume of the table radio, so that his wife could still hear it while she was cleaning the kitchen and washing the dishes. Moreover, it would prevent her from hearing their conversation about things that would upset her: politics, union struggles, and war.

On the east front, the Russians had reconquered Odessa, a strategic harbor on the Black Sea. At the same

---

[63] Haitian name for good luck charm.

time, the Red Army won the Dnieper-Carpathian offensive, commenced on Christmas Eve 1943. Twenty German and eighteen Romanian divisions had been destroyed. These German defeats were a good omen for the war to soon end.

Firmin was anxious to take part in the great invasion of the European continent, which he believed would give the death blow to the Axis powers. His desire to participate in this historic event of the twentieth century was stronger than his fear of dying. He never forgot what he and his brothers in color hoped to get in reward for their contribution to the final victory. Would the war end before their involvement in the fight, they would lose all chances of winning any recognition, any improvement of their condition as citizens, on behalf of the government or the American people.

When Maggie appeared again in the living room, their conversation switched to their two children.

Brian was serving as a lieutenant in the 5th Infantry Division, which had taken part in the invasion of Sicily in September 1943. Since then, Brian's battalion was progressing north towards Rome. As for Liz, she had joined the WAAF[64] in July 1942. Her skills and her mastery of German and French had led her to be transferred to the Intelligence Corps in the fall of 1943. At that time, she could still pay a visit to her parents during her scarce furloughs. Until she eventually was recruited by the SOE[65] in January 1944. Maggie had tried to deter her, but the young woman was determined. Hence, their only contacts with their daughter went by mail. However, as

---

[64] Women's Auxiliary Air Force.
[65] Special Operations Executive.

217

opposed to Brian's situation, the Joneses had no idea where Liz could be. In the headquarters in London, or under cover, somewhere in France or anywhere else in Europe?

Anyhow, their children's respective roles in the Army gave Maggie and John an immense patriotic pride, which helped them endure their fear of losing them. Besides, the presence of the young American soldier in their home had filled the void they had subconsciously suffered from. Now that Firmin was about to leave them, the couple began to realize the importance of their encounter. They would soon be left alone with their anxiety.

The discussion extended until late in the evening, as if each of them knew it would be the last one.

Indeed, in the following afternoon, Firmin would have to take back all his belongings at the Joneses'. From then on, he would sleep with his crew mates in a dorm, in the basement of a church in Pontypool, near the camp.

***

John was still at work. Maggie immediately understood when she saw Firmin coming home so early.

"So, here we are. This is where our destinies part," she said in a resigned tone. "John will be very sad. We'll miss you awfully."

Without a word, Firmin went upstairs to his room. It took him only a few minutes to cram into his duffle bag all the things he had carefully gathered on his bed earlier in the morning. He then sat on the side of the bed and gazed long around him at every detail of the furniture and the decoration of the room. Then, he went downstairs. Maggie hadn't moved. She stood in the corridor, waiting for him.

"Do we still have time for a last cup of tea?" she asked without conviction.

"A driver's waiting outside, sorry," Firmin lamented.

The corporal embraced Maggie.

"Greet your husband for me, and pass him my affection and my respect," he said.

"Promise me that you will take care of you," Maggie replied. "And don't forget to kiss your mother for me, when you return home ... and, when you have time, one day, send us a little letter to give us news."

Firmin released his embrace.

"God bless you both, and your children too," he said, before opening the door and stepping out. He climbed on board the truck, and looked a last time at Maggie. No word could have expressed better than his long gaze his emotion, his sadness and his deep gratitude altogether.

Firmin soon rediscovered the lack of privacy and the coldness of a dorm, which didn't leave room for introspection. Yet, despite the discomfort of his cot, he quickly sank into a deep sleep. He slept without interruption until 06:30.

From then on, he would endure four days of intensive drills. The program included balloon operating, twenty-five mile marches carrying their complete soldier's combat gear, and hand-to-hand fighting with a knife or a bayonet.

CHAPTER 35

April 21, 1944

The 320th VLA stretched in a long procession on the road from New Inn's base to Pontypool's train station. A Jeep with four headquarters senior officers on board were leading the convoy. A group of engineers and members of the medical staff was marching, sixty feet behind. They were followed by the three batteries, A, B and C, each of them composed of one hundred and ninety-five men and five officers. A second Jeep transporting four senior officers closed the convoy.

A staff sergeant was setting the pace. He checked that every man was marching in steps and singing loud and clear. Lost in the middle of A battery men, Corporal Bellegarde strove to keep up with the regular pace of one hundred and twenty steps per minute. But he didn't sing. He didn't feel in the mood for singing.

Pontypool wasn't just an ordinary garrison town for him, as it was for most of his comrades. Leaving it, he didn't leave behind a mere girlfriend, but a fiancée. More than friendship, the Joneses had brought him, almost daily, the family environment that he had missed before. Like hundreds of thousands of American soldiers gathered on the British soil.

Despite the early hour, the procession passed along a few groups of British civilians. Some people greeted them friendly, but without enthusiasm. The local population was getting tired of the presence of so many American soldiers in their country. Not to mention the frequent brawls between Yankees and Tommies. For a few seconds, Firmin thought he had seen Maggie among them. He gave the woman a knowing smile, before he realized his mistake. The staff sergeant immediately brought him back into line.

"Louder, corporal, louder!" he shouted. "Can't hear you!"

At the train station, the 320th VLA crammed into the first convoy, which would bring them to Newport. There, they took another train to Bristol. When the train entered the tunnel under the Severn, Firmin and other soldiers remembered what they had heard during their stay in Chepstow. They freaked out imagining a possible airstrike on the pump station, causing the flooding of the tunnel.

Bristol Temple Meads train station was a strategic railroad junction with multiple connections. Oxford and London to the east. Cardiff and the south of Wales to the west. Plymouth, Newton Abbot, Weymouth, Southampton and Portsmouth on the south coast of England.

All the platforms were jam-packed with American soldiers. Mostly white infantry men.

Lieutenant Colonel Reed's troops were subjected to some racist slurs, but they had been ordered not to answer the taunts, whatsoever. Moreover, the strong presence of MPs had a very deterrent effect. No regrettable incident occurred.

Several trains to Plymouth overcrowded with white soldiers left before the 320th VLA could take one. Some of Firmin's buddies couldn't help but think and assert that it was a sign of discrimination.

Firmin and Edward managed to find two places side by

side in the corridor. They spent the first half an hour standing. They chatted while watching through the window the verdant landscapes of the Gloucestershire and the Somerset County passing by. Then, they sat on top of their bags, and eventually doze.

Their train had to stop at Newton Abbot station to let other priority convoys pass along. It finally left for a last fifteen minute trip to the Torquay terminal, on the Devonshire coast.

Outside the station, they could smell the sea breeze. But they didn't manage to observe it. Two MPs inside a jeep were waiting to lead them to their final destination, a few miles away. Two other Jeeps would drive the senior officers. The remainder of the battalion would have to get there walking.

The men of the 320th VLA finally discovered the K3 camp, one of the many *sausage camps*[66] which had been growing like mushrooms in the southwest of Britain. It could host five thousand men. But it was already almost fully occupied by the 237th and 238th U.S. Engineer battalions.

These temporary camps were situated alongside secondary roads to facilitate their supply with material, fuel and food. Most often in wooded areas, in order to conceal them from aerial surveillance. The roads around were banned to all civilian traffic. No contact between the soldiers and the local population was allowed, as the American and British headquarters feared that all these troop movements may reveal the imminence of the

---

[66] Nickname given to staging camps used to gather troops before the big invasion.

triggering of Operation *Neptune*[67].

The scarce hutments were reserved to house senior officers and their mess, and to store sensitive material. All the other soldiers would be housed in tents.

Firmin and his comrades quickly understood that the good time they had had in Pontypool was well and truly over. Even for the guys like Edward and Jimmy who had been housed in dorms set up in the basement of a church or in the attic of a school. They all would soon miss the past eight weeks in Pontypool, despite the intensity of the drills.

The *Nissen* huts of Checkendon, with their corrugated iron walls and their brick foundations, looked like resort hotels when compared to the canvas tents of the camp.

In the evening, the men of the 320th VLA were informed that, from this moment on, no more leave would be granted. They would soon be involved in large-scale maneuvers in coordination with other U.S. Army units. A final rehearsal of the big European continent's invasion.

Before this, the battalion would stay for eight days on the edge of these moist woods. The lack of space made open-air activities very limited. Drills were reduced to push-ups and workout exercises. The men couldn't do anything between two meals, but stay inside their pyramidal tents, reading, chatting, playing cards or shooting craps. They would soon die of boredom, making every new day look endless.

Firmin and his crew felt relieved when the 320th VLA eventually moved to a marshaling area, where they would embark on various ships involved in the maneuvers.

---

[67] First phase of Operation Overlord.

The first thing they noticed when they arrived was the absence of balloons above the ships. Most of the guys were deeply disappointed. Some even felt betrayed. What was the use of this exercise for the balloon crews, then?

They would soon discover that one of the purposes of this last large-scale exercise was to teach the soldiers how to transship from big boats into landing crafts. Indeed, the latter were designed to carry soldiers and at most one truck or one tank. However, they weren't intended for crossing the Channel. The bigger part of the crossing would be done on board of larger ships equipped with davits. At a reasonable distance from the continental coasts, the landing crafts would be descended to the sea level. Either with men already in, or empty. In this case, the soldiers would have to descend rope ladders hung to the flank of the LST.

The exercise reminded Firmin of what they had experienced right before they boarded the *Aquitania*. Except that now they wouldn't jump onto a dinghy floating in a swimming pool, but onto a landing craft tossed by the waves in the open sea. And to make it more realistic, non-commissioned officers would shoot live ammunition above their heads.

Many of the soldiers suffered from seasickness, especially because they stayed three days long aboard. They were knocked out when they landed on May 4, 1944, on Slapton Sands, between Dartmouth and Start Point.

The site had been chosen due to its similarities with the Normandy beaches, where the Big invasion of Europe would take place. The last phase of the operation consisted in the actual landing process. The soldiers had to rush out of a landing craft. They would jump from a steel ramp into the choppy waves, and run to the wooded hill which overlooked the shore. Once again, they had to progress under a rain of live bullets and in the deafening sound of exploding charges spread on the beach and remotely triggered.

The officers of the headquarters had decided to keep the secret over a tragedy that had occurred off the same beach a few days earlier. During another large-scale landing rehearsal called *Tiger*[68], eight American LSTs[69] had been attacked by German torpedo speedboats. Two LSTs had been sunk, a third one seriously damaged. Seven hundred and forty-nine Americans had been killed. Some officers were carrying strategic information about Operation Overlord. Disclosing information about the importance of the losses could have betrayed the secret and revealed to the German the intentions of the Allied forces.

To ensure that no confidential document could end up in the hands of the enemy, the SHAEF[70], under the command of Dwight David Eisenhower, ordered to retrieve the corpses of every missing officer.

The disaster had at least had the merit of pointing out the major failures in terms of coordination. Especially the absence of synchronization of the radio frequencies used by the various ships involved. But also a misuse of the life vests and a lack of cooperation between the American and British Armies, and between the Navy and the Army.

After the exercise, the men of the 320th VLA learned that they wouldn't stay long neither as a complete

---

[68] Source: http://www.combinedops.com/Op_Tiger.htm
[69] Landing Ship Tank.
[70] Supreme Headquarters of the Allied Expeditionary Forces.

battalion, nor as a battery. They would be incorporated instead as balloon teams in various U.S. infantry units. Thus, they would lose their commandant's caring protection. Moreover, every balloon crew would be isolated among white infantry men on a ship all through the crossing of the Channel. This prospect scared many in the battalion.

On May 6, back in the marshaling camp, the 320th VLA was split into two groups. Battery C would stay in Torquay. Firmin and the rest of the battalion were transferred to another *sausage camp*. In Dorchester, further east in the bay, a few miles north from Portland Island.

Like Devonshire, Dorset was dotted with military camps. There were eighty-eight in Dorset, of which six around Dorchester.

A and B batteries and elements of the 320th VLA HQ were gathered in one of the two camps in marshaling area D, hosting almost five hundred vehicles and three thousand people.

CHAPTER 36

May 21, 1944

More than two weeks had passed since their arrival in this new camp, surrounded by barbed wire and defended by armed guards. Dozens of square tents with pyramidal tops were perfectly aligned in several rows, as far as the eye could see. Inside the tents, soldiers slept almost shoulder to shoulder.

The camp was so crowded—over three thousand men —that every activity required from the soldiers to stand in line for hours. At the sanitary block, to use the latrines or take a shower. At the mess, to have dinner or supper. Besides, the lack of space made almost all drills impossible. Therefore, Captain Taylor ensured that his nearly four hundred men were always busy. With daily sessions of dismounting, cleaning and mounting of their rifles. With series of push-ups and abs to maintain the stamina of the balloon operators.

Nonetheless, some men were continuously busy. The engineers who took care of the waterproofing of all the vehicles which would take part in the Operation Neptune. Those had no time to get bored.

Regarding recreation, there was no way to get out and pub-crawl for a sing-along or a dart game. All communication with the outside was banned. The trains and other transports were stopped. The troops were totally isolated from the rest of the world. No visitor was allowed inside the camps.

227

So, the guys killed time. Some would write to their families or read their last mail. Others would flip through comic books or old magazines. Some played poker, betting cigarettes. More seldom were those who endeavored to learn by heart a few French phrases. They all had received a French language guide filled with daily life sentences in French with their phonetic transcription and their English translation.

Bawn joor mad-mwa-zel[71] ou *juh voodray dew pang seel voo play*[72]. Firmin was probably the only one who didn't need it. Still, he didn't boast of it, as he didn't want to be turned into the camp's French teacher.

Boredom and forced lack of privacy eventually made blood boil. Brawls and scuffles would sometimes break out. Some of them ended with a stay in the infirmary, a night guard or a latrine chore.

Firmin spent most of his free time chatting with Edward. He was feeling closer and closer to him. He finally let him in on his diary. He made him swear that he would bring it back to his parents in New Orleans, together with his harmonica, in case he were killed during the war.

In Pontypool, Firmin had hidden his gris-gris in his bag, to avoid embarrassing questions from Mrs. Jones. But now that the Big day was getting closer, he kept it constantly hung from his dog tag's necklace. He claimed he did it to honor his promise to his mother. But actually, he needed to feel it nestling against the skin of his chest.

Every evening, before the curfew, Firmin wrote a few words in his diary. But also a letter to his parents, and

---

[71] *Bonjour mademoiselle.* Hello, Miss.
[72] *Je voudrais du pain, s'il vous plaît.* May I have some bread, please?

another to Ethel. Once a week, he would bring all his V- Mails[73] to the mail orderly.

Due to the last movements of troops, the mail reached their addressees most often late and irregularly.

Thus, the last bunch of letters had been delivered the day before. The first delivery since they had left Pontypool.

His mother kept on sending one letter per week.

In one of the latest, she wrote she was happy for him. However, she begged him not to get distracted by his love for Ethel. "Keep your head on your shoulders! Think first of saving your life. And come back home safe and sound. Whole and healthy!"

Judging from the dates on her mail, Ethel had fulfilled her promise. She had written every day, save on Sundays. At least until May 4. Sixteen letters delivered together on the same day. He read and reread them all. He wished he had received them one by one, day by day. Anyhow, he felt deeply relieved. She loved him, and her love didn't fade. Sure not.

In her last letters, Ethel was worried by his silence. But she didn't blame him for that. She knew from her colleagues of the Red Cross that the soldiers were held incommunicado, and were very busy with drills and maneuvers.

"Maybe Ethel has finally received my mail by now?" Firmin thought, pressing all her letters on his chest.

He decided to send to his parents and Ethel a reply in

---

[73] Victory mail. Mail process in which a preprinted letter form was filled by a soldier, then transferred to the military postal service. After it had been censored, the mail was copied to a microfilm and printed back to paper after the film had reached its destination.

the most concise way. The mail orderly was running out of V-Mail forms. Everything had to get onto a single page, avoiding every word that might be obliterated by the censorship. He would reserve his negative thoughts and state of mind for his diary and his buddy Edward.

That forenoon, Firmin didn't attend Albert White's service. He chose instead to read a verse from Maggie's bible. After they had dinner, about twenty guys of the 320th VLA organized a softball game on a narrow space between a row of tents and the fence of the camp. The shouts and cheering of the few spectators rapidly attracted others. As the clamor was growing, white soldiers of an engineer combat battalion came closer. Seeing colored soldiers playing despite the ban, two white soldiers flipped their wig and uttered threats and racial slurs at them. A lieutenant of the 320th VLA rushed in and confiscated the ball and the bats. He ordered his men to scram before all this turned into a brawl.

The atmosphere in the camp was getting tenser and more poisonous every day. It would set the soldiers' nerves on edge. At the same time, it maintained their tension, and hence their aggressiveness. Yet, if they waited further to go to battle, this aggression could soon turn against their brothers in arms.

One thing, fortunately, made this confinement more endurable. It was Spring. Beautiful days were back. The sun was shining brighter and longer, warming up the nature and the bodies. The trees, gorged with sap, were covered with a thick light-green foliage. The local vegetation didn't compare the beauty of Louisiana trees adorned with Spanish moss. Yet, it reminded him of his parents and of his native country.

Firmin loved to wake up with bird songs, long before the bugle call. The feverish agitation of the mockingbirds, great and blue tits, and other robins, inspired him the recklessness and sheer happiness of being alive. Away from the fury of the war and the murderous madness of men. But, soon after, he would fall into a deep depression when he realized one person was missing on his side. Ethel took every day a more important place in his thoughts. And now that he had received her impassioned letters, her absence was all the more painful as he didn't even have a single picture of her. Things had happened so fast between the two. And their separation had occurred so suddenly.

Edward, for his part, had bought from a photographer a souvenir picture of Clarisse and him standing side by side. It was at the exit of the movie theater, while Firmin and Ethel were strolling arm in arm in the streets of Pontypool, probably kissing each other. And yet, Edward wasn't in love at all with this girl.

"Why didn't you push me to have us photographed, on that day?" Firmin blamed him when Ed showed him the picture.

Corporal Bellegarde needed to isolate himself for a while to think about his future. He had noticed a white birch at the edge of the camp. So, after the altercation about the softball game, Firmin returned to his tent and fetched his diary and his harmonica. Then, he walked to the tree and sat at the base of it, with his back rested against its white and smooth bark.

From that point, he could admire the perfect alignment of the multitude of tents. "Nothing can resist such an organization," Firmin thought. How many GIs were there on the British soil, ready for the invasion of Europe? Ready for pushing the German armies back to Berlin? One hundred thousand? One million? Or more? Firmin couldn't tell. It was a well-kept secret. Anyhow, from what he had seen during the transfer of the 320th VLA from Pontypool to Torquay, he reckoned that the American soldiers were very numerous and well equipped.

Firmin shut his eyes to better recall the delicate features of Ethel's face. He wished he could have the skill of a draftsman. He could have made a faithful portrait of his fiancée. He had even tried once. But the result was terrible. Luckily for him, her radiant smile appeared in his thoughts with almost the same accuracy as if she were standing right before him. But how long will her image remain so precise in his memory?

He strove to reproduce mentally the smell of her skin, the taste of her tongue in his mouth, the silky contact of her breasts in the hollow of his hand.

"What are you dreaming of, Corp.? Of Ethel, I guess from your blissful smile. Right?"

Firmin recognized Ed's voice.

"Why are you asking if you already know the answer? You'd better let me dream on, instead!"

"May I sit?" Edward asked.

"Now that you shattered my dream…"

Edward sat near him.

"You've really got a crush on her, haven't you?"

Firmin sighed deeply.

"She was your first, right?"

Firmin didn't reply.

"I see," Edward continued. "You know … we all

believe we're in love when we go out with a girl for the first time…"

"It's got nothing to do with that!" Firmin objected curtly.

"Trust my experience. When you've gotten your rocks off with another bird, you'll forget her. Bet my next pay!"

Firmin turned towards Ed with a reproachful gaze.

"You're undeniably skilled in the art of shattering dreams!"

Ed realized he had hurt his leader.

"You mean it's really serious… I'm terribly sorry. I apologize … forgive me!"

"No problem. I'll be fine. Anyhow, it's no good for me to be in love. I must keep my mind clear if I want to stay alive until this damn war is over, at least."

"You can count on me!" Ed comforted him. "Every time I'll see you with this thoughtful look, I'll shatter your dream and get your feet back on the ground."

Firmin couldn't hold on his impulse to laugh. Ed first looked at him with an incredulous expression. They both eventually split their sides with laughter.

The two friends then remained silent for a few minutes.

"Are you telling about me in your book?" Ed asked to break the silence.

"What kind of interesting stuff could I tell about you?"

"Well, I … I don't know," Ed mumbled.

"Cool down, Ed. Don't feel upset. I was just kidding."

"Dang it, you got me!" Edward whispered.

"Of course, I'm telling about you. Your name will also appear in my memoirs… If you don't mind."

Edward puffed out his chest with pride. No educated person had ever given a damn about him, before.

"What kinda things are you writing?"

"Everything I'd like to remember later. And who knows? I could become a journalist or a columnist, like Ollie Stewart of the Baltimore *Afro American* or Roi Ottley, correspondent of the *Pittsburgh Courier,* or Langston Hughes of the *Chicago Defender*.

"Never heard of them," Ed mumbled, with a little shrug of his shoulders.

Firmin turned to his buddy.

"When this war is over, remind me to review your citizen's education."

"What kinda things?" Ed insisted.

"Well, things of our daily life in the army. Good and bad memories. Segregation and racism in Camp Tyson and in Southern garrison towns. But also, the way the British welcomed the Negroes. Our training and drills. Our job in this barrage balloon battalion."

"You really believe they'll let you publish all this in America?" Edward wondered.

Firmin shook his head and sighed long.

"If they refuse to publish my articles, it'll mean we fought for nothing in the U.S. Army."

"You're damn right, Corp.! What'll you do with your diary, then?"

"I don't know. I could write my memoirs and submit them to a publisher."

"Bet you no one will accept. Whites got no intention to make a hero out of a Negro!"

"In America, probably not!" Firmin agreed. "In that case, I'll find one here, in Britain."

"Aren't you scared they'd ban you from returning home, then?"

Firmin didn't reply. He nodded gently, poked his hand into his bag and took out the diary. He opened it with the bookmark. The left page was half filled. He drew a line under the last sentence, and wrote the date.

"Anyhow, if I don't do it for me and for the remainder of the battalion, who's gonna do it? Can you tell me? Wild Bill? I daren't imagine what kind of shit he could tell about us?"

"Reed!" Ed suggested. "He is our commandant, and a nice fellow too. Isn't he?"

"I agree, but, he's not always with us. And furthermore, he's not in our brains!"

"For sure, Corp.!" Ed approved, turning towards Firmin. "Alright, Corp.," he added, getting up. "I leave you alone with your confessor."

Corporal Bellegarde gave him a thankful wink, and returned to his thoughts. He needed to clear them up before writing them down in his diary.

CHAPTER 37

June 2, 1944

T he day before, the announcement of their transfer to Weymouth and Portland boarding harbors had come as a relief for the soldiers. They couldn't stand any longer to be trapped in this camp like wild animals in a cage.

Each soldier had received clear instructions and new equipment. A gas mask in its bag, an inflatable life vest with two CO_2 cartridges, and an entrenching tool and its cover.

Besides, they had received a kit including food rations for one week, two hundred French francs in "flag tickets,"[74] ten motion sickness preventive pills and water purification tablets, not to mention a service packet of *Thins* rubber prophylactics. The latter were officially supposed to help curtail the spreading of venereal diseases causing numerous infections among American soldiers. However, Jimmy and other GIs understood this extra distribution of condoms as the promise of a debauchery of sex in the great brothel that France was supposed to be, according to a rumor among the grunts. The rumor was an extension of the propaganda disseminated by some recruiting sergeants in the U.S. induction centers.

In the days preceding the departure, discipline had been

---

[74] A currency issued by the United States for use in Allied-occupied France, in the wake of the Battle of Normandy.
Source: https://fr.wikipedia.org/wiki/Billet_drapeau

slightly relaxed. Psychiatrists had been assigned to the marshaling areas. But, most of the soldiers were rather looking for the spiritual and moral support of army chaplains.

Physical support was ensured by improved food rations completed with white bread and fruit cocktails.

The staff sergeants reminded the soldiers how important it was to dig a good fox hole.

"There are three things which you should never part with: your helmet, your rifle and your folding shovel! Be it to sleep by night or to defend a strategic position, get used to dig a hole deep enough to guarantee your own protection with a minimum of comfort. It will be useful as well to watch over the moves of our enemies. If necessary it can work as a shooting station. So, even if you're knocked out, don't forget this rule. Never! Digging is a matter of life or death! Your fox hole is your life assurance! To say it short: dig! or die!"

A last backpack review had defined and standardized the equipment every soldier would take with him for the crossing of the Channel. Each of them should carry as little as possible, so as to increase the number of troops transported on the ships, and make their storming of the Normandy beaches easier and faster. The remainder of the material would follow, provided that the landing was successful, of course.

Besides the seasickness prevention pills, every soldier had received a few barf bags. It reminded them of their crossing of the Atlantic Ocean a few months earlier.

When they arrived in Weymouth Port, the men of the 320th VLA's battery A joined several units of the U.S. anti-aircraft artillery. The 16th AAA group, the 197th and

457th AAA AW[75] battalions, and the 413th AAA gun battalion. Corporal Firmin Bellegarde and his comrades were the only colored soldiers, besides the men of the 3275th *Quartermaster Service Company*, but also among all the GIs who embarked in Weymouth harbor in preparation for the big invasion. Almost two hundred and eighty thousand men, of which five hundred were African Americans, within a few days, composing the bulk of the first U.S. infantry division. The rest of it was to leave from Portland Island, south of Weymouth.

Firmin and his colleagues didn't feel at ease among all those Whites. They had suffered so much from contempt until then, especially during their preparation year in Camp Tyson. They now feared the way they would be treated, particularly by white Southerners, when they are isolated and dispersed on the multitude of boats during the crossing.

The balloon crews indeed knew they would be spread aboard hundreds of boats of all sizes involved in Operation Neptune, and would have to work in full autonomy. Needless to say the men of the 320th VLA didn't feel safe. A team of medics of the battalion would also join this first expedition.

However, their anguish soon subsided. The weather in this late spring was nice and warm. A light breeze was blowing on the town. Scents of iodized sea air mingled with the smell of the exhaust gases of the barges relentlessly shuttling in the harbor. Thousands of GIs were marching in groups of one or two hundred, almost nonchalantly, towards the docks. GIs of the famous U.S.

---

[75] Anti-Aircraft Artillery Automatic Weapon.

1st Infantry division, officially nicknamed the *Big Red One*, after its shoulder patch featuring a red number one on a khaki background.

Comforted by the calmness reigning in their ranks, Firmin was gazing at the scene with the sharp eye of a man who intended to testify for future generations. The port was teeming with American soldiers. Only a few dwellers of the town attended the live performance, sitting on public benches along the facades of the houses. American MPs were watching over the smooth flow of the groups.

By groups of fifty men, the GIs were guided towards a gangway from which they would get aboard small flat-bottomed boats designated by the letters LCVP. They were also nicknamed *Higgins boats*.

Firmin felt a pang of nostalgia, as it reminded him of his mother who had probably worked on some of those landing crafts in Higgins's factory in New Orleans.

Inside each LCVP, three crew members dressed in their Navy outfits, helped the soldiers get on board. As the sea was calm, the barges were loaded beyond their official capacity of thirty-six men. Meanwhile, several empty boats, back from a former round trip, were waiting for their turn to berth close to the gangway.

One after the other, the landing crafts would take away a load of GIs and bring it to one of the bigger ships anchored in the bay.

Aligned in three rows, the balloon crews of the 320th VLA continued their way on the Custom House Quay up to the esplanade in front of the Weymouth pavilion. The building, which housed since 1908 a theater, a ballroom, a restaurant and the Cafe Ritz, had been requisitioned by the army to house senior officers of the general staff.

There, a large space had been allocated to the preparation of the balloons before their loading on the LSTs. At the crack of dawn, the battalion's truck drivers had brought several dozens of deflated balloons, mooring material, new hand winches and hundreds of bottles of compressed hydrogen piled on platforms. This solution had been chosen to compensate for the lack of autonomous hydrogen generators.

The balloon inspectors were impatiently waiting for the arrival of the crews, to start inflating the balloons.

Not far from them, LSTs were docking, their bows heading to the quay. Their prows would then split open in two side panels, forming wide open mouths which swallowed Sherman tanks, GMC CCKW 2-½ ton trucks, amphibian GMC DUKWs, Dodge WC-51, and Jeeps, with an insatiable greed.

On the esplanade, there was just enough space to prepare four balloons at a time. Once inflated, the balloon was freed from its mooring net and progressively brought to a height of one hundred fifty feet, under the control of its crew. It would then be guided to the quay and embarked on an LST or an LSI[76].

Immediately after, another balloon crew would take its place to help prepare their balloon under the supervision of an inspector.

While waiting for their turn, the guys could take a rest, enjoying a coffee and doughnuts served by U.S. Red Cross volunteers under large tents installed on the dock.

---

[76] Landing Ship Infantry.

When he saw these warm welcoming and cheerful women, endeavoring to joke with the soldiers to relieve their internalized fear, Firmin thought even more of Ethel. Since May 20, he had received no letter from his fiancée. Most of his friends too were lacking news from their families.

Finally, Firmin's crew's turn came. One of the balloon inspectors beckoned them over to him. It was Wilson Monk[77]. A man hailing from Atlantic City. Like other experts of the battalion, Wilson Monk was attached to the HQ battery. The elite of the 320th VLA, somehow. Firmin scarcely dealt with Monk in the previous weeks. But judging from what he knew about him, he was a competent engineer and a cool guy.

"You look pretty busy, these times, don't you? Firmin said.

"Kind of, indeed!" Monk agreed, showing the pile of folded and deflated balloons.

"C'mon!" he added. "Help me bring this one to the free spot over there."

Firmin, Edward and Jimmy got rid of their backpacks and put on their protection gloves. Then, they carried the balloon to the inflation area. They unfolded it, trying not to damage the external envelope.

Firmin stayed near Wilson during his inspection.

"Don't you trust me, corporal?"

"I sure do!" Firmin replied. "But two pairs of eyes are worth more than one! Right?"

---

[77] Wilson Monk really existed. All the information about him in this book was found in Linda Hervieux's book, paying tribute to the forgotten heroes of the 320th VLA. A book titled "Forgotten" and published by Harper Collins. ISBN 978-0-06-231379-9.

"Yep!" the inspector admitted, somewhat upset.

"I've read somewhere," Firmin insisted, "that combat pilots often do the same with their chief mechanic, don't they?"

Monk remained undisturbed and continued. He asked Firmin's crew men to cover the balloon with a mooring net and tether it to the sand bags lying on the ground on both sides of the cotton neoprene coated envelope.

"Now, guys, bring these two bottles over here," he said pointing his hand to a platform loaded with dozens of cylindrical containers filled with hydrogen. "And make sure you don't fall... One spark and wham! War is over for us! But in that case, forget about a posthumous medal. Such a reward, you can earn only after you've crossed the Channel!"

The supervisor checked that the gas pipes were properly screwed to the balloon valves, then ordered Edward and Firmin to open the taps of the gas bottles by one half turn. He approached his ear to the valves to detect a possible leakage. He didn't hear any. So, he ordered to open the taps one full turn further.

While the balloon was inflating, Ed and Jimmy ensured to undo possible persistent folds. On their side, Bellegarde and Monk chatted while walking around the silver cigar which was taking its final shape.

"As you are closer than me to Lieutenant Colonel Reed," Firmin commented, "you probably know where we're going to land, don't you?"

"Don't know more than you. Besides, you'll discover it long before me," Monk replied with a regretful tone.

"Duck! You mean ... you don't go with us?"

"Nope," Monk sighed. "They need me here to keep on

242

supervising the balloons preparation. There must be someone to replace all those who'll be destroyed by enemy shots if we want to continue protecting the French shores. And before they reach their destination, they will protect other ships transporting ammunition, food and replacement troops. And only then, when the landing succeeds, I and other mechanics and engineers of the headquarters battery will join you in France. At least, I hope so. It would make me sick if I were sent back home before I could set foot on the French soil."

"I see," Firmin commented. "If you want, I can talk about you to a French mademoiselle and ask her to wait for you…"

"Don't worry for me," Monk interrupted him, shoving his hand into his pocket.

He took a picture out of his wallet and showed it to Corporal Bellegarde.

"Her name is Mertina. We've been engaged since 1941. And we intend to marry as soon as I'm back from war. We had this portrait made by a photographer of Atlantic City."

On the photograph Wilson Monk was posing in his parade outfit on Mertina's side. They looked happy and in love.

"We bought two copies of it. One for each of us. So, every evening, I look at this picture and I feel like she's in bed with me. It cost me one dollar, but it was worth it… What about you? Have you got a girl friend waiting for you at home?"

"I met her here… I mean, in Pontypool!" Firmin proudly replied. "Her name is Ethel!"

"A British girl? Don't you fear that…?"

"She's American!" Firmin exclaimed with enthusiasm.

"She's a Red Cross volunteer. And she's from New Orleans, like me. Crazy, isn't it?"

"Sounds like you've got a crush on her!"

"Sure! We love each other! We even got engaged!"

"Have you got a picture?" Monk asked.

"Don't mention it! You can't imagine how much I blame myself. We didn't even think of taking a picture of ourselves in Pontypool! We were too busy kissing in the streets and in the Empire picture house. After that, our departure came so suddenly. Luckily, I still can rebuild her image in my brain when I close my eyes."

"I think your balloon is almost ready to fly," Monk said.

A few minutes later, the balloon controller made a sign to Firmin's teammates, to let the ballon go up six feet high. He then made a last visual check of the bottom surface and of the links of the mooring cables.

The three men eventually picked up their backpacks and their rifles, and took away the balloon with its manual winch up to the LST's embarkment dock.

CHAPTER 38

June 3, 1944

During the previous night, Firmin, Ed and Jimmy had successively been on watch duty on the upper deck of their LST. One of them had to stay near the winch and the mooring cables of their balloon, amongst trucks and Jeeps.

The tanks and other armored vehicles were parked on the lower deck. Both flanks of the ship housed a row of narrow compartments, each containing nine berths. The compartments at the bow were reserved for the ship's crew, composed of one hundred men and twenty officers. The other compartments could house up to two hundred soldiers.

The bunks reminded Firmin of those of the *Aquitania*. They were suspended by hinges, on the bulkhead on one side, and grouped in tiers of three bunks high. On the other side, they hung from the ceiling at two metal chains. The spacing between two bunks was so narrow that it prevented you from sitting up. The most popular were the top beds. The two occupants under could receive puke throws during their sleep. Even when the ship was protected inside the port, some soldiers already suffered from seasickness.

June 3 passed quietly. The soldiers stayed under the camouflage tarps of the vehicles, to protect themselves from the sun while breathing the fresh sea air on the main deck.

A rumor said that the invasion was planned for the early hours of June 5. The whole fleet would leave the harbor at the first light, on Sunday June 4. Therefore, it would be difficult to organize religious services on board of each ship.

Very few soldiers had received their baptism of fire, but many knew at least one veteran who had fought during the Great War. Others had heard or read in History books about the Civil War. All were aware of the large number of victims, killed or wounded, that this war would cause, like any other.

Fear was the companion of each soldier. The fear of being killed, of course. But also the anguish of behaving cowardly when facing the enemy. The fear of killing a human being. The dread of committing a mortal sin. Some would silence their angst by dreaming of a feat of arms, that would turn them into heroes. Coming back from war with a medal would earn them a good reputation. Especially for those living out in the boondocks. However, should they, by misfortune, return in a coffin, the glory would reflect on their family.

Others, fatalistic or resigned, prepared to die soldiers, with bravery. But most of the men were terrified. Many felt the urge of praying in communion.

They needed the spiritual help and comfort of religion. Sadly, the army was sorely lacking chaplains. According to the regulation, there was one for twelve hundred soldiers. The 320th VLA had his: Albert White. But the men of the battalion were scattered on dozens of ships. Besides, there were only a little more than three hundred men aboard Firmin's LST.

Hence, on Saturday, June 3, late in the afternoon, an

officer improvised a religious service on the top deck of the LST. Standing on the rooftop of a truck, the lieutenant invited the men to come closer to him. Every available space around was soon filled. The latecomers had to climb on other vehicles to hear him.

"I know that you'd rather listen to a chaplain, given that only a man of the Church is allowed to give communion, which I'm not. However, like many of you, I was raised in the faith in God and Jesus. My father taught me the Bible, and at home, on Sundays, we used to read and study a verse from the Holy Book."

The lieutenant then opened his Bible, and started to read, with a powerful and assured voice.

"Job 36:6–7. *He doesn't preserve the life of the wicked, but gives to the afflicted their right. He doesn't withdraw his eyes from the righteous, but with kings on the throne, he sets them forever, and they are exalted.*

We know on which side are the wicked mentioned in the Bible. It is our duty to obey God and go fight and kill the wicked until they lay down their arms and surrender! Behaving like this will be rewarded by our Lord. Be it in this life or in the other."

Staying away from the others, Firmin and his crew mates listened to the lieutenant, while keeping an eye on their balloon.

"Ain't sure we, Negroes, will be rewarded for what we's done for the country," Jimmy mumbled through his clenched teeth.

"Right on the nose, Jim," Ed agreed. "Just need to see how they've been ignoring us since we came on board!"

Firmin turned his head and made them a sign to talk lower.

247

"This is precisely why we'd better stick together, and always remain free from any reproach," Corporal Bellegarde whispered. "Should we show the slightest weakness in front of the enemy, they would immediately use it to justify their racial prejudices. On the other hand, if one of us acted with bravery, there'd be no White to testify it."

"Why we's done risk our *niggers* neck, then?" Jimmy asked, surprised.

"Because it's our only chance to assert our civil rights," Firmin replied, upset. "And to make the world know it, we'll have to attest ourselves. Therefore, one of us at least should stay alive and tell what we've done and seen."

"You're damn right!" Ed approved.

Corporal Bellegarde gazed carefully at each of the two operators.

"I'll write on three sheets of paper the addresses of our families. Each of us will keep a copy. So, should one of us die, the two others would go and meet his family and tell them what we've done. The world must know that we were there. That we took part in the Big invasion of Europe! Otherwise, who else will do it? You said it, yourself, Ed! All these Whites ignore us. We don't even exist in their eyes!"

"If you die," Ed suggested, "I'll just need to publish your diary!"

"What diary?" Jimmy asked, stunned.

Firmin looked at Edward with an angry gaze.

"Couldn't you just keep your mouth shut?"

"No worry!" Ed replied. "He can't even read!"

"Thank you for reminding me!" Jimmy said, offended.

"No problem, Jimmy," Firmin comforted him. "I'll

248

teach you on our way back home!"

"Thank you, Corp.!" Private Stevenson replied, looking at Ed with contempt.

"Anyhow," Corporal Bellegarde continued, "as you could see it, we're only a few hundred colored soldiers involved in the first phase of the invasion of Europe, alongside the combat units. It's both a privilege and a huge responsibility. All our brothers and sisters home rely on us. They expect from us an exemplary behavior. They want black heroes. They hope for a hell of a lot in return. Nothing less than the same civil rights as the Whites."

"Nothing less, for sure!" Ed acquiesced.

"But if we fail," Firmin added, "we'd have gone through all this for nothing. All our brothers who will lose their lives will have died in vain. Therefore, we're gonna fight like true soldiers!"

"Like fuckin' good soldiers!" Jimmy added, in an enthusiastic tone.

"Even if we're scared," Corporal Bellegarde said. "God is on our side!"

"Amen!" his two crew mates replied, almost simultaneously.

When the prayer was over, the lieutenant wished the soldiers a good meal.

CHAPTER 39

W hile everyone around was having supper, joking or playing cards, Firmin fished out his diary from his haversack. He started writing his impressions, and drawing a few clumsy sketches of the view he had over the deck and the bay.

Firmin would never part with his haversack, which contained his precious treasure. His diary, all the letters from his parents and Ethel, a few drawing sheets, a grease lead pencil, and his harmonica. All carefully protected in a watertight bag. His fountain pen and a little bottle of ink refill were tightly sealed in a second bag. His Haitian good luck charm hanging around his neck with his dog tags. Nevertheless, Corporal Bellegarde had to remain very discreet, since some Whites hated educated Blacks more than all others. Had one of them caught Firmin writing in a diary, he would have caused him serious trouble.

Saturday, June 3, 1944
No mass tomorrow morning. Departure at dawn. This afternoon, white officer read a verse from the Bible and invited us to pray. Day after tomorrow, we'll land on French beaches. Many of us will die, officer said. I'm scared. Still got to be strong. Believe we're all scared.

Right now, my thoughts are for you, my dear parents. For you too, Ethel. I cling to the idea of seeing you again, not to sink into despair. I wonder if I'll have the courage to overcome my fear tomorrow. I pray to God to help me so. But, should I die tomorrow, or before I'm back home, I want you to know I love you with all my heart.

When the bell rang for the curfew, Firmin closed his diary and put it back into the watertight bag. The night promised to be short.

Sunday, June 4

Right after breakfast, the captain ordered the crew members back to their stations, for an imminent departure. As for the soldiers, they had to return to their compartments. Only a few men would stay on the decks to watch over the vehicles.

Firmin gazed a last time at the houses of Weymouth. They were the symbol of his happy experience on this island. He thought with emotion of Maggie and John. Then, he looked in the distance around the LST. A tidal wave of pride flooded his body and soul when he saw the armada. He could feel his temples throbbing. It confirmed and even reinforced his conviction that he was about to take part in the writing of a memorable page of the history of his country, and of the modern world too, alongside combat units of the U.S. Army.

A chance that had scarcely been given to Black Americans, and of which he firmly intended to prove worthy of. The presence on this ship of only three Blacks among three hundred people attested the privilege, but also the considerable responsibility that rested upon their shoulders.

Hundreds of ships of Force O,[78] marshaled in the bay, started to move towards the gathering area of all the armada. A zone located south of the Isle of Wight, code-named Z and nicknamed Piccadilly Circus.

The complete crew of balloon operators stayed on the deck while the LST was moving forward at the speed of eighteen knots. They could see, all around, balloons flying over other ships, but they were too far to allow Firmin to recognize his colleagues of the 320th VLA. Still, seeing them, even from afar, Firmin, Ed and Jimmy felt less alone.

The three men still worried. It was the first time they maneuvered their balloon from the deck of a moving ship. Within the first two hours, the balloon remained controllable, despite the turmoil caused by two distinct and sometimes contrary forces. The sea breeze, also known as *true* wind, on the one hand, and the *apparent* wind induced by the speed of the ship, on the other hand. They required from the balloon crew a constant surveillance. They had to ensure that the balloon was always in line with the direction of the apparent wind, so that the balloon wouldn't disturb the progression of the LST.

Things got tougher when the wind started to refresh and progressively reached 5 on the Beaufort wind scale. The crew mates were hard-pressed to prevent the rope from spinning. So, Firmin ordered to reduce the flying height before the rope could get hooked by some element of the ship, and eventually break.

Meanwhile, it started to rain harder and harder. The

---

[78] O for Omaha.

fresh wind, foreshadowing a storm, had raised a strong swell. Everywhere on the deck, the soldiers, seized by a violent seasickness, were moaning in pain. The guys would puke their guts out wherever they could. Over the rail into the sea, when they were quick enough. Into their barf bags, if not into their helmets that they would then empty overboard. On their shoes, sometimes. The smell of vomit eventually stank up the atmosphere, despite the strong breeze. Luckily, the rain was intense enough to wash the deck clean.

Suddenly, Allied aircraft flew over the convoy at low altitude, sending light signs for the attention of the ships' captains. Then, the men heard a concert of sirens coming from all the boats around, before the alarm of their LST sounded on its turn. The captain ordered to reduce the speed, and eventually start a U-turn on the port side.

The maneuver needed to be perfectly synchronized with all the ships around. Otherwise, it could end up in an utter chaos, considering the number of boats involved. With a high risk of collision between them.

On their side, Firmin and his crew mates had to redouble their efforts to fight in the same time nausea, and a raging sea, and a wind blowing in gusts. Of course they had had sessions of balloon handling by strong wind at Camp Tyson, but nevertheless nothing comparable to what they were facing at this moment.

During their return to Weymouth Bay, the captain just made a laconic announcement. "The storm that is currently raging on the Channel forces us to return to the harbor. The invasion is postponed until further notice."

The soldiers were too devastated by the seasickness to react. Yet, many must have felt relieved to know they would soon have a chance to recover some strength in a more quiet area.

When the LST finally dropped anchor off Weymouth, everyone on board was knocked out and soaked. The captain advised them to return to their berths inside their compartments to take off their wet clothes and take some rest. Most of them quickly fell asleep, without having supper. They were too queasy to swallow anything. On top of it, a strong smell of vomit still wafted in the air all over the place.

Firmin for his part had to struggle to fall asleep after his guard duty on the deck. Several soldiers in nearby berths woke up in the night, screaming or crying in the middle of their nightmares crowded with corpses and mutilated bodies.

CHAPTER 40

Leaning against the inner side of a shell crater, Firmin was desperately striving to resist his irrepressible urge to sleep. A matter of survival. He had no intention to let the Grim Reaper take his soul away during his sleep. A matter of dignity.

His two crew mates had found refuge in another hole, a few yards away from him, but he couldn't talk to them. They had received clear instructions. By night, keep silent and use no light, if you don't want to be shot by a sniper or shredded by a mortar shell. Any breach of these rules may cost you your life. Or worse and unforgivable, the lives of your brothers-in-arms.

With fully dilated pupils, Firmin was scrutinizing the cloudy sky, pierced here and there by the bright light of the full moon. All his senses on alert, his brain was analyzing the slightest suspicious noise among the rustle of leaves swept by the wind, and the sound of the waves breaking on the backwash.

A long shadow stretched over his hideout. Firmin at first thought it was just a cloud cutting a moon beam. He instantly relaxed and breathed out slowly. But, suddenly, appearing from out of the blue, a high and dark silhouette stood in front of him, pointing ahead his rifle with a fixed bayonet. Uttering a terrifying roar, the German was about to pounce on him and skewer him, when Corporal Bellegarde felt a hand grabbing his arm and shaking him vigorously. In a desperate defense reflex, Firmin screamed

255

in fear and rage, got released, and swung his fist forward to punch his assailant.

"Cool down, Corp.! It's me, Jimmy. You almost knocked me down!"

"Huh? What's on?"

Firmin rubbed his hands across his eyes. Standing before him, Jimmy was holding an insulated container in one hand.

"I thought you'd like a good cup of joe. So, I kept some hot water for you."

"Are we still in Weymouth, now?"

"Yes, Corp. But I done heard we'd leave tonight."

Firmin sighed. He wished he were in France already, safe and sound.

"How's the weather?"

"Still terrible, Corp. Just a little less windy and rainy. And it was about fifty degrees, one hour ago."

"I see… Now, before we know more, I wouldn't refuse a big cup of hot coffee," Firmin added, while vigorously rubbing his arms to warm himself up.

After a refill with warmth and energy, and a bit of grooming, Firmin and Jimmy joined Ed on the deck near the winch of their balloon.

The captain of the LST soon confirmed to all the men on board that the H-Hour had been set on the morrow, June 6, 1944.

"I know how eager you are to give the bloody fucking Nazis a damn beating! Your patience has been put to the test, lately. Especially yesterday, when a storm forced us to return. But tonight, we're gonna leave, for good this time. The decision was made this morning by General

Eisenhower, supreme commander of the Allied expeditionary forces."

The news was greeted by a few whistles of approval, but most of the men who belonged to combat regiments, were actually plagued by the fear of dying. They weren't in the mood to boast and brag. Their commandant had had the honesty to warn that two out of three of them would probably never come home again. Of course, they were prepared to sacrifice their lives for the sake of their country and their families, however with bravery and dignity. Not behaving like boxers swagging on the ring and scoffing at their opponent, to gain the sympathy of their fans.

"Tomorrow's gonna be a hard day. Probably the hardest of your short life. We'll need the strength of every one of you to ensure the success of this invasion, which will be a crucial turning point in the war against the Nazi tyranny. So, use this day in the bay to relax, because the coming night will be short. Thereafter you won't get any time to rest until we have defeated our enemy's defenses on the French soil!"

This precision confirmed what everyone had already sensed when they learned that the armada would include fifteen hospital ships, with eight thousand doctors on board.

Intending to reduce the nervousness of the one hundred and thirty thousand soldiers spread on about five thousand ships of the Allied armada, the headquarters had ordered an additional supply of food and cigarettes.

After an improved lunch, the more quiet ones—or the less aware—managed to have a little digestive nap. The others, especially the youngest who hadn't yet received their baptism of fire, were too anxious to fall asleep. They remained prostrate and shivering. Some staring vacantly into the distance, smoking cigarette after cigarette. Others reading, once more, letters from their families. Or burning their eyes through focusing on the photo of their wives or their girl friends.

Sometimes, a seasoned fighter, rescued from the Tunisian campaign or the invasion of Sicily, tried to divert the inexperienced soldiers from their fear by providing his veteran's advice. Like protecting the barrel of their rifle with a condom. "It'll protect your barrel from sea water entering it. And hence prevent rust and sand from jamming you rifle. It has saved many lives. Trust me!"

Firmin and Edward managed to sleep for a couple of hours, before eating their last meal of the day. Corporal Bellegarde took advantage of the last hour of sunlight to write a few lines in his diary.

He endeavored to hide it to his crew mates, but he was worried about what he expected to find on the other shore of the Channel. In the absence of a colored chaplain, Firmin read a verse from Maggie's bible.

Shortly after 20:00, the sun disappeared behind the horizon. Soon, a full and bright moon would appear in the opposite side of the sky. Every light on board was prohibited.

One hour later, just before the ships formed a convoy heading to *Piccadilly Circus*, the captain of the LST demanded a complete silence and the full attention of all the men aboard. He read them a *communiqué* addressed to all the troops involved in operations Neptune and Overlord by their commander in chief, General Dwight D. Eisenhower.

"*Soldiers, Sailors, and Airmen of the Allied Expeditionary Force: You are about to embark upon the Great Crusade, toward which we have striven these many months.*

The eyes of the world are upon you. The hopes and prayers of liberty-loving people everywhere march with you.

In company with our brave Allies and brothers-in-arms on other Fronts, you will bring about the destruction of the German war machine, the elimination of Nazi tyranny over oppressed peoples of Europe, and security for ourselves in a free world.

Your task will not be an easy one. Your enemy is well trained, well equipped, and battle-hardened. He will fight savagely.

But this is the year 1944. Much has happened since the Nazi triumphs of 1940-41. The United Nations have inflicted upon the Germans great defeats, in open battle, man-to-man. Our air offensive has seriously reduced their strength in the air and their capacity to wage war on the ground. Our Home Fronts have given us an overwhelming superiority in weapons and munitions of war, and placed at our disposal great reserves of trained fighting men. The tide has turned. The free men of the world are marching together to victory.

I have full confidence in your courage, devotion to duty, and skill in battle. We will accept nothing less than full victory.

Good Luck! And let us all beseech the blessing of

Almighty God upon this great and noble undertaking.[79]"

A long silence followed. As opposed to the captain of their LST, General Eisenhower had chosen the accurate and meaningful words to infuse in every man of his troops the feeling of the rightness of their fight and their sacrifice. He didn't hide that the battle would be hard. Nevertheless, he made them feel confident in the military superiority of the Allies over the Nazis.

At this moment, Firmin and his two crew members had the feeling that they were an essential part of the U.S. Army, as much as any other soldier, regardless of the color of his skin. It was the first time since they had joined the army.

---

[79] Source :
https://www.americanrhetoric.com/speeches/dwighteisenhowerorderofdday.ht

CHAPTER 41

Around 21:30, the captain ordered his crew to weigh anchor, leave the bay, and move to point Z. All around, you could distinguish the shapes of a multitude of ships heading in the same direction, without lights. On each of them, two lookouts on guard were scanning the sea to make certain their ship stayed away from the others.

Aboard their LST, Firmin, Ed and Jimmy observed the surrounding show with a mingle of pride and apprehension. Around them, as far as their eyes could see, dozens of balloons were flying in the air, one or two hundred feet above the sea level. A testimony of their involvement in the crusade against the Nazi tyranny.

Firmin nervously fingered the *gris-gris* hanging from the end of his necklace. He wondered if Ollie Stewart was aboard one of the other ships. He had read somewhere that the war correspondent of the *Afro-American* newspaper, who hailed from Louisiana like him, had stayed in London in May this year. But, had he been accredited by the U.S. headquarters to cover the invasion live? Ernest Hemingway, the famous novelist, was said to be part of the observers, together with many other white reporters[80]. But, will there be one African American journalist to witness the presence of colored soldiers during the assault of the European fortress at dawn, tomorrow?

---

[80] Among whom Robert Capa and Don Whitehead, on board of USS Samuel Chase.

With the night, a damp cold fell over the sea. Still, the young soldiers wouldn't shiver from the cold, but they would tremble in fear.

His head resting on his backpack, Jimmy was dozing off. Curled up in fetal position and huddled against a partition, he was sheltered from the wind. Firmin and Ed were watching over the balloon and scrutinizing the horizon.

As the ships were flocking in numbers towards the point Z, the armada revealed its huge power. Warships protected a myriad of troopships. The U.S. forces numbered seventeen hundred boats, LSI and LST, supported by three battleships, nine armored cruisers, nineteen destroyers, a gunboat, and dozens of squadron escorts and minesweepers. The latter were meant to open two navigation corridors down to the landing beaches code-named *Utah* and *Omaha*.

All the months spent in Britain finally found their justification.

Around midnight, the U.S. fleet eventually joined the whole east naval force under British command. At this moment, more than five thousand ships[81] were getting ready to launch the largest invasion of all times.

Only the crew leaders of the ships, and the senior officers of the assault units, knew the coordinates of the beaches where they all would land at 6:30 sharp.

Firmin's LST would not be part of the first assault wave. Nor of the second one. Its passengers wouldn't be the most exposed to danger. Nonetheless, nobody on board was spared from the gut-wrenching fear that you feel

---

[81] Figures vary between five and seven thousand ships according to different sources.

before entering a battlefield. All the less as danger was lurking everywhere around. The Germans had formidable submarines that had sunk many allied ships. Not to mention the torpedo speedboats which could appear out of nowhere and vanish as suddenly after having destroyed several ships.

And, to make it worse, there was the damn seasickness which undermined a vast majority of the soldiers. A northwesterly wind was blowing in gusts of fourteen knots, raising waves of four to seven feet high. All the troops on the sea would have to stand these awful conditions for hours before the fateful moment.

Shortly after the gathering at point Z, the armada split into five convoys, which would take different paths previously cleared of mines and marked by light buoys. Each convoy had two paths – one fast, one slow – leading to its landing beach.

Force U[82], on starboard, was under the balloon protection of battery C. All the balloon crews of battery A were under the command of Force O[83], heading towards Omaha beach. The crews of battery B had been kept as a reserve and would follow only after the complete success of the invasion.

Corporal Bellegarde wondered if the fate which had led him to the battery A of the 320th VLA would be favorable to him. Would he survive the D-Day? Would he be luckier if he had been assigned to battery C, which was now heading towards Utah beach? Would he be less deserving

---

[82] U for Utah beach.
[83] O for Omaha beach.

of respect if he were part of battery B, held in reserve on the British soil?

"Aren't you ever scared, Corp.?"

Firmin looked at Edward.

"Of course, I am! Scared stiff, to be honest! But what does it change? Our life is in the hands of the Lord. And, as the saying goes: fear doesn't avoid the danger."

"Can be. But the closer we get from H-Hour, the less I'm ready to die for people who despise us."

"It's precisely by fighting on their side that we will force them to respect us."

"Bunk! Ain't gonna be the first time we fight on their side. The Civil war, the Great War. Never heard of it? What did we get in return? Tell me! Nothin' a-tall! Zip! No! If it was me…"

"Give it a rest!" Firmin begged him. "Or you're gonna talk nonsense and put us all in a big mess!"

"What? Ain't it true?"

"It's neither the right time, nor the right place to talk about that. And remember the promise you made to me! Always watch over one another, until the end of the war!"

Edward didn't reply. At the same time, Firmin realized that the engine had stopped. He could only hear the sound of the waves breaking against the LST's hull. The wind and the swell in the middle of the Channel increased the rolling of the flat bottom ship. Suddenly, a long series of slams resounded in the metal structure, making half of the men jump with fright. But it was just the clacking of the anchors' chain links hitting the edges of the two exit holes.

An officer explained that the convoy had reached a first stage, ten miles off the French coasts. It was about 02:30. They would need to wait until 06:30 for the decisive assault to come. Four hours of an unbearable, harrowing anxiety.

Ahead of them, several LSTs and LSIs were crammed with assault forces of the 116th Infantry regiment and men of the 5th Ranger battalion. They would have the most difficult and perilous task to be the first men to storm the beaches and annihilate the German defense. Firmin could already hear the engines of the davits bringing down to the water the landing crafts of the first assault waves. The corporal thought of these poor foot soldiers, but also of the medics of the 320th VLA who would help their colleagues of the combat regiments of the 29th Infantry division protect and treat the wounded.

From the deck of his LST, Firmin couldn't distinguish the French coasts. However, Firmin feared that the German lookouts could possibly see his balloon flying one or two hundred feet above the ship. Corporal Bellegarde wasn't the only one who worried about it.

An infantry man came closer and gazed at them with a scornful and mean look.

"You boys ain't got nothing to do here!" he shouted. "We're gonna be spotted 'cause of your fun fair balloon. If I could, I'd cut the wires before the German artillery starts shooting at us!"

He would probably have done it, hadn't his superior interfered.

Meanwhile, all the ships were strongly tossed by the choppy sea. The men aboard were suffering more and more from seasickness. Their stomachs were knotted by fear as much as by nausea. Seasoned officers would regularly walk among them and try to calm down the most affected. But also to prevent some of them from panicking, hence contaminating others.

Now, Firmin could hear from the LSTs ahead officers shouting their orders to climb down the rope ladders, and jump into the LCIs. The same kind of landing crafts which were used for the embarkment of the troops at Weymouth. They would have to cross the ten miles separating them from the sand beaches, through a strong swell and a wind blowing in gusts.

How would these foot soldiers, trained to fight on solid ground, stand the coming three hours before the assault? In what physical state, will they have to face the German defenses?

Everyone aboard was probably wondering the same. But, secretly, everyone was thanking God for not taking part in the first assault wave.

In three hours, they would land on the beaches under a deluge of iron and fire. Corporal Bellegarde was more and more hard-pressed to resist fatigue and his urge to sleep. Ed was already dozing off. Firmin woke Jimmy and ordered him to take his guard duty. The corporal himself eventually fell asleep.

CHAPTER 42

F irmin was sleeping soundly. Jimmy shook him vigorously. However, he blocked the corporal's arms, for fear of being punched in a defensive reflex.

"Get up, Corp.! They're shooting at us!"

"Eh? What's up?"

"The Germans! They spotted us! They're shooting at us!"

It took the corporal a few seconds to remember where he was and realize he was not dreaming. He jumped to the blast of the cannons of the USS *Emmons.* The U.S. destroyer was backed up by the *Georges Leygues*, a Free French cruiser, and the USS battleship *Arkansas*[84].

"What time is it?"

"5:30, Corp.!"

"Suck it!" Firmin muttered when he understood he had only slept two hours and won't have a chance to get some more rest before the beginning of the landing.

He quickly figured out how serious the situation was. Particularly for the men sailing in circles aboard single barges, tossed by seven-feet-high waves, waiting for the order to storm the beaches of Omaha and Utah.

If nothing were done to destroy the German cannons and defense batteries, all these soldiers would be slaughtered without the slightest chance to survive. It would eventually compromise the whole operation *Overlord.*

---

[84] Source : https://en.wikipedia.org/wiki/Omaha_Beach

In the LST, no one was sleeping any longer. On the deck, the men waiting to disembark were soaked with sea spray and sweat. The smell of fear was mingling with the stench of vomit. Many guys, heads lowered, were mumbling prayers. Corporal Firmin Bellegarde, private first class Edward Washington and Private James Stevenson, gathered around the winch of their balloon, were now fully awake. Like all the others, they were scared to death. They were aware of the damages a bombshell dropped on their LST would cause. Even though they knew that they were still out of reach of the German artillery.

However, this detail seemed to have escaped the shrewdness of a little group of infantry men, who were staring insistently at the trio. A few hours earlier, they had already threatened to cut the balloon steel cable.

"Hey, Corp., what do we do if they jump on us?" Jimmy worried.

"Nothing, of course," Firmin replied. "For the moment, stay close to the winch, at all time! And if they come too close, yell as loud as you can to draw one of their officer's attention, which'll force him to intervene."

Corporal Bellegarde ordered them to never part with their rifle, and constantly keep an eye on these men, hoping that it would suffice to stop them from carrying out their threat.

Suddenly, at 05:50, the eagerly expected naval bombing commenced with the heavy fire of USS *Texas*, USS *Satterlee* and H.M.S. *Talybont*[85] towards Pointe du Hoc.

---

[85] HMS (His/Her Majesty's Ship): prefix of the British Royal Navy ships.

Taking advantage of the confusion, the little group of foot soldiers rushed to the winch. Caught off guard, the three crew mates of the 320th VLA could hardly protest before their balloon was only held by one strand of its steel wire rope. The guys must have found a pair of strong cutting pliers. There wasn't anything more they could do. Corporal Bellegarde made a sign to his crew members asking them to let the infantry men finish freeing their balloon. It soon went off high in the sky, and was carried away by the wind. The balloon eventually disappeared among the clouds.

An officer finally interfered. Luckily, one of the foot soldiers still was holding his pair of cutting pliers in his hands. Otherwise, Firmin could have been charged with deliberate sabotage, in order to escape his duty to land on the beach. Such an offense would have earned him to face a court martial.

The leader justified his action by screaming he had "no intention to let Negroes turn them into a target of the German artillery."

Aware of what was at stake, the officer just ordered everyone to return to his post and get ready to embark at any time on the landing crafts.

At 05:55, all the heads tilted upward to the sky. Most of the soldiers recognized the very specific hum of the Liberators. The B-24 bombers. The cloud cover prevented from seeing them. Still, judging from the intense noise they made, Firmin reckoned there must have been hundreds of them. It left no doubt in the minds of all the foot soldiers of the 1st and 29th U.S. Infantry divisions that their planes would drop a carpet of bombs on the German defenses. At least, they hoped so.

Five minutes later, the fire of the Navy focused on Omaha beach, at the foot of the hill, which was slowly appearing in Firmin's eyes, as the day was dawning. The corporal gazed at his wristwatch. A model A-11 which he had received, like every soldier, during his short stay at Camp Shanks. 6:05. Twenty-five minutes before H-hour, the general headquarters had finally decided to use drastic measures to annihilate the German defense batteries.

All the U.S. warships together sent a deluge of bombshells on the French coast. Among them was the USS *Texas* on the west flank. A battleship armed with ten 14″/45 caliber guns, six 5″/51 caliber guns and ten 3″/50 A4 caliber guns. On the east side was the battleship USS *Arkansas*, which was intensely shelling Longues-sur-Mer. Three cruisers and twelve destroyers were completing the Omaha naval forces.

"No German can possibly get through this," the infantry men might have thought with relief at this moment, while waiting for the order to get into the LCVPs.

Meanwhile, Duplex Drive Sherman tanks and 105 Howitzer motor carriage M7 Priest, loaded on the LCTs of the first assault wave, joined the naval artillery to bomb German defensive positions. Unfortunately, the pitch and roll made their shooting quite inaccurate.

But soon, the Sherman DD amphibious tanks of the 741st Tank battalion would be released in the sea with their float screens lifted. They had been conceived by engineers to safely reach the sand beaches and offer the foot soldiers an efficient protection.

The intense shelling session aimed at destroying every pocket of resistance on the coast. Within five minutes, the bombers of the 8th Air Force dropped thirteen thousand bombs. But the noise made by their explosion was reduced by the distance still separating Corporal Bellegarde's LST from Omaha beach.

Now, shells were fired from the flanks and from the back of the American fleet. Instead of shooting series of salvos, the battleships were shooting volleys of simultaneous salvos. The recoil was then such that the ship was displaced by several yards every time. The racket was deafening. The men aboard the LST could possibly protect their ears by pressing their hands onto their auricles. But there was not much they could do against the air pressure generated by thousands of explosions, which compressed their chests and lungs.

Like many other soldiers, Corporal Bellegarde and his crew mates were seeking some relief by staying huddled on the deck, their palms pressed against their ears, waiting until the flood of fire would stop. Some, however, lost control. Sometimes, they remained prostrate, with wide-open eyes, looking like zombies. Others were seized with an uncontrollable panic, shrieking with hysteria. A soldier with a teenager's face even tried to jump overboard. He was caught up *in extremis* by his staff sergeant.

The chaos went on for almost half an hour. It would only stop at 06:30. The exact time scheduled for the invasion.

Due to the smoke screens spread by U.S. destroyers to hide the armada, and the smoke resulting from the bomb explosions, the soldiers still aboard the ships couldn't see what was going on on the beaches.

Still deafened by the violent blasts, Firmin pricked up his ears, trying to perceive the signal of the takeover of the beach by the first assault wave.

The tumult of the cannon fires had left room to a deep and calming silence. Almost reassuring.

However, the break would only last a few minutes.

Sharp snaps were heard in the distance. At first, everybody hoped that they were just a few gun bursts shot by an isolated German sniper. The hope was quickly shattered by the acceleration of the shooting rhythm.

On the upper deck, the captain of the LST and his second in command endeavored to understand what was happening. They scrutinized the beach with their binoculars. But they were more than one and a half miles away. They couldn't distinguish much of it, besides dark points on the surface of the water and light dots on the ridge line.

They first thought of some MG 42 German machine guns which could have escaped from the intense Allied bombing. Weapons capable of causing serious damage because of their firing power and their strategic position overhanging the beach.

Suddenly, much stronger explosions sounded. The officers and the veterans of the African and Sicily campaigns immediately identified the dreadful 8.8 cm and 10.5 cm Flak.

The tracer bullets of the MG 42s were now drawing two red dotted lines departing from the upper east and west extremities of the hill and sweeping the sand and the surface of the water.

The Germans had waited until the very last moment to open fire on the poor fighters of the first assault wave. The coxswains of the landing crafts had lowered the ramps far from the beach to make their return trips to their landing ships easier and faster. The purpose was to increase the number of rotations with additional troops.

After they had jumped into a knee-deep water, the guys still had to run two thousand feet in the open before they could reach the beach. It was this precise moment of extreme vulnerability that the German gunners had chosen to open fire.

The bloodbath had begun.

With an effective firing range of forty-eight thousand feet with the 8.8 cm Flak, and fifty-seven thousand feet with the 10.5 cm Flak, the German resistance was about to slaughter the assault units of the 16th and 116th RCTs[86] and of the 2nd and 5th Ranger battalions.

Fearing they may be hit by a bomb shell, some coxswains released the soldiers so far from the shore that they couldn't touch the bottom with their feet. The poor guys were so overloaded that they would sink and drown.

Very soon, all the soldiers of the first wave were killed. Besides a few men who found themselves nailed down to the ground behind a beach obstacle. A steel Czech hedgehog or a reinforced concrete tetrahedron.

Terrified by the awful vision of their comrades' bodies floating on the surface like corks, the men of the second wave were forced to storm the beach. Their only chance to survive was to reach a mound of pebbles or sand dunes, where they would be sheltered from direct shots of MG 42s. But they still had to run through a two hundred yards shelf before they could reach the foot of the nearly one hundred and seventy yards high cliffs.

It was out of the question to turn back. The coxswains

---

[86] Regimental Combat Team.

had been ordered not to bring back anyone. The soldiers couldn't even count on the support of the amphibious tanks, since they had been disembarked far from the beach, where seven-feet-high waves had overwhelmed their watertight flotation screens.

Twenty-seven out of thirty-two Sherman DD tanks of the 16th RCT, 1st ID, on the east side had been drowned. All those of the 116th RCT, 29th ID, on the west flank had reached their target, because the captains of their LCTs had decided to disembark the tanks directly on the beach.

With intervals of fifteen minutes, the third and fourth waves followed.

As they approached the shoreline, the barges were strafed by the heavy fire of German machine guns. As smoke and fog reduced their visibility, the coxswains would lose their landmarks, which, added to the current, eventually made them reach the beach east of their initial target.

Several landing crafts filled with soldiers were hit and sunk before they could reach the solid ground.

Meanwhile, the tide was rising. Log ramps planted in the sand and topped with one or more mines went overwhelmed by the surf. Several barges were blown up by some of these formidable anti invasion defense devices. The tide flow was growing stronger. The waves sometimes managed to capsize an LCA or LCVP with thirty men aboard.

The crews of the landing crafts were constantly bailing out the water which would come in from all sides, because of the swell and the geysers resulting from the explosion of bombshells and mines.

Lacking the support of the Sherman DD tanks, the rare

soldiers who made it to the beach had only a few Browning automatic rifles to oppose the German machine guns. The FM Bar M 1918 A2[87] had a fire rate of over three hundred and fifty rounds per minute, but its effective firing range was less than forty-five hundred feet. Moreover, they were fed with a 20-round detachable box magazine.

The assault troops could still count on a few M2 mortars, firing three pound shells with fifty-nine-hundred-foot range, at a rate of eighteen rounds per minute. They were soon short of ammunition, for lack of supply.

Meanwhile, the naval artillery continued to aim beyond the beach, intending to spare their soldiers' lives. But, doing so, they had hardly any chance to hit enemies' positions.

The landing crafts which had escaped the intense fire were keeping on doing round trips, each time unloading men, but also ammunition, weapons, blood bags and food rations.

Soon after 11:00, came the turn of Firmin's LST to send its soldiers to the assault of the beach. The captain ordered the men to descend to the LCVPs and LCMs and join the landing crafts returning empty from the beach. Their crew members just barked out injunctions to get in, but you could figure out from their frightened gaze the tragedy which was unfolding there.

The soldiers approached the railing. Some of them would hug before joining different groups. They had spent several days on this ship. Chatting together and sharing

_____

[87] https://en.wikipedia.org/wiki/M1918_Browning_Automatic_Rifle

common memories, exchanging pictures of their families and relatives. Some may have promised, like Firmin and Edward had, to contact their respective families, would the other die on the French soil. Others would cross themselves while reciting, "Our Father."

Then, the soldiers began to climb down the rope ladders and jump on board *Higgins boats.* They were so scared that some got their feet blocked in the mesh of the net. The sea was raging. A man fell in the water between the flanks of the LST and of an LCVP. As several fellow soldiers were helping him to climb on board, a more powerful wave projected the landing craft against the LST's hull. The poor soldier's head was crushed in the middle like a walnut.

Another one, unbalanced by the weight of his material, fell heavily head first and was knocked out.

Firmin and his crew mates were gazing, powerless, at these young soldiers obeying the orders of their superiors, in a daze. They looked like farm animals on their way to the slaughterhouse. Except that they were human beings, fully conscious of what was waiting for them.

"God bless you!" the lieutenant would say to each soldier.

The crews of the landing crafts never stopped screaming at them. "Stay crouched if you want to keep your head on your shoulders until you reach the beach."

The three men of the 320th VLA wondered when they would be ordered to follow the others. They didn't belong to an assault unit, but they had lost their balloon. Hence, their presence on the LST was now unnecessary.

Like all the others, they were ready. With their full equipment. Heavy helmet on the head and life vest around the chest. Garand M1 rifle in one hand, protected by a watertight plastic cover. A backpack filled with a new model of gas mask, bandage and wound dressing, a campaign lunch box, several combat food rations, not to mention two hundred cartridges. Their entrenching tools hung outside their bags.

Firmin Bellegarde also had his personal haversack, in which he kept his diary inside a watertight bag, like an invaluable treasure.

An ultimate group of men was descending the rope ladder. When he realized there was some extra space left to fill the barge, the lieutenant turned his head towards the balloon team.

"Hey, you! You don't have your balloon anymore, do you?"

Corporal Bellegarde stood at attention. The two others did the same.

"Sir. Yes, sir!"

"Ready to show what you've gotten in your pants?"

It was not planned that the men of the 320th VLA would take part in the fight. They were supposed to stay on board the LST until the site was under full control, before they would bring their balloon on the solid ground to secure the beach. But, because of a few excited soldiers, they had lost theirs.

Now, this white lieutenant was challenging them. How could they shirk the challenge? By defying them like this, he was also offering them an opportunity to prove their courage.

Corporal Bellegarde looked at each of his partners. Both remained silent, but he felt from their determined gaze they were not opposed to go and fight.

"Sir. Yes, sir!" Firmin shouted. "We're ready!"
Then, the corporal made a perfect military salute.
"Well. What are you waiting for? Get on board!"
Lieutenant McLaughling was the last one to embark.

CHAPTER 43

Nestled at the rear of the LCVP, near his crew mates, Firmin Bellegarde thought of his mother. He was squeezing his *gris-gris* in one hand. With the other, he was tightly clenching the structure of the boat, manufactured in Andrew Higgins factory, where his mother used to work. He could almost feel her reassuring and protective presence. He convinced himself that nothing wrong could happen to him.

But no other soldiers aboard shared his confidence. Water never stopped entering the boat and everybody was requested to bail it out with his helmet. At least, those who managed to resist seasickness. The soldiers were wading in the sea water covered with traces of partially digested meals. It smelled of a foul stench which mingled with the odor of exhaust gas.

Some men cursed this damn Higgins who had built these allegedly unsinkable barges, which offered moreover an illusory protection. Indeed, besides the bullet-proof steel bow ramp in the front, the sides of the boat were made of plywood covered with metal gray paint, which MG 42 bullets could easily pierce.

The coxswain, standing behind the steering wheel, was the most exposed man. He had to constantly monitor the obstacles cutting his way to the beach, while surfing on the waves to prevent the boat from capsizing and sinking.

In the fury of the cross fire of German machine guns and U.S. naval artillery, Firmin could hear the moaning and calls for help from soldiers who had been ejected from their boat. A strong current was inexorably carrying them off, further to the east. Corporal Bellegarde took a quick look overboard. Among inanimate bodies kept afloat by their life vests, several soldiers were begging around to be rescued, while desperately clinging to floating debris.

A speedboat was zigzagging between the barges. On its board, an officer, shouting through a loudspeaker, reminded the crews of the Higgins boats of the outright ban to rescue any castaway. This was the mission of the rescue teams. The job of the landing crafts was to bring to the beach as many soldiers and refueling as possible. The key objective of Operation Neptune was to push back the Germans and take the beaches. Whatever the cost. Which meant overcoming one's compassion for the wounded.

A mortar shell landed about thirty feet on starboard. Its explosion lifted a geyser of water and scum, which almost overwhelmed the barge. Another one ended its trajectory on the port side, under the bow of an LCT, carrying a Sherman M4 *tankdozer*[88], and twenty soldiers. The barge and its crew, the tank and the twenty soldiers were blown up in the air. The next second, they fell back in a deafening crash, among screams of terror of the distraught and powerless witnesses of their last instants of life.

Coming closer to the beach, Firmin's crew discovered an awful scene of desolation. Dozens of wreckages of amphibious tanks and barges beaten by the swell. Backpacks, food ration boxes, medical care and ammunition crates drifting along with the current and the rising tide. And horror of horrors, pieces of human bodies, dismembered corpses, beheaded trunks. Dead soldiers

---

[88] Tank equipped with a bulldozer blade. It was used to sweep a track in the sand or in the dunes, while uncovering buried mines.

bathing in a water reddened by their own blood.

The sea now covered all the beach obstacles topped with mines, forcing the crews to unload their cargoes in even deeper and stormier water.

While the MG 42 bullets were keeping on whistling and tracing furrows of foam when penetrating the waves, the coxswain announced with a hoarse and powerful voice that he was about to lower the bow ramp.

He brought the LCVP as close as possible behind the wreckage of a Sherman *Donald Duck*[89], of which only the top of its flotation screen still emerged from the water.

Suddenly, the ramp went down. No time left to hesitate. The coxswain started screaming.

"Go, go, go! Hurry up!"

With his automatic pistol in hand, Lieutenant McLaughlin literally pushed the soldiers out of the boat.

"C'mon! Move your asses and run to the beach as fast as you can! The surest way to get killed today is to stay here in the middle of the water!"

When the turn of the three balloon operators came, McLaughlin addressed to Corporal Bellegarde.

"It's time for you to distinguish yourselves! Now or never!"

Terrified and yet decided to stay alive, Firmin, Ed and Jimmy rushed towards the ramp. They ran like bats out of hell and jumped into the water behind the Sherman tank, shouting at the top of their lungs.

By expressing their fear of dying without restraint, they were completely out of breath, when their heads disappeared under the water level. Surprised by the depth,

---

[89] Nickname given to the amphibious Sherman M4 Dual Drive tanks.

almost suffocating, Firmin started to panic, when he felt the sandy bottom under his feet. He looked above him. The water was riled by the stir of the waves and the current. Yet, he could still see the cloudy sky and the V-shaped hull of the LCVP. However, it prevented him from seeing his two crew mates.

Gathering his ultimate strength, he stretched his legs like two powerful springs, hoping to come up to the surface before his lungs would implode.

As he was about to finally take a deep breath of air, Firmin saw a silhouette falling from the ramp. The body sank into the waves, just a few inches off his face. Water entered his mouth as he was inhaling. In a survival reflex, his brain blocked the way to his lungs, redirecting the water to his stomach. Still, the few drops which had reached his trachea triggered a terrible cough and a deep panic attack. At this moment, Firmin thought he was living his last seconds.

With desperate movements, he tried to take off his backpack not to sink again. But it was stuck by the strap of his rifle. The words of the staff sergeant still sounded in his head.

"There are three things which you should never part with: your helmet, your rifle and your trench shovel!"

He started screaming for help, hoping that a speed boat would come and pick him up. Yet, he knew how useless it was. He had seen so many white men, tossed like corks, and whom no one came to rescue. So, who would care about a Negro?

His life vest could just enough keep his mouth above the water, but the waves threatened to swallow him at any moment. And there was this corpse drifting in his direction, with wide-stretched arms. Firmin tried to push it back, like one would ward off evil spirits. The body flipped over on its back. Firmin recognized Lieutenant McLaughlin. Shrapnel had dug a large open wound in his chest, leaving his determined face intact.

After he had swallowed a glassful of salt water, Corporal Bellegarde heard someone shouting in his back. It was Ed's voice.

"Hey, Corp.? You awright?"

Swimming like a dog, Firmin managed to turn round towards his partner.

"Ed! Thank God, you're alive! Where's Jimmy? Seen him?"

"He was forced to get rid of his backpack not to drown. Told'm to follow the others to the beach and mind his ass."

Ed extended his arm towards Firmin.

"Cling to me, Corp.! I'm gonna draw you until you can walk on the bottom."

The first yards turned out to be quite complicated. The corporal was moving his legs vertically to avoid sinking, while Ed was doing breaststroke. Their legs would constantly hit one another.

"Ain't there frogs in Louisiana?" Edward asked.

"Sure, we've got frogs, there!" Firmin replied.

"Have you seen the way they swim? Folding their legs, then stretching them out in a V-shape, and finally squeezing them together again?"

"Of course, I have! I've even caught plenty of them!"

"Well, then. Swim like a frog now! Otherwise, we'll never reach the beach!"

"Sir, yes, sir, private first class Washington!"

Ed noticed another wreckage emerging a hundred feet ahead of him.

"Hold on, Corp., and you'll get a few minutes' rest to recover a bit. But, please don't stop swimming like a frog, until I tell you!"

"Hot damn! I'm freezing!" Firmin moaned. "Don't you?"

"Shut up, Corp., and do like me! Keep on swimming. It'll warm you up!"

They progressed like this during almost one hour, carefully, wreckage after wreckage, then hiding behind every tetrahedron, every Czech hedgehog they found on their way. Then, they ran a frantic race in zigzags on the wet sand, while striving to step in previous footprints to avoid stamping on a mine. The two fellow soldiers eventually reached a shelter behind a mound of pebbles, in the east part of the beach.

About thirty guys were there, waiting for the right moment to run further across the shelf, towards the hill. They seemed completely lost. Some of them belonged to the 1st ID, others to the 29th ID, all from different units. The 16th and 116th RCT, artillery battalions, combat engineer battalions in charge of the beach obstacles demolition.

Seeing the three colored soldiers coming, one of the men gazed at them insistently. It was a white guy with a kid's face. Hardly older than Firmin. His cheeks were spotted with freckles, and his hair was the color of fire.

"You're from the 320th VLA, aren't you?"

Firmin nodded approvingly.

"Welcome to hell, guys!"

At first, Firmin and Ed didn't know how to take his

invitation. The ginger boy noticed on their faces a mingle of mistrust and astonishment.

"One of your colleagues saved my life, about half an hour ago! And not only mine, as far as I could understand. He's a medic. Corporal Woodson. You know him?"

"Waverly Woodson[90]?"

"Exactly!" the young soldier confirmed.

"I must have dealt with him once or twice in the infirmary. Besides this, we scarcely mix with headquarters' people."

"He's quite a nice fellow, anyway. Trust me. He's been seriously injured by a piece of shrapnel that cut opened his inner thigh. But he continued to help all those he could. He's risked his life to save several guys from drowning. And he's even set up a medical station!" the red-haired soldier added, pointing his hand to the east.

Firmin turned on his left and saw a little tent protected from German fire by a rocky embankment. Several guys near it were busy bringing wounded soldiers under cover. Medics had been warned that their red cross wouldn't protect them from enemy shots. German snipers, indeed, deliberately spotted them to stop them from rescuing their wounded comrades. This was meant to discourage the fighters from assaulting German defense lines. The Nazis were renowned to trample shamelessly international war conventions. Therefore, the tent had no red cross on it.

Among the men crouched near the tent, Firmin recognized Corporal Woodson and two other guys of his

---

[90] Corporal Waverly Woodson proved his courage and dedication as of the early hours of the invasion of Omaha Beach on June 6, 1944.
Read Linda Hervieux book, "Forgotten"
http://www.lindahervieux.com/the-320th-blog/2015/9/3/waverly-b-woodson-jr

unit. It reminded him of Jimmy. In the heat of the moment, he had almost forgotten his crew mate. He then thought something serious had happened to him. He started scanning the beach around. It was littered with dead and wounded men. Firmin turned round again to the young ginger.

"Seen anyone else from the 320th VLA?"

"No. Sorry. Don't even know myself where's my own unit. All my section got killed or wounded.

"Me, I lost my second crew mate after we jumped off the LCVP. He," Firmin added showing his buddy, "he's my first crew mate. Private first class Edward Washington. He saved my life! Would've drowned without him."

Forgetting the danger, Corporal Bellegarde was about to run towards the tent. Maybe Woodson knew where Jimmy was.

The soldier grabbed his backpack and violently jerked him down to the ground.

"Are you crazy?" he asked curtly.

At the same time, several bullets ricochetted behind them. Firmin realized he had had a brush with death. He looked at the red-haired soldier.

"Believe I owe you my life, too!"

The guy grinned, without a word.

"Corporal Bellegarde," Firmin added.

"Nice to meet you. I'm Corporal Connelly, 16th RCT."

"Hail from Ireland, I guess," Firmin suggested.

"Hard to deny, with such a name! Let alone the color of my hair."

"We're betrayed by the color of our skin," Firmin added in a joking tone.

Connelly seemed a bit embarrassed. He probably

thought he had lacked tact.

"This is your baptism of fire, right?" he asked, to switch to another issue.

"Correct," Firmin confirmed. "What about you?"

"I was in Sicily with General Bradley last August."

"How was it?"

Connelly hesitated a while.

"'twas hard … but less than today."

"What are we supposed to do now?" Firmin worried. "Shall we wait for the reinforcement to come?"

"No dice!" the Irish replied. "We'd be hit by a mortar shell, sooner or later."

Connelly dared a quick glance beyond the mound to evaluate their situation.

"Do you know how to use it?" he asked, looking at their Garand M1 rifles still protected in their waterproof bags.

"I was quite good at shooting training," Edward said proudly. "Ain't it true, Corp.?"

"Sure!" Bellegarde confirmed.

"Alright, then!" Connelly approved. "In this case, get 'em out of their bags and make sure no sand got into the barrel. And don't forget to fix your knife to it!"

"Firmin and Ed obeyed in full confidence. This white guy seemed to be a good fellow.

"Ready?" he asked, after they had finished.

They both confirmed with a hand sign. The Irish gazed a last time at the hill.

"At my top, you get up behind me and you rush to the next crater two hundred feet ahead, at one o'clock. And make sure you walk in my steps. The place is riddled with mines. OK?"

"Yes!" Bellegarde replied, after exchanging a quick glance with Ed to check that he had properly understood Connelly's instructions.

"Now!" the Irish yelled, jumping on his feet. "Run, run, run! As fast as you can!"

Both crew mates of the 320th VLA rushed behind the Irish and ran in his steps, so fast that Firmin hardly felt the ground under his feet. When they reached the edge of the crater, the three men realized that it was already occupied by two soldiers who shouted at them to get the hell away and find another shelter. But the Irish didn't care and jumped in, imitated by Firmin and Ed.

"Scram! Get outta here, you niggers!" yelled the stockier of the two soldiers, pointing his rifle at Firmin. The guy had an accent that both friends of the 320th VLA immediately identified. The accent of Tennessee's white bumpkins, they happened to hear during their stay in Camp Tyson. His face was sun tanned and his mitts looked so powerful that they could have mashed the butt of his rifle.

"I've never let a nigger piss me off... So, I'll never let it happen here!"

Firmin saw Edward clenching his fists and gritting his teeth. He was very close to flip his wig. And it was exactly what the white redneck was expecting, to offer him a good reason to shoot a Negro. Firmin grabbed Ed's arm and drew him backwards.

The Tennessean didn't stop gazing at Edward with a provocative look.

"Just try, nigger, and I'll rub you out like a coon! See what I mean?"

Corporal Connelly tried to blow off some steam. But he

couldn't measure up with the two big brutes. Moreover, the second guy had a higher rank than his.

"All right, guys. In less than five minutes, we'll be gone… The three of us!"

The stocky man smiled widely, revealing his teeth browned by a regular tobacco chewing.

"Hey, ginger. Are you one of those Yankee nigger's cock suckers?"

The Irish was seething with rage. His blood soon flowed up to his ears, turning his face as red as his hair.

Corporal Bellegarde feared the Irish would soon jump on the Southerner, his rifle pointed at him, and stab him with his knife.

The situation was almost getting out of hand. Firmin knew exactly where it would end for Ed and him: in a court-martial.

He carefully rose a bit and took a quick look at the hill overlooking the beach. Many foot soldiers had managed to get up there and were pushing the Germans backwards. Most of the German machine guns positioned on the heights and which had knocked down so many American soldiers since dawn had been silenced for ever.

More explosions were now caused by mine clearing personnel and demolition engineers than by German cannons.

The reinforcements of the 15th and 118th RCT would soon open a first breach on the east side. New supplies of soldiers and material continued to flock from LSIs and LSTs which had come close to the shore. Other operators of the 320th VLA would soon land on the beach with their balloons.

Firmin saw a little group of infantry men passing

nearby, walking towards the top of the hill. He made a sign to Edward, asking him to stand ready. Then, he gave a tap on Connelly's shoulder.

"Thanks for your advice, Corp. We're gonna dig our hole somewhere else."

Bellegarde and Washington left the crater and followed some other soldiers, carefully walking in their foot prints. When they finally made it to a less exposed area with a loose soil, Firmin fell on his knees and said:

"Let's call it a day! I suggest we stay here and dig our foxholes while waiting for the others to come."

"Okey-doke, Corp.!" Edward agreed, letting himself fall on his back.

Firmin took off his backpack. He then took his trench shovel out and unfolded it. He advised Ed to do the same. "It'd be too dumb to be hit now by a bullet or shrapnel."

While they were both vigorously digging the sandy ground, Corporal Connelly joined them.

"Would you accept an Irish ginger near you? I got sick of the two country bumpkins!"

Ed looked at him, without stopping shoveling the sand.

"As long as you don't ask us to dig your foxhole…"

Half an hour later, everyone was properly sheltered. They would finally be able to rest a bit and recover some strength. As they still had their respective backpacks, they could find something to eat, out of their daily K-ration safely packed in wax paper.

Never before, had they appreciated so much their canned food diet. Corporal Connelly advised his two new buddies to quickly take off their wet clothes and let them dry in the wind before the end of the day. "Otherwise, you'll be in big trouble during the following night. And don't forget to proceed to a complete cleaning and lubricating of your rifles, using the kit integrated in the butt."

After he had completed these priority tasks, Firmin unconsciously grabbed his good luck charm hanging from his dog tag necklace. He then realized that since he had jumped out of the LCVP he hadn't thought a second of his parent's, neither of Ethel. A rush of adrenaline ran down his spine. Panicked, he turned to the left, then to the right. His tension went down a bit when he saw his haversack lain on his backpack on the bottom of the foxhole.

He anxiously grasped the canvas bag and opened it to check its precious content. He felt immediately relieved when he saw his two watertight bags inside. He made sure they hadn't become leaky, due to his forced immersion in the morning. Luckily, the bags had done their job well. Everything inside was dry. His diary. The letters from his mother and from Ethel. And his harmonica, in which he gently blew the first notes of a gospel.

Firmin thought for a few seconds that he would write a few lines in his diary. He finally changed his mind. This day was far from being over. And the danger was close by, and constant. He would rather wait until the end of the afternoon. So, he carefully repacked his treasure and put it back into his haversack. But this time, he wouldn't leave it unattended anymore. He was afraid of losing it in a sudden withdrawal if the Germans came back with reinforcement units. He wrapped the strap of the bag around his neck and began a conversation with Ed, who was lying in a foxhole next to his.

When he wanted to check on his wristwatch what time it was, Firmin noticed that the inner side of the watch face was covered with condensation. He pressed the watch against his left ear. He heard the regular ticking of its mechanism. He felt reassured. However, he asked his two neighbors to confirm him what time they had. It was between 14:54 and 14:57.

CHAPTER 44

The last German soldiers had left the heights. Sounds of gunfire exchanges seemed to come from farther, beyond the hill. LCVPs and LCMs could now deliver their cargoes safely, without being targeted by the German artillery. The tide was slowly going out. In about three hours, LSTs and LSIs would be able to beach without getting damaged by trapped obstacles.

Corporal Bellegarde asked Ed to watch over their foxholes carefully, while he would return to the beach and try to find Jimmy and other guys of their battalion. He put on his jacket, still slightly wet, and grabbed his rifle and his haversack. He just left his backpack under Ed's custody.

As he was walking down towards the sea, Firmin discovered the extent of the human disaster which had taken place here since 6:30 in the morning. The withdrawing tide had regurgitated the corpses of hundreds of American soldiers, stopped by sandbanks and surfacing limestone concretions, or trapped in the wreckages of tanks, trucks and landing crafts, all sunk during the assault.

On the two-hundred-yard shelf separating the fifteen feet high seawall and the hill, corpses covered by white sheets were aligned, side by side. Other dead would be brought and placed on the ground with great care, next to each other, soon forming a second, and later a third row.

Sometimes, the shoes of the dead remained uncovered

by its shroud. On the side of one of them, it was a hand which could be seen. A white hand.

Firmin was struck by a sudden and violent anxiety attack. "Was Jimmy's corpse lying under one of these sheets? If so, was he mixed among Whites? Did the army apply the same racial segregation rules to those who died for the country?"

Firmin heard a loud voice calling him.

"Hey, you!"

The corporal turned back and saw a lieutenant of the 606th *Quartermaster Graves Registration Company*.

"What's your unit?"

"Sir, 320th VLA, sir!"

"What the hell are you doing here? I can't see any balloon over the beach."

Firmin explained to him what had occurred to his balloon and that he was searching his second crew member.

"Forget about him, boy! Either he's dead and you can't help'm anymore, or he's injured and the medics'll take care of'm. Anyhow, without a balloon, you'll be more useful when helping us carry our poor fellow soldiers over here."

Corporal Bellegarde gazed around him, desperately searching an officer of the 320th VLA who could spare him to be confronted to death so directly, in its most gruesome ways and appearances. Although, on this day and until further order, the balloon crews were independent units, left on their own, they were, however, at the disposal of the 1st ID, under the command of Major General Clarence R. Huebner.

Firmin couldn't challenge the orders of this lieutenant.

The officer summoned one of his men over, who ran to them with a stretcher. He must have been in his late thirties.

The number of soldiers killed in action that day was so high that the service men of the GRCs were overworked.

The stretcher bearer flashed Firmin a smile.

"You do what I tell you, and everything's gonna be all right!" the man said, curtly.

He then recovered his emotionless gaze. Firmin couldn't tell what the man felt, deep in his soul, watching all these lifeless soldiers lying on that beach. Did he see what Firmin was seeing? Broken puppets, frozen in unimaginable poses, most often touching, sometimes yet farcical? Corpses so horribly mutilated that they didn't look human anymore!

Corporal Bellegarde had to turn his eyes away when the service man seemed to remain indifferent. But he wasn't. He had been trained for this job which consisted in preserving the dignity of every man who died for his country. Offering each a temporary burial, near the place of his death, and safe from any desecration. Then make a record of the accurate location of the grave, so that his family will be able to decide if the remains of their beloved one should return to his home town or be buried in a local definitive memorial.

The man of the 606th QGRC was directing the operations with firmness. He still showed tact with Firmin. He would spot the less damaged corpses, if possible complete, and ask Firmin to help him pick them up and lay them on the stretcher. He would spare Firmin to be too close to the dead's face, by letting him carry the foot end of the stretcher. But sometimes one of the legs would have a compound fracture, from which a broken bone surrounded by shreds of flesh emerged. When he lifted the body, Firmin would feel in his hand the crack of the broken bone.

"Don't worry. Won't do him any harm, now!" the man would say. But it didn't help. Everything he saw or heard turned his stomach. He had to make continuous efforts not the drop the corpse and turn round to spew his guts out.

The two men were passing to-and-fro among soldiers who seemed to ignore their fallen comrades.

Wounded were sitting side by side, warmly bundled up in a blanket, with their backs leaning against the sand seawall. Some had their face or hands covered with a bandage stained with dried blood. Others had an arm in a sling, or a leg immobilized by a splint. Some would smoke a cigarette, while gazing at the sea covered with ships, unloading a continuous flow of fresh troops. Others would talk with their neighbors about their next medical repatriation. In Great Britain first, to be treated, then possibly sent back home.

Not far from them, a group of able-bodied soldiers were enjoying a smoke break. Just a few yards away, a man was lying on his stomach, his face bathing in a blood-reddened puddle, at the foot of a beach obstacle. An illusory shelter which had turned into a deadly trap.

Corporal Bellegarde was seized by a growing discomfort, as he was putting some distance between this vision of horror and him. Moreover, he felt somehow guilty of still being alive, safe and sound, while hundreds of others had been killed or definitively crippled, because their fate was to be on the front line. However, he intuitively understood why the survivors kept on living in such an apparent unconcern. Letting themselves be overwhelmed by their emotion would have been the best way to make the sacrifice of hundreds of these braves useless. Probably thousands.

"We will accept nothing less than full victory!" Ike said in his speech to all the soldiers involved in operation Neptune. The 12th U.S. Army group was still far from its final target: Berlin.

Until then, time would exclusively be devoted to the fight. Only after full victory would come the time for the commemoration and the remembrance.

After he had brought a ninth corpse to the temporary gathering zone, Firmin noticed a colored soldier who was strolling along the dune. Despite the blanket covering the man's shoulders and hiding his outfit, Corporal Bellegarde still recognized Jimmy's gait. Thus, he stopped, unexpectedly, causing a jerk to the stretcher.

"Hey! What's goin' on behind? We're not finished, yet!" the front bearer grumbled.

"I believe I found my second crew mate," Firmin replied. "Gimme two seconds to check it!"

Firmin screamed at the man afar.

"Jimmy? It's me, Corporal Bellegarde!"

The man froze.

"Corporal Bellegarde?"

Jimmy started walking faster to come closer.

"Hot damn! I really thought you'd been killed!" Jimmy shouted, gazing at his superior as if he were a ghost.

"So did I!" Firmin replied, smiling broadly.

Hadn't he been carrying a stretcher, Firmin would have embraced him. Suddenly, Jimmy's smile turned into a grin of anxiety.

"Ed?"

"He's doin' fine! Perfectly well!" Firmin shouted.

Both teammates burst out laughing, relieving their nervous tension.

"Give it a rest! Stop this outpouring now!" the man of the 606th QGRC grumbled. "We still got a lotta work to do!"

Firmin explained to Jimmy where to find Edward and ordered him to join him immediately and stay there until he returns.

He then continued his temporary mission for one more hour, and returned to his foxhole. It was past 18:00 when the three balloon operators were together again.

Two exits had been opened by the assault troops. E1 in *Easy Red* sector leading to Saint-Laurent-sur-Mer, and E3 leading to Colleville, east of *Fox Green*. A few tanks of the 741st Tank battalion had made it to the top of the hill. It was now a continuous flow of men and equipment which could safely climb to the ridge line overhanging Omaha beach.

Their mission was to secure their beachhead and achieve a connection with the British landed on the east side at Gold beach. On the west side, the beachhead should extend to the U.S. troops landed on Utah beach, and the paratroopers of the 82nd and 101st Airborne who had jumped over the Cotentin Peninsula in the previous night.

The mission of the crews of the 320th VLA consisted in placing as many balloons as possible over the beach and the hill to protect the landing sites of Omaha and Utah from potential air strikes of the *Luftwaffe*.

Therefore, the main concern of Corporal Bellegarde

now was to quickly get a replacement balloon. However, he was aware that he would need to wait for the arrival of supply ships which would succeed one another, during the following days, each of them surmounted by an inflated balloon. As they still lacked mobile hydrogen production units, the teams of the headquarters' battery, still stationed in Weymouth, would keep on inflating the balloons in the UK, prior to their crossing of the channel.

Nevertheless, Corporal Bellegarde wanted to inform an officer of the battery A where his crew was on the beach.

He soon recognized Lieutenant Colonel Reed walking on the beach together with two officers of the 320th VLA, in the search for his crews. Reed was relieved when Firmin informed him his crew was complete and in good shape. Ed and Jimmy joined Firmin to salute their commandant.

"Glad to hear you're safe and sound, soldiers!" Reed said. "I'm aware that the last hours have been quite challenging for each of you. Still, this day isn't over. We haven't yet fulfilled our mission. That is, flying as many balloons as possible along the ridge line before the end of this historic day. Therefore, I count on everyone's devotion and patriotism to achieve this goal. And hence, prove all our fellow soldiers that we didn't come here to play a minor role.

"Sir, yes, sir!" Corporal Bellegarde shouted giving his commandant a perfect military salute.

While Reed was continuing his research for men of his battalion, one of the two officers near him took note of the location of corporal Bellegarde's crew. Firmin asked him if the battalion had suffered casualties. The officer dodged the matter.

"Return to your position and wait until we give you further instructions!"

All the crews of battery A were dispersed coastwise on the five miles of Omaha beach. Many had landed without a balloon. Therefore, it would take long to locate all of them.

Lacking their balloon, Firmin ordered Ed and Jimmy to improvise a shelter with the two canvas tent-halves left. Jimmy had lost his, in the sea with his backpack. Two of them would be able to sleep in a dry place, while the third one would remain on guard duty.

The smoke of the exploded shells had completely cleared away, but the smell of gunpowder still remained very strong and stung their throats.

Gazing at the sea, Firmin noticed the comings and goings of a tank dozer, in the area where he had carried the remains of the fallen. He was seized with a sudden panic attack. How would he survive this hell? He recalled the wounded whom he had seen on the beach. Some were severely banged up. They probably would keep irreversible damage. Yet, Firmin couldn't help but envy them. Most of them would soon return to England. Far from this hell on earth. At safe distance from death. Mutilated but still alive, indeed. Nevertheless, some wounds can turn your life into an endless ordeal. Inflicting you such an awful suffering that you wish you had died instead. His late grandfather had told him of the *Gueules cassées*[91] of the Great War, in France. Not to mention those who were gassed and condemned to a slow and

---

[91] Broken faces (facially disfigured service men of WWI)

painful agony. At that time, Firmin would have nightmares.

Unknowingly, Firmin started to fiddle his lucky charm. The mechanical gesture recalled in his mind the last words that his mother told him at the bus stop, before his departure to Camp Claiborne.

"Don't you ever part with it! You hear me? Of course, it won't stop me from praying for your sake, every day. Anyhow, it'll do you no harm!"

He wondered if he was in his mother's thoughts in this very moment. Had the American newspapers and radios already reported the landing of their troops on the Normandy beaches? Would they tell the truth about the horror of what had happened early this morning? Thousands of young men taken away by the grim reaper in the wee hours of June 6, 1944. Like all mothers, she had to live with the constant fear of receiving a telegram announcing her the loss of the flesh of her flesh.

"She'd die of grief, for sure, if I were killed," Firmin thought. "She already lost Marie. She wouldn't survive the loss of her second and only child."

After the tide went out, the engineering units undertook the minesweeping and flattening of the ground leading to the three exits towards the inland. The last of them was Exit F1, at the most eastern part of Omaha beach.

A little later in the evening, the men of the 320th VLA were informed of the casualty count of their battalion. Two of them had been killed, seventeen others wounded. Although these losses were minor when compared to the global estimation—between two thousand and four thousand seven hundred killed, wounded or missing soldiers—they caused Firmin and his crew mates a real shock.

The infantry men of the 26th RCT had landed as planned, but their losses in terms of equipment were huge. Twenty-six artillery pieces, fifty tanks and landing crafts, and ten of their ships had been destroyed. Only one hundred tons of material had been unloaded so far, out of the twenty-four hundred tons initially programmed.

Yet, the worse had been avoided. Although the progression towards the inland remained slow, the Allies hadn't been thrown back to the sea, like some officers of the supreme headquarters had feared until the middle of the morning.

Firmin decided to take a short break. There hadn't been any food distribution, due to the delay in the landing program, so Firmin and Ed shared their food ration with Jimmy who had lost his backpack. As a compensation, Firmin ordered Jimmy to go and fetch fresh water to refill their two canteens. Due to all the rain that had fallen in the last days, many little creeks were continuously pouring out their runoffs from the top of the cliff. Every soldier had received water purification tablets to clean it, since you couldn't count on a distribution of drinkable water on a battlefield.

The three fellow soldiers devoured the canned pork meat, the short bread cookies and the bitter chocolate bars of their K-rations. After he had finished his evening meal, Ed suddenly felt uncomfortable.

"Can't believe I could eat all that food near all those dead bodies," he said.

Then, he looked around and realized that many other

soldiers were eating their supper greedily despite the surrounding horror.

The human instinct of survival is something natural. Why try to resist it?

"After all," Firmin commented, "don't we offer a buffet to the next of kin of a deceased, after his burial?"

It took until 23:15 to see a first balloon flying above the ridge line of the hill overlooking Omaha beach. Around E3 exit leading to Colleville. A quarter-hour later, a lonely German airplane appeared out of the clouds and started to machine-gun the troops on the ground. Ships anchored off the coast opened fire on it, but didn't manage to hit it. Its pilot made a large turn and flew away.

Corporal Bellegarde was informed by a lieutenant of his unit that they missed balloons and couldn't supply him with a replacement one. Hence, Firmin and his crew should stay in their foxholes and get some shut-eye. Easier said than done.

Although suffering from fatigue after such a very long day, many soldiers had to struggle to fall asleep in this first night on the soil of Normandy. The sound of whiffs of grapeshot hardly ever stopped. Sometimes, when an enemy aircraft was approaching, they would hear the ack-ack slams of the 16th AAA automatic weapons shooting at the sky. Besides, the warships anchored off the coast regularly shelled German posts hiding in the inland. When the racket subsided, the able-bodied soldiers could hear the heartbreaking moan of their wounded comrades waiting for their medical repatriation to Great Britain.

Additionally, the sky was strongly lightened by searchlights looking for possible enemy aircraft. Adding to the almost full moon shine, sometimes, you could feel like it was broad daylight.

CHAPTER 45

Omaha Beach, June 7, 1944

Firmin was awakened at the crack of dawn by the cold. He discovered a row of balloons flying above the ridge line of the hill. His colleagues had probably worked late after midnight. He felt proud to belong to the 320th VLA, but at the same time, he was a bit envious of his colleagues who had successfully fulfilled their job.

On the beach, combat engineer squadrons were already taking advantage of the low tide to clear the widely uncovered ground from landmines and other booby traps, in preparation for a massive landing of troops and material of the 2nd ID. The prestigious *Indian Head*[92].

The service units of the 29th ID soon unloaded their bulldozers, which primary mission was to dig a first large temporary graveyard on the shelf, between the beach and the hill.

Looking at the ordered procession of the earthmovers, Corporal Bellegarde feared he would be requisitioned with his crew members to carry dead bodies again. Despite the great respect he felt for the fallen heroes, he didn't have the guts to stand this painful task for the second time. So, he rushed to find an officer of his battalion intending to ask for a new balloon with its winch. But moving on the beach was always risky. Omaha beach was still within

---

[92] Nicknamed after their shoulder sleeve insignia featuring the head of an Indian warrior inside a five-pointed white star.

reach of the German artillery. Shells regularly fell on the beach. Every time he heard their characteristic whistling, Firmin would run and jump face down into the first crater he could find, and grasp his *gris-gris*. After he heard the blast, he would thank the Lord for sparing him, one more time.

On his way, he met one of the quartermasters of the 320th VLA, whom he asked to provide him new food rations and water-resistant blankets. He tried to coax him by telling him that one of his crew members had lost his backpack during the assault. But the guy was overworked. Anyhow, the trucks of the battalion loaded with replacement equipment and a stock of ammunition hadn't yet landed.

Before he saw an officer of his battalion, Firmin noticed that half of the twelve balloons which were flying above the hill earlier this morning had been shot down by German shots.

He felt relieved when he saw the shapes of dozens of balloons tethered to LSTs and LSIs coming from Great Britain. But before they reached the beach, the remaining six VLAs were destroyed too.

Still, some good news came from the front, which boosted the morale of all the men left on the beach. The towns of Colleville-sur-Mer and Saint-Laurent had been liberated during the forenoon. On their side, the soldiers of the British 50th Northumbrian ID had freed Bayeux, southeast from Omaha.

However, the operation Overlord was far behind the SHAEF's schedule. The beachheads established by the Allied forces had to be connected by hook or by crook. The U.S. troops which had landed on Omaha beach still had to achieve the link-up with the British army settled on Gold beach, in the east, and with the 4th U.S. ID settled in the west on Utah beach.

The latter were under the aerial protection of the balloons of battery C. Firmin was told that his colleagues had faced a less significant resistance on Utah beach. According to the information received from Lieutenant Colonel Reed, the total casualties there didn't exceed two hundred killed and about sixty missing.

The whole day again, Corporal Bellegarde and his two crew mates were left without a balloon. Yet, they didn't remain inactive.

They helped their colleagues of the 16th AAA group to position their automatic anti-aircraft weapons. Their association with the barrage balloons were highly prized by the men of the 320th VLA.

They also helped with logistic tasks or the mounting of tents which would serve as medical units or officers' messes.

One just needed to observe the landing operations to realize that the Allied troops would imminently miss reinforcement, equipment and ammunition, if things didn't run faster. After they had been emptied of their content, the LSIs and LSTs beached at low tide had to wait until the next high tide to leave and be replaced by another ship. At the end of the second day in Normandy, less than fifteen hundred tons of various equipment had been unloaded.

By the end of the afternoon, almost four hundred and sixty corpses had been buried in the mass grave. A funeral service was organized to honor them. Many soldiers attended the ceremony, among whom Firmin and several guys of the 320th VLA.

Slightly after 20:00, everyone was allowed to have a short break for supper. The day had been exhausting and backbreaking for all the units stationed along the beach. Despite the absence of a direct fight.

Firmin, Ed and Jimmy gathered in the largest foxhole to share their meal. They would be able to chat together. Which they hadn't done since breakfast. They had indeed been requested all day long by different units to perform various tasks, most often separately.

Edward looked particularly upset. You could see it from the way he was chewing his ham covered *hardtack*[93]. In an energetic and jerky way. Besides, he couldn't stop his left leg from trembling.

Jimmy, on his side, seemed rather relaxed. Almost serene. He had managed to recover a complete equipment to replace the one he had lost in his backpack during the landing.

He was now firmly decided to enjoy the mere pleasure of eating after a day of hard work.

"Whatsa' matter, private first class Washington?" Firmin asked.

"Everything's fine," Ed replied, without a look at him.

The corporal smiled. He could easily see that something was annoying his crew mate.

"Well, then. Relax and rejoice! We're still alive. And, as our combat units will push back the German troops, the front will move away. Then, we'll be sent back home, safe

---

[93] Long-lasting crackers (sea biscuit) made of flour and water. It replaced bread in a soldier's food rations.

and sound. A matter of a few days. Or a few weeks, at worse."

"Yep!" Jimmy agreed. "Wish I was already far from this damn place, on my way back home."

Edward rushed to swallow his last mouthful, then gazed at Firmin.

"Awright, Corp. I'm gonna tell you what's wrong!"

He leaned forward to him and continued in a tone of confidence.

"Are you aware of what's been goin' on since we landed on this beach? We've been asked all day long to perform low-grade tasks. Always the same. They think we Negroes are no good at, but carrying crates and dead bodies. We're balloon operators! Not quartermasters!"

"What the hell are you talking about? We don't have a balloon any more. We got to help in some way!"

"Who's fault? Because of those crackers who shit in their pants and claim that our balloons served as targets for the German artillery!"

"They were just scared. We all were! Not you?"

"Bunk!" Edward reacted with a muffled voice. "It was an excuse to challenge our role in the war. They'll do all what they can to downplay our involvement in the landing."

"Won't happen, Washington! There were civilian witnesses with us. Journalists, photographers, and even a writer!"

"Oh yeah? There was none of our balloons tethered to the solid ground before 23:30. No picture taken before that time would testify to our presence on the beach on June 6. People will say that we landed long after the fights. And yet, we know how close we were to be hit by a bullet or shrapnel when we assaulted the beach in that Higgins boat, filled with white infantry men. We even almost drowned before reaching the beach! Didn't we, Corp.?"

"But you forget our commandant. Do you remember what he told us when we met him in the afternoon?

You've done a great job, guys! I'm proud of you!

Reed will tell the world that we were there and that we endured the heavy fire of MG 42s. And two of us were killed!"

"Maybe, Corp.," Ed agreed. "But there's no reason why we should be asked to do all kinds of shit jobs."

"Don't ever say this again! Do you hear me, Washington?

"So what? Ain't it true?"

Corporal Bellegarde sat up and looked straight at his first crew mate.

"Listen to me well, Washington!"

Firmin took a long and deep breath, and continued.

"The work of our brothers in the quartermaster units is neither despicable nor degrading. In no way. There would be no possible military victory without them. Burying the dead means paying them and their families the tribute they deserve. Building ports, bridges, roads; transporting troops, supplying combat units with food, arms and ammunition, and God knows what, are all important tasks. Besides, by doing their jobs, our brothers will often get very close to the front, hence within shooting range of German shells and bombs. They will risk their lives to support their fellow soldiers of the combat units.

Therefore, I can't let you suggest that the quartermasters are doing second-rate jobs. Shit jobs, as you call them."

The corporal stopped talking and remained silent for a while, forcing Ed to think over the issue.

"Did I make myself clear, Washington?"

"Yes, Corp.!"

"This said," Firmin added, "if tomorrow at noon we still haven't got a replacement balloon, I'll give you a chance to join a combat mission… If you decide to volunteer for that, of course! I wouldn't force you to."

His superior's proposal left Edward speechless. He didn't even ask what kind of mission he meant. Firmin deduced that Ed was probably a braggart, who wished to be considered a hero when he's back in his hometown, but wasn't ready to pay the price of it.

However, Firmin could understand what Edward meant. He had also felt the same feeling of frustration. Several times during the day, he had felt like he was kept away from the fighting.

Why did he have to go through all these training and drills of hand-to-hand fighting and rifle shooting, if it was just to wait for a balloon and watch it fly in the sky above his head?

He remembered the demands of the *Double Victory Campaign* published in the *Pittsburgh Courier*, two years earlier. He thought of their conversation, right before the crossing of the Channel, about the importance of fighting for their country, to earn in return the same civil rights as the Whites. Even Jimmy was eager and willing to fight.

Although the German resistance was stronger than expected, news from the front was rather reassuring. The 115th Infantry Regiment heading towards the southwest had reached Formigny. The 175th IR of the 29th ID, which had landed earlier this morning, was progressing towards Isigny.

Firmin determined the order of the guard duties for the night. Then, everyone returned to his foxhole, still with some fear. The veterans had warned the rookies. The Allied air force had relentlessly bombed strategic places like road crossings and railroad junctions, all day long, intending to slow down the arrival of reinforcement German tanks. At night, they would return to their bases in Great Britain. Hence, the airspace would be more vulnerable during the night to potential raids by enemy planes still able to fly.

The veterans had given a name to such night visits. *Bed check, Charlie!* An ironical way to wish the young soldiers a good night.

In his diary, Firmin wrote these few words:

Omaha beach. June 7, 1944. D-Day + 1. Second day without a balloon for my crew. Feel useless as a soldier. Luckily, our officers always find a way to keep us busy with all kinds of menial tasks. (unloading crates, mounting tents, digging holes)

Corporal Bellegarde always kept in mind that his diary might end up in the hands of a white officer. Therefore, he avoided, most of the time, to write too critical comments about the army or use a too ironical tone.

When the night fell, twenty balloons were flying over Omaha beach. The corporal and his crew mates hoped they would still be there in the morrow. Then, they would have more chance to get their own balloon from one of the ships which would beach and unload with the low tide.

CHAPTER 46

Omaha beach, June 8, 1944

The front was only a few miles away from the beach. Several times in the night, Firmin had been awakened from his sleep by sporadic gunfire coming from the inland. Commandos of the 1st and 29th IDs were harassing pockets of German resistance. They needed to catch up and quickly establish a junction with the 4th ID departed from Utah beach. At all costs.

All the men stationed on the beach woke up tired from the lack of sleep. And yet, none of them had the indecency to complain about it. How many of their comrades in arms nearby had fallen under enemy fire?

Firmin's whole body was aching, suffering from his uncomfortable sleeping position inside his foxhole, and from the high air humidity. He stretched his limbs and his back, then stood up on his knees, and cast a quick gaze around his shelter. He looked over at the ridge line. Most of the balloons had survived the fire of the German artillery. A few of them had already been lowered, not to hinder the firing of the naval artillery and the raids of Allied air forces, which had now full air supremacy.

Corporal Bellegarde called his two crew members. But none of them would reply. So, he rose out of his hole and looked into their shelters. Jimmy's was empty. In his, Edward was snoring like a bear. He was wrapped in his canvas shelter half turned into a blanket. With a kick, Firmin lifted a spray of sand which partly ended in Ed's

313

open mouth and on his closed eyelids.

Washington jumped up, screaming and desperately searching his rifle. He finally got rid of the sand in his eyes, and eventually calmed down.

Meanwhile, Jimmy reappeared.

"Where have you been, Stevenson? You were supposed to be on guard duty, and wake us up?"

Jimmy proudly raised his arm and showed two canteens filled with hot water.

"Everybody around was awake. So, I thought I'd let you sleep a bit longer, while I'd be looking for some stuff to prepare a good strong joe. I even found some extra sugar!" Jimmy added, tapping a pocket of his jacket.

"Well, next time, wake up at least one of us before you go anywhere!" Firmin rumbled, upset.

All three lingered with delight over their instant hot and sweet coffee, while admiring the beautiful and reassuring show of the Allied armada anchored off Omaha beach.

The skyline was saturated with the shapes of dozens of U.S., British, and French destroyers and cruisers. In front of them stood a steel behemoth: the American battleship *USS Texas*. The latter, together with other warships positioned further west, off the *Pointe du Hoc* and Utah beach, would soon pour a deluge of fire and steel over targets previously spotted by ground observers and reconnaissance aircraft.

Waiting for the end of the receding tide, dozens of LSTs and LSIs, each surmounted by a balloon, were preparing to be beached, and unload their cargo of ammunition and material. A race against the clock was about to start, for the ship crews, and for the troops stationed on the beach. All available forces would be requisitioned. As far as they were concerned, the three operators of the 320th VLA would finally recover a balloon.

Corporal Bellegarde and his crew spent their last moments of respite filling their hungry bellies with their breakfast ration set. Canned ham and scrambled eggs, biscuits and fruit paste.

Once satisfied, they would take care of their personal hygiene. None of them had shaven nor washed since they had left Weymouth. Firmin ordered his crew men to go and fetch one or two clear water jerrycans. Edward tried to offload the chore on Jimmy, but the compensation the latter asked in return—two Camel cigarette packs— seemed too high for him. He finally had to accept to go with him.

During their absence, Corporal Bellegarde was approached by a lieutenant of his unit, who wondered why he was alone.

"As soon as you get your crew back, go down to the beach and take over a balloon!"

"Sir. Yes, sir!" Firmin shouted, with an assured voice.

He watched the officer walk away, hoping he wouldn't hang around the area. But apparently, the man wouldn't drop the case so easily. When Ed and Jimmy reappeared, twenty minutes later, carrying two jerrycans filled to the bottleneck, the officer was still near, staying alert, making sure that none of his men was shirking his work. Corporal Bellegarde asked them to bury their precious containers deep into their foxholes and cover them up with their shelter halves. The morning toilet would wait.

Wearing their rifle slung, the three men walked to one of the beached LSTs. Firmin also kept his haversack filled with his precious belongings. They ran into other crews of the 320th VLA, with whom they could share their feelings. They talked about their two fallen comrades. They were all moved by the loss, but they also knew that their job here was not over yet.

Firmin's crew was waiting for the full completion of the LST's unloading before they could get on board. Meanwhile, Lieutenant Colonel Reed paid them a short visit to congratulate them for their job and encourage them to keep on honoring their unit and their weapon.

Corporal Bellegarde's crew had to wait one more hour to take possession of their new balloon. They had hoped to be allotted a jeep to carry the balloon up to the position pointed by their lieutenant, on the ridge line of the hill. Unluckily, no vehicle was available for them. Thus, they would have to bring it up on foot, holding the balloon by its mooring wires.

Once they had reached their target, at the cost of exhausting efforts, they strongly tethered the balloon to the ground. Then, they went down once again to pick up all their equipment and their two jerrycans of water. They eventually returned to their balloon and dug new foxholes.

When they had finished installing their final post, somewhere between D1 and D3 exits, twenty additional balloons were flying above the five miles of Omaha beach.

They eventually could enjoy a well-deserved dinner break, while observing the incessant procession of soldiers, vehicles of all kinds, and equipment, newly unloaded on the beach.

Squadrons of bombers coming from Great Britain would regularly fly over the coast towards the inland, intending to drop the full content of their bomb bays on strategic targets.

Every new wave was preceded by a humming, which would grow as the planes were getting nearer. The noise would become deafening when the squadrons passed right above Omaha beach.

After he had checked that the lieutenant wasn't watching them any longer, Firmin asked his crew to assemble two shelter halves, in order to build a rain cover for the following night. Meanwhile, he found a place nearby to do his toilet. At last.

Sitting on top of one of the jerrycans, he used the second one to fill his helmet with water. Although the air was fresh, he took off his shirt and started brushing his teeth. Inevitably, like each time he performed this ritual, Firmin thought of his mother. All through his childhood, and even later, as long as he lived under her roof, she would remind him: "Don't forget to brush your teeth carefully, and say a prayer before you go to sleep!"

Before he left New Orleans, when he heard these words, Firmin would grumble: "Enough with that, Mom. I'm not five anymore." But today, he would give a lot to hear them again. She would surely lecture him if she knew her son had only the bottom of a *Marvis* mint toothpaste tube left. He hadn't forgotten to buy a refill of ink and extra letter sheets before departing from Abersychan, but he had neglected the issue of hygiene which worried his mother so much.

He then took time to shave carefully. But, when he closed his eyes, he no longer thought of his mother. When he left New Orleans, he still was a beardless teenager. Since then, his beard had appeared. He was a man now, even though he wasn't legally an adult. He had experienced love with a woman. With Ethel. Far from home.

The remembrance of this first time was so strong that Firmin thought he could feel her breath, smell her skin and the fragrance of her rose petal blend *eau de Cologne*. He could almost feel the delicate contact of her warm and silky skin on his neck. A powerful desire started overwhelming his entire body. But the magic of this erotic dream suddenly broke when he cut his cheek with the dull blade of his GEM razor.

"Well," Firmin thought, while wiping the cut with his towel soaked with some aftershave lotion, "it's definitely time to renew my hygiene kit."

The corporal continued his toilet by washing his upper body, and in particular his armpits, his neck and his ears. As for the rest, he would wait until the field showers have been installed.

He then let the two others thoroughly wash, before asking them to go and get the jerrycans refilled and find anything that could improve their lives on the beach.

He, on his side, would stay near the winch, fifty feet beneath their balloon. He could take it easy. Even if his lieutenant came and saw him unoccupied, he wouldn't give him any kind of chore. Someone had to look over the balloon to bring it higher in the sky in case of an enemy airstrike. He used this timely pause to write one or two pages in his diary.

Then, he started two letters on V-mail forms. One to his parents. Another to Ethel. He would need to carefully choose each word, as he had only two pieces left. But he thought it would be a good training for later. Journalists were also limited by time constraints and by the number of words allocated. If he intended to join one day the limited circle of African American news reporters, it wasn't too soon to learn how to be accurate and concise.

While writing, he realized he hadn't received any news from them, since May 21, of which the latest letter had been posted on May 4. How much longer now would he be deprived of his parents and Ethel's letters? He couldn't tell whom of his mother or Ethel he missed the most. Still one thing was sure: he was suffering a lot from their absence.

Suddenly a huge explosion resounded below. Strangely, it hadn't been preceded by any whistle which usually announces the arrival of a fired shell. Firmin raised his head and saw a cloud of black smoke above the wreckage of a ship tumbling on its side. After the ship had sunk, her upper deck still emerged above the water level.

Shortly after, a double blast torn apart the hull of a second ship, which was anchored in the continuation of the first one, in parallel with the beach. Again, the shipwreck tilted on its side. A third boat soon suffered the same fate, still on the same line as the two others.

Corporal Bellegarde understood what was going on. More ships would surely be scuttled to turn them into breakwaters and create sheltered water between the sea and the sand beach, in front of E1 exit. Firmin had already heard of these block ships, which were deliberately sunk in estuaries to ban their entrance to enemy submarines, but it was the first time he saw it done. He didn't see the necessity of doing this in such a configuration. Were they going to do this along the five miles of Omaha beach?

He didn't have time to think about it. His crew mates

were back. Besides the jerrycans of water, they were carrying armfuls of things.

"Get a load of this, Corp.!" Jimmy shouted, pointing at a part of his loot, wrapped in his left arm.

With a cheerful expression, he dropped the whole at his feet. He explained how he had run by pure chance into a guy who hailed from his home neighborhood. A soldier of the 3207[94] QSC. Their common origins earned him to get things which would significantly improve their comfort. Besides K-rations for two days, Jimmy had received six cigarette packs, three bars of *Ivory* soap, two boxes of razor blades, two *Colgate's* toothpaste tubes, a pack of condoms. And, height of the luxury, two packs of *Jeyes'* hygienic toilet paper. But the trophy of which he was prouder was an "abandoned" shelter half, found in a bush.

"This one is for you, Corp.!" Jimmy said with a triumphant smile. "You can add it to your half, and build your own tent! It'll keep you away from the rain … and from Ed's snoring like a bear!"

The military situation at the end of this day was overall positive, despite a terrible weather, alternating downpours and short sunny spells. The beachheads of Gold beach and Omaha beach were now linked together at Port-en-Bessin. The soldiers of the 26th Infantry regiment were pushing back the German 726th Grenadier to the east, between Bayeux and Port-en-Bessin. Ninety survivors of three companies of the 2nd Ranger battalion under lieutenant-colonel Rudder's command who were stuck at Pointe du Hoc since June 6 were eventually relieved in the morning of June 8 by fellow rangers of the 5th and 2nd Ranger

---

[94] Quartermaster Service Company.

battalions, and elements of the 116th Infantry Regiment. And the 29th IR, progressing towards Isigny-sur-Mer, had taken Grandcamp.

Shortly before the night fall and after the return of the last Allied aircraft to their British air bases, all the balloons of the 320th VLA were raised in the sky of Omaha beach at an altitude varying from three hundred to six hundred feet. Firmin started to count them. He stopped at fifty. It was too dark to distinguish more of them in the far distance.

Like the night before, Corporal Bellegarde would take the first guard duty. From 23:00 to 01:00. After that, he would sleep, with the feeling he had fulfilled his duty. He thanked God for having spared their three lives, one more day.

CHAPTER 47

June 9, 1944

T his third night on Omaha beach was more quiet than the previous ones. Firmin managed to sleep five hours, almost straight. When he woke, he couldn't remember if he had had a bad dream. Was he getting used to his war environment? Anyhow, he had stopped fearing continuously that he might be killed anytime. And yet, the risk was real. Thus, neither he nor his crew mates could relax their vigilance. Fear can paralyze a soldier. But it can also save his life by putting all his senses on alert when it is properly mastered.

Corporal Bellegarde thus started this new day in the Normandy Theater of operations with a reminder of the basic safety rules. After they had lowered their balloon and had their breakfast, he ordered a meticulous cleaning and lubricating of their rifles.

In the morning, a new wave of ships unloaded their lots of equipment and fresh troops. Once the ships emptied, the wounded of the previous night were carried on board to be repatriated to Great Britain, where they would be cared for in military hospitals.

With the rising tide, all the refloated LSTs and LSIs could finally leave. When the beach was fully cleared, the extension of the artificial breakwaters resumed. A dozen cargo ships, nearing the end of their careers, had been sunk in parallel with the beach to build what the British code-named *Gooseberry*.

The teams of combat engineers even sacrificed the *HMS Centurion*, an old battleship of the Royal navy, inaugurated in 1911.

Firmin and his crew saw strange constructions floating in the distance, towed by tugboats. They would later be told that they were reinforced concrete caissons designed to float during the whole crossing from Weymouth, where they had been gathered with the utmost secrecy.

A first two hundred feet long and fifty feet wide Phoenix breakwater was brought until it would form a right angle with the old battleship, west wise. The movements of the waves, and the strength of the tidal current made the maneuver extremely tricky and dangerous. As opposed to block ships, the Phoenix caissons were not sunk by explosive charges placed under the waterline. They were filled, instead, with water by powerful pumps until they would touch the bottom. Only a few feet would remain above the waterline at high tide.

This gigantic port installation, code-named *Mulberry A*, was the work of the 128th U.S. Task Force. Its goal was to build, in less than two weeks, an artificial harbor capable of supplying the U.S. military forces, whatever the weather conditions, and independently from the existing harbors still under German control. The construction of a second harbor, named *Mulberry B*, was planned to start on the following day in the Gold beach sector, under British command. Undoubtedly, a competition between the two main Allied armies would be used to motivate their troops to complete both military engineering infrastructures in the shortest possible time.

Meanwhile, the forces fighting inland were facing many German pockets of resistance. A single German sniper would often cause heavy casualties on his own. Without the support of a tank or an armored vehicle to blow up the house or the bell tower in which the sniper was hiding, a squad or a platoon could be annihilated within a few hours.

In the best cases, it would stay put until the arrival of reinforcements. Then, men from other units could be solicited for a support operation.

This is what happened by the end of the afternoon. A lieutenant was looking for volunteers to "knock off a Kraut." Their mission was to drive a sniper out of a farm, a few miles away from the beach. The officer explained that he was looking for excellent shots. Edward spontaneously volunteered. Firmin tried to protest. They couldn't let their balloon unattended.

"You don't need the three of you to keep an eye on that balloon!" the lieutenant replied, curtly. "It's really quiet, today, isn't it?"

Corporal Bellegarde didn't want to be left behind, so he volunteered too. He ordered Jimmy to stay and watch over the balloon until they return. "Just a matter of a few hours," he said.

"Take your backpacks, anyway," the lieutenant added. "Just in case. Might take longer. Never know with those damn Krauts."

The lieutenant checked that Firmin and Ed each took all the necessary equipment with them. Their rifles with their combat knives. Two K-rations, a canteen of water, a few water purification tablets, two boxes of ammunition with a second Garand *en bloc* clip loaded with eight rounds. Plus a trench shovel, their heavy helmet, an individual first-aid kit, and a shelter half each to protect them from cold and rain. Firmin added his personal haversack.

The officer soon managed to constitute a group of ten men, besides him and a driver. All colored. Only the lieutenant was white. Except Firmin and Edward, they all belonged to a dump truck company. The same kind of unit in which Corporal Bellegarde had started his military training in Camp Claiborne. Firmin thus took advantage of it to make friends and chat with them during the trip in a covered 2½-ton truck. A 6x6 GMC CCKW.

The lieutenant reminded everyone of the safety rules before they reached the target zone. The sniper had already shot seven soldiers. Besides, there was an uncovered nine hundred feet wide strip between the house where he was hiding and another building were the five survivors of a U.S. combat section were taking shelter.

The road was narrow, and lined on each side by a hedgerow, and a ditch in which rainwater was collected. The bushes were so dense and leafy that you could hardly see anything through. Being hidden from both sides by two vegetation curtains made you feel safe. But actually, the hedgerows and ditches would easily turn into a deadly trap. Would an enemy tank or armored vehicle suddenly appear ahead or behind them, they would have no way of escape. And if they jumped out of the truck, they would be shot like sitting ducks before they could reach the hedgerows.

During their short trip, one of the guys sitting in front of them carefully sharpened both edges of his knife. His friends tried several times to convince him to put the dagger back in its leather sheath. Unsuccessfully.

"I'll tell you. You can miss a game with a rifle. But if you know how to use this well," the man said, brandishing his knife, "and if you can get close enough to the animal before he sees you, then, you just need to jump at its neck and cut its throat. Fast and clean," he added, while simulating the move of a throat cutting.

"It's a man you'll have to kill, Andy, not an animal!" his friend replied.

"Neither a man nor an animal, but a bloody fuckin' Nazi!" the dude sneered stupidly.

Everyone then went silent. Besides that guy, no one wished to run into another man and kill him with his knife. Firmin looked at Ed, without a word. They probably remembered the same thing. After the first hand-to-hand fight drills they had in Scotland, Edward had been deeply shocked by the idea of killing a man in cold blood and watching him die. Firmin had made Ed promise that he wouldn't hesitate to drive his knife into the heart of a damn German if that man were about to kill him.

Ed nodded, implicitly confirming he didn't forget his commitment.

The driver stopped the GMC at the start of a last turn before a straight line leading to the barn where the five infantry men were waiting for them. One of the guys had crawled towards that safe place to warn the reinforcement team about the danger. The lieutenant knocked at the rear window and asked his men with a hand sign to get down the truck. Then, he jumped out of the cabin and went to the lookout man, who explained to him briefly the current situation. The main problem was that several inhabitants of the house were held hostage by the sniper. A woman, her parents and her three children. It was thus out of the question to move out the German by lobbing one or two hand grenades inside the house, or asking for artillery fire.

The Normans had already been badly hit by Allied bombings since the big invasion.

Among the soldiers killed by the German sniper, one was a trained marksman using a riflescope-mounted Garand M1C. Unfortunately, he had been killed very quickly. The rifle could be taken back, but two other men were killed while trying to use the rifle against the sniper. Now, none of the five survivors was a good shot enough to hit the German without fail. And none had ever used such a gun before.

Immediately, Edward Washington volunteered to help eliminate this obstacle which banned the way to Trévières, where a unit of the 2nd ID was stopped by determined and heavily armed Germans.

The lieutenant accepted. Yet, before going any closer to the shooting area, he asked the infantry man to tell him more about the surroundings of the house.

There were two ways to approach the sniper. First one was getting through the hedgerow on the left, and run under cover to the barn. The second way was to go through the right side hedgerow, out of the sniper's eyesight, and walk to a position situated six hundred feet from the sniper's position. From there, it would be easier to reach the target, knowing that the effective firing range of the Garand M1 was fifteen hundred feet.

The officer had received special training in fighting techniques, and he would never send one of his men to a certain death. White or Black. Turning to Corporal Bellegarde, he asked him if he had camouflage face paint sticks on him. As they were mostly supposed to remain static, the men of the 320th VLA hadn't received such kinds of things with their package. The lieutenant gave them one set, with two colors. Green and ivory.

"Don't believe the color of your skin makes you invisible to a watchful sniper! And don't let him see your teeth."

He insisted then on the vital importance of blending into the landscape. So, he explained to them how to cover themselves with fresh green foliage, stuck in the net of their helmet, in the straps of their backpacks, and even wrapped around their rifles.

After he had given his recommendations to the whole group, he assigned the roles. Two men would hide in the ditches on both sides of the road, in order to watch their backs. Six others would join the soldiers waiting in the barn by the left side of the road. The lieutenant would approach the house by the right side of the road, under cover of the hedgerow, together with the infantry man and the two operators of the 320th VLA.

But before they all left, he warned them that he intended to let private first class Washington fire a few test shots, so that he would get used to his new weapon.

"So, guys, don't shoot back at us, like idiots!"

After he got the scope mounted Garand M1C rifle in his hands, the lieutenant took Washington apart with him. He pointed at a fruit tree in the middle of a field. He reckoned the distance at almost one thousand feet. Looking through his M16 field binoculars, he recognized an apple tree. In the middle of the trunk, he noticed a twisted protuberance. Probably ten inches wide. He gave Ed his binoculars and pointed his hand at the gnarl.

"Now, soldier, lay down in prone position and aim at that burl on the apple tree!"

Edward obeyed unflinchingly, as it was the first time a

white officer didn't ask him to perform a demeaning chore! This time, he was asked to show his combat ability. He wouldn't spoil this opportunity. He looked over his shoulder.

Crouched along the hedgerow, Corporal Bellegarde was observing him.

"Ready, soldier?"

Edward placed his dominant eye in line with the ocular lens of the rifle scope and adjusted the focusing ring until he could see an accurate image of his target.

"Suh, ready, suh!"

"Now, aim, breathe deeply and gently, and at my signal, empty your lungs, keep focused on your target and pull the trigger progressively until it releases the hammer!"

The first shot was a miss. It didn't even hit the trunk.

Edward blamed himself, but the officer didn't lose his composure.

"All right, soldier. Relax, and try again. Be more flexible with your finger when you pull the trigger."

Washington was reassured. He corrected his shooting and managed to reach the trunk.

"That was much better, soldier! Are you sure the target was well aligned with the center point of the scope?"

"Suh, yessuh!"

"Well, soldier. Then, aim about four inches left and two inches below the target. Got it?"

"Yessuh! Four inches left and two inches below the target!"

"So, take your time, and make sure it'll be a hit at the first shot! Cause if you miss the sniper, he'll surely spot and kill you in return."

The private first class Washington was fully aware of the issue. He applied himself like a student having an exam. This time, the shot hit the target. The officer could distinctly see the entrance point of the bullet. He asked Edward to try again until his *en bloc* clip was empty. The result was a nice shot grouping. Six impacts inside a seven inches wide circle, the lieutenant reckoned.

"Good job, Private Washington," said the lieutenant, giving him a friendly pat on the shoulder.

When he stood up again, Ed realized his uniform was soaked. The ground was still moist with last days' rain. Still, he was too focused on his mission to care about this detail.

Both men returned to Corporal Bellegarde and the other soldier. The officer ordered the latter to go to the other side of the road and join his comrades behind the barn. They would have to create a diversion, to force the sniper to move and look in their direction, while Edward would spot him in his line of sight from the better position on this side of the hedgerow. The diversion time was set fifteen minutes later. The four men synchronized their watches.

Meanwhile, Firmin and Ed carefully camouflaged. The lieutenant stayed with them to provide them with ultimate advice. Once on the spot, lying flat on the ground, Washington had to remain completely motionless. The slightest movement could betray his presence and cost his life.

The lieutenant and Corporal Bellegarde sheltered behind the bushy vegetation of the hedgerow. The lieutenant could clearly see the sniper's hideout with his binoculars. Their field of view allowed him to watch over the whole facade at once. He eventually guessed the most likely place from where the German would shoot. One of the windows of the second floor had lost half of its sheets of plate glass. Washington would need to react very quickly when the German would show up at the window and start shooting.

"Private Washington! Do you see the second window, starting from the right side of the first floor?"

"Suh, yessuh!" Edward replied, adjusting his line of sight on the window.

"This must be the place from where the son of a bitch will shoot. So, keep your eye focused on it and stay ready."

"Yessuh!"

"And don't forget what I just explained to you! Breathe calmly. Empty your lungs, and slowly pull the trigger. And of course, remember to aim slightly left and below his head."

"Yessuh!"

"Now, relax, soldier. I will warn you one minute before the diversion time. Then, I'll give you a count down of the last ten seconds."

Firmin was surely more anxious than his crew mate. While he, himself, was well protected by a mound of earth and a hazel hedge, Ed, for his part, was exposed to the response shot of a formidable enemy sniper. At this moment, Firmin was feeling what every combat soldier could feel in such situations. The fear of losing a comrade in arms. A man with whom he had lived and shared so many things. Often tough, like the storm during the crossing of the Atlantic Ocean, aboard the *Aquitania*, or the systematic discrimination they had suffered in the United States. Sometimes pleasant, like the warm welcome they had received at their arrival in Great Britain or during their night trip at the *Palais de Danse* in Barry.

Corporal Bellegarde was very proud of his teammate, but also a bit envious. If Edward succeeded in eliminating that isolated shooter and freeing the inhabitants of the house, he would surely earn a citation, and probably a medal too. Yet, the glory would likely be credited to the whole battery and indirectly to himself, Corporal Bellegarde.

When the lieutenant announced the last minute before the signal, Firmin's heart started racing. His chest compressed itself. His gaze was irresistibly attracted by his friend. In a mechanical reflex, he brought his hand to his chest and searched the contact of his Haitian lucky charm. He grasped it and fingered it nervously, while his lips were murmuring an almost inaudible *Ave Maria*.

"Get ready, Washington," the officer whispered… "Ten seconds, nine, eight…"

Corporal Bellegarde had more and more difficulty in breathing. His prayer to the Holy Virgin resounded in his head at an accelerated rate. Yet no sound came out of his mouth.

"Three, two, one, zero…"

Nothing happened. The lieutenant knew there could be a time lag of a few seconds between their watches. While waiting for the first shootings to start, he kept his binoculars focused on the house and centered on the window with missing glass panes.

"Stay focused, Washington. Right on the target!"

Suddenly, a first salvo broke the silence. The officer noticed a movement in the embrasure of the window. The sniper was about to spot a new victim. The barrel of his rifle was visible. Thanks to his binoculars, the lieutenant could now distinguish his head and shoulders under his helmet.

"Can you see him, soldier?"

"Yessuh!"

"When you like, Washington!"

With a self-control he had never suspected, the private first class inhaled a deep breath of fresh and moist air. The head of his enemy was placed at the very center of his rifle scope. Instinctively, he aimed at the nose, then shifted a few inches left and below. He maintained this position, his finger slightly pressed on the trigger. He had noticed before that the previous owner of the rifle had modified the trigger tension to make it softer and more progressive than on standard Garand M1 rifles.

The lieutenant had warned him to shoot only if he was fully sure he would hit his target. However, he knew that waiting too long would let the sniper enough time to kill several more of his fellow soldiers. Thus, he decided to act as quickly as possible. While the diversion shots were digging holes on the walls of the house, the sniper remained under cover. Edward was pricking up his ears, while keeping his scope focused on the window. His intuition was correct. After a few seconds' pause in the shooting, the German lifted up to aim at a GI.

Washington adjusted his target a last time, emptied his lungs, and gently pulled the trigger. The shot went off.

"Got 'em!" the lieutenant said, with a contained voice, his binoculars still focused on the window.

Ed recovered his normal breathing.

"Don't move yet, Washington! Maybe he's only

injured. Keep your position until we have secured the house."

The officer walked back, and crossed the road to join the others behind the barn. Meanwhile, the corporal and the private first class of the 320th VLA remained motionless on their posts.

"Hot damn, Ed!" Firmin said. "You got that son of a bitch! You're the best, man!"

"Did you hear, the lieutenant? He might just be wounded!"

"Oh yeah? So, why did he stop shooting, then?"

"I don't know. Maybe he's waiting for us to show up. Then, he'll rub us out one by one!"

The two crew mates waited there for about ten minutes before the officer called them back with a long and powerful whistle.

The sniper had been severely hit. He had surrendered without resistance. But the lieutenant had had to interfere to stop the survivors of the 2nd ID combat unit to lynch him in retaliation for the death of their seven brothers in arms.

By sparing his hostages, the man had acted like a soldier, not like a war criminal. Therefore, he deserved to be treated in compliance with the Geneva convention.

CHAPTER 48

W hen they entered the house, the soldiers found the three children and their mother sitting on the ground, with their feet and hands bound with a rope. The grandparents had been tied to their chairs around a table in the center of the main room. They all had crazed eyes. Except the grandfather who "had seen much worse." He had "fought the Krauts in Verdun!"

"*C'était autre chose, ça, monsieur. Mais vous êtes bien trop jeune pour avoir connu ça. Pas vrai, lieutenant ?*"

But the lieutenant couldn't understand. There were no such sentences in the French phrase book.

Once everyone was freed from his bonds, the old man offered a general round of his *Calvados*[95] brandy reserve.

"*Vous m'en direz des nouvelles !*"

"I don't understand a single word, Grandpa!" the officer muttered.

"He wants to celebrate our arrival, sir!" Firmin said.

"You understand French?" the lieutenant asked, surprised.

The corporal realized he had just betrayed a secret that he had better kept for himself. He would serve as an interpreter from now on. He still tried to downplay his skills, but the lieutenant was too happy that he could have such a precious asset with him.

"Ask him if the Germans might have hidden some weapons and explosives in his house?"

---

[95] Apple brandy.

Firmin approached the old man.

"*Bonjour, monsieur. Mon nom est Firmin Bellegarde. Le lieutenant voudrait savoir s'il y a des armes ou des explosifs cachés quelque part chez vous.*"

Hearing this, the face of the man lit up. His features relaxed. His eyes started shining.

"*You're back!*" he said, still in French, looking alternately at Firmin and at the other colored soldiers in the room. "*At that time, you didn't speak a word of French.*"

Corporal Bellegarde understood that the family patriarch was talking about the Great War and the African American soldiers of the 93rd ID, which had served in the spring of 1918, under the command of the French army.

"*We already had our Senegalese riflemen in our army. So, it made us no problem welcoming American Negroes. They were mostly brave men. They had a lot of moxie! I still remember the fright in the Germans' eyes when they saw these big black fellows screaming and pouncing on them, with their bayonets fixed on their rifles. The guys of the 369th Infantry regiment were quite ferocious. The Harlem Hellfighters! This is how the Germans used to call them. We used to call them the* Black rattlesnakes*, after their sleeve insignia. They were with us, the men of the 161st Infantry division, in the trenches in Champagne, then in Alsace. What a beating we gave those damn Fritz!*"

"*My grandfather too was in France,*" Firmin said. "*You may have known him.*"

The old man wiped a tear drop with the back of a sleeve. Then, he got up, painfully, and stood at attention, in front of Firmin, and gave him a perfect military salute.

Corporal Bellegarde felt confused. Not by the mark of

respect of the old man, but because of the presence of an officer in the same room. A white lieutenant.

"*Son, I suggest we toast together to our reunion*," the old man said with a quavering voice.

Then, addressing to his daughter:

"Genevieve, bring us clean glasses and a few bottles of my special reserve."

The woman protested. Her brother, her sister-in-law and their two children were in danger in the village nearby. They surely needed some help. The Germans were capable of the worse.

The lieutenant used her reluctance as an excuse to decline the invitation.

"Well, corporal. Explain to them that we have to go, and that we'll come back later to share a drink."

The soldiers of the 2nd ID left first towards the village of Aignerville, less than six hundred yards away, and where their comrades were still strafed by machine gun shootings.

The lieutenant suggested to the woman to accompany them in the GMC. He left the custody of the German to two of his men, although the old man could easily have accomplished this task alone, considering the importance of the prisoner's wound. Maybe he feared a savage execution of his prisoner in his absence.

When they arrived, the sound of strafes had stopped. A disturbing silence was hovering in the air. The soldiers jumped out of the truck and dispersed on both sides of the street. The lieutenant helped the woman to get down of the cabin. She was so overwhelmed with emotion that the lieutenant feared she could faint. He held her arm to prevent her from falling.

The fighters of the 2nd ID were carefully walking towards the center of the town among the rubble of houses. The bombing by the Allied artillery hadn't left much intact. Almost nothing. A machine gun was standing in the middle of the town square. A German soldier was lying on its side. There was no living soul.

The woman started to call her brother.

"*Jean, can you hear me? It's me, Genevieve!*"

Nobody answered.

"*Jean, Yvonne, can you hear me? It's Genevieve. I'm with the Americans. The Germans are gone! You can get out now! No need to be afraid anymore!*"

Someone finally showed up. A man in his fifties. He came out of his hideout, under the limekilns of the village. Incredulous and suspicious, he was holding one arm high, while using his free hand to protect his eyes from the bright daylight.

"C'est bon. Vous pouvez sortir, maintenant. C'est les Américains !"[96]

About forty others showed up, one by one. Among them an American wounded paratrooper. The inhabitants had welcomed him, cared for him and hidden him for three days. He would soon be transferred to a medical unit before being repatriated to Great Britain.

It took the villagers several minutes to be convinced they had nothing to fear from the Germans anymore. Conscious that they had probably escaped a retaliation execution, they timidly approached their saviors. An officer beckoned the male villagers over to him. He wanted to ask them questions about the German troops

---

[96] It's alright! You can get out now! The Americans are here!

and the presence of members of the resistance or collaborators in the area. The prejudices about the French being collaborators or reluctant to fight were widespread in the U.S. Army.

Finally reassured, the women threw themselves in the arms of the GIs. White and Black, indistinctly. For them, they were all heroes. Fascinated by these big dark-skinned fellows, the children immediately forgot their fear and nagged them with questions. Unable to understand a word, the soldiers answered with the only arguments at their disposal: chewing gum and chocolate bars.

Firmin and his fellow soldiers enjoyed this moment with an intense emotion. So much that they didn't even notice the contemptuous gazes of some infantry men of the 2nd ID. Like the British, the French showed them respect and seemed to ignore racial prejudices.

All the soldiers were knocked out by the fights of the day. The officers decided to stay in the town to regain strength, before going further to Trévières, a thousand yards south.

According to rumors circulating among the soldiers, the 175th Infantry regiment of the 29th ID, which had landed on June 7, had captured Isigny, setting up at once a link with the 101st Airborne and Utah beach. The 1st ID, landed on Omaha beach on June 6, launched in an offensive west of Bayeux, had liberated the towns of Tour-en-Bessin, Etréham and Blay.

The lieutenant and his men could have returned to Omaha beach, but when the officer offered his help to his counterparts of the 2nd ID, they accepted. So, it was decided that the little group of colored soldiers would stay overnight in case the capture of Trévières would turn out to be harder than expected. The guys were split in groups of two at strategic points of Aignerville, where they would spend the night before departing to Trévières at dawn.

The officer requisitioned Firmin to serve him as a translator. He needed him to get some drinking water and some extras to improve the supper menu. He also kept Edward close to him. As a sharp shooter, he could be very useful.

Firmin and Ed dug a common foxhole and covered it with their two shelter halves. The lieutenant, on his side, found room and board in the *Château d'Aignerville*, only three hundred yards from the two crew mates of the 320th VLA. The castle was of a modest size actually, still pretty comfortable, given the circumstances.

Firmin used the last glows of daylight to write a few lines in his diary, and complete the letters to his mother and Ethel.

Ed soon fell asleep, his head filled with dreams of glorious deeds. He had rubbed out a German. Even better, a sniper. He had probably saved the lives of five soldiers, who, without him, would have been killed. He longed to meet Jimmy and the other men of his battalion again to tell them his feat of arms. However, he had to face a dilemma. He now had two rifles. Would he be allowed to keep the scope mounted Garand M1C in exchange with his standard M1 rifle? No dice, for sure! Who would accept to leave such a gun in the hands of a balloon operator! Moreover, a Negro operator!

The two crew mates didn't hear a group of scouts of the 2nd ID leave for Trévières before midnight.

Soon after they woke, on June 10, all the soldiers were asked to shelter immediately. A barrage of the naval artillery was about to fall on Trévières.

Once the shelling was over, a convoy moved forward.

When they entered the town, the soldiers discovered piles of rubble. Most of the inhabitants had flown to the nearby swamps. Three quarters of the town had been destroyed. It had already suffered a lot from the bombing of the night prior to the invasion. The last shooters had been eliminated. The other German soldiers surrendered.

The town was freed, now. But at what cost?

"Ain't sure that the people here see us like their saviors!" Firmin thought.

He wouldn't have time to check it.

The lieutenant thanked Edward for his efficient help. He promised he would mention his name in his report. He finally entrusted the two soldiers of the 320th VLA with a last mission. Returning to Omaha beach to report to the headquarters the capture of Trévières. He found two places in another GMC truck for them.

Before he let them go, he asked them for the M1C rifle back. Edward tried to negotiate to keep it. "I deserve it, after all." But the officer remained inflexible.

"You wouldn't have a great utility of it on the beach, would you?

They didn't even have the pleasure to stop at the old man's house in Aignerville. One hour later, they found their post back on the top of the hill, overlooking Omaha beach.

They were coldly greeted by Jimmy, who was particularly upset. He had been forced to stay there continuously, watching over their balloon, day and night. Needless to say he wasn't in a mood to listen to Ed preening himself with his feat of arms. Nor would he accept any chore whatsoever for the rest of the day.

CHAPTER 49

During the following days, Corporal Bellegarde's crew settled into a daily rut. Almost immutable. Every morning, they would get their balloon down to the ground. Then, they would take off the bomb after replacing its pin, cover the balloon with its net, and attach the mooring cables to sand filled bags.

They would then have their breakfast, which came with their daily C-ration. A significant improvement when compared with the K-ration, which was still served to the troops on the front line. Nevertheless, you still needed to find a way to warm up the canned cooked dishes. For that, and for many other things, Omaha beach was a place for resourceful people. A place where Jimmy felt particularly at ease. Out of an ammunition crate, he had made a table where the three of them could eat at a sufficient height to prevent the sand from mingling with their food. Thanks to some accessories recovered here and there on the beach, he had made a portable stove above which they could warm up a can within a few minutes, and even boil water to prepare their morning instant coffee.

He had also managed to get from his friend of the QSC, two canvas water buckets, which were very useful and convenient to wash themselves.

When they weren't requisitioned for a chore, they would observe the construction of Omaha's artificial harbor, which continued relentlessly until June 18.

Sometimes, when they were having dinner, the three balloon operators would see kids coming from a nearby village or farm. They were most often intrigued by the balloons flying above the ships. Yet, their technical questions would soon be replaced by negotiations to get from these black GIs chocolate bars or chewing gum. The older boys didn't hesitate to beg for blond cigarettes, if not for nylon stockings, intending to impress their girl friends.

The young girls, for their part, would ask to be taught the steps of the last fashionable dances in America.

Even though these spontaneous contacts were somehow guided by personal interests, they were for all these black GIs a source of comfort and recognition, which their white compatriots strove to deny them. Besides, they experienced the same absence of prejudices from the Normans—children or adults—against them, as from the British. It confirmed them that the segregation and racism they had to suffer in their own country were in no way natural. And therefore, they deserved to be fought.

For educated Negroes like Firmin, it proved that the idea of the supremacy of the White race over the Black race was just an invention of the racist Whites intending to justify slavery, then discrimination, and finally segregation. The first one had been fought, and eventually abolished at the end of the Civil War. The second had recently been banned in the army and in public services.

It was now possible to hope that segregation—the last violation of the dignity and equal rights of colored people—would soon be eradicated, under the pressure of colored unions and of the Negro press.

In the end, on June 18, the harbor stretched from under their balloon, somewhere between E1 and E3 exits at the level of Colleville, towards the west as far as the eye could see, in front of the D1 exit towards Vierville. Firmin managed to count the elements forming the breakwaters. Thirty-four Phoenix caissons, one battleship and thirteen cargo ships, all sunken. Inside the protected zone, three pier heads were linked to the beach by three floating roadways, code-named Whales. They would allow the unloading of a continuous procession of trucks filled with crates of various supplies. The Phoenix breakwaters were topped with Bofors 40 mm anti-aircraft guns, which served only on few occasions.

The idea of this transportable harbor grew in the mind of Louis Mountbatten, Vice-Admiral in the British Royal Navy, after the fiasco of the operation *Jubilee* in Dieppe, on August 19, 1942, under his command. The two big harbors of Le Havre and Cherbourg being too far from the chosen landing zone, the officer had stated: "As we have no harbor at our disposal, we shall bring our own."[97]

The construction of all the prefabricated elements had been entrusted by the end of 1943 to three hundred companies and had required them to hire forty thousand workers. On June 4, 1944, all the elements were ready. They were launched and towed by tugboats to the middle of the Channel.

Planned to be operational at D-Day + 21, the Mulberry A actually started working on June 16. Two days later, it became the biggest European harbor, with a daily unloading of eight thousand tons of goods. Which was on June 18, at D-Day + 12.

Firmin was fascinated by the performance achieved by all the engineering teams, which comprised many colored soldiers. Particularly the four[98] companies of the 494th Port

---

[97] Source: https://musee-arromanches.fr/ports/index.php?lang=uk
[98] 238th, 239th, 240th and 241st *Port companies*.

battalion attached to the 6th Engineer special brigade. A demonstration of the strength and efficiency of the U.S. Army, as much as the confirmation of the usefulness of African Americans among them. Ed and Jimmy considered them with envy. Those fellows would return home with a technical know-how and a useful skill for their civilian life. Much more useful, anyhow, than knowing how to handle a static inflatable balloon.

As for Firmin, his future was not an issue. He would be a reporter or an author. And, while waiting to become famous, he would make a living by working as a musician in a club, like his father. Of course, he would first need to practice again, starting with his harmonica. Later with a saxophone.

This prospect aroused a deep nostalgia.

Nobody had received any mail since May 20. It was obviously not a priority for the staff, given the circumstances. The troops were now complaining about this.

Edward couldn't help boasting to other soldiers of the 320th VLA for having knocked off a German sniper. The anecdote eventually came to the ears of Reed and his second in command. The latter—Captain Taylor— eventually came to meet Bellegarde's crew, to check the facts by himself, as he had never received such information from the staff headquarters so far.

As a direct witness of the event, Firmin confirmed the statement of his teammate. He indicated the name of the lieutenant of the Dump truck company who had supervised the support mission to the infantry men of the 2nd ID in Aignerville.

When Captain Taylor checked the story, it appeared

that the lieutenant had been killed, on the following day, before he could write his report. As he had no other witness than his crew leader, private first class Washington couldn't claim a citation for his bravery anymore. He was even requested to stop talking about it in public.

The 320th VLA had already it's hero in the person of a medic named Waverly Woodson. Due to his severe injury, Woodson had to be repatriated on a hospital ship. Three days later, he asked to be sent back to the front. Meanwhile, the press had seized the story of this shy and modest hero, who had ignored his own wound and pain to help almost three hundred soldiers[99]. That was good enough in Wild Bill's mind and for all the Southern White officers.

One more thing came to the ears of Lieutenant Colonel Reed. Corporal Bellegarde's mastery of French, which earned him a series of missions as an interpreter with the local people or to convey messages between the beach and units on the front line. On his way back, he would barter with local farmers. Exchanging chewing gum, chocolate bars, cigarettes and nylon stockings with eggs, milk, poultry and cider. However, he could never return to Trévières, where he would have enjoyed meeting the grandfather again.

On June 13, the supreme commander, Ike himself, paid a visit to his troops on Omaha beach. Firmin and his friends saw him in the distance, talking with a group of Black service men of some logistics units.

Every day, news was returning from the front. Before

---

[99] Source: *Forgotten* by Linda Hervieux, Harper Collins publishers.

they were embarked on LSTs, the wounded could talk to the medics, hence feeding informal word of mouth talk.

On that day, 502nd and 506th regiments of the 101st Airborne managed to capture Carentan. The soldiers of the 1st ID freed the village of Caumont, after a fierce battle with the German 2nd *SS Panzer Division*.

On June 14, General de Gaulle landed from *La Combattante*, a destroyer of the French navy, intending to meet with British General Montgomery. He then went to Bayeux, where he was welcomed by the local population with the singing of *La Marseillaise*, before announcing the creation of the provisional government of the French Republic.

Concurrently, the British were forced to give up the encirclement of Caen, and stop the offensive of the 1st Corps in the northeast of the city.

On June 15, the progression of the Americans was significantly slowed by the fierce resistance of the Germans. The capture of the deepwater port of Cherbourg was the major priority. To achieve it, the U.S. Army had to prevent the arrival of enemy reinforcements at all costs, and isolate the Germans stationed in the north of the peninsula. Their plan was to reach the West Coast, in order to split the Cotentin. Thanks to the back-up of a new army corps which had landed that day on Utah beach, the 9th and 90th ID, attached to the 7th Corps, managed to capture Bonneville, a village south of Valognes, less than thirteen miles southeast from Cherbourg.

On Friday 16 and Saturday June 17, the 7th Corps, under the command of General Collins, continued its progression to the east, liberating several villages on its way. Orglandes, Magneville, Néhou, Saint-Sauveur-le-

Vicomte. In the evening of June 17, the West Coast was only six miles away.

The advance was slow, but inexorable. And all this under awful weather conditions.

When repatriated, the injured soldiers would tell the medics the hell of the fights. The thick hedgerows that they had to bypass or get through. Their fear of seeing a *Tiger* Panzer appear at any time with its dreadful 8.8 cm *Flak* gun. The nights they spent in foxholes hastily dug in the ditches along the roads. Most often without managing to sleep. The impossibility to wash themselves or even change clothes. Not to mention the constant gnawing hunger they felt because of the cold and tasteless food of their K-rations.

"You can't even imagine the hell we're going through! You, the servicemen, are just a bunch of chickens and goof-offs!" This is what was often heard in the mouth of the survivors.

The most severely injured were transported by air across the Channel. The planes would take off from temporary airfield A1, built by the engineering battalions of the 9th Air Force, at Saint-Pierre-du-Mont, about three miles west from Omaha beach[100].

The dead couldn't talk, but the guilt they aroused was all the stronger. More painful. When body bags were lacking, the corpses were wrapped in recovered parachute silk to hide the expression of terror on their faces, when they hadn't been distorted by shrapnel or a bullet.

On June 18, the main objective of the 7th Corps had been achieved. The Cotentin Peninsula was cut by a line

---

[100] ALG (Advanced Landing Grounds). The prefix A designated the temporary airfields built by the Americans. B was for the British airfields.

linking Utah beach in the east to Barneville on the West Coast. Almost forty thousand Germans, assigned to the protection of Cherbourg, were trapped.

The U.S. ground forces increased their pressure towards the north, while the Allied armada was taking position in the north of the peninsula, in preparation for a massive shelling of the fortifications of the city and its port.

Simultaneously, and since June 17, a new depression was progressively growing over the Channel. In the morning of the 19th, it strengthened and reached the Norman coast.

On that day, and during the two following days, the Channel was swept by a violent storm, caused by a northeast wind. A kind of storm which the Normans were long used to weathering, several times a year.

The crews of the 320th VLA had to keep their balloons on the ground for three days, and reinforce the mooring with additional ballasts of all kinds. As they missed sand filled bags, they wrapped the wires around wooden crates filled with wet sand and pebbles.

The soldiers stationed all along the beach attended the most distressing show. What had been achieved thanks to fifteen days of tenacious and relentless work by the teams of the military engineering was annihilated by the nature in three days.

Obviously, the British Admiral Lord Mountbatten and his engineers hadn't seriously considered the warning of U.S. Navy's Admiral, John Leslie Hall Jr., who stated, when the project was announced:

"I think it's the biggest waste of manpower and equipment that I have ever seen. I can unload a thousand

LSTs at a time over the open beaches. Why give me something that anybody who's ever seen the sea act upon 150-ton concrete blocks at Casablanca knows the first storm will destroy? What's the use of building them just to have them destroyed and litter up the beaches?[101]"

The facts confirmed he was right. Winds, reaching 6 or 7 on the Beaufort wind scale, rose up to ten feet high waves and tossed the floating elements of the Pier heads and roadways, as if they were just small fishing boats.

The floating roadways, code-named *Whales*, were made with metal bridging units. Each of them of eighty feet length and weighing sixty-two thousand pounds. These units were supported by metal or concrete pontoons, code-named *Beetles*, anchored to the bottom of the sea by steel ropes.

The storm raised such a powerful swell, that it subjected the steel frames to torsions and mechanical constraints, which twisted and dislocated the roadway elements.

Breakwater caissons, meant to protect the harbor, were also battered by the swell, and they eventually beached at the foot of the cliff. Even the block ships, which had been sunk leaving too wide intervals between them, proved inefficient against the power of the nature.

Within these three days, almost no ship could approach the beaches of Omaha and Gold, causing an increased delay in the unloading of material planned since June 6. The deficit caused by the storm was estimated at twenty thousand vehicles, and one hundred and forty thousand tons of other supplies.

---

[101] http://www.skylighters.org/encyclopedia/mulberry.html

On June 22, when the storm was over, the Supreme headquarters' staff could only notice and report the extent of the damage. The artificial harbor of Omaha beach was completely out of order. So much that it was decided not to rebuild it. *Mulberry B* in Arromanches had suffered less from the storm. It had indeed been protected by an alignment of caissons on its east side, meant to protect the harbor from northeast wind rather than from west wind. Moreover, the British had left the least possible space between the block ships, thus preventing the waves from penetrating the harbor. Plus, the British engineers had used four anchor cables on each pontoon, whereas the Americans had only used two.

Elements of *Mulberry A* which could still be used were transferred to Arromanches, renamed Port Winston.

In Omaha, it took fifteen hundred soldiers a week to dismount and clean the port. However, the unloading of new supplies resumed on June 23, with the good old method of LST beaching on the gentle slopes of Omaha beach.

Intending to ensure a minimum protection of the ships, the *Seabees*[102] reinforced the existing breakwaters with twelve block ships and twenty-six additional Phoenix caissons.

Very soon, Omaha beach recovered its position as the biggest European port. At the end of June, forty thousand two hundred tons were unloaded daily there. Seven thousand tons in Utah and thirty-six hundred tons in Port Winston.

Firmin, Ed and Jimmy didn't resist making fun of the

_____
[102] Engineering units.

white officers of the engineering units, who had invested so much time and money in this project of artificial harbor, which eventually proved operational for just three days.

"Thank God, this idea didn't come out of a Negro's mind. The poor guy would have been court-martialed for treason and hanged, for sure," Jimmy commented, ironically.

CHAPTER 50

Although the supplies were stopped during the storm, the advance of the troops inland still continued.

On June 19, the British had freed Tilly-sur-Seulles, six miles west from Caen. On the following day, the 7th U.S. Corps had moved forward to Cherbourg. In Sottevast, ten miles south of Cherbourg, the Americans had discovered a launch pad of V2 rockets under construction. On June 21, in the thick of the storm, the troops of the 7th Corps had entered Cherbourg, where the Germans had retreated to defend the port as long a possible. The latter had been riddled with remotely controlled mines. Cornered and quickly in numerical inferiority, the garrison commander of Cherbourg, Lieutenant General Von Schlieben ordered the complete destruction of all the port facilities.

Finally, on the following day, June 22, while the storm was over, the troops of the 22nd Infantry regiment continued to harass the German defenses. But the latter still put up a fierce resistance. The Americans were compelled to withdraw for a while, to allow a new massive shelling of the city by the combined action of the 8th and 9th Air Force, and the naval artillery stationed off the coast of Cherbourg.

Yet, the Americans had to wait until June 26 to obtain the unconditional surrender of Von Schlieben. And on the 27th, they eventually took possession of the port, yet after it had been ravaged by its sabotage by the Germans.

However, on the same day, one hundred and sixty-seven Allied vehicles could be unloaded in Cherbourg.

***

As of the day after the storm ended, the troops stationed on Omaha beach recovered their usual daily routine. Yet, an event would disturb this return to normal.

There were rumors about a rape which had been committed by a Black soldier, named Clarence Whitfield, on June 14, at Vierville-sur-Mer, nearby Sainte-Mère-Église[103]. On June 20, six days after the fact, after a speedy trial, Whitfield had been convicted and sentenced to death. Private Whitfield had acted in the grip of alcohol, and under the influence of three fellow soldiers of a logistics unit.

The case raised strong reactions in the ranks of the U.S. Army. It even revived racial tensions, by awakening old prejudices among Southern segregationists. Like the alleged inability of colored people to control their emotions, particularly with regard to sexual relation.

The headquarters staff wanted to avoid by all means that such kind of behavior would spread. The military tribunals were determined to severely punish them. Especially since rapes had already been committed in Great Britain. The African American soldiers Willie Smith and Eliga Brinson had been accused of the rape of Dorothy Holmes, a sixteen-year-old teenager, on March 5, 1944. They had finally been convicted and sentenced to

---

[103] Source: https://www.cairn.info/revue-vingtieme-siecle-revue-d-histoire-2002-3-page-109.htm

death by an American court-martial on April 29, 1944[104].

Shortly after, another rape charge against Corporal Leroy Henry had raised vivid emotions in the British public opinion, shocked by the inequity of American military tribunals towards colored soldiers. The case had rapidly extended beyond the British borders and turned into an international cause.

Despite a unanimous conviction by an American court-martial, General Dwight D. Eisenhower had decided to pardon the African American non-commissioned officer, under the pressure of the NAACP and the American Negro press. Leroy Henry was finally acquitted on June 17, 1944[105].

At all times, soldiers have been involved in rapes, most often gang rapes. In enemy territories, the military authorities are generally quite tolerant towards such acts. But in this specific case, like previously in Great Britain, the American soldiers were in a friendly country. The repeated bombardments of the last months had considerably shaken the confidence and recognition of a part of the local population for their American liberators. Such behaviors not only corrupted the public morals. They also threatened to seriously complicate the progression of the troops towards Germany.

Corporal Bellegarde was outraged by the demeanor of drunk soldiers, which was inappropriate at the very least.

---

[104] https://fr.findagrave.com/memorial/114441963/eliga-brinson. Both men were executed by hanging on August 11, 1944, in HM Prison Shepton Mallet in England, by the British home office executioners Thomas and Albert Pierrepoint.

[105]   Source : www.rochester.edu/newscenter/wp-content/uploads/2016/03/1847_Leroy-Henry-Poster_PrintInHouse1.pdf et https://muse.jhu.edu/article/669874

He had already experienced it with one of his crew mates, in the person of Donut. He had also felt relieved when he was given the opportunity to reduce his team from four to three people, which allowed him to get rid of this "chucklehead."

Yet, some African Americans considered this exemplary punishment as a new manifestation of racism within the army.

They all feared that it would lead the SHAEF to refuse leaves to colored soldiers. No furlough or overnight pass had been granted since the marshaling of the troops, in early May, on the British ground. The men needed to relax and have fun. Including the service men stationed far behind the font line. But the whole region had been devastated by bombs. They were far from Great Britain, which was relatively spared by the war. Far from its fish and chips, its pubs and its *Palais de Danse*. Even the mail distribution had been suspended during all that time. The soldiers' morale was at its lowest ebb.

With the return of nice weather, and after the capture of Cherbourg, the living conditions of the American combat troops would significantly improve, hence boosting their morale.

The men received their first C-rations, after one month of K-rations. Cooks of the messes could buy fresh produce from local farmers, who were very happy to sell a production they could no longer sell to Paris. Fresh food was most often traded for gasoline and material coming from army storage sites.

The U.S. Red Cross could install *Clubmobiles*[106] near

---

[106] GMC U.S. Red-Cross trucks were fitted with a kitchen consisting of a built-in doughnut machine and a stove for heating water for coffee. It also

the camps. Each GMC truck was run by three young American women, who would serve hot coffee and doughnuts to the soldiers.

The first Post Exchanges in France opened, where the GIs could buy some extra chocolate, cigarettes, wash and hygiene grooming kits, and many other products likely to improve their daily life.

On July 4, Independence Day, nobody was in a mood to celebrate and rejoice. In Sainteny, the boys of the 83rd ID were confronting the SS *Panzergrenadier Regiment 38* of the Division Götz von Berlichingen and the German paratroopers of the *Fallschirmjäger Regiment 6*. The day resulted in one thousand American casualties for a progression of only seven hundred feet.

However, the 4th of July was celebrated in Trévières, on the initiative of Charles Pommiers, notary and mayor of the village, in honor of their liberators. A few official representatives of the U.S. Army attended the ceremony.

On the following day, the American troops continued to progress towards Périers and La Haye-du-Puits, at the cost of five hundred more casualties.

But for everyone, the greatest source of comfort came in the late afternoon of July 6th with the mails from their families. The first mail delivery for more than forty-five days.

Corporal Bellegarde received fifteen V-mails on that day. Through the window of each envelope, he could recognize the handwriting of its sender. He sorted them out and separated his mother's letters from Ethel's. He

---

contained a Victrola with loud speakers, current music records, books, candy, gum and cigarettes. Source:
https://en.wikipedia.org/wiki/American_Red_Cross_Clubmobile_Service

started to open the first ones and ordered them chronologically. There were six sheets. He had been waiting for them for so long that he could have read them all in one go, within a few minutes. But he didn't want to spoil this moment of communion with his parents. An opportunity to escape the pressure of the war. He would take time to enjoy every single word. Each letter filled a single page, as required by the V-mail format. With her delicate handwriting, Celestine managed to fit in twenty-four lines. In his, Firmin hardly succeeded inserting twenty.

In her first letters, Celestine told her son about gossip of New Orleans, in the way of a column in the *New Orleans Item-Tribune*. She would strive not to appear too worried to spare him more sorrow. She would write about her long working days at Mr. Higgins's factory, explaining it was good for her savings. That, with that money, when the war is over, she would start her own business. His father, Joe, continued to work as an unskilled worker on renovation sites during the week, and as a musician in a bar of the French Quarter.

Firmin wondered if his father had started boozing again on Saturday evenings, like before, when he would come back home, drunk, then beat his wife. If it were the case, his mother wouldn't tell anyhow.

In her third mail, Celestine wrote that she had received a touching letter from Mrs. Jones, in which she mentioned Firmin with affection. Saying that she considered him like her second son, and prayed for him every Sunday in the church. She also referred to a charming young woman named Ethel, who had strongly impressed her, the day Firmin and she had shared a dinner with them at home.

"*I hope, Son, that you will not change yr mind about that woman, when you meet another one in France. Mrs. Jones seems to be a wise and pious woman. If I had some doubts about yr judgment, I have none about hers. I wish I could meet Ethel. Do you write to her, at least, to tell you care about her?*"

In the two following mails, Celestine had recovered her gossip style. She wrote about her meetings with other mothers at St-Paul's Lutheran church. About their neighbors, the Davises, who wouldn't talk to her, as they were jealous, because none of their sons had been deemed fit to serve in the army. About the Robinsons, on the ground floor. The husband who was getting worse, due to his illness. His dignified wife, who kept on taking care of him at home. If she decided to send him to a nursing home, she wouldn't be able to pay the rent and would be forced to follow her husband, in what people used to call a deathtrap. She hoped God would call him back to him one night, in his sleep. Every day, she asked news about her "dear little Firmin." Celestine did her shopping twice a week to prevent her from starving or getting tired.

Reading this, Firmin felt heavyhearted. He had forgotten how caring Mrs. Robinson was with him. He almost was ashamed. He wondered if she would live long enough to see him again when he comes back home, after the war. Of course, he would invite her for his wedding with Ethel.

His mother's last mail overwhelmed him. It was dated June 8. D + 2. Her writing was clumsy, trembling, and sometimes cut in the middle of a word, showing her deep concern.

"My beloved son. Since yesterday, the whole press tells only about operation Overlord, D-Day, Bloody Omaha and Utah beach. They showed pictures of 320th VLA balloons flying over Normandy beaches. Yr battalion! I don't even know on which of the beaches you landed. Yr dad is proud of you. He tells everyone around his son is a hero. That you took part in the D-Day! But me, I can't sleep. Every morning, I go to work with great fear, thinking that in the evening I might receive this damn telegram from the army, which every American mother dreads. 'The Secretary of War desires me to express his deepest regret that your son, Firmin Bellegarde, corporal in the 320th VLA, was killed in action on 6 June 1944, in France…' I pray to the Lord that this letter will reach you, safe and sound, and I beg you to send me news ASAP. Yr mom, who loves you more than anything else."

Still deeply moved, he folded his mother's six V-mails and carefully put them inside the bag where he kept each of the mails he received.

Then, he gazed at the stack of Ethel's letters. There were nine.

"Nine only, since May 4!" Firmin thought, disappointed. "This is less than two a week. Maybe she stopped long ago, for she didn't get mine?" he worried.

He couldn't stand waiting any longer. He opened the envelopes, checked the dates, and sorted the mails, placing the oldest on top of the pile.

The first one was dated May 9, the last June 20. She didn't forget him. He breathed a deep sigh of relief.

"Firmin, darling. Every day without you hurts me

terribly. All the more, given that I don't receive news from you anymore. Several colleagues at the Red Cross are in the same situation. So, we support each other. The troop movements must be kept secret. The outcome of the war depends on it. Enemy ears are listening… Good! Still, I've started worrying. Maybe you just forgot me? The idea hurts me so much that I wish I'd never met you. I never thought before that loving someone as much as I love you could be so painful. Yet, what can be more beautiful than to love and be loved in return? For I know you love me. I could feel it. I'm so scared for you. I look forward to seeing you and snuggle into yr arms. Write soon! Ethel."

Firmin shut his eyes and pressed the letter against his chest. Ethel's face was forming in his mind. Vague in the beginning, her facial contour became more precise. Progressively, by little steps. Like a portrait under the brushstrokes of a painter, revealing, one by one, the details of her eyes, her mouth, her cheeks, and her hair.

V-mails were only the copies of the original letters, assembled on a microfilm, sent to their destination to be reprinted on paper, slipped into an envelope, and eventually delivered to their recipient. To the greatest regret of the soldiers in love, they couldn't carry with them the perfume fragrance of their beloved partners.

Firmin still tried to recall his smell memory, hoping it would help him recreate Ethel's perfume in his mind. But the only thing he managed to smell was the odor of his own perspiration. He might have washed every day, his dirty clothes were impregnated with it. No one had received any clean spare clothes so far. He smiled, thinking of Ethel's reaction if she were before him, right now.

The three following mails had been written every fourth day. In the letters of May 12 and 16, Ethel told him of her work days, of her fear of losing him, and her eagerness to see him back. In the evening, filled with love and romanticism, she would devour pages of Jane Austen's novel, *Sense and Sensibility*. Ethel would identify, by turns, with the passionate Marianne and with the wise Elinor.

Firmin felt no attraction for that kind of literature from another time. Reading wasn't his passion anyhow. Besides African American newspapers, he didn't read. Music was his hobby. Yet, he was proud of knowing that the woman he loved was educated. "Mom's gonna like it, for sure!" Firmin thought.

"Good news, Corp.?"

Firmin looked up. It was Jimmy. Standing upright on the edge of his foxhole, he was holding an open can, stirring its content with a fork.

Firmin didn't reply and resumed his reading.

"You'd better eat something, Corp. If you want, I can warm up your can. The stove is still burning. We've got spaghetti with beef today. Could be worse."

Corporal Bellegarde accepted. He laid down the pile of mail, opened his C-ration, and took out the can containing the main course, which he handed over to Jimmy.

"Well. Thank you. Put it on the stove. I'll join you in ten minutes."

Firmin started reading Ethel's next mail. It was dated May 20.

"*Firmin, my love. I couldn't sleep for the last two days and nights. Recently, I started suffering from nausea, which I believed was linked to my being in love and sad. I feel so unhappy without you. I tried to hide it, but Clarisse caught me twice vomiting in the bathroom. We talked about those women things. Everything fits. The dates. The delay. I'm pregnant, my love. Pregnant by you, of course, as I haven't had any other partner. We've done it just once, but it was enough. Bad luck! Clarisse told me. Is it really bad luck? Or is it a sign of destiny? The prospect of having a baby with you fills me with happiness, but it scares me too. I hesitated to tell you the truth now, or wait until you return. I even had ugly thoughts. May God forgive me! How do you feel when you read this mail? Are you happy? Or, will you rather try to forget me and our child, like so many inconsistent men would do? But you're not like them, are you? Whatever you decide, my love, let me know. Quickly. Even if it's gonna hurt me more. With all my love, Ethel.*

The news knocked him down. Firmin let his hands fall on both sides of his legs. He was dazed. Paralyzed. Like a rabbit caught in the lights of a car driving in its direction. Unable to react. Due to his young age—he was just twenty —he had never imagined having to cope with such an event. Especially now. Under such circumstances. How could he be so irresponsible? He who used to lecture his crew mates about not drinking too much, to stop them from having an inappropriate demeanor with women! Why didn't he use a condom? Easy to say, afterwards!

Images of the scene were now scrolling in his head. All this had happened so fast. They had spent so much time together, that day. Their mutual desire was such that they had lost their minds.

"It's ready, Corp.! Your meal is hot, now."

His memory of that night was so strong that Firmin felt like he was living it one more time. He then realized that their lapse in judgment was inevitable. Such was their destiny.

"Whatsa' matter, Corp.?"

Firmin jumped with surprise. He looked up and saw Jimmy who was holding his smoking can of spaghetti and beef.

"Enjoy your meal, Corp.!" he said with a radiant smile.

Corporal Bellegarde gazed with disgust at his meal.

"Oh! Sorry, Stevenson. I'm afraid I ain't hungry anymore. Can you get me a good hot Joe, instead?"

"What's cooking, Corp.? Anything wrong?" Jimmy asked, gazing at the letter in Firmin's hand?"

Firmin didn't want to pour out his personal life. The only man with whom he could do it was Ed. Anyway, not now. Tomorrow, maybe.

"I'm all right!" lied the corporal. "I just fear I may not digest this delicious meal well."

Jimmy burst out laughing and returned in his foxhole with the untouched canned spaghetti with beef portion.

Firmin returned to his reflection. He wondered how his mother would react when learning the news. She would surely start by giving him an earful. "Knocking up a girl when you're not sure you'll be there to raise your child and see him grow! Not to mention the shame that will fall on the poor girl when she comes back home pregnant, and yet unmarried! Did you just think it over, Son?"

His father, Joe, would react otherwise. "Let that gal!

She should have refrained. When you don't wanna get preggy, you don't sleep with a man. She got what she deserves. Forget her and live your life! You're way too young to bother with a woman and a baby…"

Anyhow, Firmin was deeply in love with that girl. And he was determined to take his responsibility. Therefore, he would have to be much more careful from now on. He had to stay alive to take care of his two loved ones.

Firmin felt a long thrill running through his whole body when he remembered the mission Ed and he had accepted a few days earlier. He could have been killed. Then, this mail would have been returned to Ethel without an explanation. Indeed, Firmin hadn't yet mentioned to the battalion headquarters Ethel's contact information, as one of the people to be informed in case he were killed or injured.

From now on, he would stay back from the fight and just do his job as a balloon crew leader.

After he had finished reading all the mails from Ethel, he swallowed his hot coffee together with a few crackers and a dessert. Far from distressing him, the prospect of becoming a father restored his appetite. Still, not to the point he would ask Jimmy to warm up his canned spaghetti with beef, once again. Besides, Jimmy had probably swallowed it up, already.

He didn't even say a word of it to Edward, when the latter expressed his concern about his refusal to eat his meal. He would talk to Ed later, when he's alone with him.

For the time being, Firmin would only write his feelings in his diary. While he was doing it, he remembered his little sister Marie. He could see her, sitting on a heap of straw, on the bottom of the wheeled crate their father had built. Firmin, clad like a farmer, would draw the crate. Marie laughing out loud when a bump or a hollow would bounce the little cart, almost making her lose her balance.

A wave of emotion flooded him, but he strove to suppress his tears. His sister was gone way too early. He wished he had seen her grow old, cherished her, and given her the protection of a big brother.

Now, he was hoping that Ethel's baby would be a girl. "We'd call her Marie. Ethel would surely accept. Mom's gonna be happy… As for Dad, he'll be so touched that he'll be pleased to welcome the three of us!"

CHAPTER 51

The following days were punctuated by the continuous inflow of material and men unloading, day and night, all along Omaha beach.

Two days after the reception of Ethel's mail, a lieutenant of a logistics unit who had heard of Ed's shooting skills asked Corporal Bellegarde to lend him his crew member to carry out a mission. Edward immediately seized the opportunity to express his feelings to the white officer.

"You don't lack nerve! When it comes to award me a citation or a medal, you send me packing because the officer who could've testified of my accomplishment was killed! But now that you need me, you come back to me as if nothing had happened…"

"Let's call it a chance to remedy this injustice, soldier!" the lieutenant replied. "I'm offering you an opportunity to stand out, once more."

"If Corporal Bellegarde comes with us, I accept," Edward replied, looking at Firmin with a questioning gaze.

Ed's request caught Firmin off guard. He hadn't told him of his situation of future dad, so far. He had no intention to play the hero. But, on the other hand, he feared to be seen by his crew as a yellow belly.

"Not this time, sorry. Go without me, Washington."

Ed couldn't believe his ears. Yet, he refrained from making his superior feel uncomfortable. Now, if he refused to follow the lieutenant, the latter would make a report to his hierarchy, which would in return blame the corporal for refusal to comply. Only Lieutenant Colonel Reed's intervention could have saved him in this moment.

Ed gave Firmin a once-over with a gaze of utter incomprehension, then turned to the officer.

"Alright, lieutenant. I'm yours. Hope I won't regret it."

***

After he returned from his mission, late in the evening, private first class Edward Washington demanded to his superior the reason why he had suddenly changed his mind.

"Is this the way you expect to gain the Whites' respect? By doing your job and nothing more? Let me remind you what you said on the LST, during the crossing! Even if we risk our lives, we have to fight like the Whites, because it's our only chance to assert our civil rights!"

Corporal Bellegarde thought he could justify his decision by only confessing to Edward he would soon become a father, and hence had no right to risk his life. Instead, the excuse made Edward angry.

"You mean you don't mind if I die here, do you?"

Firmin tried to get out of this awkward situation, but it wouldn't work.

"What about our promise to always watch over one another, until the end of the war? Wasn't it a mutual commitment?" Edward added.

Firmin took Ed away from Jimmy, who was dozing in his foxhole. The two men discussed for long. Firmin apologized profusely, and agreed he shouldn't have let his buddy leave alone for a dangerous mission. Edward finally cooled down and congratulated the future dad with a warm handshake.

"Hope you're gonna buy us a round of drinks, next time we get a leave," Edward said before returning to his foxhole.

His mission had sharpened his appetite, although he hadn't had a chance to stand out on the battlefield with a new act of bravery.

The 320th VLA had been protecting the two beaches of the American sector for more than a month, although the battalion was originally planned to stay for just seventy-two hours in Normandy. However, despite the danger, nobody complained. To the contrary, most of the balloon operators were happy. It proved that their presence was useful. At least, as long as the Allies hadn't overcome the German resistance.

The major obstacle for the American troops was the particular topography of the Norman countryside. Besides the almost impassable hedgerows, there were the marshes of the Cotentin, in which the troops and the tanks would get bogged down. Not to mention the damn *Panzer Faust*. These German rocket launchers could easily pierce the armor of any American tank. When they were stuck between two hedgerows or in the middle of a swampy area, they were turned into easy targets for German SS foot soldiers. Many Sherman tanks had been destroyed like this.

In the British-Canadian sector, the advance of the front was stopped by German Panzer divisions. The British troops waited until July 10, before they could liberate the northern part of Caen, although it had previously been reduced to piles of rubble by massive Allied bombardments.

It resulted in pushing the Germans, the next day, to focus their counter-attack further west, in the Cotentin.

On July 12, a rumor spread about Roosevelt's death. Some, at first, believed it was about the US president, Franklin D. Roosevelt. But when his burial in the military cemetery at Sainte-Mère-Église was announced, it became obvious that the dead was Theodore Roosevelt Jr., the nephew of former president Theodore Roosevelt.

Generals too could die on a battlefield. Or almost. Indeed, the soldiers soon learned the general had died of a heart attack, in the middle of a blanket drill.

"Betcha my bottom dollar that guy's gonna get a posthumous medal for that!" Edward joked, making everybody around laugh out loud.

On July 13, the remainder of the 320th VLA landed on Omaha beach. The major part of the HQ battery, and the whole battery B.

On that occasion, Corporal Bellegarde met once more with Wilson Monk, the balloon inspector. When he recognized Firmin, he came over to greet him.

Although he hadn't really made friends with that man, Firmin couldn't resist to tell him about his new personal situation. Monk congratulated him, then left to join the HQ camp of his battalion.

CHAPTER 52

July 14, 1944

F or the Allied Supreme Headquarters, Bastille Day, was considered a golden opportunity to strengthen the ties between American soldiers and the French people of Normandy, who had been severely affected by Allied bombings since the day before the invasion.

While battles were raging on the front, sometimes just a few miles away, ceremonies were organized jointly by military authorities and local city halls, in various Norman towns.

However, only a privileged few would be allowed to attend the ceremonies. Men deemed worthy to represent their army and their country. Corporal Bellegarde's crew had the chance to be part of them. They had been granted one day leave under the command of a white officer, and they intended to enjoy it. Their balloon would be left under the control of a member of another crew.

Before they could climb on one of the trucks, a lieutenant checked their outfit. Although they had almost no chance to be allowed to parade alongside white soldiers, they had to take care of their appearance.

Discipline wasn't the only reason, nor the major one. For six weeks, all these men had experienced suffering, fear, fatigue, sleepless nights, lack of hygiene, of recreation or even mere pleasure. Many of them hoped, either openly or secretly, that usual popular rejoicing and celebrations would follow the official ceremonies of July 14.

Firmin, Ed and Jimmy had spent a long time to prepare in this prospect. They had built a makeshift shower and had scrubbed their bodies from top to toe, despite the chilly temperature, before putting on the replacement uniforms which had recently been delivered by the supply units.

In his haversack, Firmin had brought his diary and his harmonica, in addition to all the good things he intended to offer to the Normans he would meet.

As a team leader, Firmin had reminded his crew mates of the rules of good behavior they should apply with the French, based on what he had read in the *pocket guide to France*[107].

"Stay out of political discussions between French people. Always be polite. The French like to use courtesy words. Please. Thank you. They also shake hands on greeting each other and saying goodbye. But they are not back tappers. It's not their way.

If you are billeted with a French family, treat the woman in the house the way you want the woman of your family treated by other men while you're away. Be sure you thank them for their hospitality and show your appreciation.

France has often been represented as a frivolous nation where sly winks and coy pats on the rear are tolerated. You'd better get rid of such notions if you want to keep out of trouble. French girls have been saying NO to the Nazis for years now. They expect the men in the American army to act like friends and Allies."

---

[107]   Source :
https://archive.org/stream/PocketGuideToFrance/APocketGuideToFrance#page/n0/mode/2up

Corporal Bellegarde also reminded them of elementary secrecy rules.

"Be as friendly as you like with anyone who wants to share your friendship; just don't discuss anything connected with the operations of our unit, or of any other. Remember the wolf in sheep's clothing.

Beware of prostitutes. You might catch a venereal disease and become a less healthy soldier in our fighting forces. Plus, they are often undercover Nazi agents."

The trio joined a convoy of three trucks loaded with Black American soldiers from engineering and logistics units. During the trip, the three balloon operators were overwhelmed with questions about their involvement in the D-Day landing, which had been reported in several articles of the British press, and of Stars and Stripes[108]. Jimmy was the most talkative of the three when it came to tell how he had reached the beach under the heavy fire of German batteries. Firmin and Ed had heard the story ten times before, but each time, Jimmy would add some romantic details.

Firmin's mind was far away. With Ethel in Great Britain. He imagined her with a round belly, watching out for his arrival, hoping he would be back before the birth of their baby.

The prospect of this unforeseen responsibility scared him. And yet, he was firmly decided not to follow his father's example. And therefore, he could count on his

---

[108] Originally published in Great Britain, the official newspaper of the U.S. Army in Europe's theater of operations was printed as of July 4, on the rotary presses of *La Presse cherbourgeoise*, then as of mid-August by the daily newspaper *Ouest-Éclair* in Rennes.

mother's support and wise advice.

Firmin didn't even notice that the two other trucks had left the convoy. His truck was heading towards Isigny-sur-Mer.

An MP officer finally ordered the driver to stop the GMC. The lieutenant asked his men to get out. The driver would stay inside the cabin and watch over the rifles.

Two columns of trucks and jeeps were parked on both sides of the roadway. The officer ordered his men to line up on two perfect rows.

On his sign, the little group headed to the center of the village, marching in rhythm.

When they reached the main square, they discovered an impressive gathering of American soldiers and French civilians. Among them, many MPs ensured the positioning of the different units. One of them, noticing the twelve Black soldiers, approached their lieutenant and assigned him a place apart from the crowd.

"Here we are," Ed muttered. "Even in France, they don't want us to be seen with 'em!"

"Shut up!" Firmin whispered, while kicking Ed's ankle. "Be happy to be here and enjoy the show!"

The notables of Isigny-sur-Mer had carefully prepared the event. The street was decked out with American and French flags, and banners welcoming their liberators.

A heavy atmosphere reigned over the village. The present moment was dedicated to meditation and affliction. First honor and mourn the dead. Then only, comfort the living.

On the narrow sidewalks, the villagers were gathered in small groups, waiting for the religious procession to pass by. Suddenly, the murmur of private conversations stopped, leaving room to the muffled footsteps of the little altar servers, who opened the parade. At its head, the youngest, dressed in a red outfit, was holding a smoking censer in one hand. The child was followed by half a dozen altar boys wearing a white surplice over their red cassock. Last came the priest of the parish.

The image reminded Firmin of his school years at the *Holy Cross Junior High School* in New Orleans. He leaned forward to have an overview of the whole parade.

Behind the priest, he could see senior officers from different units involved in the Battle of Normandy. All these people were parading silently in front of emotional and admiring civilians.

Turning his head to the left, Firmin saw a film crew of the U.S. Army, which was busy capturing this historic moment.

A U.S. Navy marine with a trumpet in his hand was heading a parade of the Great War's veterans, proudly displaying their medals pinned to the flap of their dark coats. A few younger men were walking behind. Their blue, white and red armbands claimed their membership in the French resistance.

When U.S. GIs and Marines finally appeared, marching in rhythm, the lieutenant ordered his men to stand at attention and get ready to follow them at the end of the parade.

The procession stopped a first time in front of the war memorial. A little group of veterans of 1914–1918, paid tribute to the sons of the village who died for the homeland.

The priest then invited the crowd to pray for the salvation of their souls. Hearing the words *Notre Père*, a man dressed in civilian clothes near the priest started praying Our Father in English. The American officers and soldiers, most of whom were Christians, could join the French in this prayer. Then, the priest continued with *Je vous salue Marie*, in French. The man near him translated. *Hail Mary...*

Heads down and holding hands, Americans and French said the prayer to the Holy Virgin together, three times, in their respective languages.

Then, the procession continued, heading to the temporary graveyard, where the soldiers fallen since June 7, were buried. All along the way, civilians were watching, silent and admiring, at the military parade. Old women were smiling at the camera.

Firmin was fascinated by the man operating an imposing camera supported by a tripod and standing inside a jeep. The camera was fitted with several lenses mounted on a rotating disc. As an aspiring news reporter, Corporal Bellegarde was aware of the power of images in the diffusion of information. He was easily captivated by the news from all over the world shown in dark rooms before the projection of the film.

On top of the camera, the two film magazines reminded both ears of Mickey mouse. Which Jimmy didn't miss pointing out, with the high-pitched voice of the little Walt Disney's character. He probably hoped it would draw the cameraman's attention. But when the operator realized the twelve colored soldiers were close to enter the camera's range, he stopped its panoramic movement and turned the other way round.

"Forget it, man," Ed muttered between his teeth. "Film is too expensive to be wasted filming Negroes like us!"

His partner's deeply sensible comment instantly broke

Firmin's dream of being entrusted with a motion picture camera by a television channel, one day. He would have to be satisfied with a notepad and a pencil to do his job as a journalist. "At least, it'll be much easier to carry," Firmin thought, ironically.

Finally, they reached the temporary graveyard. Hundreds of tombs had been hastily dug. Each one was indicated by a mere white painted stick, topped with a metal plate with the engraved identity of the soldier. Here and there a white cross would replace the stick.

The priest started to bless the deceased, then said a prayer for the dead. Children and soldiers were invited to lay their floral wreaths. Some were hesitating between several graves, sometimes moving the flowers from one to another location.

A few officers gathered here and there in front of the tombs of fellow soldiers of their respective units, while a bugler was playing "Taps" bugle call.

Firmin wondered which of the graves contained the remains of a Negro. Even though less than two thousand of them had landed on D-Day, and if a majority of the Black contingent was assigned to service units away from the front, they still had suffered losses. Starting with the two men of the 320th VLA. Besides, the guys who continuously supplied ammunition and food to the front couldn't hide in a foxhole from enemy shots and shelling, as opposed to the fighters.

After all the dead had been honored by their brothers in arms, the procession moved back to the village, where the mayor would give a speech in the honor of the Americans.

Once again, the twelve African Americans would be requested to stay behind. Fortunately, a platform had been installed in the middle of the main square. The twelve men wouldn't miss anything of the show.

The mayor, his wife, a few officers and other notables of the village climbed onto the platform. The mayor greeted every officer, who then took a seat. Yet, one of them remained standing in front of a microphone fixed on a mike stand.

Firmin heard a voice announcing in French that colonel Scott was about to read the English translation of the mayor's talk. The officer unfolded a sheet of paper and started to read:

"For the second time, we unite to celebrate liberty. On the fourth of July, knowing you could not commemorate your independence, since you were engaged in the war, we wished to observe the day, and you joined with us. Today you have associated yourselves with our national holiday. The fourteenth of July is a legal holiday, and a day of rest for all Frenchmen. But we are prouder to observe it today. What a difference between the 14th of July 1939 and the 14th of July 1944! In 1939, we were not aware of our happiness. One must have suffered for more than four years under the German boots to know the value which we now attach to the word liberty. On this 14th of July 1944, we wish with one accord to manifest our joy being free once again."

Then, another officer stood up and approached the mike to read a speech in French. It was Lewis H. Brereton, lieutenant general of the 9th Air Force.

"Monsieur le maire, dear friends. I can't express how happy I am to be back again in France, on the 14th of July.

A hundred and fifty-five years ago, the Bastille was stormed. It was a big blow. A great victory in the name of freedom. At that time, everybody in the world was watching France. Today, the world is watching you, one more time. For it is on your ground and on your side that the German armies will be defeated. This time, completely and for ever. Nobody can ignore the links which unite our two countries. You know it well. And we never forgot how much Lafayette and Rochambeau contributed to our independence. It's a debt which can never be paid back.

But in 1944, like in 1918, we are proud to fight again in France the German tyranny. We offer you not only a material relief, but also something which isn't less important: friendship, sympathy and hope. Like you did for us in the past.

It isn't the right moment to make great speeches. However, I wish to tell you how much we feel sorry for the damage this damn war is causing to your beautiful homeland.

We admire your courage. We admire your temperament and your spirit. Soon, very soon ..., we will win full victory.

Now, I would like to greet you, on behalf of our government, of the U.S. Army, and the 9th Air Force, which I have the honor to command. Vive la France!"[109]

Hearing the last three words, the crowd applauded loudly.

Firmin had understood every single word, especially since the general strove to speak distinctly and calmly,

---

[109] Source: Youtube14 juillet - Grandcamp-les-Bains - Normandie - 14/07/1944 - DDay-Overlord

without excessive emphasis. He had obviously learned his speech by heart, since he didn't need to look at his text more than two or three times. Unfolding the sheet of paper, quickly glancing at it, folding it again in his hand, then resuming his talk.

Several times, Edward pulled Firmin's sleeve, begging him to translate the speech. The corporal, however, waited until the end to sum up its general idea in a few words, before the first notes of the American national anthem sounded. In a same impulse, the officials on the platform stood up and the officers saluted the star-spangled banner raised in the middle of the square, near the French flag.

All the soldiers stood at attention and made a perfect salute. Firmin couldn't hide his emotion. All the humiliation he had suffered, segregation, discrimination, contempt of the Whites for Blacks, were erased by much stronger feelings.

Patriotism, respect for the flag and the conviction he belonged to the American Nation in its entirety, beyond prejudices and community divisions.

A thunder of cheers and applause of the crowd burst out at the end of the anthem, showing the deep recognition from the French for their liberators.

Then, a man announced that a children's choir would sing *La Marseillaise*, under the direction of their old teacher. All the men of the village took off their berets and hats. Men, women, children, old people, civilians, partisans, veterans of the Great War, all stood at attention. The soldiers of both countries made perfect hand salutes. Palms facing down for the Americans. Palms facing forward for the French.

Among the choir members, a few little girls were clad

with dresses, specially made for this event by their mothers, which recalled the American flag. A white five-pointed star was sewn on a blue square of canvas covering their chests. And the lower part of their dresses were made of a white fabric sewn with horizontal red stripes.

At the signal of the choir conductor, the children started to sing *a cappella*. Once again, all the soldiers, American and French saluted at attention. Everyone listened to the choir respectfully, until the end, without singing.

A new salvo of applause and cheers marked the end of the official ceremony.

From then on, the atmosphere became less formal and started to warm up. Soldiers, dispersed in the crowd, brought boxes and distributed all kinds of treats. Children of all ages rushed to them, shouting, hoping to collect a maximum of chewing gum, chocolate bars and candies.

Young girls walked among the soldiers with a basket full of tricolor cockades they would pin on the soldiers' shirts. The latter were pleased to receive these civilian decorations made of canvas or wool, in their honor.

The twelve Black American GIs were observing with envy this feverish agitation from afar, when they saw three girls making their way to them through several MPs.

"Get a load of this!" Jimmy said loudly.

The three girlfriends, with long brown and curly hair, spoke out the dozen English words they had learned since the landing, punctuated with nervous giggles. This unexpected mark of attention reminded the twelve men of the best moments they had spent in Great Britain.

It made them instantly forget the previous warnings of their lieutenant asking them a minimum of self-control. All, starting with Jimmy, boasted about to curry favors with the prettiest, or, at least one of them. All but Firmin and a private first class of the 2nd *Quartermaster Company*, attached to the 2nd ID, who looked shyer or less interested in dead-end relations.

Unwittingly, Firmin became the center of interest of the three girls, when he offered his fellow soldiers to serve as their interpreter. Yet, he would soon escape this embarrassing attention. Feeling the hostile gazes of several MPs, their lieutenant told his men it was time to leave the town and return to Omaha beach. Some tried to protest, but the officer brought them back into line. On their way back to the truck, Firmin negotiated with the lieutenant to stop on the road near the villages of Aignerville and Trévières, before driving back to Omaha. The officer was aware of his men's frustration, so he accepted.

CHAPTER 53

In the GMC, the guys were overexcited. The fifteen minutes they had spent with the three young girls had awakened their instinct of vigorous and fiery males. Their reptilian brain had gained the ascendant over their cortex. The braggarts started to compare their records and their power of seduction.

One of them preened himself of having slept one night with two English birds. Two girlfriends. In the same bed.

"Believe me, they loved it. We fucked like bunnies, all night long."

"Big deal, Darik!" his neighbor replied. "English gals are frigid. Or they pretend! Believe me, man. No woman on earth compares to the French!"

"Indeedy, man!" another guy confirmed. "That's why I joined uncle Sam. In the induction center, in Atlanta, a sarge told me French girls are easy, especially with Negroes."

Firmin was stunned by all these ridiculous prejudices. He even worried about it. Ed and Jimmy noticed it from his gaze. He had warned them before leaving Omaha beach. Therefore, they refrained from taking part in the male boasting contest with their brothers of the logistics unit, although they didn't see any harm in it.

Such kind of sexist comments didn't always lead to consequences, as long as the men stayed sober. Yet, after several drinks, alcohol could easily push a man to satisfy his fantasies. All the more a bunch of drunken men.

"Give it a rest, will ya! Or we return straight to Omaha beach."

"Can't we have a little fun?" Darik grumbled.

"Having fun, you said? You'd better read again the pamphlet you received before you left Great Britain. Treat the French women the way you would like your wife or your mother be treated. Otherwise, you'll end up like all the Negroes convicted of rape, or just suspected of rape … swinging on the end of a rope! Court-martials are ruthless with Negroes who show disrespect to white women. Have you ever heard of Clarence Whitfield?"

Corporal Bellegarde's warning chilled everyone in the truck. They all kept silent until it stopped.

When he recognized the farm where Edward had driven out the German sniper, Firmin asked the driver with a sign to reduce speed. One could hear bursts of voices and laughs in the distance. The occupants of the farm were likely enjoying a holiday meal, Firmin thought, when he realized it was 13:00 and that he hadn't eaten anything since 07:00 this morning.

He preceded the lieutenant inside the farm.

From the porch, the two men saw people sitting around a long table covered with a white tablecloth. Firmin immediately recognized the old man and his daughter Geneviève. Near them, ten people were so busy relishing the content of their plates that they didn't notice the presence of the two Americans.

"*Bon appétit!*" Firmin screamed.

All the heads turned towards the porch. Firmin greeted them with his hand. It took a few embarrassing seconds to the family patriarch to recognize him. He then turned to his daughter.

"*Ne restez pas là !*[110]" she screamed in French, wiping her hands on her apron.

"*Come closer and join us!*" she added. *"We've just started!"*

"They're inviting us!" Firmin said.

The lieutenant tried to stop him.

"Did you tell them we're not alone?"

Firmin didn't reply and walked to the table. He first greeted the old man and his daughter, then introduced himself and the lieutenant to all the guests. He explained to them they were accompanied by twelve other GIs like him, who would be pleased to share their rations to celebrate the French national holiday together.

The patriarch welcomed the proposal with enthusiasm. He stood up from his chair, stayed at attention, and proudly introduced himself to the lieutenant, looking at him straight in the eyes.

"*Sergent-chef Eugène Leroyer, mes respects, mon lieutenant!*[111]"

The latter returned his salute and thanked him for his hospitality.

Meanwhile, Corporal Bellegarde was gone to fetch his comrades. In order to keep an eye on the rifles, the driver drove the truck inside the farm's courtyard.

When she saw the twelve imposing shapes of the Black GIs jumping down the platform, Geneviève worried.

"*Gee! What am I gonna do with all these big fellows?*"

"*Don't worry, ma'm!*" Firmin reassured her. "*They're gonna be small. I will ask them to give you a hand!*"

---

[110] Don't stay there!

[111] Staff Sergeant Eugène Leroyer, with my respects, lieutenant.

Geneviève asked her brother Jean to go to the barn and bring back what he could find to welcome their last minute's guests appropriately. Like in all farms in the region, wedding parties were opportunities to gather much larger tables than the present one. They would just need to forget about the missing tablecloths. As for the seats, a few planks nailed on logs of wood would easily make it. Corporal Bellegarde didn't have much pain to find volunteers to help the mistress of the house with this task.

All the soldiers were invited to unpack their food rations on the table. Everyone had bought more than his C-ration for this special day. When they saw the chewing gum, candies and other treats piling up on the table, the youngest guests whooped with joy. There were Geneviève's three children, who seemed to have well overcome the trauma of their being held hostages. Plus two cousins, the children of uncle Jean and aunt Yvonne, Geneviève's sister-in-law.

Firmin didn't want his fellow soldiers to remain isolated on their side. Therefore, he offered to Geneviève to insert each soldier between two other guests.

"That's a great idea!" Eugène exclaimed, without worrying about his daughter's opinion.

"C'mon kids. Leave some space for our American friends!"

The children didn't need to be asked twice. One of the boys took advantage of the joyful confusion during the placement of the soldiers to steal a handful of candies.

For this holiday meal, the mistress of the house had prepared an assortment of farm produces, based on eggs and cooked meat, accompanied with boiled seasonal vegetables. Carrots, eggplants, zucchini, spinach, turnips, peas. As well as raw vegetables, like pink radishes, onions, cucumber, endives. Not to forget bread cooked on the farm, and fresh butter.

For the dessert, Yvonne had made three cakes of her own. The canned stew meat and fruit cakes brought by the soldiers would be welcomed by everyone around the table.

The kids were exceptionally granted one glass of sweet cider each, while the adults would accompany their meal with hard cider at will. For lack of glasses, the soldiers would be served in their aluminum canteen cups. Everyone around the tables would soon be filled with a growing good mood and a communicative joy.

Firmin was constantly solicited by someone to translate a story told by the old man or a question asked by one of the soldiers. One of them, hailing from Virginia, who was raised in a family of farm laborers, couldn't tire of questioning about Mr. Leroyer's family farm.

"How many acres have you got? What are you growing? How many heads in your cattle? How many dairy cows? How much milk do they give?"

As he feared to offend their host, Firmin avoided translating the remarks of his fellow soldier about the absence of modern agricultural machines, and the dilapidation of the premises. And the disparaging comments about the noisy and uncomfortable clogs worn by all these farmers.

Every answer of the old man disappointed the Virginian soldier, which one could read on his face. All these questions eventually became embarrassing to Firmin who feared they could upset their host. Thus, he decided to put an end to the conversation and asked the soldier to change the subject. Which the lieutenant approved, since he didn't want to spoil this moment of friendship with the local people.

"Don't you guys have a phonograph?" the officer asked.

Firmin didn't know the word in French, so he translated the question, using gestures.

"*Don't worry, Son,*" the old man replied in French. "*We've also got phonographs in France. But not here, at the farm! We've only got a wireless set. Which is far more useful here. Phonographs are for people in big towns. There's one at the village party hall, but it must be at our mayor's house, currently.*"

"You never dance, then?"

"*Do you believe you're the only ones who know how to have fun?*" the old man asked, with a mocking smile.

Eugène Leroyer placed his thumbs under the top of his suspenders, and made them slip downwards, while stretching the elastic straps.

"*Geneviève, bring us two bottles of my personal Calva… And you, Petit Jean…*" he added to the eldest of his grandsons, "*bring my accordion here … and watch your back if you let it fall! Is it clear?*"

The kid was already gone. His mother soon returned from the pantry with two bottles of moonshine cider brandy. She passed around the tables, serving every adult a small dose of the precious alcohol.

"*Watch out, guys! This ain't cider!*" the old man warned.

Then, he stood up and raised his glass.

"*I suggest we toast … the Franco-American friendship, and the victory against the Krauts!*"

Corporal Bellegarde stood up and invited his comrades

to get up and toast with Eugène. Somewhat suspicious, the lieutenant sniffed the golden liquor. The strong vapors of the Calvados foreshadowed a pretty high level of alcohol.

"*Long live the United States and long live France!*" Eugène shouted, before gulping down his brandy.

"God bless America and *vive la France!*" Firmin echoed, raising his quarter.

The swallowing of Eugène's rotgut triggered a concert of coughing and throats clearing. The kids burst out laughing at the sight of all the Black soldiers' faces distorted by the burning sensation caused by the seventy percent ABV brandy. The whiskey which some of them had drunk in Great Britain probably seemed bland in comparison.

Fearing the devastating effects of such a strong booze on his men's behavior, the lieutenant ordered them to refuse any additional dose. He instructed Firmin to beg Eugène and Geneviève, politely but firmly, to put the bottles back in a secured and secret place. He then asked him to explain why.

"War is not over, yet. We must keep our minds clear to defeat the German army and annihilate Hitler! Then, only, we will be pleased to celebrate full victory with you like it should be."

The old man didn't insist. With a nod, he asked his daughter to bring the Calvados back to the pantry. Meanwhile, Petit Jean reappeared, wearing his grandpa's accordion slung. The straps were too long for him, causing the instrument to bounce on his thighs at each footstep.

Seeing the little boy proudly carrying the squeeze box, too big and heavy for him, Firmin saw himself back at the same age, the day his father had put his tenor sax in his kid's hands. Firmin had already seen a *Hohner* accordion in New Orleans. On one side, it had a piano-like keyboard with black and white keys. On the other side, it had a dozen black buttons. Eugène's was different. It was made of varnished blond wood, and had pearly buttons on both treble and bass sides.

Eugène took the instrument off the kid's hands and asked everybody to follow him to the barn, on the other side of the yard facing the house. He sat on the edge of a stone water trough, attached to the building's wall. The children started swinging from one foot to the other and spinning to the rhythm of imaginary tunes. A few soldiers proposed to help Geneviève to move the chairs to form the arc of a circle around an improvised dance floor.

The old man played a series of scales on his accordion to warm up his fingers. After a few minutes, he played the first notes of a song which moved the hearts of the French, exasperated by the German occupation. Geneviève would soon hum its melody, then sing.

"*Il revient à ma mémoire des souvenirs familiers,*
je revois ma blouse noire lorsque j'étais écolier,
sur le chemin de l'école je chantais à pleine voix,
des romances sans paroles, vieilles chansons d'autrefois.
Douce France[112], cher pays de mon enfance,
bercé de tendre insouciance,
je t'ai gardée dans mon cœur !
Mon village au clocher aux maisons sages,
où les enfants de mon âge ont partagé mon bonheur,

---

[112] 1943, Douce France, lyrics by Trenet and Rghioui, tune by Trenet, Pleche and Grandjean.

oui je t'aime et je te donne ce poème, oui je t'aime…[113]"

Everyone imitated Geneviève. Jean, Yvonne and the children… And even the GIs who, at Firmin's sign would sing phonetically the first words of the chorus, then continue humming along the melody.

Cheered up by the enthusiastic applause of the spectators, Eugène continued with other hits of the moment. *Frou-frou*, sung by Berthe Sylva. *Mon légionnaire* sung by Marie Dubas.

One of the GIs found two tablespoons and turned them into a percussion instrument. Several of his friends accompanied him by tapping their thighs. Others sat astride and started to beat the measure on the back of their chairs.

Firmin couldn't resist taking his *Hohner* harmonica out of his haversack. He then improvised a solo on Marie Dubas' song.

Intending to honor his guests, Eugène announced the following song. *J'ai deux amours*, by Josephine Baker.

Everybody sang with him and Geneviève.

"On dit qu'au-delà des mers, là-bas sous le ciel clair,
il existe une cité au séjour enchanté,
et sous les grands arbres noirs, chaque soir,
vers elle s'en va tout mon espoir…"[114]

---

[113] Lyricstranslate.com. *Familiar memories come back to my mind, I recall my black blouse, when I was a student on the way to school, I sang aloud ballads without lyrics, old songs from the past…*

Sweet France, dear country of my childhood, cradled in tender carefreeness, I have kept you in my heart! My village with the bell tower and with noble houses where children of my age have shared my joy, yes, I love you…

Then one soldier asked:

"Josephine Baker? Isn't she the one who sings dressed in a banana-made skirt?"

Corporal Bellegarde begged him not to make a scene and consider Baker's costume with humor. Fortunately, the noise made by the audience quickly covered the mockery of the touchy soldier.

Eugène eventually invited Firmin to play with him the following song, dedicated to his favorite instrument. *L'accordéoniste*[115] sung by Édith Piaf in 1940.

The atmosphere was slowly losing its festiveness. All the songs of the French repertoire didn't really inspire the African American guests of Eugène. So, he made a last try with a tune which sounded more like the standards of Black American music. *Swing Valse* by Gus Viseur[116]. Yet, the soldiers' heart was not in it. Their applause, at first prolonged and enthusiastic, became more polite, almost forced.

Geneviève, who didn't want to end the celebration on a sad note, asked Firmin:

"*Why don't you play us one of those swinging tunes? This hit of Glenn so-and-so, for instance. In ze moon?*"

"*In the Mood* by Glenn Miller!" Firmin corrected.

"*Exactly!*" Geneviève confirmed, excited.

"*I'm sorry, ma'am, but this tune requires a brass band, and we've only got an accordion and a harmonica. However, I could play one or two pieces of blues specially*

---

[114] Lyricstranslate.com They say beyond the seas, there beneath the pale sky, there exists a city, an enchanted escape. And under the big black trees, each night, towards it go all my hopes.

[115] Lyrics and tune by Michel Emer.

[116] Belgian accordionist (1915–1974) and jazz musician.

composed for this modest instrument."

"*Can one dance on them?*" Geneviève worried.

"*Sure!*"

"*Good. Let's play some blooze, then!*"

Firmin looked at his comrades. After a few seconds of reflection, he asked them:

"You all know *Shotgun Blues* by Sonny Boy Williamson[117]?"

Several guys nodded. Firmin moistened his lips and started to beat the measure with his right leg. After a few notes of introduction, he began to sing:

"You ought a heard my grandmother
When she got my grandfather, told me."

One of the soldiers in the group, who reminded Firmin of this good old Donut, as much by his chubbiness as by his joyful gaze, immediately sang with him. He knew the lyrics by heart. Firmin gave him a wink, and started playing his harmonica.

"She said get away from me, man
I swear you've done gotten too old..."

The others slapped their hands and stepped their feet to beat the rhythm. The kids moved, more or less in the tempo. The youngest son of Geneviève took his eldest cousin by the hand and invited her for a dance. Boosted by their audacity, her mother stood up and tried to make her husband dance with her. But the latter wasn't ready to make a show in front of all these strangers.

"Now when my baby left me
You know she left me with mule to ride

---

[117] African American blues harmonica player (1914–1948).

Now when the train left the station
You know my mule laid down and died."

Firmin quickly gained confidence in his play. Borne by his comrades' enthusiasm, he would extend the melodic parts of the song with effects of trill, vibrato or syncopation, under the fascinated gaze of Petit Jean. He tried to push the old man to accompany him in the melody with an accordion improvisation, but the rhythm must have been too quick for him.

Between two pieces, one of the GIs asked the lieutenant if he could invite Geneviève to dance with him. The officer firmly rejected it.

"This woman is married. Her husband is a war prisoner in Germany. It would be against decency for her to have any physical contact with another man! Especially in the presence of her children and her next of kin."

Feeling that things could suddenly go wrong, the officer announced time had come for them to return to Omaha beach.

"We've got a job to do, guys!"

Firmin translated the order of their leader. The children expressed their great disappointment. The lieutenant felt compelled to let Firmin play a very last piece before leaving.

Firmin decided to give his utmost best in a memorable performance of *Whooping the Blues* by Sonny Terry[118].

When the moment had come to leave, Petit Jean asked Firmin if he would soon come back to teach him to play this magical instrument.

---

[118] African American blues singer and harmonica player (1911–1986).

"*It sounds a bit like an accordion, but it's so much lighter!*" the boy sighed.

His little cousin, who had danced a lot on his music insisted he took her in his arms to give him a kiss.

He lifted her. She seemed as light as a bunch of flowers. Her curled hair was flattened on her wet temples. When she smiled, her upper lip would rise and reveal an open space where she had recently lost two milk incisors.

"*What's your name?*" the little girl asked.

"*My name is Firmin. And yours is Pauline, isn't it?*"

The girl nodded. Then, she stroked Firmin's cheek.

"*Are you married?*"

"*I'm engaged.*"

Pauline looked at him with a pout of disappointment, then recovered.

"*Will you soon marry?*"

Firmin looked over the delicate lines of her face. He wondered if the baby whom Ethel would give birth to in a few months would be a girl and if she would look like his little sister Marie. Or would it be a boy to whom he would teach to play the saxophone or baseball? But in that case, he would one day go to war, like him, and like his grandfather in 1917!

"*Will you come and see us again before you return there, in America?*"

Firmin didn't want to disappoint her by making a promise he wouldn't fulfill.

"*Maybe. Who knows?*"

The lieutenant and his men recovered their respective positions and jobs on Omaha beach one hour later.

For a few hours, the war had seemed to suspend its

course for a short truce, but it would soon recall itself to them.

CHAPTER 54

At nightfall on July 15, the Allies had unloaded one and a half million soldiers and three hundred thousand vehicles since June 6[119]. Every day, fifty-four thousand tons of material were unloaded at Utah, Omaha and Arromanches, where the only operational artificial port was running twenty-four hours a day.

On July 18, the British finally succeeded in liberating the whole plain in the southeast of Caen, at the cost of heavy losses. Fifteen hundred men and two hundred seventy tanks. Caen was completely under Allied control, yet one month behind schedule.

On the American side, the 29th ID, commanded by General Norman Cota, entered the ruins of Saint-Lo that day. However, it was blocked by the German artillery, positioned in the south of the town, and by elements of the 3rd German parachute division. The town was finally freed on July 19, thanks to the reinforcement troops of the 35th ID. The road to Coutances and Vire was open.

On July 20, due to strong rains, the ground troops were deprived of aerial support. In Saint-Lo, isolated German snipers continued to cause a large number of casualties, both civilians and soldiers. Eighty percent of the town was destroyed and dead bodies were rotting among the rubble.

On July 21, continuous rain stopped any significant progress. During this forced respite, the Allied headquarters prepared operation *Cobra*, which aimed at

---

[119] Source of all the information in this chapter: www.dday-overloard.com.

breaking the German defense lines. The American 8th ID organized reconnaissance missions.

On July 22, the British operation *Goodwood* turned out a failure. On the American side, the 358th Infantry regiment also failed in its attempt to make a breakthrough towards Saint-Germain-sur-Sèves, suffering heavy losses. Seven hundred casualties among the soldiers.

On Sunday 23, the weather didn't improve. Operation *Cobra* had to be delayed. However, the American units were positioned and the staff used this lull to provide the troops with new equipment.

On Monday, July 24, the weather significantly got better. Operation *Cobra* could finally begin. Three divisions of the 8th Air Force launched sixteen hundred bombers in an air raid, intending to clear a four miles long and two and a half miles wide strip, northwest of Saint-Lo. But the cloud ceiling was so low that the bombs partly fell on units of the 30th ID, killing twenty-five GIs and injuring a hundred and thirty others. And yet, despite this tragedy, operation *Cobra* was maintained the following day.

July 25: *Cobra* was relaunched concomitantly with the British and Canadian operation *Spring*. Thirty-three hundred tons of bombs were dropped between Montreuil and Hebecrevon, in the northeast of Saint-Lo. Once again, several dozens of GIs were killed by "short bombings." Five hundred wounded, and one hundred and eleven killed, including Lieutenant General Lesly McNair[120].

The bomb carpet also buried twenty-five hundred German soldiers of the *Panzer Lehr*[121]. Immediately after,

---

[120] The highest-ranking American killed in action in Europe.
[121] German armored division, under the command of General Fritz Bayerlein.
    Source: https://fr.wikipedia.org/wiki/Panzer_Lehr_Division

the Americans launched six divisions in an assault between the two towns. However, in the evening, the front had moved less than one and a half miles forward. On the British side, the German defense had inflicted fifteen hundred casualties. Nevertheless, their sacrifice had compelled the Germans to maintain part of their troops in the area of Caen, hence relieving their American allies.

As the first massive bombing hadn't been sufficient, the American command decided to renew it on the following day and pursue operation *Cobra* with four additional infantry divisions. In the evening of July 26, the southern front of the Cotentin was open.

During all that time, the British and American logistics units had been working relentlessly on the beaches of Normandy to dispatch a continuous flow of fresh troops and material.

In the rear, Firmin and his comrades of the 320th VLA didn't limit themselves to their job as balloon crews. All the less as German airstrikes had stopped since D + 1. When they weren't helping with the unloading of thousands of crates filled with ammunition, food and medical material, they would be used for various tasks on the spot or for missions between the beach and the front.

The mail was delivered more regularly. Firmin received a second lot of letters from his mother and from Ethel. He wished he could embrace the future mother of his child and return home to New Orleans to see his parents again. He didn't dream of heroic acts, but merely of starting a family and living the best possible life in his country. Unfortunately, it wasn't yet time to return home, although the initial plan for the 320th VLA was to stay seventy-two hours on the continent.

Against all odds, on July 27, considering the very low risk of airstrikes over Omaha beach, the U.S. general staff decided to transfer A and HQ batteries of the 320th VLA to the port of Cherbourg. Battery B would remain on Omaha, while battery C would continue to protect Utah beach.

All the guys concerned by the transfer looked forward to enjoying the pleasures which this port city would offer them. Around Saint-Laurent-sur-Mer, there was no recreation available. They had all heard of the balls of July 14, which had been organized in the center of Cherbourg. Nothing comparable to the party improvised in the Leroyer's farm. Not to mention the numerous bars and call-girls you could find, like in every port city in the world.

They would have to work hard, but at least they would have the opportunity to ease up. To forget the horrors of the war for a while. To soften the homesickness which grew in them every day. The guys of battery B watched with envy their colleagues of battery A getting in the trucks of the 320th VLA, and driving away from the beach. They eventually vanished behind the ridge line of the hill.

Halfway through their trip, the convoy stopped shortly after crossing Montebourg, near a farm. Several men of the battalion were appointed to barter gasoline or other equipment prized by local peasants with good Norman food. As usual, Jimmy volunteered. His natural ease and self-confidence largely compensated his ignorance of the French language. While some would comfortably lie down on the tall grass fields, before lunch time, others would stretch their legs, while relieving their bladders.

Caught by a more serious need, Ed walked away from the road towards a haystack in the middle of a freshly harvested wheat field. Firmin, who was observing him from afar, saw the silhouette of a farmer heading towards the stack with a pitchfork in his hands. Expecting to see Edward rushing out of the improvised latrines, with his pants around his ankles, Firmin invited a few friends to attend this live comedy. Instead of this, the peasant planted his pitchfork in the ground, rested his hands on its handle, and started what looked like a friendly conversation with his visitor. Ten minutes later, Firmin saw his buddy reappearing, tucking his shirttails back into his pants, while the farmer was giving him a friendly pat on the shoulder.

"Did you see this?" Ed grumbled, when he saw his friends roaring with laughter. "I was just busy dropping a deuce when that hillbilly stood in front of me and started chatting with me. He didn't seem to bother watching me in this humiliating position! Besides, I couldn't catch a word of it! Those French are really weird!"

CHAPTER 55

O n their way, while approaching their destination, Firmin and his friends of the 320th VLA could measure the importance of the job done by the U.S. service units. What must have been a peaceful landscape two months earlier was becoming a gigantic military warehouse. Probably the biggest in the world.

Grass meadows, where dairy cows used to be grazing, had been requisitioned to serve as storage places. Huge quantities of material had been accumulating since D + 1, because of the delayed progression of the Allied troops.

Here, tens of thousands of food ration crates were piled in four feet high stacks. There, a concentration of tires was sorted out by size. Elsewhere was a fuel depot, where servicemen were filling hundreds of jerrycans out of tanker trucks. A little farther was an ammunition dump.

The balloon operators even saw a true open-air car assembly line, when they passed along the village of La Cambe, south of Grandcamp. The men of the 148th Motor vehicle assembly company were busy assembling $2^{1/2}$-ton GMCs.

Yet, this was just a sample of what they would discover in the port of Cherbourg in the following days.

The port had been rehabilitated by engineering units. Especially by the 1056th Engineer Port Construction and Repair Group, helped by American and British mine clearers, and the divers of the Royal Navy salvage units.

Many shipwrecks sunk and sometimes mined by the Germans had to be refloated. A sabotaged swing bridge, which blocked the entrance of the commercial port, had been dismounted. Wharves had been assembled. Quays of the Atlantic dockage had been repaired to allow the docking of Liberty ships. The goal of the U.S. Army was to gain efficiency. From an initial capacity of eight thousand tons a day, they would reach eight thousand six hundred tons in August, eleven thousand tons in October, and fourteen and a half thousand tons in November 1944.

The teams had been working non-stop, day and night, since the liberation of the city. On July 16, four Liberty ships arriving from the United States could anchor off the coast of Cherbourg. In the first days, the unloading was done by DUKWs which ensured the transfer of material from the ships to the outer commercial port.

On July 25, a first tanker, the *Empire traveller*, moored at Querqueville terminal, west of Cherbourg. The supply of gasoline was crucial for the advancement of Allied armored vehicles, and the installation of the undersea pipeline conceived by the British, code-named PLUTO[122], was seriously behind schedule.

The fuel, transported by ship to Querqueville terminal, had to be stored in reservoirs before being carried through a land pipeline to an open depot in La Haye-du-Puits, or by truck to intermediate storage places. Until then, the gasoline tankers were anchored off the coast of Sainte-Honorine-des-Pertes, and from there the fuel was transferred to the land by flexible pipes maintained on the surface by floats.

The port of Cherbourg was about to become the number one harbor in the world in terms of freight traffic,

---

[122] Acronym of Pipeline Under The Ocean. Source: Wikipedia.

whereas it was at the 32nd rank before the war. Firmin and his comrades were very proud to be involved in this colossal project of Europe's reconquest.

Of course, they weren't facing a determined enemy on the front line, but they fulfilled a crucial role. And many of them were African Americans.

Among the all-Black units were Engineer Dump truck companies, Quartermaster truck companies and Ports companies attached to the 490th Port Battalion, and the 100th Ordnance Ammunition Battalion.

The logistics teams worked twelve hours a day to feed the Allied war machine. They had to ensure the unloading of material as planned by the SHAEF, which had been severely delayed by the mid-June storm and the fierce resistance of the Germans.

Besides, they would have to transport all these goods to the front, which would have to move forward until it has reached Berlin. But the French railroad network had been dramatically damaged by massive bombings, and its trains were old and insufficient.

Therefore, the Allies decided to bring locomotives and cars from Wales and America. They were shipped, mounted on rails, on board of Liberty ships. The first trains were then transshipped on LSTs, and later unloaded on wharves fitted with railroads. Since the port had been repaired, the railroad material was carried by two British ferries, the *Twickenham* and the *Hampton*, which had been transformed to allow a bow unloading. Besides, a hoisting system allowed to lift the heavy locomotives and set them down on rails alongside the *Homet* dike.

The heaviest locomotives would arrive aboard two American *sea trains.* The *Texas* and the *Lakehurst.* By the end of July, fifty locomotives and two hundred cars had been unloaded in Cherbourg, thus allowing the resumption of trains' circulation between the port and Lison, and later Molay-Littry, on the Cherbourg-Paris railroad.

However, the bigger part of the freight transport continued to be provided by road, at the cost of constant repair of the roadways, damaged by bombings and ruined by the incessant flow of trucks. By the end of July, thirty thousand tons of supply transited daily on these roads.

Like on Omaha beach, the balloon crews were spread on a wide area around the port. Between Querqueville and Tourlaville. Firmin's crew had been positioned close to the wharf, alongside the docks.

One day, Firmin and Ed went to the Mielles platform to watch the unloading of the *Twickenham*, on the invitation of two guys of the Transportation Corps whom they had made friends with, during a previous lunchtime at a mess. Edward had had passionate talks with them, about different Negro baseball leagues. The first one, Josh, hailed from Philadelphia, Pennsylvania, and claimed to be an unconditional supporter of the *Philadelphia stars*. His friend, Satchel, hailing from New York, was all about the *New York Black Yankees*. Edward had wisely refused to stand up for any of them. Even more easily as he had lost interest in baseball competition since the disbanding of the *Bacharach Giants* of Atlantic City in 1942.

As far as he was concerned, Firmin had never been a fan of this game. The last time New Orleans had had a baseball team in a minor league was in 1932, with the *New Orleans Ads,* also known at that time under the name of *Caulfield Ads*. Besides the multiplicity of Negro baseball leagues, clubs would form one year and disappear the following year.

"My stuff, you know, is music!" Firmin had said to avoid taking a stand.

Josh had arranged with his corporal to let Firmin and Edward come as close as possible to the raised bow of the *Twickenham*. The ferry had a built-in bridge crane specially conceived to lift the cars, one by one, carry them outside the ship, right above a railroad connected to a classification yard.

"Our job," Josh explained, "is to help the crane operator to bring down the car smoothly with its wheels strait in line with the rails. Looks easy, like this, but after you've unloaded ten of these wood and steel masses, you get a damn sore back!"

"Aren't you afraid of getting your feet crashed?" Edward asked when he saw the two guys trying to align the car still hanging in the air.

"No need to worry about that! It's a piece of cake compared to unloading locomotives. Like to see one?"

Josh dragged Firmin and Ed a bit further on the *Homet* quay. He pointed his hand at a huge ship equipped with a lifting mast.

"This is the *Texas*!" John explained. "It can carry up to thirty-eight steam locomotives like the one you see there, plus their coal tenders. They're so heavy that we had to bring over from Wales the crane vessel there: the *Lapland*. When we tried to unload the first engine, the lifting mast of the *Texas* broke, and *Miss Liberty*[123] fell in the water. It

---

[123] 1,323 copies of the 141R (Miss Liberty) locomotives would drive after the war on the French railroad network. Source : http://www.antiqbrocdelatour.com/les-anciens-trains-de-legende/locomotive-

made a hell of a racket! It took us a week before we could take it out of the water and bring it back on the rails with the others."

As the crane was bringing the 141R from the *Lapland* upright above the boarding wharf, the crane vessel would lean dangerously, emitting a metallic creaking, which chilled their backs. Firmin wondered when the locomotive would fall on the quay, making the *Lapland* capsize.

The steel monster was only hooked to a balancing beam, by a system of pulleys and chains placed above the center of gravity. While Firmin was anxiously observing the slow descent of the engine towards the railroad, Edward was staring at the soldier who was controlling alone the single motor used to wind out the crane's rope and bring down the load. He thought about their original eleven hundred pounds gasoline-powered winch they used in Camp Tyson to control their first balloons. He smiled. "Jimmy would be green with envy if he saw this!"

The most dangerous part of the maneuver was when, a couple of inches above the ground, twenty guys were aligning the seventy-five tons of *Miss Liberty* with the rails. Amazingly, the final contact of the wheels with the steel tracks went almost silent, except a dull vibration of the ground under the weight of the heavy dark engine.

Before returning to Jimmy and their balloon, Firmin and Ed suggested Josh and Satchel to meet again soon at the *Liberty club* or in a bar of the *rue de la soif*.[124]

---

legendaire-141-R-1944.php

[124] Literally "thirst street." Street fitted for pub-crawl.

CHAPTER 56

While the days of the 320th VLA and other American service units were going by in a well-oiled routine, the fighting units continued to weather the fierce resistance of the Germans.

Yet, an event would strike the minds of Lieutenant Colonel Reed's men, as much as the remembrance of June 6, 1944. On July 27, Reed read to his troops a message he had just received from General Eisenhower himself:

"Lieutenant General Omar N. Bradley, commander in chief of the 1st Army, has drawn my attention to the remarkable job you've achieved during your mission since June 6, and until July 10, 1944… Despite the losses sustained, the battalion carried out its mission with courage and determination, and proved an important element of the air defense team… I commend you and the officers and men of your battalion for fine effort, which has merited the praise of all who have observed it."[125]

This commendation, highlighting the courage and merit of their unit, boosted the enthusiasm and pride of most of the members of the 320th VLA. Firmin and others imagined the reaction of their families and neighbors, who would read General Eisenhower's comment, in one of the

---

[125] Source: https://historyofyesterday.com/the-african-americans-who-hit-the-beaches-of-normandy-on-d-day-ab8b95077e4f

many daily Negro newspapers.

"*It seems the whole front knows the story of the Negro barrage balloon battalion outfit, which was one of the first ashore on D-Day… They have gotten the reputation of hard workers and good soldiers.*"

There was no doubt that they would be welcomed like heroes when they return home.

On July 28, as part of operation Cobra, the 4th Armored division achieved a six mile breach towards Avranches, through the lines of the 84th German Corps[126], whereas the British were ordered to hold their position in the southeast of Caen.

On July 30, the 2nd AD and the 30th ID which now controlled the south of Saint-Lo, were progressing to the southeast, while the 6th AD captured Granville, in the west. Under the combined pressure of the 4th, 8th and 79th ID, and the 3rd, 4th and 6th AD, the Germans abandoned their positions, allowing the Americans to capture the bridge of Pontaubault, and hence open the road to Brittany.

However, the success of operation *Cobra* had cost many lives. Five thousand American soldiers killed in action, more than thirteen thousand five hundred injured. Plus, the successive bombings involved by the operation had caused fifteen thousand casualties among the civilians.

On August 2, General Patton's 3rd Army managed to free the Mont-Saint-Michel. The next day, Patton reached the German defenses in Rennes.

Every day, news about the progression of the front came to the soldiers in the rear via the *Stars and Stripes*

---

[126] Sources of all military information in this chapter: https://www.dday-overlord.com/bataille-normandie/

newspaper. But it wouldn't suffice to reassure them. Field hospitals were overcrowded by the daily arrival of new wounded soldiers. Graves Registration Companies were also working relentlessly.

While waiting for their evacuation to Great Britain, some soldiers didn't miss the opportunity to blame the soldiers of the service units, especially the African Americans, for being fight dodgers and chickens. They just ignored that most of the Negroes hadn't chosen to be inducted into service units instead of combat units. On the contrary, many colored soldiers had been denied access to combat units, because of racist prejudices.

For the rest, Firmin's daily life was punctuated by the meals which offered a prized moment of relief.

The location of Firmin's balloon team was close to the HQ encampment. Therefore, the trio often enjoyed a B-ration meal served under a mess tent. As opposed to individual C-rations, a B-ration consisted of canned or frozen meat, dried vegetables, fresh bread, milk and coffee, prepared for groups of five to ten soldiers. Sometimes, the meals were enhanced by local fresh food traded with Norman farmers. Although such practice was officially prohibited. This, for excellent reasons.

The slow progression of the front combined with the continuous inflow of supply had caused congestion and a multiplication of the storing areas on the Norman territory. Firmin and his comrades had gotten a little overview of it during their transfer from Omaha beach to Cherbourg.

Now, because of the hedgerows and the inaccurate maps, trucks would sometimes drive around for hours in the countryside before they could reach their destination. It wasn't uncommon that cargoes were lost. All the less as

411

the delivery points were numerous and sometimes changing. Soldiers' camps, maneuver fields, repair workshops, field hospitals, not to mention POW camps. Every storage place was likely to be the subject of theft or trafficking.

A strange confusion eventually reigned over Cherbourg and the Cotentin.

By the end of July, eight hundred thousand GIs were crammed in the bridgehead, covering the area of both the Calvados and the peninsula with a local population of two hundred fifty thousand civilians. In some places, GIs would number three vs. one Norman.

Yet, the soldiers stationed in the city of Cherbourg didn't have much difficulty to find a place to sleep. Many dwellers had fled to the inland when they had been informed of imminent bombings, thus leaving many empty buildings and houses behind them. In the countryside, the luckiest had found refuge in a farm or an abandoned barn. Yet, most of the soldiers were accommodated in tent camps. Especially the colored soldiers.

Even after an exhausting working day, the men stationed in Cherbourg would take advantage of every recreation offered by the Army.

In Cherbourg, the *Eldorado* movie theater was opened since July 18. It would mostly play old movies, except once. On August 5, *Casanova Brown* was played there as a world premiere, in the honor of the American soldiers who had landed in Normandy since D-Day. A comedy romantic film featuring Gary Cooper and Teresa Wright, directed by Sam Wood and produced by Nunnally Johnson.

As for the colored soldiers, it was rather film

projections on white sheets inside a barn, using a defective equipment which often earned the operator a volley of insults. Nevertheless, everything was good to take their minds off things.

The U.S. special services would organize various recreations in any sort of place, and with rudimentary means. Open-air dance shows on wooden dance floors simply laid on the ground. Theater plays, concerts. The soldiers would watch, sitting on the grass or on their helmets.

The special services also supplied radio sets sometimes, so that the GIs could listen to BBC music programs. Whenever he could, Firmin would connect to *Radio Cherbourg* which broadcast news in French.

After a long working day, the soldiers could read the *Stars and Stripes,* which the kids were distributing in the streets of the city. Once a week, the luckiest could get their hands on a copy of the *Yank Magazine,* filled with illustrations and articles telling the feats of arms of American soldiers.

Religious services were held under big tents. Carrying out the promise he had made to his mother, Firmin would attend a mass almost every week. Otherwise, he would read a verse in Maggie's bible.

Corporal Bellegarde used every short moment of rest after lunch or in the evening to write a few lines or make some sketches in his diary.

When he lacked inspiration, he used to read the last mail from Ethel, once more. Then, a series of feelings would run through his body. It started with a deep nostalgia. But then came melancholy, dark thoughts, anguish and eventually the fear of dying. Dying without knowing his coming child. Dying without being convinced his child would have a chance to live in a better world, thanks to the sacrifice of his father and of all the ones who will fall before the end of this war.

Then, to escape this depressed state, Firmin would take out his harmonica from his haversack, and improvise a melody which he thought he would later dedicate to his child.

The moments of rest were also an opportunity to make friends with African Americans of armed service units. Engineer Dump Truck Companies, Quartermaster truck companies, and other Port companies attached to the 490th Port Battalion.

Inside the port, one out of three soldiers was Black. In other places, many of them worked for the roads maintenance, the repair of railroads and telephone lines. For healthcare, as stretcher bearers or medics. And of course, in transportation companies, namely as drivers of $2^{1/2}$-ton trucks. The men of the Army special forces were also in charge of the custody of German POWs. Besides, the latter were often better considered and treated by Southern Whites than the colored soldiers.

After two weeks of this routine work, boredom started to get on the nerves of Firmin and his crew mates. The front continued to progress, but too slowly according to many soldiers.

Luckily, despite all the suffering they had endured since the night of June 5 to 6, the Normans hadn't lost their love of partying. The celebration of the 14th of July had rung the revival of popular dance in the liberated zone.

Sunday afternoon dance parties were opportunities of

meetings and flirtations between American soldiers and French girls. Like in the Welsh *Palais de Danse*, one could see the girls dancing equally with Whites or Blacks. At supper time, good girls would return to their parents', and the soldiers to their camps.

In other places, night balls were organized, where the soldiers could dance, drink and have sex with a professional or occasional prostitute. They often ended with brawls and scuffles between soldiers, sometimes involving civilians, which would be stopped by a quick and aggressive intervention of the MPs.

Firmin, Ed and Jimmy, like most of the guys of the 320th VLA, avoided these places like the plague. They didn't want to end up their military path in jail or worse, after a hasty trial by court-martial.

This Sunday, August 6, Firmin and his friends taught young Norman girls how to dance the *Lindy hop* and the *Jitterbug.* Meanwhile, General Patton, head of the 3rd Army, was progressing with the 8th Corps in Brittany, up to the boundaries of Brest and Nantes, and in the south of Normandy with the 15th and 20th Corps towards Laval and Le Mans. Simultaneously, the British 2nd Army, in the south of Caen, was moving slowly towards Thury-Harcourt and Condé.

On August 7, taking advantage of a thick fog, the 2nd SS *Panzer Division Das Reich* launched one hundred and forty-five *Tiger* tanks in a large-scale counter-attack[127] against Avranches. It took until noon before the rocket-firing Hawker Typhoon fighter bombers of the RAF Second tactical Air force could take off. Yet, a vast

---

[127] Operation Lüttich.

majority of the sixty German tanks destroyed were actually knocked out by gunfire from ground forces.

On the same day, the Canadians in charge of Operation *Totalize* achieved a six mile breakthrough, hence forcing the 5th *Panzergruppe West* to withdraw to the south.

On August 9, the 8th Corps of Patton's 3rd Army besieged the city of Brest, while Le Mans was freed by the 5th ID.

On their side, the British continued their progression with operation *Totalize*.

On August 10, the 15th Corps, which included the French 2nd Armored division, was advancing towards the north of Alençon, with the intention to encircle the soldiers of the 9th *Panzer Division* in the Falaise pocket.

As part of Operation *Totalize*, the 1st Canadian Army of General Crerar was approaching Falaise, at the same time.

In the evening of August 11, the French 2nd AD of General Leclerc besieged Alençon and would capture it one day later.

The American and British fronts were about to join in Falaise, catching the Germans in a pincer movement. However, facing each other, the Allies risked shooting one another. Therefore, General Bradley decided to refuse to General Patton the permission to bypass Falaise, and hence close the pocket. He ordered him instead to stop his progression for a few hours, and secure the surroundings of Argentan. As a result, thousands of German soldiers could escape the trap and withdraw towards Paris.

On Saturday, August 12, Firmin's crew was granted a first twenty-four hours' leave.

CHAPTER 57

Cherbourg, Saturday, August 12, 1944

T he trio had been eagerly expecting this moment. Their last true furlough was in April, in Pontypool. The short trip on July 14 wasn't really a free time pass. You can't talk of freedom when you are under the constant surveillance of an officer. Moreover if he's White.

The three men took great care of themselves and dressed to the nines before heading downtown, slightly before noon. Jimmy was the last to be ready. Firmin and Edward had to threaten to leave him behind to make him stop polishing his shoes. "Anyhow, after five minutes walk in the streets covered with rubble, they'll be dusty again!"

They had no intention to lose one more minute of their free time. Yet, they would soon regret to be gone with an empty stomach. Normandy surely didn't lack food, but rationing was still in force. The only few active restaurants were stormed by officers. Besides, they couldn't find anything equivalent to the *fish and chips* they had enjoyed in Great Britain. All the less, since the massive presence of warships off the coast banned all local fishing activity.

The three balloon operators hence decided to walk to the PX of Cherbourg, where they would buy some good things to nibble and drink. Besides, they would also purchase various precious products they would later trade with the Normans.

The streets were teeming with people. And yet, as opposed to what they had experienced in Pontypool and other places on the other side of the Channel, there were only few civilians among them. "We're gonna have a hard time to invite a cookie for a dance tonight!" Jimmy joked, when they saw three young girls scrolling arm in arm, under the lustful gaze of a group of soldiers.

The excess of testosterone accumulated during months of sexual deprivation made many soldiers excessively harassing with women. The military authorities were very nervous about it. Therefore, the MPs were constantly showing up to discourage outbursts. The French authorities had alerted the staff of the Allied forces about the increasing number of inappropriate behaviors and rapes committed by some soldiers, especially those intoxicated with *Calvados* brandy, which they drank without restraint.

Culprits were court-martialed and severely punished. The first one among them in France, Clarence Whitfield, was waiting for his execution[128] in the following days. Yet, this didn't suffice to stop all these males in heat. Their sexual appetite still needed to be satisfied. The staff couldn't avoid breaching the morals and the laws of their country. Although prostitution was illegal in the United States, the American command decided to tolerate brothels, yet under the surveillance of doctors and the military police. One of the cathouses was "reserved for Whites," the other was said, "not segregated." In other words: "reserved for Colored."

But this wasn't the only reason for the massive

---

[128] He will be hanged on August 14, 1944, by a British home office executioner, employed by the U.S. Army.

presence of MPs in the city. The ratio of colored soldiers in Cherbourg was three times as high as in the United States or in Great Britain, which caused a significant increase in racial tensions.

According to their internal rules, the American Red Cross had organized two distinct recreation centers. The *Victory club*, reserved for Whites and the *Liberty club*, reserved for Blacks.

While wandering in the streets of Cherbourg, Firmin and his friends were surprised by the small size and dilapidation of the houses and buildings, which height didn't exceed four levels, including the attic.

After they crossed La Fontaine Street, they walked down Albert Mahieu Street to the south, until Gambetta Street, which they went up to the east towards the commercial port. They finally stopped in front of number two on Gambetta Street.

The four-story building, which housed the *Ratti*[129], distinguished itself from the neighboring old houses, by its modern *Art deco* architecture.

On the top of its cut-angled facade, one could read the name of its owner on a colored earthenware background.

Above the main entrance, at the corner of Gambetta and Des Portes Streets, a semicircular sign announced the new function of the building: *American Red Cross, Liberty Club*.

Two MPs were watching over the access. Black GIs walked out, grinning, their arms loaded with paper bags filled with their purchases.

Firmin, Ed and Jimmy entered through the wrought

---

[129] The Ratti was the biggest department store in the west of France. It was inaugurated in 1929, and was created by the architect René Levasseur.

iron swing door. They were immediately welcomed by the benevolent smiles of two African American hostesses, dressed in their Red Cross outfits. This vision instantly warmed the hearts of the corporal's crew mates. But it had a completely different effect on him. It revealed in him a deep lack. Much deeper than he could admit.

When he missed Ethel, he just needed to recall the lines of her face that he still could remember, or the smell of her skin, to feel her presence. This capacity of his mind managed to reduce the sensation of distance between them. A distance however amplified by the body of water separating Cherbourg from Plymouth, and, moreover, by the war, which outcome remained uncertain and distant. The two young women and their radiant smiles made Ethel's absence more real and even more painful. Summoning up his remembrance of her would never replace the joy of holding her in his arms, smelling her, and feeling the softness of her skin with his senses rather than with his mind.

Another familiar scent wafting in the air got him out of his bout of melancholy. The smell of donuts. A sweet scent which reminded all these young soldiers of their families and their beloved country. It had accompanied them at every key moment of their transatlantic journey. On the Pier 86 of New York Harbor, last November, before embarking on the *Aquitania*, or on the quay of Weymouth, on June 2, before getting aboard their LST.

The three buddies let the waft of donuts lead them by the nose to a booth, where other Red Cross volunteers served donuts and hot coffee at will. Once filled up, they strolled through the various departments, which abounded with clothes, hygiene products, and various accessories highly prized by the Normans. Such as nylon stockings, which the French didn't yet know and had conquered so many British women. Jimmy bought several pairs, with the firm intention to test their power of attraction on a pretty Norman girl.

"If you catch a bird with that, then beware! And don't forget to put on a condom before you stuff your dong in it!" Edward warned him, laughing.

On the second floor, they walked along a mess reserved for officers. They continued strolling in the aisles. They finally noticed a poster at the entrance of a big room, announcing that an amateur band performed here every evening at 20:00.

The three friends promised to come back. Until then, they needed to find something hearty to eat. The few donuts that they had swallowed earlier had only whetted their appetite. As they couldn't find anything inside, they left the store, and started searching for a place to have a bite. The scarce grocery stores, bakeries or dairy shops, still open, had been sold out in the morning. Moreover, they were monitored by the French police which had been instructed to stop the black market and fake rationing tickets.

Firmin finally entered a small café. A few customers were leaning over the counter, lingering over a drink. One of them babbled words behind his teeth in a language the corporal couldn't understand. Firmin greeted the boss and his clients in his best French. The grumpy customer lifted his head to see who had the nerve to bother them like this. Firmin still couldn't understand the words of the guy, who was obviously drunk. Still, it sufficed to see his angry gaze to understand he didn't welcome them. The corporal didn't get discouraged. He smiled at the man and turned his head to the boss.

"*Good afternoon, sir,*" Firmin said in French. "*My friends and I would like to eat something. Whatever you've got. Is it possible?*"

The man behind the counter hesitated a few seconds, giving his three regulars a questioning look.

"*Please serve these gentlemen another drink, will you!*" Firmin added.

The magical sentence immediately relaxed the lines on the three men's faces.

"This is a good fellow!" the grumpy customer approved, in a French which Firmin could understand.

Relieved by his customer's reaction, the café owner cheered up. As opposed to other businessmen in the city, he didn't take a real advantage of the unexpected windfall brought by these tens of thousands of soldiers. His business was located in a bad spot, compared to his colleagues of the *rue de la Soif,* which bars were always full. The soldiers used to pay in dollars, for the French had a very limited trust in the *Flag-ticket Francs* banknotes, which the GIs were trying to get rid of when buying drinks.

The boss offered Firmin to prepare them a cold plate each. An assortment of cooked meat produced in his parent's farm, cheese and bread, the whole served with hard cider.

Firmin, Ed and Jimmy devoured these delicious produces with such an appetite that the boss had to serve them more. The three buddies paid him generously in return, and promised to send him new clients.

With a full stomach and a high morale, they left in

search of another recreation place. They decided to try the *Eldorado* movie theater. Maybe it would play one of these Hollywood super-productions, from which you come out with a head full of dreams and a cheerful heart. But when they arrived, they had no more desire to shut themselves in a dark room. In Pontypool, they were with their girlfriends. But here, they were sadly alone. If the film were a dud, they would miss a girl to kiss, and get bored to death.

Moreover, the oppressing presence of MPs and the palpable tension between white and black soldiers made them feel uncomfortable. Firmin sometimes felt like he was back in a Southern state of America. In Camp Tyson, or in the streets of Memphis. It made him fear very dark days ahead when he returns home, after the war.

Claiming there was no enticing film showing today, Firmin suggested to his buddies to find another way to spend their free time. As he was out of ideas, Firmin let himself be convinced by Jimmy's enthusiasm, who desperately wished to make a tour in the tenderloin district. "If we have to do it, better do it in broad daylight!" Firmin thought. However, he warned Jimmy.

"OK. But not more than two or three drinks, then!" he agreed.

Corporal Bellegarde didn't want to lose one of his crew members in a street fight or arrested by an MP patrol.

Before going to the *rue de la Paix* and the *rue de l'Union*, which formed the major part of the *rue de la Soif*, Firmin insisted on going to the Holy Trinity basilica to pray. Ed and Jimmy followed him grudgingly. But when they went closer to the stately building, they immediately stopped grumbling in his back. They had never seen a church of this size before. The only places of worship they had attended in America were modest wooden buildings, belonging to groups of a few dozen faithfuls. In Great Britain, Protestant and Anglican congregations were gathering in stone or brick buildings, yet most often of decent size. The three balloon operators had likely seen a postcard showing Westminster Abbey in London or Notre-Dame cathedral in Paris. But it was the first time they saw a real one with their own eyes.

Firmin invited them to follow him inside the monument. The smell of incense which permeated the place reminded him of his years at the Holy Cross Junior High School in New Orleans. Mechanically, he dipped his fingers in the font, and piously crossed himself, touching his fingers to his forehead, his chest, his left shoulder, and then the right one.

Then, he started walking counterclockwise in the side aisle. A few soldiers were praying, seated or kneeling, in different spots of the nave. A fresh breeze caressed his neck and blew through his collar inside his jacket. Firmin shivered. He looked up and noticed that entire frames of stained glass windows were missing, letting a bright white light penetrate the cathedral. Passing along a series of side chapels devoted to a few saints, Firmin explained their functions to his two friends. When they reached the transept, Firmin approached the front of the chancel. He turned towards the high altar, and once more crossed himself, while making a quick genuflection.

Firmin silently admired the chancel and the impressing and richly decorated sculpture, behind. It was flanked by six marble columns, and topped with a great monstrance.

In the middle of this set, a large fresco illustrated the baptism of Jesus.

Fascinated by the beauty of the painting, Jimmy couldn't hold in a cry of admiration. Firmin kicked his ankle to remind him of the rules of respect inside the House of God. He then turned round to make sure nobody had heard Jimmy.

A few rows behind, another African American soldier was observing them with reproachful eyes. He motioned him to keep silent, while cocking his head slightly to his left. Firmin looked at the opposite side of the nave. Two groups of soldiers occupied a few rows. They all were Whites. Commissioned and non-commissioned officers. Two of them glared at them. Firmin turned again to the high altar and whispered in Jimmy's ear.

"Let's scram. Right now! And keep quiet!" Firmin murmured.

CHAPTER 58

Half an hour later, the three balloon operators reached the beginning of *rue de la Paix*. The street was teeming with soldiers in uniform strolling with hesitant and sinuous steps from one joint to the next one. Some would run into each other while walking by, hence causing aggressive reactions from the most smashed ones. Luckily, at this time in the afternoon, the explicit threat of an MP pounding his billy club on the palm of his hand sufficed to stifle any temptation of engaging a brawl.

Further in the street, a group of four white MPs was blocking the way through.

"You guys stay on your side! Alright?"

Looking beyond this human roadblock, Firmin and his crew members noticed that this section of the street was only frequented by Whites.

"Hot damn! Can't believe it!" Edward grumbled in his clenched jaws.

The highest-ranking MP, a staff sergeant, stepped forward to Edward, pointing his billy club at him. Ed proudly lifted his head, and stared at the MP right in the eyes.

"Segregation in not allowed here, sir!"

The MP moved closer until his club would press Edward's chest. He increased the pressure several times, punctuating the first syllable of each word of his question.

"Are you looking for trouble, private first class Washington?"

As a crew leader, Firmin was aware that things could

easily turn into big trouble for both of them.

"No, staff sergeant. Private first class Washington won't make a fuss."

Firmin grabbed Ed's arm firmly, and forced him to turn back.

"Let's go. It's an order!"

On their way back, Firmin endeavored to calm down Edward.

"I can't tolerate this injustice either, but you know like I do that we don't have any chance to be heard, right now. For the moment, the only thing we can do is keep quiet, and watch our step."

Suddenly, Firmin perceived a familiar sound of music, which instantly woke a feeling of nostalgia for his hometown. It was coming from a little bar.

"C'mon guys, you're my guests!" Firmin said, entering the bar, first.

Despite the lack of light and the narrowness of the room, the atmosphere inside was warm. Near the counter, standing on a pedestal table, a U.S. Army phonograph was playing a *V- disc*. Laid on a shelf fixed to the wall, a pile of 78 rpm recordings were waiting to be selected by a GI in charge of the sound system.

V-discs[130] were produced by the U.S. Army and contained a wide variety of music genres. Classical music, swing, jazz, big bands… White artists, as well as Black singers and musicians. Yet, in compliance with segregation rules, the soldiers made their own selection of discs, and not only based on their personal musical tastes. You could bet your bottom dollar that most of them were

---

[130] Source: https://archive.org/details/V-discs1-991943-1944

recordings of African American artists.

The title which was playing when they entered was *Mood Indigo* by Duke Ellington and his orchestra.

Above the mirror, behind the counter, one could read in white letters painted on a slate: "*La maison ne fait pas crédit.*"

Under it, the bar owner had written his personal translation: "Payment in cash. In US dollars only."

Firmin ordered three glasses of hard cider and laid three dimes on the counter, which the bar tender rushed to put in the front pocket of his apron.

Corporal Bellegarde grasped the three glasses in his hands and joined his buddies, already installed around a table. Still outraged by the incident with the MP, Ed was staring ahead of him with a dark gaze.

"Cheers!" Firmin said, raising his glass.

Jimmy imitated him, smiling broadly. Ed brought his glass to his lips and emptied it in one gulp, without a word or a look at Firmin.

"Ease up, man, and enjoy the moment!" Firmin said. "Listen to that music! Aren't you feeling good with us?"

They stayed there, sitting around their table, listening to the titles chosen by the disc jockey. Between two discs, one of the GIs in the room would sometimes say his feeling about the artist.

The man at the phonograph was quite good at switching the various styles of music with or without voices.

Instrumentals like *Bouncin' on a V-disc* by the organist Fats Waller, or *Boogie Woogie Man and Pine Creek Boogie* by the pianists Pete Johnson and Albert Ammons, were alternating with songs by performers like Hazel

Scott, a singer and pianist, who had recorded several titles for the U.S. Army.

At the start of the recording, you could hear Hazel Scott introducing herself.

"*Hello, fellows. This is Hazel Scott. I'd like to make a V- disc for you. And I'd like to play a tune I did in one of the pictures I just finished, written by Johnny Green, very beautiful, Body and Soul.*"

Body and soul was followed by *C Jam Blues*, in which Hazel Scott was accompanied by the jazz drummer Sidney Catlett. Several guys in the room started to beat the measure. Some, by tapping their feet on the ground, others by drumming the tables with their hands.

When the DJ announced *People will say we're in love*, a piano solo, two or three guys expressed their disapproval by booing loudly.

"Ain't you got some swinging stuff, instead?"

But they were quickly silenced by other guys in the room. A love song could do you no harm in such a violent world! To tell the truth, Hazel Scott was quite famous and had many secret lovers among Black American soldiers.

Firmin thought of Ethel, while listening to the tune, until Jimmy shattered his daydreaming with a bawdy remark.

"All those nice feelings sound good, but what I need, right now, is a poontang! It's been three months now since my dong met something other than my calloused paw. I'd like to stuff a cookie, now!"

His loud comment triggered a series of dirty approvals, each dirtier than the previous one, punctuated by raucous laughter.

After they finished their third drink, Firmin suggested

returning to the *Liberty club* to have a bite before the concert. As they were about to leave the bar, two white soldiers showed up in the doorway.

"*Patron, deux calvas pour mon ami et moi!*"[131] one of them shouted, with a strong American accent.

"This is a colored place. Get the hell outa here!" replied a customer hidden in a dark corner of the room.

"Lookin' for trouble, you nigger?" muttered the White, while searching around where this voice came from.

The slur was enough to arouse an instant reaction of anger.

Several soldiers stood up in a same impulse and rushed on the two Whites to throw them out. Without thinking of the consequences, some of them started to beat them up. After thirty seconds of a severe beating, half a dozen white MPs came to the rescue of the two guys. Billy clubs started to rain, falling preferably on curly heads.

The other clients understood they risked being indiscriminately arrested and would end up in jail. Firmin asked the bar owner if there was another way out. All those who had stayed inside the room could escape through the backyard.

The three crew mates slowly recovered their calm, while eating at the *Liberty club*.

When time came to go to the concert room to attend the evening performance, Jimmy announced to his two colleagues he'd rather spend the rest of his overnight leave with a French dolly. Or, said with his own words: "I'm sorry, guys, but my balls are at the brink of explosion!"

"Don't forget to put on a condom!" his corporal warned

---

[131] Boss, two Calvados brandies for my friend and I.

him. "And if she asks anything about our job, you shut up! Hear?"

CHAPTER 59

On the following day, everyone in the 320th VLA recovered his working routine, while helping with the loading of hundreds of dump trucks which continuously supplied the troops on the progressing front. The battalion also made its trucks and drivers available to back up the transportation units.

The three crew mates hence had a chance to make friends with guys of various service units, some of whom had been trained in Camp Claiborne, where Firmin had first been inducted.

Once, he confided to a little group of truck drivers his regret of having been transferred to another activity. But the guys of the dump truck company laughed at him.

"You guys of the 320th VLA hit the headlines in the newspapers. People will long remember you as a combat unit, whereas we're just good enough to transport goods of all kinds. When we arrive in a battle area, loaded with things intended to support or relieve white fighters, they most often show us indifference, when not contempt!"

Firmin didn't share his confidence.

"The only ones who're gonna be honored will be those who are still alive at the end of the war and have taken part in the final fights. And you guys of the transportation and engineering companies will have the front-row seats, just behind the front line. Whereas we'll long be back home!"

Every evening, official news from the front came back to the rear bases. They were mingled with rumors brought by the wounded, in transit in Cherbourg, before their repatriation to Great Britain, or reported by the truck drivers in charge of the troops supply.

August 13: the pincers formed by the 19th Corps, U.S. 1st Army in the east, and by the 7th and 9th Corps, reinforced by the 2nd AD in the south, was tightening on the troops of the German 7th Army.

Four divisions, of which one armored. However, at the end of the day, almost ten thousand soldiers of the 12th *SS Panzerdivision* succeeded in escaping the pocket and were heading to the Seine River.[132]

August 16: whereas the Falaise pocket wasn't yet completely closed, the 12th Corps of General Patton's 3rd Army reached Orleans and the Loire River. The 20th Corps was in Chartres, and the 15th Corps in Dreux.

When the British Field Marshall Montgomery ordered the complete closing of the pocket, the bulk of the German forces had already escaped from the trap.

August 19: the 1st Polish Armored division, settled on mount Ormel, which overlooked the road to Vimoutiers, shelled the German Armored units fleeing by the *death row* between Trun and Chambois. Meanwhile, Patton's 3rd Army reached the Seine River, near the village of Rosny. On its side, the French 2nd AD freed the village of Exmes, east of Argentan.

August 20: the escaping Germans left behind them hundreds of wreckages of charred vehicles and tanks, thousands of corpses[133,] and as many wounded soldiers. Three German generals were captured. Yet, many SS units

---

[132] All information in this chapter, related to the Battle of Normandy, comes from the website:
https://www.dday-overlord.com/bataille-normandie/journees

had managed to flee east, towards the Seine, under cover of the morning mist.

August 21: one hundred and sixty-five thousand Germans could escape, but the Americans continued their progression to the east. Patton's 15th Corps managed to cross the Seine, thanks to the bridges installed by the engineering units, and eventually reached Mantes. Other American units, at the same time, were heading to Melun, Fontainebleau and Sens.

On the same day, American troops landed[134] in Morlaix, on the coast of Brittany, in the northeast of Brest.

The daily edition of the *Stars and Stripes* delivered news about the various fronts, on which their fellow soldiers were fighting. The colored GIs stationed in Normandy were informed of the hanging of Clarence Whitfield, on August 14, in the Chateau de Canisy, near Saint-Lo, intending to send everyone a strong message. Other rapes had been committed on June 20, 23 and 29, angering the local population and the French authorities. The American military courts were ruthless, yet with an increased severity when the culprits, convicted or alleged, were colored.

Tuesday, August 22: aware of the inexorable progression of the American troops towards the west, the Parisians started rising up against the occupants on August 19. Acts of rebellion multiplied. Yet, the German garrison of Paris, numbering sixteen thousand men, had received the Führer's order to quell the insurgency, at all

---

[133] Killed German soldiers numbered around six thousand on June 21, according to the same source.

[134] Source: website https://www.france-histoire-esperance.com/23-aout-20-septembre-1944-bataille-de-brest/

costs. On their side, the members of the resistance had very few weapons at their disposal. They rested their last hope on a short-term arrival of the Allied forces. They couldn't hold on more than a couple of days.

However, the American staff had no intention to go to Paris. Their targets were clearly Germany and Berlin. Therefore, General Leclerc, head of the French 2nd AD, was ordered to rush to Paris. The tank unit would enter Paris two days later. The French soldiers received a triumphant welcome from the people of Paris.

A few days after the Allied landing in Brittany, a platoon of balloons of battery A was detached to ensure the aerial protection of the bay of Morlaix. Firmin's crew would take part in the mission. On board of a few trucks of the 320th VLA, the platoon joined a supply convoy for the troops involved in Operation *Cobra*, engaged in the battle of Brest[135].

Like B and C batteries, battery A was composed of three platoons, of each fifteen balloon crews. The platoon was under the command of a sergeant, who was supported for this mission by a medic, five men in charge of the logistics, and the vehicle drivers. A jeep, a command car, and six $2^{1/2}$-ton trucks for the crews and the material, besides the balloons.

Fifteen inflated balloons were transferred from Cherbourg to the bay of Morlaix by DUKWs. They were then transported by truck to various strategic positions

---

[135] The battle of Brest started on August 23, and would end on September 19, with the surrender of General Ramcke to General Middleton, head of the 8th Corps of the U.S. Army. The fierce fights would cause the destruction of the town and its port facilities. The latter were not repaired in time to take part in the war effort.

designated by their sergeant. Firmin's balloon was placed on the east bank of the Morlaix River, near a small village. Once again, Firmin's crew would be left on its own. It would still be supplied daily with water, food, and equipment by a truck of their battalion.

Immediately after they arrived on site, the three men dug their foxholes and settled as comfortably as possible, given the location and the circumstances.

They soon regretted the long working days they were used to on Omaha beach, and in Cherbourg. Now, they were isolated. They had no chance to help with the unloading of the ships landed on the beaches of Brittany with various supplies intended for the troops of General Patton's 3rd Army.

Intending to kill time and break the monotony of his days, Firmin devoted more time to writing in his diary. Once a week, he would give his V-mails for Ethel and his mother to the truck driver. When he was lucky, the guy could deliver a handful of late letters and a few copies of the *Stars and Stripes* newspaper.

In the evening, before nightfall, Firmin would take out his harmonica and play a few pieces of blues or Gospel. Sometimes, the three friends formed a chorus and sang, contemplating the sunset. They shared the same homesickness, and, moreover, the same disgust for the canned food supplied by the army. So, they liked comparing the cook skills of their mothers.

Firmin made their mouths water by describing the feasts of Cajun fried chicken drumsticks, of shrimp and onion gumbo with rice and Worcester sauce, or crayfish-stuffed baked potatoes with onion and ground black pepper. All types of Louisiana recipes revisited by Celestine Bellegarde.

Jimmy depicted his mother preparing various catfish-based recipes which she used to improve with "cooks' secrets" of her own. She alternated southern style fried catfish, spicy grilled catfish, and other local specialties. On special occasions, she would replace catfish by trout. Jimmy would sometimes describe each element of a menu, from the starter to the dessert. His favorite was the melting strawberry cake, coated with strawberry custard.

Edward, for his part, recalled with emotion Chicken Bones Beach, south of downtown Atlantic City, where he used to picnic on Sundays, in the Summer, with his parents and his five brothers and sisters. On these occasions, his mother used to prepare full baskets of finger-licking good fried chicken, soaked with gravy. "Just thinking of it makes my mouth water!"

Yet, it also reminded him of a darker side of his childhood.

Until 1900, Jim Crow laws, which ruled racial segregation since 1876 in the former Confederate States, didn't apply to Atlantic City. His grandparents told him how Whites and Blacks, at that time, attended the same beaches. But, step by step, with the flow of tourists coming from the south, hotels were forced by their white customers, viscerally racist, to push back the Negroes further south of the beach. Segregation eventually imposed itself.

Like his two crew mates, Edward had always lived in a segregated place. He was used to public washrooms and water fountains for colored. To being compelled to step off the sidewalk when a white woman was walking in his direction. To be denied the access to a school reserved for Whites only. Luckily, he didn't experience being banned from the best universities, since he never went beyond the ninth grade.

By going to war, they had hoped in return to gain the respect of the Whites, but this hope seemed to get a little bit further away every day. They now wondered how they would be treated when returning home.

Would they relive what their grandfathers had experienced when they had returned from Europe in 1918 and 1919? Who had suffered the worse violence from white supremacists when they dared walking in the streets dressed in their uniforms. Or would they finally have access to the same jobs and the same schools as the Whites? Would they be allowed to resume their studies and become engineers, doctors or foremen?

Firmin still had the ambition to become a journalist or an author. At least, he could get a job as a truck or bus driver. Ed and Firmin knew that their experience in the army wouldn't be of much use in the civilian life. Yet, Edward had high hopes of resuming his career as a salesman, which he had started in an APEX store in Atlantic City. He was even convinced he would become his own boss, as the manager of a shop of Sarah Spencer Washington's chain of stores.

Jimmy's situation would be more complicated. During his service time, he had received no training which might be useful in his civilian life. He couldn't imagine working in his parent's farm. Too tough and too ungrateful. Staying in the army wasn't a conceivable option. He was definitely allergic to orders, especially when they were barked by racist white officers.

And until now, the highest ranks were reserved for Whites. With the exception of Benjamin O. Davis, the first Black brigadier general in the U.S. Army. Yet, the latter couldn't give any order to a white soldier, according to the military rules still in force. Moreover, he didn't have the function of a brigade commander. He was actually the assistant and advisor of the inspector general, on Negro troops' policies, especially on integration and discrimination issues in the European theater of operations. Yet, the official ban of any kind of discrimination in the Army didn't prevent it from applying the segregation rules enforced in the Southern States after the abolition of slavery in 1865. Segregation which implicitly authorized all sorts of contemptuous behaviors and remarks towards the colored soldiers, which the latter deemed insulting and provocative. All this resulted in racial tensions, all the stronger that in this small part of France the ratio of colored troops was unusually high, which worried Firmin a lot.

CHAPTER 60

September 12, 1944

From their position, the three balloon operators could see the roof of a farmhouse. In the beginning, Firmin was reluctant to go to the farm and buy some fresh food. He was aware that the Norman peasants were quite upset by the demeanor of some soldiers in the search for booze and sexual intercourse, whether consensual or not.

A few days after they arrived, Firmin tried a first contact with the farmer, who was observing them from his field. As a soldier, Firmin had to keep his gun constantly with him, especially in a battle zone. So, his rifle slung, he gently walked towards the man. Fearing for his safety and his daughter-in-law's, the farmer brandished his pitchfork in Firmin's direction, and shouted:

"Stop! Go bac or eye col ze police!"

Firmin instantly stopped and stayed put. He then tried to reassure the man, in French.

"Don't be afraid, sir. We just want to buy your fresh eggs and some food to eat!"

The man stayed on guard.

"We know the guys like you!" the man replied in French. *"You always end up getting drunk with Calva, and then you dishonor our wives and daughters!"*

Firmin tried to convince the man of his honorable intentions, but he wouldn't trust him. So, the farmer threatened him once more to call the police if he refused to return to where he belonged. Firmin obeyed without protesting, knowing that he would face big troubles if the incident were reported to the U.S. military police.

Three more days were gone when the old man came to them, driving his horse-drawn cart. Sitting beside him on the seat was a young woman, holding a wicker basket on her knees, and an older man, who couldn't take his eyes off the balloon flying seven hundred feet above their heads. His lower jaw was hanging open, as if it was about to unhook from his head.

"*You still want to buy my eggs?*" the old man asked Firmin, without saying hello.

The peasant then introduced Jeanette, his daughter-in-law. Her husband had been sent to Germany, as a forced laborer, the man explained.

"*I warn the three of you. Don't come too close to her, or you'll have to deal with me!*"

Firmin swore none of them would disrespect her.

Then, the old man presented his elder son, Jacquou.

"*He's halfwit, but he's not mean. That is, as long as you don't hurt a member of his family.*"

The son was doing his best to control a giggle by pressing his hands on his mouth. Then, he grabbed and pulled his father's sleeve, whispered something in his ear, and burst out laughing. His father shook his head, and addressed Firmin again.

"*Forgive him. It's the first time he sees a real Negro! So, you know…*"

In the following days, Jacquou came back alone, carrying a basketful of provision. The three soldiers traded them with cigarettes, chewing gum, and sometimes a jerrycan of gasoline. Gaston, the old man, had stolen half a dozen of them in a nearby depot. Intending to avoid arousing suspicion from the military police, Firmin made an agreement with his colleague of the headquarters to trade, at every delivery tour, one or two full jerrycans with empty ones. Hence, Firmin refused to give away a full can unless Gaston came with an empty one, which made his father upset, as he didn't know how to store all this gasoline. Firmin didn't want to know, either.

Rain and cold made the GIs life pretty much painful in Normandy, especially during the night. Foxholes became waterlogged, and threatened to bury their occupants.

One evening, the old peasant took pity on his neighbors and suggested that they sheltered in his barn. The three operators of the 320th VLA immediately accepted. After they had firmly tethered their balloon to the ground, they went to the farm with their bags and rifles. As they were completely soaked, Gaston invited them in his house. They would have supper together, and warm up in front of the fireplace.

They followed the old man inside a large kitchen. In the middle of the room stood a long solid wooden table surrounded by six chairs.

"*You can add three more plates!*"

They recognized Jeanette who was taking care of the cooking of the evening meal on a wood stove, under the supervision of another older woman, whom the three GIs had never seen before. Her dress was as dark as her eyes. She gave the three soldiers a once-over, without a smile.

"*This is Valentine, my wife,*" Gaston said without a gaze at her.

When she noticed their boots covered with wet mud, Valentine pointed a threatening hand at them and shouted:

"They're gonna muck up my home! Couldn't they take off their shoes, at least?"

Firmin immediately understood and asked the two others to take off their boots like him. They were immediately seized by the icy contact of their bare feet on the soil covered with terracotta tiles, but they endeavored to keep smiling, hoping it would coax the mistress of the house.

On the wall, opposite to the stove, two burning logs were crackling in the fireplace, providing a comforting warmth, and a surplus of light, to the main room of the ground floor. Besides, the kitchen was lit by two hurricane lanterns hanging from a beam above the table.

The old man suggested that his guests made their socks and their coat dry before the fire. They would surely have taken off their wet pants too, but the presence of two women forbid them to undress further.

Before sitting at the table, on the patriarch's invitation, the three GIs took out of their bags a few cans of food that they offered to his wife. She accepted and granted them a hardly audible, "sankiew."

Firmin had noticed a crucifix hanging on the wall above the fireplace. Therefore, he expected their hosts to say grace, like the Joneses. Instead of this, the old man, sitting at one end of the table, grabbed with one hand half a circular loaf of bread lying near his plate. With the other hand, he made a cross sign on the bread with the tip of his knife. He eventually cut a piece for everyone around the table. Firmin deduced it was probably their way to bless the meal.

The dinner took place in a reverent silence, broken by the noises of swallowing, the tinkling of spoons on the plates, and the clearing of throats. Yet, from time to time, Jacquou, who was sitting on a stool, unwillingly brought some joy by giggling for a reason unknown but to him. But the dark gaze of the old man sufficed to stop him. Until the next time.

Intending to relax the atmosphere, Firmin complemented the cook on her soup. Gazing at her plate, Jeannette lowered her head and gave a slight smile. Firmin thought he had seen her cheeks turn rosy.

He tried to guess which different ingredients gave this soup its particular flavor and taste. After the soup, they shared an omelette with chive and onions.

When the old man proposed to serve them cider of his own production, Firmin accepted, precising:

"One glass, but not more."

Valentine seemed to appreciate this mark of courtesy, which was also a sign of temperance.

For the dessert, Jeanette served cooked apples, which had been kept warm in a cauldron hooked up inside the fireplace. The farmer enhanced his dessert with Calvados brandy poured in the middle of the hollowed-out apple. This time, Firmin categorically refused the old man's proposal, which earned the corporal Valentine's approval.

"You'd better follow the example of these gentlemen," she said to her husband, ending her sentence with a broad grin at Firmin.

When the meal was over and the table cleared, the two women left the men and went to sleep.

As the rain finally stopped, Gaston asked his son to accompany the soldiers to their sleeping place in the barn, which was only a few meters away from the house.

The night was already pitch-dark. They took their

flashlights out of their bags. Jacquou was elated. He had never seen such type of lamps before.

"*I also want one of these!*" he exclaimed. "*Give me yours!*"

Firmin had to promise Jacquou that he would soon get him one, to make him stop shouting.

On their way, the three GIs relieved their bladders in the puddles which strewed the ground of the courtyard, making Jacquou giggle, once again.

Inside the barn, he showed them the wooden ladder they needed to climb to reach the platform where the straw used to feed the cattle was stored. Finally, he wished them a good night, and left the barn, still overexcited by the prospect of getting his own American flashlight, soon.

The comfort on the platform was quite rudimentary. Firmin recalled with emotion of his bed at the Joneses'. What a change, since then! A change consistent with the difference between the ways people welcomed them.

In Great Britain they had been coddled. Here, in France, some French were exasperated, when not frankly hostile. But Firmin quickly realized that this reaction didn't specially target the colored soldiers, but all the GIs. The main reason was the massive Allied bombardments, which had destroyed many villages and towns, and made a large number of victims among Norman civilians.

However, in this building, they would remain dry. They had no right to complain. At this very moment, their fellow soldiers, engaged on different fronts, were suffering terribly, shivering with cold and fear in their muddy foxholes.

"I suggest we say a prayer for all the fighters," Firmin said suddenly.

His thought for the Joneses probably reminded him of Maggie's deep faith, and the bible she had offered him.

After they had laid their sleeping bags on a thick layer of hay, the three men slipped their bodies inside with delight. Edward and Jimmy quickly fell asleep.

It took Firmin longer, despite his great fatigue. His mind was focused on Ethel. She had been pregnant for five months now. How swollen was her belly now? He had often seen pregnant women in the Lower Ninth in New Orleans, but he had never tried to guess their stage of pregnancy by the roundness of their bellies. He only remembered they could be enormous a few days before the delivery. Sometimes they remained so after the child's birth. So, Firmin came to imagine Ethel would never recover her graceful silhouette. Would he still love her then? And what about his child? Was he going to be smart and handsome? Or will he look like one of the Davises rascals? Could he be halfwit like the poor Jacquou?

Firmin struggled to remove his dark thoughts from his mind. Therefore, he tried to recall his childhood, when he was sleeping on the mezzanine in a shack, which used to be their home in Baton Rouge. Thinking of this, he realized this Norman farmer wasn't actually wealthier than his Black parents living in New Orleans.

Despite the concert of snoring, Firmin managed to fall asleep rather quickly. He couldn't afford to wake up late on the morrow. He and his crew mates had to hold their post, and their sergeant could appear anytime after the sunrise, during his inspection tour.

Dawn was still long ahead when Firmin was torn from his sleep by Jimmy who was shaking him and shouting:

"Wake up, Corp.! I'm afraid there's something serious happening in the old man's house!"

CHAPTER 61

It took Firmin a few seconds to recover his senses. Several loud voices intermingled. Those of a woman shouting. He could recognize Jeanette's voice, and distinctly perceived a few words. "Help … please … no … mercy…" Covering her begging for compassion, deep voices were yelling:

"Don't make a fuss, you bitch! … Let's get the hell outta here." "That's enough, now! Hurry up, man!"

Firmin didn't need to hear more to understand what was going on in the farmhouse. He had to interfere immediately to prevent his countrymen from doing something irredeemable. He shook Ed, who was still sleeping, and ordered his two crew mates to take their rifles and follow him to rescue the young woman. It was so dark that they almost fell from the ladder when they descended from the platform.

As they ran out of the barn, Firmin saw a ray of light coming out the house's main door, surprisingly left open. Suddenly, two human forms rushed out of the doorway.

"Hey, you!" Firmin screamed.

One of the two men pointed his flashlight in his direction. He was holding his rifle in the other hand.

"Mind your own business!" he warned, pointing his rifle ahead, while slowly walking backwards.

The two groups of GIs were aiming each other. They knew they would be in big trouble if they started shooting. Firmin ordered his crew mates not to try anything.

"Everyone's kindly going back where he belongs and

everything's gonna be fine," said the guy. "Is that clear?"

"Loud and clear," Firmin replied, lowering the barrel of his rifle.

The two shapes continued to walk backwards without turning round, then suddenly ran like rabbits, and vanished in the murk of the night.

Firmin immediately rushed inside the house, followed by Jimmy and Ed.

A glittering light coming from behind the table was projecting its moving shadow on the wall. The three men bypassed it, lighting the ground with their flashlights. Standing on the kitchen tiles, an oil lamp diffused its yellow and swaying glow on Jeanette's motionless body. The bottom edge of her dress was pulled up over her belly. The top had been torn up, uncovering her chest. Her panties had been ripped open. Her inner thighs were stained with blood and semen.

"Fuckin' bastards!" Firmin exclaimed. "Should've killed them!"

Ed instantly felt nauseous. He rushed outside and chucked up.

Jimmy was paralyzed. He couldn't take his eyes off that vision of horror.

For just a few seconds, Firmin thought of hunting the two rapists. He immediately changed his mind. It was pitch-black outside. It would be a waste of time. Even worse, anyone seeing him running away from the farm would suspect him of being the perpetrator of the crime. Suddenly, he felt stunned that no one in the house had rushed down after hearing Jeanette's calls for help. He started imagining the worse. "They must have been assaulted in their sleep." He motioned for Jimmy to search the house and check the three other occupants.

Corporal Bellegarde strove to stay calm, while his brain was running at full speed. "If they all were killed by those two guys, nobody will be able to get us out of this trap!"

Indeed, the mere presence of the three friends inside the farmhouse would be enough to find them guilty. Returning to their foxholes right now, to hide their presence on the spot at the time the crimes occurred, wouldn't help. Their position in the vicinity of the farm would be enough to turn them into suspects. And, for the military police, suspect and colored is a synonymous expression of guilty.

Mechanically, Firmin kneeled near Jeanette. He grabbed the hemline of her dress, and delicately lowered it until it covered her soiled and tortured private parts.

"Espèce de salauds ! Qu'est-ce que vous lui avez fait ?"[136]

Firmin almost had a stroke. His heart started racing. He jerked his head on the side and saw Jimmy, hands up, whose eyes seemed like almost getting out of their sockets. Behind him, the old man was holding him at bay, by pressing the barrel of his shotgun onto his ribs.

Corporal Bellegarde could precisely tell what was going on inside the brain of the boorish peasant, at this very moment. What that man could see was a black soldier bent over the inert body of his daughter-in-law, lying on the ground in a position which left no doubt about the heinous assault she had just suffered. Who would blame him for using his gun to avenge this woman, and restore the honor of his son at once? After all the rapes that had been perpetrated so far by GIs in the region since D-Day!

---

[136] *"You, fuckin' bastards! What have you done to her?"*

Firmin begged the old man not to shoot.

"*We didn't do that, I swear!*"

He gently raised his hands and pressed them on top of his head. Then, he ordered Edward to lay his rifle on the floor, put his hands over his head, and calmly get on his knees.

"*We've been awakened by the screams of your daughter-in-law, so we rushed over here!*" Firmin continued to explain in French. "*There were two soldiers. We saw them running out of the house. They disappeared!*"

"*You're lying!*" the farmer yelled.

"*I swear! They spoke American and had their rifles!*"

"*So do you!*"

"*We didn't do anything! You must believe me!*" Firmin begged, with a quivering voice.

"*You're gonna tell this to the gendarmes[137]!*" the man replied, screwing his rifle barrel onto the flank of Jimmy, who jerked his head towards him.

With a firm gesture, he ordered him to kneel down near Edward.

"*Stretch out on the ground, face down, and keep your hands crossed behind your heads, so that I can see them!*"

Firmin obeyed and ordered the two others to do the same, without resisting. The patriarch then called his wife and his son, who were waiting for his signal to come down.

Valentine was the first who appeared, with a lit storm lamp hanging from her stretched arm. What she

---

[137] Gendarmes are members of the French Gendarmerie, a military force in charge of law enforcement among the civilian population.

discovered confirmed her what she had foreseen. However, the shock was such that her legs gave way under her. She fell on her knees. Her mouth opened in a long and silent scream.

It was a miracle that the lamp didn't escape from her hand, then set fire to the kitchen.

Her body and soul were torn by a dreadful pain. Yet, what came out of her throat was just a slight whistle, almost inaudible. A flood of tears gushing from her eyes, she gazed at each of the three GIs, one by one, with a bewildered look. Then, her gaze, filled with incomprehension, melted in Firmin's, who seemed to beg her to believe in his innocence.

Meanwhile, Jacquou's muddled brain was trying to bring order in the confusion of images and sensations, which was flowing in his mind from all sides. The vision of his brother's wife, lying in this strange position on the kitchen's tiles, was turning his mind upside down. Fortunately, he hadn't yet made the link between Jeanette's state and the presence of the three soldiers in the room. Otherwise, he would have sprung at their throats and killed them with his hands.

"*Go to the village and fetch the gendarmes!*" his father asked him. "*And bring them back here, as fast as possible! Did you understand?*"

"*She's dead? Jeanette's dead? Is she dead?*" Jacquou repeated, while nervously swinging back and forth on his feet.

"*Do what I say, Jacquou. Hurry up! And tell them to come with Doctor Vendeuvre,*" he added, to reassure his son.

While waiting for his return, Firmin twice tried to tell

Gaston his version of the facts. But the old man wouldn't listen.

"*Give it a rest! Keep your saliva for the gendarmes, you, bastard!*"

Sometimes, Jimmy and Edward talked together in English.

"Are we going to stay here until they come and lynch us?"

The farmer immediately made them stop with a threatening voice.

"*Shut up or I shoot you like the rabid dogs you are!*"

Firmin then ordered them to stay put and keep quiet, and begged the old man in French not to kill them.

His wife, sitting on the floor, had lifted up the head and shoulders of her daughter-in-law. She was caressing Jeanette's hair and rocking her gently like a mother would do with her baby to make her sleep. She was humming a lullaby, sprinkled with uncontrollable sobs.

Suddenly, a little sigh escaped from Jeanette's pale lips. Her mother-in-law leaned over her head to check that she had indeed heard a tiny breath of life. Jeanette's chest now heaved itself faintly, yet perceptibly.

"*She still can breathe! Hallelujah!*" Valentine whispered with a sob.

She lifted her head and looked at her husband with incredulous and tearful eyes.

"*Can you hear me, Gaston? Jeanette is alive!*" she screamed.

"She's alive! Hallelujah!" Firmin exclaimed.

"Hallelujah!" repeated Ed and Jimmy, who felt relieved as much for Jeanette as for themselves.

The young woman would be able to establish the truth,

and therefore exonerate them from the crime. Thereby, it would avoid them to swing on the end of a rope, like Clarence Whitfield.

Nevertheless, the farmer didn't lower his guard. He made them shut up, once more.

Shortly after, Jacquou came back with three gendarmes. The doctor was busy with a difficult delivery. He had promised to come as soon as possible.

The *brigadier-chef* scanned the crime scene with a roving glance. He ordered his two assistants to handcuff the three GIs, who were still lying face down on the floor. Then, he gently came closer to the farmer and said:

"*You made the right decision, waiting for us, Gaston! It's up to the American military justice to take care of these Negroes. And trust me, their courts have no mercy for rapists!*"

Gaston's hands were still clenched on the barrel and the butt of his shotgun.

"*Come on, Gaston. Be reasonable. Give me your rifle, now!*"

His eyes still focused on the three Americans, he let the brigadier-chef take his shotgun, without resisting.

The gendarme took a second storm lamp, which Jacquou had brought in the meantime, and lifted it above Valentine and the victim. Bruises now appeared on Jeanette's face, neck and forearms.

He crouched to get closer to her.

"*Can you tell me what happened tonight?*"

"*Can't you see it by yourself?*" Gaston yelled.

The gendarme looked at him and frowned.

"*This is the procedure, Gaston! Please, let me do my job.*"

The brigadier-chef resumed his questioning in the heat. Noticing the young woman was wincing in pain, he comforted her.

"*The doctor will soon be here. Do you think you can still answer a few questions before he arrives?*"

Jeannette nodded.

"*What happened?*"

The woman struggled to sit up, backing on her stepmother. She uttered several plaintive wails. All her body was aching.

"*I was sleeping upstairs when I heard some noise coming from the kitchen. Then ... then I heard men's voices...*"

"*Could you hear what they said?*"

"*I ..., I don't know. The ..., they were speaking English!*"

"*And then?*"

The young woman sucked her breath in convulsively, then breathed out long and deep.

"*I stood up ... and I went downstairs to see who it was.*"

"*Alone? Why didn't you ask Gaston? Or Jacquou?*" the brigadier-chef asked, stunned.

"*I ..., I thought it was them,*" she replied in a sorry tone. "*I thought they must have been still hungry and that...*"

"*Still hungry? What do you mean?*"

"*My step ... stepfather invited them for supper yesterday.*"

The gendarme turned his head briefly towards Gaston to get his approval. The latter confirmed with a nod of his head.

"*So, did you recognize them when you saw them?*"

"*I can't tell,*" she said, crying and shaking her head. "*It*

455

was so dark… They had flashlights."

"*What did you do, then?*"

"*I … I asked them wha … what they were doing here. What they were looking for…*"

"*Can you speak English?*"

"*No. But I knew one of the three GIs of yesterday could speak French, so…*"

"*Can you remember which one?*"

Jeanette painfully extended her right hand and pointed it at Firmin. Once again, the gendarme looked at Gaston, who confirmed silently.

"*And? What did they reply?*"

"*Nothing. They said things in English, making noises with their tongues, like boys do here, sometimes, when they are drunk. Well, you … you know what I mean…*"

"*I see,*" the gendarme replied. "*What did you do, then?*"

"*I begged them to leave…*"

"*Why didn't you scream?*"

"*I … I … didn't have time … they grabbed me and made me fall … my head hit the floor, and I…*"

"*Yes? What?*"

"*I think I fainted.*"

"*Aw! For long?*"

"*I don't know, sir. I don't think so. They … they were tearing off my dress when I opened my eyes again.*"

"*So, you could see them!*" the brigadier-chef exclaimed. He was so happy to wrap up his investigation so quickly.

"*Well… I mean…*"

"*What?*"

"*I'm not sure. It was dark and their faces were dark as well…*"

"*Of course ... well, they are Negroes. It's understandable that you couldn't recognize them in the dark. Can you see other Negroes in the room?*"

Firmin didn't miss a word of the interrogation. It was obvious that this French policeman was racist, and that he was ready for anything to hand over perfect culprits to the American military authorities.

"*I beg you, please, miss!*" Firmin screamed. "*Try to remember what those men looked like! And you'll realize it wasn't us!*"

"*You, shut up!*" the brigadier-chef ordered. "*You'll talk when I ask you something.*"

Then, addressing Jeanette again, he asked:

"*Where they black, yes or no?*"

"*Black, green, brown, I can't remember ... but they had strange colors on their faces. Something like...*"

The gaze of the gendarme focused on some traces on the woman's neck. Traces he had first thought of being starting bruises.

"*Tell me when it hurts!*" the gendarme said.

He rubbed Jeanette's skin with two fingers, on the brown and green spots. Then, he looked at his fingers lit by the lamp, which Jacquou was now holding. They were covered with brown, black and green fat residues.

"*Something like camouflage paint?*"

"*Can be.*" Jeanette sobbed, exhausted.

"*You see. I told you it wasn't us!*" Firmin intervened, without waiting for the question of the gendarme.

The latter turned towards the three GIs.

"*Regardez*[138], monsieur le gendarme…" Firmin said.

---

[138] Look.

"Brigadier-chef!" the latter corrected.

He then asked Jacquou, with a sign, to point his lamp at the three suspects.

"*Come on guys! Show your faces to the policeman!*" Firmin ordered his crew mates.

"*Look carefully, brigadier-chef. None of us has camouflage paint on his face!*"

The gendarme checked each suspect's face. He grasped Firmin's lower jaw with his right hand and twisted his face to the left, then to the right, roughly. He did the same with Edward.

Jimmy couldn't let a White man disrespect him like this. When the gendarme grasped his jaw, Jimmy jerked his head to escape from his hand.

"Don't touch me like this. Ain't no nigger on a slave auction!" he exclaimed, upset.

"Stop it, Jimmy. He's just looking after traces of camouflage paint on your face."

"What?"

"Shut up, I said."

"*It is indeed true,*" the brigadier-chef agreed, turning to Gaston. "*I'm sorry, but they aren't the guys who assaulted your daughter-in-law!*"

Hearing this, Firmin emptied his lungs in a deep exhalation.

"We're safe now, guys! We've been exonerated."

Relieved by this unexpected reversal, Edward cracked.

"Thank you, Lord!" he whispered, with a trembling voice.

Firmin turned his head and looked at the old man. He couldn't blame him for having suspected him. Instead, he could understand him. His son's wife had been assaulted in his own house by American soldiers. What the man had seen when he had arrived in the kitchen accused him and his crew mates, without a shadow of a doubt.

"I'm truly sorry for your daughter-in-law and for you, sir. I'm ashamed of my compatriots. If we can help in any way..."

"By the way," the brigadier-chef intervened, *"I'll have to make a report to the American military police. You're no longer suspects, but you still remain witnesses. And we still need to investigate with our army counterparts to identify and arrest the offenders."*

Once again, a pang of anxiety and fear overwhelmed Corporal Bellegarde. He was terrified by the MP's brutality and intolerance. All the more as he was faulty of having left his post unattended to shelter in a farm, be it just for one night. His sergeant will surely give him a damn earful. Yet, Firmin managed to put things into perspective, knowing that all three had been very close to a tragic end, which would have been particularly dishonorable for his parents, and especially for Ethel and their upcoming baby.

When he left his country, Firmin wished to fight against racism and segregation. Today, he witnessed the racism of this gendarme, and the strength of prejudices against Black people, on the other side of the Atlantic Ocean. And this almost ended up with him swinging on the end of a rope, like many other Negroes in the Southern States, under the Mason-Dixon line. His dream of equal rights was far from coming true.

CHAPTER 62

After a short stay at the gendarmerie, the three GIs were retrieved by the MP to be heard as witnesses of the felony. However, the hearing was quite challenging. One of the police officers was convinced they couldn't be innocent.

"You think you're smart? Don't even think of fooling me…"

Luckily, none of the three cracked. At the end of the day, their sergeant came to pick them up. He reminded them of their outright ban to leave their post.

"You could be court-martialed for this breach of the military rules! Abandonment of your position in a combat zone! Have you lost your mind?"

Corporal Bellegarde stood up for his crew mates, and claimed the full responsibility of his decision.

"We were soaked. It was raining cats and dogs. The farmer wanted to offer us a shelter for the night. His house was less than six hundred yards away…"

The sergeant decided to show understanding. He still took measures against them.

"You're lucky that I need all my men. Now, you're gonna return to your balloon. But if I see one of you at more than one hundred yards from your post… And of course, I am cancelling all your passes until further notice. Is it clear?"

Even Jimmy didn't say a word. He was fully conscious of the gift the sergeant was making them. None of the three complained about his order to avoid all new contact with civilians. Therefore, the sergeant himself went to the farm to retrieve his men's equipment, which they had left in the barn.

Firmin was relieved when he recovered his haversack untouched. He realized he could have lost his letters and his diary forever.

As of the following day, they resumed their routine job. Yet, things were different after the tragedy. They had stopped hoping that their lives could improve. Be it at home, in America, or in Europe, they were doomed to suffer the same prejudices. They were convinced that everyone in their battalion now knew what had happened. But their isolated position prevented them from knowing the feeling of their comrades. Would they support them? Or, would they avoid them like the plague, instead, for fear of being associated with this nefarious act, although they had been wrongly suspected?

During the whole day, Corporal Bellegarde endeavored to show self-confidence. He wanted to prove Ed and Jimmy that he wasn't a man who could easily be destabilized. That he deserved his rank and position as a crew leader!

Yet, when he found himself alone that night, sheltered under his tent, and when the tension had eased, he eventually cracked. Images of the previous night formed in his head. Recalling the facts, he realized how close he had been to a dreadful tragedy. What upset him the most deeply wasn't that he could have faced the same fate as Clarence Whitfield, but that his parents, Ethel and their child would have been devastated by his absence. And, moreover, by the look of contempt of their neighbors. His

461

head sunk inside his sleeping bag, he cried for a long time, then fell asleep like a child.

A few days later, their sergeant informed them that another sexual assault had been reported to the military police. It had occurred in the area, in similar conditions. The two victims had also talked of abusers, which faces and hands were covered with camouflage paints. As a consequence, the incident wouldn't be mentioned in the activity report of their unit. The serenity and reputation of 320th VLA had to be preserved until the end of its mission in Europe. In return, the three members of the crew would never refer to the event in the future.

Although the testimonies of the new victims completely exonerated them, Firmin and the two others remained morally deeply affected. They comforted themselves with the thought of their upcoming return home. Each new battle won against the Germans brought them nearer to that day.

After the capture of the Crozon Peninsula on September 17, the German General Ramcke was compelled to surrender on September 20 to Brigadier General Charles W. Canham, thus, putting an end to the battle of Brest, after twenty-nine days of fierce fights.

It was a great relief for Firmin's balloon crew. They would soon be allowed to leave their post and return to Cherbourg.

Once there, they met a dump truck unit, whose men had been trained at Camp Claiborne, Louisiana, where Firmin had first been inducted. They told them of their endless rounds on the Red Ball Express roads between Cherbourg and Chartres[139].

The express road was open since August 25. On the day Paris was freed. Some of the drivers fantasized about the City of light and its promiscuous girls. The truth was that the drivers had no time to extend their trip to Paris. Right after unloading their truck, they would drive back to Cherbourg. The traffic was carefully marked and controlled by the U.S. 793rd MP battalion, and sometimes with the support of the French police. It never stopped, day or night. The drivers had to take a ten minutes' pause every two hours. Ten minutes before each even hour, all the drivers at a time would stop in a synchronous mode. There were two separate tracks, one towards Paris, one for the return trip to Cherbourg. The round trip was completed in about fifty-three hours.

***

Firmin could write again in his diary. At the date of September 12, 1944, he mentioned:

"We're soaked by heavy rains. Been invited by Norman farmer for supper. Slept in a dry place in the barn. Had a quiet night. Slept well. NTR."

Any reference to the incident could have earned him the worse trouble, would the diary fall in other hands. He had never before used the acronym of *nothing to report*. Later, if he decided to write his memories, he would feel free to tell or not this painful episode of his war experience.

---

[139] Source: https://fr.wikipedia.org/wiki/Red_Ball_Express

In his letters to his parents and Ethel, he strove to be reassuring. They surely worried enough about him. Telegrams from the Army announcing with deep regret the loss of a son, a brother or a husband, kept arriving with an increasing frequency since June 6.

How many blue stars on the service flags hung behind the windows of American houses had been replaced by golden stars in the memory of a male in the family killed in action? How many masses had been celebrated in Saint Paul's Lutheran church, on Annette Street in New Orleans, to the benefit of a member of the congregation? The one Celestine Bellegarde belonged to.

On the European theater of operations, the soldiers who had escaped from death or serious injuries were exhausted. On top of a great fatigue came the fear of being killed, which the vision of their unlucky fellow soldiers constantly reminded them. The cases of psychological trauma were multiplying among the fighters of the front lines.

In the rear, nostalgia and homesickness were sometimes so strong that some soldiers would cry like babies. Everyone dreamed of being back home, soaking in a warm bath, eating mom's delicious food, and sleeping round the clock in a cozy bed.

On August 15, another landing had taken place in the bay of Saint-Tropez, on the Mediterranean coast of France. Since then, the progression of the American and British troops towards Germany was unstoppable.

The battle of Metz, highlight of the Lorraine campaign, had started on August 27.

On their side, the British troops of Field Marshall Montgomery, backed up by the 82nd and 101st Airborne, launched Operation *Market Garden*[140], on September 10. The operation aimed at liberating Belgium and the Netherlands, in order to bypass the *Siegfried* line, and strike Germany in the Ruhr region. It was ended on September 25, with a failure at Arnhem Bridge, north of Nijmegen in the Netherlands.

Eisenhower's hope to win the war before the end of 1944 was inexorably fading away.

On October 2, B and C batteries were transferred to Octeville, where they would join HQ and A batteries. On this occasion, Firmin, Ed and Jimmy found their former crew mate back, Douglas Murphy, who seemed to have gained some more weight.

It was also the signal for all the men of the battalion that they wouldn't stay much longer in France.

On October 24, the 320th VLA returned to Great Britain aboard landing ships.

Firmin hoped to meet Ethel again, on the occasion of a furlough, but he learned from her last mail that she had already left the island to return to the United States, due to her pregnancy. It's term was foreseen around January 20, 1945.

The battalion finally embarked on November 11, 1944, aboard the *USAT Excelsior*, which would reach New York Harbor on November 26.

Edward and Jimmy reminded Firmin of his promise to go back to New York city after the war, and have a couple of drinks at the *Copacabana*, in Spanish Harlem, or at the *Cotton Club*, in Negro Harlem. However, Firmin declined

---

[140]   Source : https://www.secondeguerre.net/articles/evenements/ou/44/ev_marketgarden.html

his buddies' invitation, arguing that he was looking forward to seeing Ethel again, and introduce her to his parents. Which was only partly true. In fact, he wasn't in a mood for partying. Maybe he was afraid of getting lost in alcohol, like some of his friends, starting with Jimmy and Donut.

He had seen the impact of alcohol on his father. As a future dad and husband himself, Firmin didn't want to repeat this frequent scenario.

A few days after their arrival in New York, all the men of the 320th VLA were granted a long furlough for resting and celebrating Christmas with their families.

CHAPTER 63

Saturday, December 2, 1944.

The return by train to New Orleans lasted almost thirty-six hours. Nothing had changed since his departure from Camp Tyson in November 1943. At the train connection in Washington, D.C., station, he and other colored soldiers had been denied access to an almost empty car. It was only occupied by two or three white travelers. The controller had informed them this car was for Whites only, but there was another one behind reserved for Colored people. The latter being jam-packed, a few black soldiers wearing uniforms protested, arguing discrimination was illegal.

But it was a waste of time. Indeed, according to the local laws, the services supplied to colored people on board this train were equal to those proposed to Whites. Therefore, it wasn't a point of discrimination, but a point of segregation. The controller eventually reminded them, calmly but firmly, that travelers aboard this train had to comply with the rules prevailing in the state crossed by the train, and applied by the train company. If they feared to lack space, they could take the next train.

Considering the inflexibility of the controller, Corporal Bellegarde had chosen to follow his requests. He couldn't wait to return home. After all, war wasn't yet won. Perhaps did they have to wait until full victory before they could see the end of segregation in their civilian lives.

When he finally made it to Union Terminal in New

Orleans, Firmin took a streetcar line which drove up Rampart Street, then Saint-Claude Avenue, up to the crossing with Elysian Fields Avenue. From this point, he took a bus until the entrance of the bridge, which crosses the canal separating the Upper from the Lower Ninth ward.

Despite the cold, Firmin decided to finish his trip back home on foot. As he reached the other bank of the canal, he took a deep breath to fill his lungs with the air of his neighborhood. At last, he was feeling safe.

On his way, he crossed a few familiar faces grinning at him. He replied to them with a smile, while striding forward. A hundred yards from the family home, Corporal Bellegarde stopped a moment to adjust his parade uniform, which was rumpled by his long journey by train.

Raising his head, his eyes were attracted by the facade of the house. All its surface on the ground floor had been decorated in his honor with tricolor garlands and cockades. The upper half of the frontage, where the Davises lived, had kept its usual appearance. Sad and devoid of fantasy. Like its occupants.

Behind one of the two windows of the Bellegardes's living room hung a service flag with a blue star. Above the door, a banner read, "Welcome Home Firmin, our hero!"

Corporal Bellegarde felt an uncontrollable emotion swelling inside him. A mingle of pride and apprehension. He stopped once again on the paved path, which led from the sidewalk to the entrance. From the corner of his eye, he noticed a slight movement of a curtain behind a window on the first floor. The Davises were probably at home. Firmin didn't even look up to check it. They didn't deserve such an honor.

As he was slowly moving forward, trying to control his emotion, the door suddenly opened widely.

Celestine was standing motionless in the doorway, her hands tightened together under her chin, as if she was begging for mercy. She stared speechless at her son with the gaze of a worried mother. A little behind, her husband was holding her by the waist.

Firmin understood that someone had recognized him in the streets and had rushed to the house to warn them of his imminent arrival.

He observed them, silently, for a long time. His father hadn't changed much. His mother, however, seemed to have aged more than he. The small wrinkles in the corner of her eyes now looked deeper. A few gray locks lightened her temples. Firmin felt a pang of guilt. He, her own son, was to blame for making her lose a bit of her physical freshness.

Celestine observed him carefully from top to toe, lingering over each limb, then focusing again on his face. She had been fearing so much that he would come back dead or crippled, like many fellow soldiers returned before him.

"Good heavens! God bless your commandant, you're safe and sound!"

Firmin smiled, remembering the fate his mother had promised to his commanding officer if something serious would happen to her son.

"What are you waiting for instead of kissing your poor Mom?" she added in a firm tone, lest she would start crying.

Firmin dropped his duffle bag at his feet. While walking clumsily towards Celestine, he gently moved to

469

his back his haversack hanging around his neck. As soon as he stepped on the threshold, Celestine encircled him with her arms and squeezed him as tightly as she could. Firmin closed his eyes and deeply breathed her fragrance of wild flowers, which memory had accompanied him during his long absence.

Standing slightly behind her, Joe was gazing at his son, as if he was seeing him for the first time. Firmin felt like he had never before noticed such an expression in his father's eyes. After a few seconds of this mute communication, Joe nodded and gave his son an admiring smile and a solemn wink. Firmin understood and returned his smile. Without a word, his father had told him how proud he was of him. Not the kind of pride centered on himself, which he must have felt when his son graduated high school with highest honors. No! What Firmin saw in his father's eyes now was admiration and a sincere respect for what his son had achieved.

Firmin had overcome so many challenges, since he had left Camp Tyson, survived such horrors, and experienced so many new and moving things too. Yet, he was deeply stirred by his father's reaction.

Celestine loosened her embrace.

"Let me look at you, my son!" she exclaimed with tears in her voice. "I can hardly recognize you! You've changed so much! I've let a teenager go, and it's a man I see back!"

She wiped her tears away with the back of a sleeve.

"Please don't cry, Mom!" Firmin begged. "Or I'm gonna cry too, like a little boy. A man doesn't cry!"

His eyes drowned in tears, Firmin noticed that other people were waiting in the entryway.

He recognized Mrs. Robinson, visibly moved too.

Firmin was surprised not to see her husband near her. He searched him around among the silhouettes standing in the corridor, who were expecting to greet the hero of the house. But he couldn't see Zachary. So he looked at Rosa again, and noticed that she was all dressed in white. When she saw his face break up, Rosa knew that Firmin had understood. She extended a hand to him and fondled his cheek, tenderly, to comfort him, like she would have done with her own grandson.

"Zack would have been so glad to see you again, for a last time! He loved you dearly, you know! Sadly, the Lord called him back too early."

Celestine invited everybody inside her apartment. "It's out of the question to warm up the draft!"

Firmin took time to get filled with every detail of the decoration, as if he wanted to make sure he was actually in the house of his teens. Nothing had moved, save a framed photo which wasn't here when he left. Getting closer, he recognized the portrait his parents had asked to a downtown photographer to make of him dressed in his uniform.

A sweet scent was wafting in the air. He closed his eyes, and inhaled slowly and deeply, hence awakening his memory of family holiday meals. He started to salivate, while distinguishing the aromas of his favorite desserts. Cheese cake served with red fruit coulis, dried fruit cookies, and pecan nuts brownies.

Firmin was both annoyed and intimidated by the reception committee his mother had organized. Besides Rosa, she had invited a friend of her congregation and their pastor, whom Firmin immediately identified, although he had met him only once before. He would never forget his speech dedicated to the virtues of knowledge, in tribute to Celestine and another mother, whose education had allowed their child to graduate high school.

Joe had invited one of his musician friends. This time, Joe easily found the words to say his pride of having a son who had fought in Europe, and had kicked the asses of those damn Nazis sauerkraut eaters. He couldn't stop praising his son, at the point Firmin was embarrassed.

Firmin had wished to celebrate this family reunion in strict privacy. At the most, he could have accepted the presence of Mrs. Robinson, whom he considered as his substitution grandmother. Since Celestine's parents were still living in Baton Rouge, about eighty miles from New Orleans, Firmin didn't see Rosalyn and Jean-Baptiste more than two or three times a year.

He was exhausted by his return trip. What he really needed, besides his parents' welcome, was a nice hot bath, a hearty meal, and a good sleep around the clock. To recover his strength before he would dare to explain the situation of his relation with Ethel. With these people around him, it was unthinkable.

"My! You're looking odd!" Celestine said, seeing her son's annoyed face. "Aren't you glad to be back home?"

"I'm sorry, Mom, but I'm so terribly tired. I just need some rest."

Celestine looked at the pastor.

"Or is there something you need to confess, instead?"

"Wh … what do you mean, Mom?" Firmin stammered.

Celestine crossed her arms on her chest and frowned severely.

"Didn't you forget to tell me something in your mail?"

Firmin bit his lower lip. Ethel was seven and a half months pregnant. Had she been reckless enough to pay them a visit, while he was still away? It was one thing to get engaged without both parents' agreement. But having a baby before being married, this was unacceptable to a devout believer like her.

"I'm so sorry, Mom. Neither Ethel nor I wanted that… We did it only once… Just once… I swear!"

"Do you realize the shame I felt when the parents of this young girl knocked at my door? When they introduced me to Ethel, with her pregnant belly?"

Firmin missed the words to say how sorry he was. Things were going worse than he had feared.

"Her father wouldn't calm down. So, I was compelled to show him your letters, in which you wrote that you loved Ethel and that you intended to marry her."

"It's still my intention!" Firmin confirmed with an assured voice.

"All the better!" Celestine approved. "This is exactly why I asked Reverend Carter to be here with us today! But before talking about this, I suggest we take a little break. All these emotions made me hungry, not you?"

CHAPTER 64

Sunday, December 3, 1944

Celestine had insisted on announcing her son's engagement before the Lord and the members of her congregation, in the respect for religious tradition. Reverend Carter had accepted to receive the two young people and their families to introduce them to his congregants as future bride and groom.

Celestine had convinced her husband to make a clothing effort. She also had made him promise to stay sober, at least until the wedding day. Joe had asked his musician friend to drive the three of them in a Chevrolet pick-up, borrowed from the garage where he worked as an assistant mechanic.

When they arrived at St. Paul's Lutheran church, Firmin saw Ethel flanked by her mother and her father. The latter was tall and burly. An impressive man with a stern expression on his face.

"Looks hard to get along with!" Firmin thought, worried.

The mother looked all the opposite. She was a solid build woman with chubby cheeks on a round face illuminated by her sparkling eyes and a shy smile.

Ethel was clad in a loose dress, which hemline exceeded under her woolen three-quarter-length coat. Seeing each other, Firmin and Ethel exchanged faint smiles, although they actually urged to throw themselves in each other's arms. They knew they had upset their respective parents. Therefore, they would have to wait until the end of the mass to embrace and kiss each other.

Both families were invited to walk to the front rows and take one of the seats reserved for them on each side of the central aisle. In an unspoken agreement, Ethel and Firmin didn't look one another until Reverend Carter finally mentioned their names. In his speech, the pastor called the audience to show understanding to the two lovers, who had failed to resist their mutual passion before their wedding day.

"May he who has never sinned throw the first stone at them!" he said, paraphrasing Jesus.

Firmin couldn't see the reaction on the faces of the faithfuls sat behind him. However, he could hear many "amens" of approval. Although he didn't care much about others' opinions, he felt relieved. He wouldn't stand that his parents, especially his mother, suffered from the reject of a part of the community.

The service ended with a hymn in honor of all those who were fighting in Europe, and in the Pacific against the forces of evil. When he heard the first notes of Amazing Grace, sung by the gospel choir, Firmin's mind was carried one year back. He saw, with a stunning precision, the images of Christmas Evening 1943, in St. Peter and St. Paul's church in Checkendon, where he had conducted a short-lived vocal ensemble on the invitation of the villagers. At this moment, he felt a much stronger emotion than in England. He was back in his family, safe and sound, accompanied by the woman of his life. He could thus still believe in the advent of a better world for him and all the colored people in his own country.

Wasn't this religious song also an invitation to keep

hoping, despite the trials of life? John Newton, the author of this hymn, former captain of a slave ship, hadn't he renounced his trade and fought slave trade at the end of his life? Why wouldn't all Firmin's white countrymen follow the example of the British, the French and all other people in Europe for which they were currently fighting?

The frank handshake with the father of his fiancée comforted Firmin, as far as his relation with his in-laws was concerned.

Later, the six went to a little restaurant for colored people serving excellent hamburgers for five cents. They sat at a table for six near the window, which looked over the street. While the parents discussed the date and formalities of the wedding, Firmin and Ethel made fun of the way how they considered them as irresponsible minors. They didn't seem to realize that their children had both lived an experience which had deeply transformed them. That they had matured far beyond the appearances. Of course, the parents could observe this war through the newspapers, the radio or images from all over the world in movie theaters. They had been afraid for their children. Yet, none of them had been directly confronted with the reality of the war. Neither Joe nor Ethel's father had fought in the Great War. They were too young at that time. They were too old now to take part in the Second World War. Therefore, they didn't have the legitimacy of their children to claim for equal civil rights for all Americans, Whites and Blacks. For a society without discrimination nor segregation. Moreover, Ethel and Firmin would soon be adults, and hence would no longer be accountable to their parents.

***

The date of the wedding ceremony was fixed on Saturday, December 23, knowing that Firmin's furlough would end on the following day after Christmas.

The war was not over yet, and their battalion remained operational. The 320th VLA would soon gather again in Camp Stewart, Georgia. However, Celestine and Ethel wouldn't need to fear for the life of their dearest one. It was no longer a question of returning to a fighting zone, but only resuming drills.

For simplification purposes, and to reduce the cost, the parents agreed that the wedding meal would take place on Christmas Eve.

***

On January 20, 1945, Ethel gave birth to a beautiful baby of eight pounds and three ounces. A boy named Jesse.

The 320th VLA was officially disbanded at the end of August 1945, after a last mission, commenced in May, on Oahu Island in Hawaii Archipelago.

Corporal Bellegarde, like all his comrades of the 320th VLA, was demobilized in September 1945.

Firmin finally returned home, where he joined Ethel and their son Jesse, hoping that a new era would start for them, and all the colored people of his country.

He was aware that the change wouldn't come without a strong resistance from most of the Whites. Yet, he was firmly determined to fight until full victory.

Epilogue

New Orleans, March 7, 1965

F irmin Bellegarde was forty-one. He hadn't become
a journalist, like he had dreamed of when he was
young. His taste for music had led him to open a record
shop. Occasionally, he would host a live music broadcast
on a local radio station. He also wrote little articles in an
African American newspaper about concerts and artistic
novelties.

He had, of course, tried to write some more political
and polemical columns, but Ethel was too scared it might
earn them serious trouble with the police and the
authorities. Not to mention the insane white supremacists
who constantly assaulted black activists, and even the
Whites who supported them.

Ethel was a head nurse at the Charity Hospital, on
Tulane Avenue. The couple had had two more children
after Jesse. John, born in June 1948, and Nora, born in
December of the following year.

Joe, Firmin's father, died in 1958. He was stabbed
during a brawl in the bar where he used to play every
weekend with his band. Since then, Celestine was living
with the couple and their three kids. Aged sixty-three, she
still worked in one of the modern hotels recently built in
the French Quarter. She also liked to prepare the evening
meal for her family, as often as she could.

Jesse was just twenty. He was a student in his third year

of law studies at the SUNO[141]. He rapidly got involved in the fight for the rights of the Negroes. As of his first year in college, he had joined the CCGNO[142], an organization founded in 1961, after the boycott of the Dryades Street shops, which was meant to protest against their refusal to hire colored employees in qualified positions. In the following year, Jesse had become a member of the SNCC[143]. And, to complete his status of the perfect activist, he had recently joined the CORE[144]. But when he realized the huge amount of work accumulated by both his studies and his militant actions, he eventually resolved to temporarily leave the CCGNO.

This evening, the whole family was sitting in front of the television set, to watch an event of the highest importance: the Selma to Montgomery march for civil rights. The march, organized by the Civil Rights Movement, intended to protest the killing of a Black activist, Jimmy Lee Jackson, by the police on February 26, 1965. The killing had occurred during a peaceful meeting held to denounce the restriction measures taken in Marion, Alabama, to stop African American voters from getting registered on voters' lists.

At the head of the procession, one could see distinguished figures like James Bevel[145], Hosea Williams[146] and Martin Luther King Jr. The protesters had

---

[141] Southern University at New Orleans.

[142] Coordinating Council of Greater New Orleans. Source: Global Nonviolent Action Database

[143] Student Nonviolent Coordinating Committee

[144] Congress for Racial Equality

[145] One of the heads of the CRM. 1936 - 2008. Source: Wikipedia

[146] An ordained minister and Civil Rights Movement activist. 1926 – 2000. Close to Dr. Martin Luther King Jr. Source: Wikipedia

left Selma to join Montgomery, Alabama's capital. The police had installed a road block a few miles away from Selma, at the exit of Edmund-Pettus Bridge. The procession first slowed down on the top of the bridge. Finally, it moved forward towards the road block.

Suddenly, the police rushed forward and assaulted the demonstrators with club blows and teargas. They were backed up by a mob of hateful Whites. The images showing on the television screen were terrifying and rabble-rousing too.

Firmin's elder son couldn't hold back his anger.

"If this is what we can harvest with non-violence," Jesse exclaimed, "let me tell you that Malcolm X was right, when he asserted our right on this earth to be a man. To be a human being. To be respected as a human being. To be given the rights of a human being in this society, on this earth, in this day. Which he intended to bring into existence *by any means necessary*."

"Don't be stupid, Jesse!" his mother intervened.

"I should be there too now, instead of sitting in this chair!"

"Your Mom's right, Son!" Firmin said.

"Sure, Dad. Let's not make waves. Better turn the other cheek and pray to God that it will stop one day…"

Firmin preferred not to reply. Their relationship with Jesse was already pretty complicated.

"You don't say anything! As usual," Ethel snapped curtly.

Then addressing her son:

"Let me remind you that your father fought for our rights!"

"Enough, Mom! I know the story. He's made war. He

was at Omaha beach. He almost died there... Great! But what did he earn from it? What did it change for me? For John? For Nora?"

"To start with," Firmin replied, "you received a better education than me. Thanks to what I did before you, you could attend college. Segregated, indeed, but of excellent quality. And next year, you'll become a lawyer. And, thanks to Dr. King, your brother and your sister will likely attend the same university as the Whites."

Jesse was reluctant to listen to his father. He kept his eyes focused on the black and white television screen.

"The path is gonna be long," Ethel added. "This is why we need to be patient, yet without ever giving up. Without losing faith, nor succumbing to the fascination for people like this Malcolm X!

We must follow the example of those who made the choice of non-violence. Like Rosa Parks, on December 1, 1955, in Montgomery, who refused to sit in the colored section of a bus. Her courageous act led to the boycott of the buses, which lasted until December 21, 1956, when the Supreme court of the United States declared that segregation in buses and in all other public places was illegal.

Like Dr. Martin Luther King Jr, then chairman of the SCLC[147], who on August 28, 1963, led a march organized by Asa Philip Randolph[148] for the defense of our civil rights. The protest, departed from Washington Monument, managed to gather 250,000[149] activists at the *Lincoln*

---

[147] Southern Christian Leadership Conference founded in January 1957.

[148] Founder of the first Black trade union in the United States. He was born in Crescent City in 1989 and died in New York in 1979.

[149] Among whom, 20% were Whites.

Memorial. The place where Dr. King held his famous speech *I have a dream...* Here again, we had to wait for one year until we received the reward of this peaceful action, which was the vote of the *Civil Rights Act,* on July 2, 1964.

Some say that this victory was partially the result of a momentum of sympathy raised by the images of police brutality against the protesters..."

"Look at that!" Jessy yelled, pointing at the television screen. "Do you call this a momentum of sympathy?"

The images were showing men and women, lying on the ground, with their faces covered with blood, smoked by a fog of teargas, beaten with golf clubs, whips or clubs rolled in barbed wire[150].

"Alright!" Jesse agreed. "Dr. King was granted the Nobel Peace Prize, three months later. Big deal! Believe me. It'll never stop! Unless," Jesse added with an ironic look, "I go and fight for democracy in Vietnam, who knows? What do you think, Dad?"

The D-Day veteran didn't know what to reply. Discrimination in public accommodations and federally funded programs had been prohibited by the Civil Rights Act, one year before.

Nevertheless, police brutality against Black people was going on. Moreover, each little victory of the African Americans made the anger of White supremacists grow stronger.

Twenty years after the end of World War II, Firmin had the feeling his dream of equal rights would never come true. Besides the veterans, no one had any consideration

---

[150] This Sunday, March 7, 1965, would be remembered in the history of the Civil Rights Movement as bloody Sunday.

for what he and his comrades had done. The Double Victory campaign had ended with a failure.

***

The first march would be followed by a second one, on Tuesday, March 9. This time, despite the withdrawal of the police road block on the other side of Edmund-Pettus Bridge, Dr. Martin Luther King decided to make a U-turn. Which would earn that day the name of *turnaround Tuesday*.

The third march, departed from Selma on Sunday, March 21, 1965, made it to Montgomery on Thursday, March 25. From three thousand two hundred protesters at its start, the procession numbered twenty-five thousand at its arrival. Some Whites joined and supported them.

One of them, Viola Liuzzo[151], paid for it with her life. She was assassinated by the Ku Klux Klan[152].

A few months later, on August 6, 1965, President Lyndon B. Johnson signed into law the *Voting Rights Act*, passed by the Congress two days earlier, which banned any kind of obstruction whatsoever to the voting rights of racial minorities.

---

[151] Viola Greg Liuzzo, White activist of the Civil Rights Movement in the Michigan April 11, 1925—March 25, 1965.

[152] Source: fr.wikipedia.org/wiki/Marches from Selma to Montgomery

Afterword

In Steven Spielberg's film, *Saving Private Ryan* (1998), which is for a large part a re-enactment of the D- Day, more specifically on Omaha beach, you won't see any Black face on the screen.

However, on that day, among the 29,714 men composing the assault forces, there were five hundred African Americans. The latter belonged to a section of the 3275th *Quartermaster Service Company,* and to battery A of the 320th *Antiaircraft Barrage Balloon Battalion* (VLA).

On the same day, among the 31,912 American soldiers who landed on Utah beach, about twelve hundred were Blacks. They belonged to the battery C of the 320th VLA, the 582nd *Engineer Dump Truck Company*, the 385th *Quartermaster Truck Company*, and the 226th, 227th, 228th, and 229th *Port companies* attached to the 490th *Port Battalion*[153].

As Alice Mills highlighted in the introduction of her book *Black GIs, Normandy, 1944*[154]:

"In 2004, the official album of the 60th Anniversary of the Landing, published by the Caen Memorial—or Museum for Peace—failed to show or mention any Black GIs. And of the 120 photographs in the album Regard sur une libération,[155] published by the Archives

---

[153] Source: The employment of Negro troops, Ulysse Lee, p 637 and 638.

[154] Bilingual French an English, Edition Cahier du temps.

[155] Images of a Liberation.

départementales de la Manche, only one shot made it possible to identify their presence.

Beginning in 2004, however, our historians started to mention Black American troops, and came to two startling conclusions: first, that Black GIs did no fighting in Normandy and, second, that they thoroughly terrorized the Norman population.

The first references to Black troops were associated with the terms murder, rapes, pillage *and* barbarian acts.

[...] *Some historians suggested that these Black American GIs refused to risk their lives in a white war and took vengeance on the Normans for what the United States made them suffer."*

The reality was that African American unions had demanded in 1941 that Black troops be integrated in the U.S. Army, and their soldiers entrusted with combat missions.

In 2016, I personally noticed, in the visitors' center of the Normandy American cemetery and memorial, that the reference to the 320th VLA was limited to a portrait of the medic Waverly Woodson, who stood out in the D-Day landing with courage and devotion. The man rescued soldiers on Omaha beach, under the heavy fire of German batteries, despite a wound in the back of his thigh, which made him terribly suffer. And, height of contempt, the portrait was displayed in a section dedicated to logistics! Although we know that the 320th VLA was a fighting unit attached to the 49th Antiaircraft Artillery Brigade.

It was in Europe that the U.S. Army had the highest number of colored soldiers. About 154,000.

Normandy was only a stage on the road to Berlin. A

long way was still ahead. It would give other Black American soldiers the opportunity to prove their bravery and their efficiency in combats.

It was the case of an armored battalion, the 761st *Tank battalion,* also known as the *Black Panthers*, trained in Camp Claiborne[156].

Landed on Omaha beach, on October 10, 1944, with six White officers, thirty-six Black officers and six hundred and seventy-six African American soldiers, this unit was placed under the command of General Patton. Attached to the 26th Infantry Division, they were quickly engaged in the battle of the Bulge, where they proved their courage and fighting skills.

General Patton first had some doubts about this Black battalion, which he expressed in his welcome speech, with his famous personal tone:

"Men, you're the first Negro tankers to ever fight in the American Army. I would never have asked for you if you weren't good. I have nothing but the best in my army. I don't care what color you are as long as you go up there and kill those Kraut sons of bitches. Everyone has their eyes on you and is expecting great things from you. Most of all your race is looking forward to your success. Don't let them down and damn you, don't let me down! They say it is patriotic to die for your country. Well, let's see how many patriots we can make out of those German sons of bitches."

Indeed, he wasn't prepared to accept them in his army. However, he desperately needed reinforcement. They wouldn't disappoint him. On the contrary!

---

[156] Source : https://www.revolvy.com/page/761st-Tank-Battalion-%28United-States%29

The men of the 761st TB received their baptism of fire on November 7, 1944, and took part in the combats, without interruption, during one hundred and eighty-three days. The battalion lost one hundred and fifty-six men, of which forty-four killed in action. It received many decorations. A medal of honor granted to staff-sergeant Ruben Rivers (awarded in 1997!), 296 Purple Hearts, 11 Silver Stars and 69 Bronze stars[157].

Here again, the American Film Industry endeavored to erase the traces of those Black American soldiers.

In the war film by Ken Annakin (1965), *The Battle of the Bulge*, with Henry Fonda, Robert Shaw and Robert Ryan, you won't see any Black. You won't see any reference to the involvement of the 761st Tank battalion.

Besides, the importance of the casualties among the fighters forced the SHAEF to accept employing Black American volunteers, coming from service units. This was how two thousand colored soldiers were selected on January 3, 1945, and gathered in Compiègne, France, on January 10. Whatever their previous rank, these guys had to give them up and accept to be demoted to the rank of private, because no Black soldier was allowed to give an order to a White soldier.

---

[157]Source :https://en.wikipedia.org/wiki/761st_Tank_Battalion_(United_States)

Acknowledgments

This book is undeniably the one in which I invested the most heart, personal conviction, time and research efforts. Between the day when the idea came to me to pay tribute to the Black American GIs of WWII, and the day I completed the French version, three years had gone by, sometimes interrupted by periods of doubt and short getaways dedicated to other writing projects.

Two years after the release of the French version, on the request of many American visitors of the WWII memorials in Normandy, I decided to write this English version of my book. I thank you for buying this copy, and I hope you enjoyed reading it.

The first person I would like to thank is Martine-Alice Mills, former maitre de conférence at the University of Caen (Normandy, France), former W.E.B. Du Bois Fellow, Harvard University, author of *Black GIs, Normandy, 1944* (Éditions Cahier du temps, 2014), for her invaluable advice and her very nice foreword.

I also wish to thank Linda Hervieux, freelance journalist and photographer, author of *Forgotten, the untold story of D-Day's black heroes, at home and at war*, published in 2015 by Harper Collins, whose testimonies collected from veterans of the 320th VLA inspired some biographical elements related to the characters of this historical fiction.

I would like to add special thanks to:

Bill Davison, son of George A. Davison, veteran of the 320th VLA,

Vinnie Dabney, son of William G. Dabney, veteran of the 320th VLA,

Joe Wilson Jr, son of Joseph E. Wilson, veteran of the 761st Tank Battalion,

and Andrew Biggio, U.S. Marine veteran, and Massachusetts police officer, best-selling author of *The Rifle*, for their kind support and encouragement.

Last but not least, I thank my wife Nathalie, and my sons Yann and Antoine for pushing me to complete this story despite the numerous difficulties.

With this new edition, printed in Bayeux, France, I would like to express my deep gratefulness to Andy Campbell who made a thorough proofreading of his copy of the initial version and pointed out errors that have now been corrected.

Andy Campbell is a private Normandy tour guide NBTGA. If you intend to make a guided tour of the major sites of the D-Day Landing Areas before 2025 (when he will retire), I recommend that you contact Andy Campbell through his website:

explorenormandytours.com.

Index of references

Black GIs, Normandy, 1944, by Alice Mills, Editions Cahiers du temps (2014)

Forgotten, the untold story of D-Day's black heroes, at home and at war, by Linda Hervieux, Harper Collins publishers (2015)

The employment of negro troops, par Ulysses Lee, published by Amazon media EU

What soldiers do : sex and the American GI in WWII France, by Marie-Louise Roberts, Univesity of Chicago Press publishers.

The US Army barrage balloon program, by James R. Schock, published by Amazon Createspace Independant Publishing Platform

The African American experience during WWII, by Neil A. Wynn, Rowman & Littlefield Publishers

Les Américains en Normandie, by Jean Quellien, Éditions OREP

Les Rescapés du Jour J, by Elizabeth Coquart and Philippe Huet, Éditions Albin Michel

The 761st « Black Panthers » Tank Battalion in WWII, by Joe Wilson Jr, McFarland & Co Inc publishers.

Internet sources:
On the 320ᵉ VLA:
http://www.skylighters.org/barrageballoons/
Barrage balloons in WWII. From Camp Tyson to Omaha Beach
http://lestweforget.hamptonu.edu/page.cfm?
uuid=9FEC3327-B2FB-E987-04E6361B4835AFA5
Lest we forget, website by Bill A Davison in tribute to

his father, George A. Davison, veteran of the 320ᵉ VLA
http://www.skylighters.org/barrageballoons/
davison.htm
http://www.europebattlefieldstours.com/
OmahaSector/OmahaSector11.html

On other subjects:
https://www.dday-overlord.com/ Website dedicated to
the chronology of the battle of Normandy and Operation
Overlord, created and developed by Marc Laurenceau.
https://www.dday-overlord.com/bataille-normandie/
journee
La bataille de Normandie jour après jour.
http://www.polishresettlementcampsintheuk.co.uk/
checkendon.htm
Campement de Checkendon
Reminiscences of Pontypool.
https://oldpontypool.wordpress.com/
https://en.wikipedia.org/wiki/Omaha_Beach
https://www.cairn.info/publications-de-Lilly-J.--
5846.htm
*L'armée américaine et les viols en France, juin 1944 –
mai 1945,* by J. Lilly and François Le Roy.
https://fr.wikipedia.org/wiki/
Viols_durant_la_libération_de_la_France
http://www.rfi.fr/france/20140606-france-
debarquement-soldats-noirs-gis-armee-americaine-viols-
segregation/
http://worldhistoryconnected.press.uillinois.edu/5.1/
gough.html
*"Messing Up Another Country's Customs:" The
Exportation of American Racism During World War II,*

par Allison J. Gough, Hawaii Pacific University

https://www.youtube.com/watch?v=1mmC1WQKjC4

Film of the US Army (ref M.F. 10-7942) over the functioning of the *Grave Registration Companies.*

Film sources:

GI noirs et oubliés. A film written by Pascal Vannier, directed by Jean-François Claire. A Coproduction Tarmak Films.

The Negro soldier 1944, African Americans in WWII US Army. Film directed and broadcast by the US Army to encourage the induction of Negro soldiers. YouTube. 40'21''.

A welcome to Britain 1943. A film produced by the US Army and shown to the GIs stationed in Great-Britain, which explained the differences of mentality and customs between Americans and British, and teach them the elementary rules of courtesy they should respect during their stay in this country. YouTube. 38'2''.

Cérémonie du 14 juillet 1944 à Grandcamp : YouTube, 11'3''

Other sources :

The Afro-American Newpapers Archive and Research Center, Baltimore, Maryland, USA.

BBC programme index of 1944 :

http://genome.ch.bbc.co.uk.

BOOKS BY THE SAME AUTHOR :
(French edition only)

Genèse de l'enfer, (éditions LNA/Prisma), 2011, readers' award of the Prix VSD du polar.

L*a Nuit du Nouveau Monde*, (City éditions), 2013.

Échec et Maât, independently published on Amazon.fr, 2018.

D-Day Un jour noir, independently published 2019, Prix Grandcamp-Maisy 2020.

Passager clandestin, independently published on Amazon.fr, 2021.

Operation Noah, new version of Genèse de l'enfer, independently published on Amazon.fr, 2022.

L'Armée des Anges, new version of La Nuit du Nouveau Monde, independently published on Amazon.fr, 2022.

If you like, you can contact me through my blog:
https://lanuitdunouveaumonde.wordpress.com

This book was printed by IMB, Bayeux, France

Legal deposit at BNF (France): March 2022

Printed by *Imprimerie Moderne de Bayeux*
ZI, 7, rue de la Résistance - F14400 Bayeux
Legal deposit : 73571 - Mars 2023